His Dreams Come True

By Barbara Scott

barbarascott@myauthor.co

Cover Design by More Visual, Ltd.

Book ISBN: 978-1-7333438-2-4

Published by Barbara Scott, October 24, 2019

For my mother, Frances, without whose love and support my dream would not have been possible.

Thank you, Mom.

His Dreams Come True

Prologue

The Gold Dust Saloon
Somewhere in the New Mexico Territory
1873

Charlie Maklin was holding one hell of a hand, and damned if it wasn't dealt to him honestly. He was hard pressed to keep his poker face neutral and took his time situating his cards in order. He looked at the pot which had grown progressively during the last few rounds of betting and considered the odds of his winning it.

A full house was always a good hand and he was holding Kings over tens. The only problem was the hand being held by the well dressed and possible hustler sitting across from him. Well dressed? In this God forsaken part of the territory? Charlie knew he was dealing with a traveling card sharp, much like himself. Only *he* didn't advertise it. He made it a point to look dusty and well worn when he came into town. He wanted to look like he was just stopping on his way through to somewhere else. Looking at the man seated across the table, Charlie wondered who was the better sharp and decided it was worth finding out.

"Well, mister, are you going to call my raise or just sit there lookin' ignorant?"

Charlie was unfazed by the insult and replied, "Oh, I'm sorry," he grinned, "I was thinking about the woman I bedded a couple of nights ago. She sure was pretty, mm mmm. I'll call," and he placed the appropriate amount of money into the pot.

The other man laid his cards on the table and Charlie stared in amazement at the four Aces staring back at him. *What!?* He had been outsmarted by a cheater that was better than him. The man was slick as a whistle because Charlie had been keeping an eye on any suspicious movements or dealing from the bottom of the deck. He laid his full house on the table and said, "I guess that beats the hell out of my full house. It's been a pleasure," he said as he stood up to leave.

"Aww, don't leave just as the game is getting interesting. You have plenty of time to win it back. I've got all night," said the other man as he gathered his winnings.

"Nah, I best be going. I have to make it to Fort Worth within the next couple of weeks. Take care now," he said as he tipped his hat to the winner. He sauntered to the bar, downed one more whiskey, and left through the batwing doors of the saloon. He mounted his horse, Nocount, and rode slowly out of town. Damn! That was a beautiful full house! *Damn, damn, damn!* He was getting sloppy. He should have been able to detect the other man's underhanded skills. It was time to either get his mind back in the game or give it up, and he was mighty tired of traveling and of the game. Surely life had to be better than this.

The sun was almost a memory in the western sky and to soothe his nerves and the loss of practically the last dollar he had, he sang to Nocount about happier times. It was his habit to make up songs as he rode along. Sometimes they were funny, sometimes sad, sometimes extremely ribald, and sometimes about love unrequited, but always a balm to his otherwise boring and sometimes tense existence. It was almost time to stop and make camp for the night. Charlie guessed he and Nocount had been riding for at least four hours when he heard the thunder of pounding hooves behind him. It sounded like at least four or five riders. Stopping and turning in the saddle to see who was coming up on him fast as lightening, he saw one of the men take a pistol from his holster and aim it squarely at his chest. Deciding that running at this point was futile, he put his hands up and waited for them to say what was on their mind.

"Evenin', gentlemen. What can I do for you?"

"We're takin' you back for hangin', that's what we're gonna to do for *you*. You murdered Bret Calhoun in cold blood and we aim to hang your ass for it. Now come along nice like and don't make any trouble for us."

"I didn't murder anyone, and who the hell is Bret Calhoun, anyway?"

"He was the gambler you lost that big pot to back in town. You shot him dead in the forehead, we all saw it, and we aim to make things right."

Apparently, one of the men in the group was tired of the charade and blurted, "Cut the bullshit, Oscar. We owe him at least the dignity of the truth before he swings."

"And what truth would that be?" Charlie asked, trying to get a handle on the situation.

"The truth is, one of our own killed that cheatin' sumbitch but, you know, we just can't let him hang for it. He's one of us, right boys? So, the circumstances surrounding your arrival and short stay in town make a good story and a convenient fall guy. Feel any better now?" the man asked as he grinned like an ape.

In all of Charlie's years as a gambler, he had never encountered a situation like this, and he wasn't going to take the fall for any crime he didn't commit.

"Well, gentleman, it seems as though we have a problem. You see, I'm not stupid, and I am definitely not going to let you hang me. You know why? Because…" and within a split second, Charlie had both of his pistols out of his holster, and started shooting them one by one in rapid succession. His speed and accuracy with a gun had always been what he considered an unfortunate skill. It came naturally to him; a natural instinct. Men saw him wearing two pistols on his hips and figured he was a gunslinger. These were the first lives he had ever taken. *Now* he was guilty of murder although he personally considered it self defense. But who in this God forsaken territory would agree?

His best bet was to ride fast out of the territory and cross the border into Texas. "Come on, Nocount. Let's get the hell out of here. Ride on to Texas, you no count piece of dung!" Nocount was aptly named because of his stubborn attitude and inconsistent listening skills. One day he was right as rain and the next he was useless, and no amount of yelling or chastising would sway him.

Damn, just when I was thinkin' to give up the game and try to go straight," Charlie thought. Oh well, instead of singing on the ride to Texas, he better come up with a workable alternative plan. One thing he knew for sure; he was headed back East. He would go to the Atlantic Ocean if he had to, maybe ride north, way up north, and find a new place to call home. A place where it was a certainty no one would recognize him or have wanted posters with his face on them tacked up in every town.

What Charlie didn't know would worry him for a long time to come. The men who would have hanged him were wanted by authorities in three territories. Instead of running and hiding, he was rightfully owed a hefty reward for their demise. Charlie would bear the burden of his actions without knowing the truth of the matter. But not knowing is what motivated him to change his life. God certainly did work in mysterious ways.

Part One

Chapter One

Colleen Newcomb lit the candle that was on her bedside table and sat on the edge of her bed, severely dreading another day on the boat. It was times like this she would curse her late husband for leaving her and his children, plus the one they made together, in such dire straits. Jacob had left them with barely enough money to keep food on the table, let alone live the life he had promised her before they were married. He had been twenty years her senior but promised the moon and stars if Colleen Darcy would just consent to be his wife. From the first day of their marriage, Jacob taught her everything about fishing boats and the fishing industry, hoping that one day, should anything ever happen to him, she and Mason, could take over and at least make a modest living.

It was true that Jacob Newcomb came from a long line of Newcombs who had settled in the Northeast. He had inherited the old house in which they lived, and by some standards it appeared they were well off because of the size and beauty of the dwelling. But on the inside, the furniture was faded and threadbare, and with paint peeling off the walls because of the wretched humidity from Penobscot Bay.

Everyone in their community knew that Jacob had tried several endeavors in which to make a living because he hated the boat and he hated fishing. Unfortunately, he had failed at each one and they would always fall back on what they knew best. Jacob's oldest child, Mason, had learned everything one needed to know about boats and fishing when he was just a wee lad, and if not for him, they would truly starve. He was now almost twenty and toiled just as hard as she six days a week to keep everyone fed, and that included their milk cow, pigs and chickens, and their beloved dog named Stern, a terrier of dubious parentage, so called as he always followed behind the family wherever they went. Stern even followed them to church on Sundays, waiting at the bottom of the church steps so he could walk home with the family he so dearly loved.

Her stepdaughter Edith, who was seventeen, took care of the home front and watched her little brother Caleb, who was only four years old. She found it hard to believe he was four already. Life was whizzing past her with incredible speed, she thought, and they never got any further along than in years past. When she looked in the mirror each day she promised herself to take better care of her hair and skin which were always so dry from the wind on the water. But she never kept the promise. She was just too tired to even keep trying.

Colleen, whose nickname was "Sherry" because of the color of her amber eyes, stood up from her bed and felt around the floor with her feet for her slippers, as the hardwood floors were freezing this early in the morning. She scratched her head and pushed her auburn curls out of her face as she descended the back stairs to the kitchen. God bless her, Edith had started a fire in the stove and put on a pot of coffee for her and Mason. A cup of strong black coffee should get her heart pumping and ready for another day of back breaking work.

"Good morning, Sherry. Sit down and drink your coffee while I make you some breakfast. I called for Mason to wake up but you know how he is." So saying, she walked to the bottom of the stairs and yelled, "Mason! Mason you wake up this instant if you want any breakfast. I'm fixing pancakes!" Then she laughed because she knew the thought of hot pancakes would surely bring him flying down the stairs.

"What would I do without you, Edith? This family would be lost without your care. I hate to burden you with so much but I don't know what else we can do for the time being. When Mason comes to breakfast, I'm going to talk to him about hiring another man to work on the boat. One more man hopefully means a bigger catch each day." On a heavy sigh, she continued, "Something has to change. We can't keep going on like this. We're all miserable and constantly on the edge of ruin. Perhaps I *should* sell *The Fetching Mermaid* to Dirk Jamison. Maybe we could take the profits and start another venture." Realizing what she had just said, she continued, "Oh God, what am I saying? That's exactly what put us in this shape to begin with! Augh!" *The Fetching Mermaid my foot,* she thought. A more likely name would have been, *"The Albatross."*

Just then, Mason came bounding down the stairs looking much the same as Sherry, sniffing the air for pancakes. "Sis, you promised pancakes! It's so unfair of you to trick me like that!" Disappointed, he flopped down on a kitchen chair and started drinking his coffee.

"Mason, we need to talk. I think we need to hire another man to work with us on the boat. One more man could mean a great difference in our income from the fish." Then Sherry started crying and hung her head to her chest as her shoulders jerked with sobs. "I...I don't know how much longer I can...do this. I know you're just as miserable as I am. We need to do something different in an effort to bring some change into our lives. Look what happened to your father! He was so tired that day he fell overboard, he just didn't have the stamina to keep up. I don't want that to happen to us, Mason." She sniffed and wiped her nose on the sleeve of her robe for lack of anything else absorbent, and continued through her tears, "Young Caleb is only four years old! He's just a wee lad and he needs his Ma. What will happen to him if I die too young?" Then she cried in earnest, moaning loudly and keening as her dear Ma had done back in Ireland. "Do ye ken, Mason? Do ye understand how I'm feelin'?"

She had been a young girl of seventeen when she landed on the shores of Penobscot Bay, her brother having died on the voyage from an infection of some sort that brought on a dangerously high fever. The captain buried him at sea and she drifted rudderless through her days until she got off the ship and found Jacob Newcomb. Many were the times since Jacob's death that Sherry would berate herself for not loving Jacob like a good wife should have done. Even though she and the children were now struggling, it was Jacob who took her in upon her arrival in America, and cared for her in exchange for a mother for his children. Sometimes at night, just as she would fall asleep, she would whisper, "I'm sorry, Jacob. I'm so very sorry."

Mason, who was a big strapping young man over six feet tall and well muscled, came around the table and took Sherry into his arms, patting her back and swaying from side to side while she cried. "Don't cry, Sherry. We'll figure something out. Maybe we'll pray this Sunday for a miracle. How does that sound? If we all pray together, surely God will hear us and grant us ease and prosperity, hmm? Come now. Eat your breakfast and we'll talk about hiring a new man on the way to the Mermaid. I vow to you, and you too, Edith, that I will do whatever it takes to make things better for our family." Edith walked over and hugged both he and Sherry, and they all swayed together in comfort. Caleb walked down the stairs one at a time, rubbing the sleep from his little eyes, and asked, "Why are you dancing?" It was enough to the dispel the pall that had fallen over the kitchen that morning, and they all began to laugh long and heartily because it felt so darned good.

***

On the way down the path toward the dock, Sherry and Mason further discussed the idea of hiring another man to help with their business. It was decided that she would tack notices to the pilings of the dock, stating Sherry's name and the name of their boat with instructions to inquire at their house on the hill directly west of their trawler.

Dirk Jamison watched their progression toward the bay and once again appreciated the sway of Sherry's hips as she walked, the color of her youthful complexion and her lips that were pink and looked so utterly kissable. Were it not for his feelings for the woman, he would have done away with her long ago, taking over her boat and business. The Mermaid would be a welcome addition to his fleet. However, she rebuffed not only his romantic attentions, but also his offer to purchase The Mermaid. One day he vowed to own both, the woman and the boat.

He noted with interest that she was tacking a notice on a piling of the dock. Perhaps she was finally putting The Mermaid up for sale. When she sailed far enough away from shore, he would walk over and take a look. When he did, he was surprised to see she was advertising for additional help for her business. It was enough to put Dirk in such a foul mood as to hastily make his way into town for a visit with his favorite painted lady. Ruby was strong and could take his roughness in stride. She was strong enough to take the sexual beating that would ease his desire for a certain auburn haired siren that was never far from his mind. He had trained Ruby to anticipate his desires and she well tolerated the heat and madness of their sessions. Actually, it never mattered whether she tolerated them or not. He took what he wanted and couldn't have cared less about her as a human being.

***

"Eastward Ho!" Charlie said each morning after packing up his camp and mounting Nocount. "Eastward Ho, Nocount! Every day brings us closer to a new life." Talking to Nocount was one of the only things that kept Charlie sane during the days and weeks on his trek East. "But remember, my name is Cullen Westover now." Cullen Westover. He liked the name. It had a certain charm, he thought. Having never assumed a counterfeit identity before, he was rather concerned about messing up when he introduced himself, or when someone called him by the new name. What if he forgot to answer? So he started singing it. In a rich baritone, he sang, "Cullen Westover, Cullen Westover, la la la, that would be me, Cullen Westover, yes indeed, Cullen Westover, la la la."

The farther away from the New Mexico territory he traveled the more relaxed and secure he felt that once he reached the East coast he would be free from capture. He had been quite paranoid while riding across Texas, and hated having to stop for any reason. However, he had to eat which meant he had to make some quick cash with which to purchase supplies. Once, while riding through the plains of Texas, he stopped and introduced himself to an older gentleman who was mending fences, and asked for short-term work. The pay wasn't too bad but the work had been back breaking. He never complained, though. It kept him moving eastward.

After crossing the Texas line into Missouri, Cullen felt easier about stopping in towns to partake of a little whisky and card playing. Before his first stop for such reasons, he talked with Nocount about it and twisted it this way and that to suit his purposes. "Yeah, I know. I've put gambling behind me, or I'm supposed to. But I might need some stake money for when I settle in a new place. Plus, you need a new set of shoes, my friend, and they don't come cheap. So stop twitchin' your ears in judgment and keep walkin' on."

Nocount was the damnedest, most judgmental animal Char…*Cullen* had ever met. Just as the thought flitted through his mind, Nocount cow kicked the air close to his stirrup which made Cullen laugh like hell. Damned if he didn't believe the horse understood every word he said.

After another couple of days riding and nights camped beneath the stars, Cullen road into a fair sized town in the middle of Missouri. It had everything he needed; a blacksmith for Nocount, a general store for supplies, and his choice of three saloons in which to gamble the last of the pay he made in Texas, digging post holes. He could sure use a bath, too. Maybe just this once, *if* the cards were kind, he could afford a bath and a room at the local hotel for a night. He thought he might as well check out the saloons first and see if his sixth sense for gambling establishments worked to his favor. After finding one in which he felt comfortable, he ordered a shot of whiskey and scanned the room for what he thought might be card sharps, and sauntered over to a table that appeared in need of a fourth player in a game of poker.

"Afternoon, Gents. Need a fourth? Mind if I take a chance?" The three other men looked him up and down, considered the way he was dressed, the stupid smile on his face, and immediately considered him a rube. "Sure," one of the men said as he pulled out the empty chair. "Have a seat. You *do* know how to play, don't you?" Cullen rolled his eyes and exclaimed, "Why a'course I know how to play, mister. What do you take me for? A green farm boy?" He hyucked a couple of times and could tell by their faces that was exactly what they took him for.

Three hours later, he was making his excuses and gathering his considerable winnings. "Damn, I ain't never won this much money in my whole life! Bartender! Bring these fella's a bottle of your finest whiskey, will ya?" Smiling like an idiot, he held his hand out to shake those of each of his competitors, tipped his hat, and walked out of the saloon. Now all he had to do was disappear quickly before they had the time to question their initial impression of him.

The first thing he did was ride Nocount to the blacksmith and livery. "Now don't you go giving this nice gentleman a hard time, ya hear?" Patting the horse's flanks, he next made his way to the hotel and paid for a room and a bath. Before heading upstairs to his room, he ordered supper in the dining room and ate like a starving man. It was so damn delicious that he closed his eyes and savored each and every bite. The coffee was strong and black, just the way he liked it, and the steak was almost bleeding. Yes sir, a mighty fine meal, it was.

Before climbing the stairs, he inquired at the front desk about laundry services and found that if he left his clothes outside his door by six o'clock that evening, they would be washed and ready by eight the next morning. He carried his gear upstairs, went in his room, locked the door, and counted his winnings from poker. Seventy-six dollars. Not the best pot he had ever won, but certainly not the worst. Tucking it safely in a special compartment of his saddle bag, he headed down the hall for a nice hot bath. As he lay in the steaming water, he went over a to-do list in his mind for tomorrow so he could get the hell out of town. Pick up Nocount, get supplies from the store, and try, if he felt he could afford the time, to get some breakfast. He knew one thing for sure. As much as he had enjoyed a hot meal, a hot bath, and a comfortable bed, he would be glad to put some miles between him and this town.

Back in his room, he stared at himself in a mirror over the wash stand and couldn't believe his eyes. The man staring back at him bore absolutely no resemblance to what he actually looked like. He looked like a straggly bum. His wavy hair was now bleached by the sun and hung an inch or two below his collar. His beard was the worst of it, though. It was long and hadn't been shaped since he started growing it, and felt a certain sadness that the beard covered his dimples. His dimples always made his mother's heart melt, and many a woman was taken in by them; those and his ice blue eyes. He took a few moments to mourn the loss of his old appearance and then shrugged it off, knowing when he was finally safe and permanently settled he would clean up just fine.

The next morning brought evidence that his luck was holding out because everything he needed to get done went off without a hitch. He was even able to order two fried egg and sausage biscuits to eat for breakfast when he was finally on the road. Nocount seemed happy with his new shoes and was looking quite spiffy from the good grooming he received while at the livery overnight. And so they headed east. Always eastward.

***

Four days later, Cullen picked up a dirt road that obviously led to the next town. It was pretty well tended and headed east, and that's all he cared about. After a mile or so, he saw in the distance a large farmhouse with a massive barn not far away. Damn, the road led to a farm and not a town. Cullen had been watching the sky all day, noticing storm clouds gathering in the south. He looked at the farmhouse and then looked at the sky. It was simple, really. He much preferred a roof over his head during a storm than being soaked like a drowned rat, so he headed toward the farmhouse hoping the owner was at least hospitable enough to offer him the hayloft in the barn for the night. Nocount lifted his head in the air, sniffing and snorting, and broke into a canter toward the farm which confirmed his decision to stop for the night.

Arriving at the premises, he noticed a woman beating a rug on a clothes line between the house and barn. "Excuse me, Missus, is your husband around? I'd like to speak to him, if you please." The woman was short and well made, and had no trouble at all beating every last speck of dust and dirt out of the well worn rug. Shading her eyes with a hand, she looked up at Cullen, and replied, "Yes, he's here. Ride around to the back of the house and you'll see him at the paddock." Cullen tipped his hat and smiled, "Much obliged, ma'am." He reined Nocount in that direction but the animal had other ideas. He headed straight for the woman and her rug. *Oh shit!*

"Nocount! Behave yourself!" Nocount was having none of it. He sidled right up to the woman and began nuzzling her face and chest. "Ma'am, I am so very sorry. Nocount isn't known for his polite behavior and sometimes he just won't listen." The horse was acting mighty odd. Cullen had never seen him be so affectionate with a person.

The woman just smiled and rubbed the horse between the eyes and ears. "He's charming, really. How fortunate you are to own such a kind and gentle animal." *What?*

"I'm sure glad you think so, ma'am. But truth be known, he's the most ill mannered animal I've ever owned." Her eyes twinkled as she replied, "Well of course he's ill mannered with a name such as Nocount! We must be careful what we name our horses, sir. The name must bring out the best in the animal." *Sure, all right.* "Just leave him with me while you speak with my husband. He'll be fine." Cullen dismounted and handed her the reins. *If this isn't the damndest thing,* he thought as he walked to the paddock fence.

"Sir, my name is Cullen Westover, and I was wondering if I might sleep in your barn tonight. I've been watching the clouds all day and I believe we're in for quite a storm this evening." The man was at least ten years older than the woman who was making over his useless horse, but Cullen liked him immediately. He had a knack for that; sizing people up within seconds. The man held out his hand in greeting and said, "Of course you can sleep in my barn. I've been watching those clouds, too, and I know it'll probably be shortly after suppertime when it finally gets here. Make yourself at home. Charlotte will have supper on the table around five o'clock. You're welcome to share a meal with us."

Cullen smiled brightly at having found such a nice couple. It wasn't often during his travels that people treated him with kindness and generosity. "Thank you, sir. I would love to join you."

The man looked in the paddock once more and then turned to introduce himself. "The name's Kenneth Hutchinson, and you've already met my wife, Charlie," the man said as she thrust his hand out to shake Cullen's. *Charlie.* The nickname sent an immediate chill down his spine and he quickly banished it with self recriminations to not be so silly and to have some faith. It was just hearing his real name, was all. Just a bit of a jolt.

Kenneth looked in the paddock one more time and continued to stare at the most beautiful chestnut horse Cullen had ever seen. He had no earthly idea what breed it was as he had never seen the like before. "He's a beaut," Cullen said admiringly. Kenneth nodded and replied, "Yes, he is. Too bad no one wants to buy him. I was wondering what I'm going to do with him when you walked up."

Cullen couldn't believe no one wanted him. "How much are you selling him for?" Kenneth sort of laughed and said, "Whatever the market will bear, and there's no market for the animal. He's the worst purchase I've ever made. I guess you'd say he's a lesson learned. Bought him off a fella that comes down from Canada once a year. He runs a circuit through a few states every spring and sells horses like no one around here has ever seen."

Cullen replied, "I hate to be ignorant, but what breed is he? I've never seen anything like him." Kenneth grinned and said, "He's what they call a Percheron. Some Frenchie breed. Strong as an ox, loyal to a fault, and gentle as a lamb. Smart as a whip, too." Then Kenneth turned and walked toward his wife. Cullen followed but really wanted to stay at the paddock fence, admiring the chestnut giant. As they walked, Cullen asked, "How tall is he?" Kenneth grinned and said, "Eighteen hands. Think you could handle that?" They both laughed and stopped while Kenneth told Charlie they would be having company for supper.

The meal was delicious and the couple was most gracious. Heck, one would think Cullen was royalty for the way he was treated. He wasn't used to it but loved it just the same. Charlie was clearing the table and fixing a pot of coffee to go with blackberry pie when Cullen asked, "What's his name?" Kenneth knew he was talking about the horse and replied, "Honor." Cullen grinned and said, "Isn't that a strange name for a horse?" Kenneth laughed, "There's a story behind that.

"When I met my wife, she was breaking and training horses for her father a few miles north of here. Never met a woman, or man, for that matter, who had such a way with horses. When we married and she moved in with me, she renamed all my horses, every last one of them. She said their names made them what they were and that negative names brought out bad dispositions and manners." He shook his head gently upon remembering those first days. It was obvious to Cullen the couple was very happily married. They appeared very much in love if the looks between them were any indication, and it suddenly expanded the empty hole in him he was never able to fill.

Charlie came back into the dining room with coffee and pie, and picked up on the conversation. "That's right. It's absolutely true. The name you give any animal will make a difference in its performance and attitude."

The rest of the evening was beyond pleasant but it was soon time to bed down for the night. "Ma'am, that was a mighty fine meal, and the very best blackberry pie I've ever eaten. Kenneth, you're a lucky man." Charlie blushed and then put her arm around Ken's waist. "I do believe that is the nicest compliment I've ever received, Mr. Westover," she gushed. Cullen shook Kenneth's hand and excused himself to head for the barn. As he walked away, Charlie whispered, "Ask him to stay, Ken. He won't stay long but I want you to ask him all the same." Her husband said he would ask. He knew better than to run counter to his wife's intuitions. He noticed her staring at him during supper and knew something was milling around in her mind.

Ken kept Cullen working close to the farmhouse, giving him odd jobs and repairs to do while his wife pondered what it was about the fella that held her interest. Had the man been better looking, Ken might have been a tad jealous, but truth be known, Cullen looked like a saddle tramp. But he had a pleasing personality and a certain way with words which Ken hoped would help him during his journey, wherever that might lead.

Right now, Ken was watching him walk over to Charlie, digging his hand in his pocket. Now, what was that all about?

"Miz Hutchinson, when will you next go into town for supplies? I was hoping you would buy me a good supply of sugar cubes. I've got the money right here," he said, pulling the change out of his pocket. Charlie took the money and said, "Of course, Cullen. I'll be glad to add sugar cubes to my list, although I can't imagine why you would need so many." Then she winked at him and looked toward the paddock where Honor was grazing with the other horses. Cullen grinned sheepishly and blushed, "Much obliged, ma'am." Then he turned and walked back to the barn to finish mucking out stalls and replenishing hay and water.

Ken walked over to her and smiled. "What's he up to now?" Charlie merely smiled in answer and that was no comfort to Ken. "Sweetheart, I don't have anything to worry about as far as he's concerned, do I?" Charlie laughed, "Oh, Ken, after all these years, you have to ask such a question? You know you are the only man in the world for me. It's just that Cullen has captured my imagination and I see happiness coming his way for the first time in his life. I mean true and lasting happiness and it just brings me some joy, that's all." Then she kissed him soundly right out in the yard for any and all to see, and whispered in his ear, "We'll finish this tonight," and walked back into the kitchen. *Damn woman*, Ken thought. She'd always keep him dancing to her tune until the day he died. He loved her beyond measure and would do anything to please her, even if that was to foster whatever plan she had for Cullen Westover. He chortled to himself as he walked toward the barn, thinking of what might happen that night in bed with his woman. It was enough to keep him grinning the rest of the day.

Cullen had watched the two kissing and envied their marriage. It was plain to anyone who noticed that the couple was still madly in love after being married for several years. It was kind of magical, in a way. And he wanted the same for himself.

He didn't have much of a recollection of his parents. He had no idea if they loved each other or not. His mother had died giving birth to her second child, his little sister, who had not lived long past his mother's death. He missed his Ma something fierce. He thought of her each and every day, and had since the day he marched off their land. She had been a school teacher and taught Cullen how to read and write, and made sure he wasn't lacking in knowledge of any kind. In her honor, Cullen continued his studies by himself after her untimely death.

His father was never the same after she passed, and had very little emotionally to give to his only child of ten years. Cullen spent his days following his father around the farm, offering to help with chores and the like, hoping to be noticed and appreciated. It never happened and Cullen, Charles Maklin, that is, left home at the age of sixteen and never looked back. Life was hard but he kept going through the pain, often physical from defending himself from older boys and men, and the sadness of being alone. He once rode on a cattle drive and learned how to play cards in the evenings.

One man in particular was an excellent poker player and taught him how to play, bet, and win at the game. It had been his saving grace over the years when jobs weren't available and it also gave him a sense of accomplishment when he won, by whatever means.

As he grew older, his looks matured and most ladies thought him quite handsome. He trifled with their hearts here and there, but mostly he paid for physical affection. It used to be enough when he was eighteen and even twenty, but as the years flew by, he knew an emptiness that couldn't be filled with winning hands of poker, and whores who only loved him for his money. So he kept going, always looking for something he couldn't even identify until now. He wanted what Ken and Charlie had. He wanted it all and had been through enough lessons in life that he knew he would have to work like the dickens to get it.

"How's it comin' along, Cullen?" Ken brought him out of his reveries as he realized he was just standing there leaning on a pitchfork, lost in fantasy. "Oh, I'm sorry, Ken. I was just thinking and kind of got lost in it. I'm almost finished with the last stall. What's next on the list?" Ken looked as if he was considering the next chore when he finally said, "That'll be all for today. But I would like you to saddle Honor and walk him around a bit. I need to see how he moves and try to figure out some different selling points. I can't keep the animal as a pet for the rest of his life. He needs to work. Percherons are in the same category as draft horses, you know. They need a job or a close relationship with a human or they'll get bored and act up. Just like a child, you might say. So, there's a saddle and girth hanging on the left side of the tack room that's just for him. Won't fit any other horse I've got, or probably ever will have. Let's go."

Cullen felt like a child on Christmas morning. He was grinning from ear to ear and it wasn't lost on Ken. It wasn't the horse Ken wanted to see in action, it was the man. He wanted to witness the relationship between Cullen and Honor, and now was as good a time as any. He felt like maybe Honor had a lot to do with Charlie's good hearted manipulations and so called her out of the kitchen to watch the ride.

They watched as Cullen walked over to Honor, and as he rubbed the horse's muzzle, he began talking sweetly and breathing into the horse's nostrils. Honor sniffed around Cullen's pockets and found the one that had sugar cubes in it. Cullen laughed as he pulled out a few and offered him the treat. Then he ran his hands down one side of his body, around the back, and then up the other side. Honor stood stock still and appeared to relish the attention.

Saddling him was another matter, entirely. The horse was huge! But Cullen managed to lift the saddle high enough to put it in place and then arranged the rest of the tack. It was finally time to put his foot in the stirrup and climb aboard. Being a few inches over six feet, Cullen never had any trouble mounting a horse. But this one? It would take some practice.

"Don't be afraid! He'll take care of you!" Charlie yelled. Cullen reined him over to the paddock fence and Ken opened the gate. "Looks like you two might become good friends. Take him for a ride in that field yonder. See what he can do," Ken said as he watched horse and rider take off. Cullen let the horse have his freedom to run as long as he wished and it was a magnificent ride. Honor was frisky and excited and Cullen threw his head back and laughed, "That's it, boy! Let it all out!" Finally, they reluctantly rode back. Ken and Charlie were all smiles and had learned a lot about Cullen in those few minutes.

Chapter Two

Sherry had always enjoyed the trip out to sea and the trip back. It was what had to be done in between that was unpleasant and exhausted her. She and Mason had cast the net and secured it, and now it was time to see if Sherry's intuition had hit upon a good sized school of cod. "Mason, I'll steer this one. I've got a good feeling about where to go." Mason stood next to Sherry, always amazed at how often she was able to guide them to a good spot and how well she knew how to navigate it. For someone who wasn't born to life at sea, she sure knew what she was doing. She was a quick study and had learned everything necessary about sailing and trawling after marrying Jacob.

At first, she stayed at home with Edith, and took care of the house and gardens, occasionally sailing with Jacob and Mason to put into practice what Jacob had taught her. Then Caleb came along and her work seemed to double. But she didn't mind because she loved the little boy with all her heart and soul. The only part of his arrival that wasn't joyous was the fact that her dear parents couldn't be there to see their first grandchild being born. Jacob had promised her he would do all in his power to bring them over from Ireland. That promise was a lot of what had kept Sherry going each day.

Sherry was used to hard work. She was the oldest of her mother's children and had learned about child rearing and farming when she was just a young girl. However, there came a time when there was nothing to farm. The potato famine struck the heart of Ireland, and it was all her parents could do to recover from the heavy losses and keep any food at all on the table. When Sherry was sixteen, they sold a family heirloom of great value to pay for her and her brother's trip to America.

She had always been her Pa's favorite and he cried like a baby as he watched her and her brother ride away in a neighbor's pony cart for the ship that would take them away from him, possibly forever. But he was willing to take the chance in letting them go so they might find happiness and prosperity in a new land.

While Mason stood beside her, she asked him, "If you could move anywhere in America, where would you move?" Mason had never allowed himself the thought of such a possibility and had to think about it for a few moments. "Somewhere that's no so darned cold! I've lived through these winters long enough. I just want to be warm." Sherry smiled and replied, "I can certainly understand that, but where do you think you would want to live? Name a state."

"Sherry, are you thinking of selling and moving to another state?" He sounded a bit panicked because he was born and raised in Maine. He had never traveled out of state and it was a frightening proposition…at first. Then he started warming to the idea. "I mean, would we have enough money from the sale of the house, the land, and The Mermaid to start over again in another place? Or maybe we could sail her down the coast?"

"I'm just daydreaming, Mason. It's just a dream, but you know Dirk is pressing me to make a decision. I've put him off so far but I'm afraid he's getting tired of my answer. He's a powerful man in these parts and most folks do his bidding without argument."

"Is he threatening you, Sherry?" Mason would kill the man with his bare hands. Someone had to take a stand against the crooked bastard and he wanted to be the man to do it. "When he finds out you're asking for help on the boat, he'll pop his cork! I'll have to keep a closer eye on him. I'll protect you. I swear I'll do my best."

When Sherry felt the need to check on the catch, they both worked the pulley hoist to bring the net up and estimate the number of fish caught in the area she had navigated. Once again she had picked an excellent spot and they wouldn't have to go back out again that day. They could go back out and make more money, but to Sherry, it was more important to spend the time together as a family. A good "one catch day" was a happy day as she could go home and enjoy her children. It also gave Sherry extra time to go over their finances and consider other ways to make extra income that wouldn't keep them separated.

Edith walked out onto the porch and sat in an old wicker rocker, waiting for any sight of The Mermaid. She was between chores and thought she would enjoy the summer heat and write a letter to the grandparents she had never met in Ireland. Sherry had encouraged her and Mason to write as often as they could but there was never much time for it. Holding pencil to paper, she tried to start the missive but was distracted by the delicious warmth of the sun.

It was days like this one she would remember while milking the cow or gathering eggs come winter. Caleb was down for a nap, and she enjoyed the time alone where she could indulge in dreams that all seventeen year old girls often do. Her dreams were simple but hard to realize in Castine. She didn't want to live the sea life anymore but everyone in town made their living that way. She wanted to marry a farmer and have three children. She wanted to have enough money so they never worried about food or other necessities. She wanted to know true love. She wasn't sure she had ever witnessed it but felt sure she would recognize it if it came her way. The closest thing to love she had ever experienced came from Sherry and Mason, her father having been somewhat cold and distant. She could tell Mason had similar thoughts of changing his life but was too caught up in the responsibility of keeping the family afloat.

Just as she would finally start the letter, she spied The Mermaid in the distance and went to the kitchen to get the evening meal started. Caleb would be up soon and he would be hungry.

*****

Five weeks later, after their evening meal, Sherry brought up what had been painfully obvious. No one was applying for the job on The Mermaid.

"We've got to consider that Dirk has scared anyone away who might want the job. Autumn isn't far off and we've got to make some extra money to keep us for the winter months. Edith, I'm so proud of you, dearest. You've been putting up all the food from the garden and it will be of tremendous help. However, we will still need staples. Lord knows how many days the ice will cover the bay and keep us from fishing this winter."

Sherry hated to ask even more of Edith but it had to be done. "Edith, I'm going to start taking Caleb on the boat with us. Once the garden is gone and the canning finished, you'll need to get a job at the fish cannery. I'm so sorry to have to ask, but we all have to do whatever is necessary to get by." Tears formed in her eyes as she placed her hand over Edith's at the table. "I'm sure that any day now a man will come asking for the job on The Mermaid. Once that happens, we'll reconsider our plans." She sniffed a couple of times and heaved a huge sigh before further asking, "Do you object terribly to getting the job, Edith?"

Edith tried to hide her dismay. "Can we afford boots, gloves and a coat for me to wear in the factory during the winter months? I've heard stories about how cold the cannery gets during the winter." Biting her tongue, she continued, "Its fine with me, Sherry. I know it has to be done and I'm glad to do it for the family." Her tremulous smile was answer enough for Sherry, and it broke her heart. She bid them to all hold hands around the table and then began praying. "Dear God, please, in your infinite wisdom and mercy, bring us a man to help on The Mermaid. Please have him be big and strong and willing to work hard. Our family needs your assistance very soon. Winter is coming and You know what that means. Please know that our gratitude for what You already provide is boundless, and we know that You will always provide more should we ask in earnest. In Jesus' name we pray, Amen."

Sherry glanced at Edith, and promised her, "I can only imagine what your dreams are, darling. One day they will come true, I know it. We just have to concentrate on tomorrow and the next day. But dreams do come true, love. They do!"

Chapter Three

Working for the Hutchinsons had been a blessing. He was well treated and the work had not been back breaking. He considered the amount of money he had saved during the last two months and knew it was time to leave, though he hated to do so. Ken and Charlie were good and loving people and he felt blessed to have met them. But it was time to go.

"Ken, can I talk to you for a minute?" Ken looked at the young man and knew what was coming. "Sure, Cullen. Let's sit down for a spell and chat." Ken sat down on a bale of hay and waited for the words that would hurt like hell.

"It's time for me to go, Ken. I need to keep on heading east and I've been here longer than I ever wanted to be. Lord knows I don't want to leave, but I've got to. I want you to know how much I appreciate your kindness and generosity. You and Charlie have become my dearest friends." Tears came to his eyes as he continued to pour his heart out. "I want what you and Charlie have together. I never much considered actually finding a woman to love but now that I've seen what good marriage truly looks like, I want it. You taught me what love looks and feels like, Ken. You and Charlie have given me something to work toward and I'll be forever grateful. I'll write when I can." Then he handed Ken a box of leftover sugar cubes and said, "Please make sure Honor gets these. He'll miss his treats, I imagine."

Ken got up, put his arms around Cullen, and hugged him tight. "Boy, you do what you have to do and go with our blessings. But please don't go until tomorrow morning. We sure would love to share another meal with you before you leave." Cullen nodded, swiped at his nose and started mucking stalls again.

Ken walked away, feeling as though he had been gut punched, and headed to the house to tell Charlie. She was going to be heartbroken, too. They had some things they needed to discuss before supper.

The meal was uncomfortable for all three of them. It was quiet and no one had much of an appetite. Cullen spoke up and said, "I'll be leaving first thing tomorrow morning. I would appreciate a little food and some supplies to take with me if you can spare them." Charlie nodded, and said, "Nocount is lame right now so you can't take him. You'll have to take Honor." Then she started crying and had to leave the table.

The next morning was even worse for Cullen. After he had saddled Honor and walked him to the kitchen door, he saw that his supplies were in a sack on the porch with a note stuck in it. He couldn't even read it. He would have to wait until he was far away and his sadness wasn't so fresh and cutting. He looked in the paddock at Nocount one more time and then headed up the dirt road that would have him traveling ever eastward.

By the time Cullen made it to North Carolina, he felt he might be ready to read the note from Ken and Charlie. It was silly that he had waited so long. What he experienced while staying at their place was nothing more than working for some nice people; people who treated him kindly and with respect. People who he had come to love, and that wasn't part of the experience he had counted on. He stared at the folded note and once again fell into the fantasy of finding love and a family. *Don't be such a ninny. Open the damn thing.*

Dear Cullen,

Take good care of Honor. Treat people with all the respect and love you want for yourself, dear friend. Once you do that, love will come your way. Be and act like what you want in your life and it will appear. May God bless and protect you during your travels.

Love,

Ken and Charlie
PS: Please write often. We miss you already.

Cullen smiled through his tears and carefully folded the missive, placing it back in his pants pocket. The loving words they had written would play over and over in his mind during his times of solitude along the trail. "Honor, no wonder you're so gentle and loyal. Charlie spoiled you, didn't she? She loved on you until you turned to jelly," he grinned and then patted the horse's neck. "She has that affect on men, that's for sure."

Cullen was anxious to reach Virginia, and by his calculations, he would probably cross the state line in about a week or ten days. He was born and raised in Dinwiddie County, and thought he might pass through his hometown and see if his father was still alive, though he didn't want to see the man, particularly. He just wanted to know if he was still living and what had happened to the farm.

The closer he got to Virginia, the more he thought about his father and the hurtful years he had spent with him after his mother's death. Then he wondered what would happen to Ken if Charlie died and suddenly knew what had happened to his pa. Ken wouldn't be able to live without Charlie. He would spend the rest of his days mourning the loss and probably wouldn't care if he lived or died. Could that be what happened to his father? Had he just given up on everything but the farm after his mother died? For days he contemplated what his father might have been experiencing during the years between his mother's death and his departure at sixteen. These ruminations occupied so much of his time that he hardly realized when he crossed the Virginia state line, but soon he began recognizing the scenery and knew he wasn't far from the land of his youth.

It wasn't long before he was riding into town, noticing the familiar and the changes, when he thought to stop at the sheriff's office. If anyone would know about deaths in the community, it would be the sheriff.

People all up and down the street were looking at him, or at least it seemed as though they were looking at him. They were probably looking at Honor, admiring the beast and wondering what breed he was. He didn't blame them. Honor had caught his eye the moment he had first walked up to shake hands with Ken.

Cullen suddenly had the urge to stay overnight. He had noticed a boarding house on the edge of town and thought some home cooking would taste mighty good. It would give him a chance to inquire about his neighbors and old friends.

He dismounted Honor and tied his reins around a hitching rail in front of the sheriff's office. Brushing the dust off his clothes with his hat, he opened the door and went inside, hoping not to see a wanted poster with his face drawn upon it.

"Afternoon. My name is Charlie Maklin," he said as he reached out to shake the sheriff's hand. "I grew up in Dinwiddie County, and my father has a farm not far from here. I'm inquiring about his health, or status…I mean, if he's still alive."

Sheriff Barley looked him up and down and then offered him a seat. Fanning himself with a thin stack of wanted posters, he said, "I'm sorry to be the one to tell you this, but your pa ain't doin' so good. His heart has done give out on him and the only ones takin' care of the farm are two old coots that's been workin' for him. You might want to go out there and check on things see'n as you're his heir and all."

For some reason, Cullen felt a rush of adrenaline that left him feeling weak. What had he expected? That his father would still be hale and hearty after all these years? Why had he even stopped in town? Damn! Old feelings were rushing in and he didn't know what to do with the information.

"Uh, I don't know. You see, I'm just passing through and only thought to check. I haven't seen him in years. Hell, I don't know why I even stopped. Thank you for the information, Sheriff. Much obliged." Cullen stood up, put his hat back on his head, and started for the door when the sheriff said, "Son, we only have one set of parents in this life. I've heard the rumors about how old man Maklin lost his family and what a mean codger he became, and I can't say as I blame you for striking out on your own. He's a hard man, is Jessup Maklin. But he's your father. Just sayin'."

Cullen gave what he said a few moments of thought and replied, "I don't think so. I'll have to pass this time as I have a goal to reach on the coast. But I'll send telegrams periodically to check on him. Is it all right if I send them to you, sheriff?" The man nodded in reply, "Yes, I 'spect that would be all right." Just as Cullen reached the door, he looked back and asked, "Do you know if the farm has any taxes that are overdue?" The sheriff shrugged his shoulders, "As far as I know they're all paid up." Cullen nodded and thanked the man, opening the door and walking toward Honor. He took the reins and mounted the horse, saying, "Ain't that somethin'? The old man is still alive," and together, they walked slowly toward the boarding house. Cullen knew he should just ride out of town and call it a day, but something made him sign his old name on the register at the boarding house, anyway. He figured he was five times a fool for staying but, what the heck, he'd done plenty of foolish things over the years.

***

Cullen reined Honor to a halt on a rise just a couple hundred yards from the farmhouse. His heart sank at the familiar sight. In the end, it had just been too hard to leave without seeing his childhood home. He didn't really know what he expected but it wasn't *this*. The porch roof was sagging in the middle and two window shutters were hanging cockeyed. And what was that big lump on the front porch? The grass in the front yard was knee high and the fields were left fallow. How in the heck had he kept the place going? How was he paying his taxes? Well, he had come this far. He might as well walk Honor the rest of the way. *Turn around! You can still leave without being seen!*

The closer he got to the farmhouse, the more he recognized the lump on the porch to be a person, sitting in a wheelchair, huddled under a blanket. It was his father. Honor stopped just feet from the porch and stood stock still as Cullen stared at the man. "Who goes there?" his father said weakly. "It's me, Pa. Charlie." The old man's demeanor changed immediately, and he croaked, "What in the hell do you want after all these years? Come to see your old man brought so low, have ya? Well, you can just turn that beast around and leave the way you came in."

"Pa, I was just making my way toward the coast and thought I would stop in and say hello. But I can see you're still angry with me. For what, I don't know, but you were always angry with me. I'm sorry to see you in bad health.

I'm also sorry to see what's become of the farm. How are you making an income? I don't see anything happening here that would bring in any money."

"I got some cattle in the north pasture, not that it's any of your damn business. Hell, why should I believe you're my son, anyway? Can't see nothin' but a scraggly beard and hair that's way too long."

"My ma's name was Beatrice, and she died giving birth to my little sister."   The old man seemed to collapse into himself upon hearing such validation. "Is there anything I can do for you before I go? Anything you need?" His father's head dropped to his chest and Cullen could see his shoulders jerking as he sobbed. "No, I'm just waiting here until I can go home to Bea. Pray God it's soon."

Cullen didn't know how to feel right then. He only knew he had to make the offer. "I've told the sheriff that I'll keep in touch by telegram to see if you need me. Will that be all right with you?" His father drew a disgusted face and said, "I don't care what you do. I've got a last will and testament with you as my heir. Who else will I leave it all to? So you can leave now. Go on, get the hell out of here."

"I loved you, Pa. With every breath, I loved you." Then Cullen turned around and walked Honor slowly toward the rise and back into town. He would take Honor to the livery and make sure his shoes were snug and that he was fed well. He would be groomed and rested, and then Cullen would ride him hard the rest of the way to the coast. He was growing impatient, as if the miles separating him and his father would heal old wounds.

Several days later, Cullen noticed a change in the air. It was a bit heavier and smelled differently. He also noticed the ground was softer and thinner. It could only mean one thing. He was near the ocean. He had never smelled ocean air in his life, but he told himself that's what it must be, and rode on.

He had zig-zagged over the Virginia/North Carolina boarder several times within the last leg of his trip and stopped in towns along the way, asking how to get to the Virginia shore. Mostly, people didn't really know so he kept riding east, stopping in towns big enough to have a saloon in which he could gamble for enough funds to keep him going and add to his savings.

One stop in particular found Cullen looking at an enormous pot and a man sitting across from him wearing an oily grin. He looked at the man and then looked at his poker hand. This time *he* was the one holding four aces. He called the raise and when the cards were laid out, his aces beat the hell out of the other man's three jacks. As always, he thanked the man, gathered his winnings, and made his excuses. When he and Honor had made camp for the night, Cullen counted his winnings, stacking it neatly before the campfire. He was amazed to find he had won two hundred and twenty dollars. He vowed he would keep the bulk of the amount intact, spending only what was absolutely necessary for his and Honor's survival. He would save most of it to pay taxes on the farm if it became necessary.

Chapter Four

It was the beginning of June when Cullen made it to the
Virginia coastline. He was mesmerized by the ebb and flow
of the waves as they crashed against the beach on which he
and Honor stood. How long he stood there marveling at the
peacefulness and majesty of the water, he wouldn't
remember. Finally, he let go of Honor's reins and sat down
in the sand, running his hands through the warmth of it and
enjoying the sound of the waves. He never wanted to move
from this spot. He wanted to stay forever in the peace and
contentment he felt at that moment. After a few hours, he
looked around for Honor and found him lying on his side,
basking in the sunlight. Cullen whistled and Honor lifted
his head for a moment and then decided he was going to
finish his nap, his big head dropping once again in the sand.
Apparently, the ocean had the same affect on the horse as it
did his master.

"Can I help you, son?" The voice startled Cullen so that
he almost drew his pistols from their holster. Fortunately,
his mind dismissed the thought just in time. Cullen turned
toward the voice and smiled at the man who stood with his
pant legs rolled up showing bare feet nestled in the sand.
"Are you all right? You've been sitting here for hours and I
just thought I should check on you. The name's Bradley
Cummings," the man said as he offered his hand in
greeting. "That's my home over on the hill there. You look
a mite tired and hungry. When's the last time you've eaten
anything?" It wasn't until that moment that Cullen felt his
hunger and answered, "I guess it was yesterday around
noon. But I'm fine, Mr. Cummings. This is my first time at
the ocean and I was just enjoying myself a bit. I've been
looking forward to this for a very long time and I hope I
didn't alarm you in any way."

"Alarmed? Heavens no. Actually, I was curious about that beast lying on my beach. How about you introduce me?" *His beach?* As they walked toward Honor, Bradley said in a friendly manor, "This isn't the ocean, by the way. This is the Chesapeake Bay. I own an oyster trawling business. Look yonder at my fleet of boats." Cullen's gaze followed the direction of the man's outstretched hand and drank in the sight of the most beautiful boats he had ever seen. "They're beautiful, sir. You must be mighty proud." Cummings smiled and answered, "I am. They are my pride and joy next to my wife and family."

As the men approached Honor, he deigned to rise and greet them. "This is my friend and companion, Honor. I know he attracts a lot of attention wherever we go so I'll answer your first question. He's a Percheron. Part of the draft horse family. He looks like a brute but is as gentle as a lamb. Smart, too." Cullen reached into his pocket for a couple of sugar cubes and handed them to Cummings. "Here, give him these and he'll be your friend for life." Honor munched on the sugar cubes and Cummings laughed as he said, Well, I'll be tarred and feathered. He is gentle, isn't he?" He then picked up the reins and started walking him on the beach in the direction of his house.

"Come on up and join us for supper. Mother is frying some flounder and making corn fritters. Oh, and coleslaw, too. I think you'll really enjoy it."

How could this be happening? Cullen knew the shape he was in and what he looked like. He looked like a damned saddle tramp. Lord only knew the last time he had shaved, and his hair looked like a family of rats had nested in it. Still, just as the Hutchinson's had, this man welcomed him to dine with his family, not knowing one thing about him. If he had been a religious or spiritual man, he would have to think that *someone from above* was looking out for him. If it were true, he would be eternally grateful. Still, he couldn't sit at this woman's table looking and smelling like he did.

"Nice to meet you, ma'am," he said as Cummings introduced him to his wife. "I sure do appreciate a good meal but I'll take mine out on the porch, if you don't mind. I'm not exactly fit to sit at such a lovely table." Mrs. Cummings smiled and said, "Nonsense, my boy. We come from humble beginnings and remember those years vividly. However, you *can* wash your face and hands before we sit down. Go on, now. There's a pan of water on the side porch. There's soap and I'll get you a clean towel."

The days spent with the Cummings family were full of learning and new adventures. They treated Cullen with friendship and respect and spoiled Honor rotten. Bradley took Cullen out into the bay and showed him how his operation was run. He tutored and mentored Cullen and found him an apt student, full of curiosity and with a good head on his shoulders. He enjoyed Cullen's enthusiasm, watching him soak up the information like a sponge.

Cullen had no idea he would be so strongly attracted to the trade. His initial intention had been to see the ocean and travel northward along the coast, away from the possibility of capture for the murders of the men who would have hanged him. His new loves were the gentle waves and salt air that brought him so much peace and contentment. Sure, fishing was hard work but he had never been afraid of exerting himself for a living.

Bradley had given him the name and address of a cousin who settled in Penobscot Bay, Maine, and who had written of how plentiful the fish were in the bay. He liked the sound of it…Penobscot. Penobscot Bay. He might as well settle there as anywhere else. Stretching his muscles, he contemplated his growing feeling that it was time to move on.

The Cummings were sorry to see him go but knew he was itching to hit the road. Mrs. Cummings stood with him while he packed his belongings and wouldn't take no for an answer when she packed extras, including warm socks, long johns, and plenty of food. She also packed a good supply of sugar cubes for Honor. Lord, how she would miss the gentle giant.

Bradley gifted Cullen with books on trawling that he could read along the way, helping him to remember everything he taught the young man. Together, the Cummings family took three days to make sure Cullen would have everything he needed. Thankfully, Honor was big and strong enough to carry the load. They all shared a last meal together where there were many prayers said for Cullen's health, safety and prosperity during the saying of grace. Cullen was sad to leave them but it was nothing like the pain of leaving Charlie and Ken. This time he left with only gratitude and excitement, not the pain he suffered at having to leave his beloved friends.

It was the end of July, and he had a long road to follow to Penobscot Bay. Although he promised not to push Honor, he found himself adhering to a daily schedule, setting goals toward how many miles they would travel per day. The more he thought of Maine, the more he thought he wanted to buy a boat of his own. The more he thought of buying that boat, the more he knew he would have to make a lot more money than he had in his saddlebag at present. So he talked with Honor about it as they rode along. "My friend, we have what you call a conundrum. Despite my previous promises to the contrary, I find myself in need of extra funds, see what I'm sayin'? It's like I'm damned if I do and damned if I don't. Well, not actually, but you get the gist of it, right? I need to find places along the way to play cards; gamble, that is. How 'bout we set aside one hundred dollars for the venture. Sound about right? I'll not go one penny over that amount, I promise; cross my heart." Honor just plodded along. He was bored and Cullen knew it. "Tell you what. If you agree with me, I'll find us a place this evening with an open field nearby and you can run like the wind, sound good?" Honor kept plodding along. Cullen was beginning to feel the same way. Nothing but road stretching before them, nothing but canned meals and silence. What he wouldn't give for one of Charlie's fluffy biscuits once in a while. Shading his eyes as he glared into the westward sun, he gazed upon a sign that read, "Philadelphia, 40 miles," and figured there must be several saloons in a city that size.

***

Dirk Jamison had never been a patient man and what little patience he had was wearing thin. Even though he was controlling and a cutthroat, he knew better than to rush Sherry into a decision. But, dammit! This was becoming an infected thorn in his side! He knew how the people of Castine felt about him and usually he couldn't have cared less. However, bullying her and then taking over her business might be the last nail in his coffin in the community. He still had to do business in town and biding his time seemed the most prudent way to handle her despite his ever growing desire to have both Sherry and her boat. Life would be damn near perfect and he could move on to coercing and swindling other trawlers into his way of thinking. One day Castine would belong to him lock, stock and barrel. He wouldn't rest until it was done.

***

Three weeks later, Cullen was sitting by a campfire counting his winnings. True to his word, he had used nothing but the amount he had set aside for gambling and smiled like a cat dripping cream from its whiskers when he finished his tally. "Not bad, my friend, not bad at all," he said to his faithful companion. "A few more pots like the last one and we'll be pretty much set for a good while. But mind you! We'll have to scrimp along to make sure the bulk of it stays untouched. So you have to be a really good boy to get anything extra, ya hear?" Cullen laughed and folded up the money good and tight before placing it in the hidden pocket of his saddlebag, knowing that he would continue to spoil the horse. Apples and sugar cubes, excellent livery service, and the occasional deep rubdown when Cullen had the extra energy. He loved the animal and was glad Honor was such a young horse. He looked forward to many years together.

When full darkness was upon them, Cullen rested against the back of his saddle and let his mind wonder, as it often did, on his good fortune over the last few months. He tried not to jinx it by letting unfamiliar thoughts and feelings flit around in his head, but images of lots of money, good food, and a brand spanking new trawler kept appearing in his mind's eye before he could stop them. Sometimes such musings would make him chuckle. Sometimes he would feel perplexed by the possibility of it. Sometimes he would stop himself from tempting fate by even contemplating it further and just told himself he had been on the receiving end of a tremendous streak of luck ever since stopping at Ken and Charlie's place. Thinking of Charlie and Ken, he owned them a letter.

***

Sherry tacked yet another notice to the pilings asking for help to make life a bit easier for her and Mason and, hopefully, to increase her catch. She knew the wind could be blustery at times but what she really thought was that Dirk Jamison was removing the notices for spite. It was getting increasingly difficult to avoid Dirk on two levels. One, he wanted her boat badly and, two, he wanted her. The thought made her want to vomit over the pier. Dirk was a good looking man on the outside. On the inside, he was the devil incarnate. She wished she could remember some of her great granny's hexes because she would throw one on him this very second. The thought made her giggle that she would go so far as to stoop to tomfoolery to be rid of Dirk Jamison. Then she thought, *"Just keep praying, Sherry. Just pray harder."*

***

Cullen noticed the difference in weather as he traveled farther north. The leaves were a splendorous array of yellows, oranges, and reds. They fell like brilliant rain as he and Honor made their way through the last leg of the trip. While he enjoyed the beauty and majesty of the land, he was getting impatient to reach his destination.

He kept a running list of things to do and crossed each item off as he accomplished a task. His winter clothes were purchased and his cache of money had grown tremendously, much to Cullen's amazement and delight. *And*, he made the money honestly! He hadn't cheated one man during the entire trip! What were the odds? Amazing…

"Get along you old beeves, get along down the trail, I'm parched as cotton and need to meet my buddies at the bar rail…for whiskey, although sinful, and painted ladies even worse, I'm loaded with my monthly pay and want to lighten my purse!" Cullen burst out laughing. " Ha! How was *that,* old buddy? Getting better and better all the time, eh? I'm a poet, don'tcha know it?" *Clip clop, clip clop, clip clop.*

Honor was not impressed. Cullen racked his brain through the long hours of travel to come up with anything he had learned and memorized over the years to ease the boredom and entertain Honor, but only one surprising thing came to mind, "*Our Father who art in Heaven, hallowed be thy name . . .*" After repeating the prayer aloud in its entirety, Cullen felt a sense of longing the likes of which he could not remember. *What is it? What am I looking for? Right now I feel like the luckiest man alive so why am I also feeling so empty? WHAT THE HELL IS IT????* Looking farther up the road, he noticed a sign. Prompting Honor into a trot, he saw the sign read, "Penobscot Bay – 25 miles." *Thank God.*

"Look yonder, Honor! We made it!" Cullen's heart was racing as he expanded his lungs with the cold salt air. *Now what?* Honor stomped and blew for a second as if in answer. First things first, he guessed. To his left were some houses, the inhabitants of which would surely have answers to his questions regarding the area. One had a sign *Penobscot Inn,* and Cullen dismounted and wrapped Honor's reins through the hitching post outside the first building which had a funny sloped roof. He pulled an apple out of his coat pocket and gave it to Honor, the horse's huge mouth never ceasing to amaze him as he chomped away. "That'll keep you busy for a minute, eh, big fella?" After several pats and
scratches behind the ear, he was climbing the front steps.

Upon opening the door, Cullen was met with the welcome and familiar smell of burning oak in a potbellied stove in the middle of a small room. There was a little bell on a counter against one wall and he rang it, hoping for service. "Ayuh?" said a wizened old man who tottered into the room and gaped with his jaw slacking open. "*Ayah?*" Cullen answered. ""Ayuh, uh huh," the old man answered. *Well I'll be horse whipped! Don't they speak English up here?* Just then a rotund little woman walked through the door from what looked like the kitchen and started giving the old men holy hell. "Hiram, for goodness sake! Don't be such an old coot. Don't torment the boy!" Cullen smiled, "Oh, thank heavens! I thought maybe he didn't speak English. You *do* speak English, don't you, sir?" The old man grinned and said, "Ayuh."

Ya ain't from around heuh, are ya boy? I believe I d'tect a fereign accent, ain't that right, Ma?" Cullen smiled and made to shake the old man's hand. "I'm originally from Virginia, but I've traveled all over these United States over the years. Had a hankerin' to come north for the cooler weather and good fishing. A friend of mine has a cousin who lives in Castine, and has made his living trawling for cod. Says he's making a good living up here." Hiram was skeptical and didn't much care for outsiders, *feranuhs*, as he called them. The expression on his face told a man exactly what he thought.

"I was wondering if you could help me by answering a few questions." In answer, Hiram shouted, "Ma? Ya got some extra chowduh in the pot?"

Evidently, that meant Cullen was invited for a meal where he hoped to find out all he could about the bay area.

***

Sherry was particularly exhausted and found her bed us soon as was possible after the evening chores. The weather was getting colder by the day and as she donned her flannel nightgown, she dreaded the cold sheets. Heating bricks would become yet another nightly chore if she wanted the comfort of snuggling under warm covers.

She fell into a deep sleep as soon as her head hit the pillow and it wasn't long before she was dreaming vividly. *It was colder than she could ever remember as she walked down the hill to The Fetching Mermaid. She could see Dirk Jamison talking to a tall man with a sheepskin coat and cowboy hat, and could almost hear them arguing. The closer she got to the pier, the clearer was their conversation. Dirk stood with a ripped sheet of paper in his hand and told the strange man, "You might as well go on down the road, Mister. I'm tellin' you, the job has already been filled." Dirk saw her from the corner of his eye and stepped in front of the strange man as if to hide him from her sight. "Dirk, don't lie to the man." She pushed Dirk aside then turned and looked into the most piercing blue eyes. The man was tall and built like a fella who was no stranger to hard work. "Mister, are you looking for work?" Just then, Dirk pulled out a pistol and aimed it at the man's heart. She screamed "NO!" and then jumped in front of the stranger to save his life, the bullet hitting her instead . . .*

Sherry sat straight up in bed in a panic. She searched her body for gunshot wounds and finding none, she tried to calm her racing heart by saying aloud, "It was only a dream, it was only a dream." Still, in her Irish heart, she wondered if it was an omen.

Chapter Five

Hiram and Prudence had been wonderful hosts, as it turned out. Cullen asked Hiram all about the bay, the best way to get to Castine, and what his chances might be in getting work. Prudence clucked over him like a mother hen and knitted him a thick wool scarf for the nor'easters come winter. All Cullen's questions had been answered, the most important of which was the best way to travel across the bay to Castine. There were two choices; travel directly across the bay by boat, or travel around the bay by horse. Cullen chose to travel by horse so as to get a better feel of the land and the people. Although he hated to spend money for an overnight stay in a boarding house, he thought it a better idea than chancing Honor's reaction to a boat on the water.

He and Honor had rested for four days with the old couple. It was time to pay his bill for the room and board, and hit the road. Shaking Hiram's hand and pulling him in for a manly pat on the back, he thanked the old man for all of his advice and then reached for Prudence. She was such a little mite that he had to bend down to hug her, but he made sure it was a good one. She had taken wonderful care of him during his stay. "I hate to leave you both. You've been kind and generous and I'll never forget it was the two of you who were my first acquaintances upon my arrival. I'll never forget you and, who knows, we just may meet again. Miss Prudence, thanks for the apples for Honor. You know how much he loves them. Y'all take care now, here?" Hiram smiled and said, "Ayuh."

***

According to the owner of Ackermann's Mercantile, Castine was only about eight more miles east. Cullen took a few minutes to look at Mr. Ackermann's wares and spied a sheepskin horse blanket. "Sir, what size is the horse blanket and what's the price?" Mr. Ackermann scratched his chin whiskers and thought a minute. "Dahndest thing you should ask, Mistuh. The wife bought it from a woman what makes'em in Vermont, ya see. Don't know what got into her, no suh. It's the biggest blasted thing ya evuh did see, it is. Can't sell it. Been sittin' theah for ages, it has. If'n it fits ya horse I'll sell it to ya fuh ten dollahs." Cullen shook it out and estimated whether or not it would fit Honor, and decided he'd take it. It was handsomely made and well worth the price. Looking further around the store, he spied the candy counter and decided to buy a good supply of peppermint sticks, wondering if Honor might enjoy a change of pace in treats. Then he eyed a large canvas bag that might have several uses, one of which might be to store Honor's new blanket.

"Tell me, Mr. Ackermann, what would a man need in the way of clothing and such if he was to work on a trawler?" Cullen could see dollar signs in the man's eyes while he gave it some thought. "Well, ya gonna need some rubbuh boots, ya ah. Then a rubbuh slickah and rain hat. Then ya gonna need some wahm clothes fer against ya skin, Union suits and the like." Cullen considered the purchases and decided to wait and see what panned out in Castine. "Thanks for the advice but I think I'll wait a bit and see what happens when I look for work."

Disappointed, Mr. Ackermann added the amounts of the blanket, canvas bag, and peppermint sticks and said, "That'll be twelve and a half dolluhs" And Cullen was back on the road.

He judged it was about four in the afternoon as he hitched Honor to a rail near the closest pier. There were some trawlers in their slips but it looked like most of the boats were still out in the bay. Cullen leisurely strolled up and down the dock, stopping to chat with a few men who were preparing their catch for sale at the cannery. Then he ambled on, taking in all the sights like a sponge. Several feet farther down the dock, he noticed a sheet of white paper tacked to a piling, flapping in the wind. He grabbed the paper and tore it off the tack. Upon reading it, his face lit up and he was smiling from ear to ear. He turned around and walked back the way he came and asked one of the men he had talked with where he could find the owner of The Fetching Mermaid. "Ayuh, that would be Sherry Newcomb, it would. She lives in yondah house on the hill, see? She's not in yet but she usually makes it back by faw-thirty a'so. Ha dawtah Edith, is up theah now. Go on up and you can wait." Cullen shook the man's hand and headed up the hill.

Edith was peeling vegetables for dinner and stopped to add another piece of wood in the stove. Wiping her hands on her apron, she heard heavy footsteps on the front porch and wondered who it might be. Mason and Sherry always used the back door on work days. Stern was barking and jumping up and down which meant the person was definitely a stranger.

"Yes, may I help you?" Edith asked as she stared at the tall figure at the door. The late afternoon sun was shining behind him and all she could make out was his silhouette.

"Afternoon, ma'am. My name is Cullen Westover, and I'm looking for work. I saw your sign looking for a man to help with the trawling. Am I in the right place?"

Edith was charmed by his Southern accent and replied, "Yes, that's right. My family is looking for help. Please come in and wait for my stepmother. Her name is Sherry, and she's the one who put up the notice. Please, do sit down. They shouldn't be much longer." Cullen sat down in a wing back chair that had seen better days and nodded his thanks.

"I'm in the kitchen getting ready to fix dinner. Would you care for some coffee?"

"I'd love some but I'd rather drink it in the kitchen, if you don't mind. I'd hate to spill any on your lovely furniture." Edith smiled and motioned for him to join her in the kitchen.

Cullen sat down at a huge oak table and waited while the girl fixed his coffee. The smell of yeast dough rising made his stomach growl. Feeling he might want to start some conversation to make the girl more comfortable, he said, "I notice that you don't have the heavy New England accent, Miss . . ." The girl blushed and said, "My name is Edith. Edith Newcomb, and no, we don't have the heavy accent. Although the Newcombs have been in Maine for generations, my father was educated in Maryland. He made sure none of us spoke with the heavy accent. I don't know why it was so important to him, but it was." Bringing him a steaming cup of coffee she asked, "Would you like crea…Oh, my gosh! I forgot to milk Sadie today! Oh no, she must be hurting something awful! Please forgive me but I have to go milk our cow." Edith put on her jacket and picked up the milk pail on the side porch. Before she could get out the door, Cullen took the pail and said, "I'll do that, Miss. You go on and start your supper. I'll be right back. Just point me in the right direction, okay?"

It had been many years since Cullen milked a cow but felt sure it was something one never forgot how to do. Sadie was a docile old girl and he found a good rhythm while singing her a song.

Meet me by moonlight alone
And then I will tell you a tale
Must be told by the moonlight alone

In the grove at the end of the vale
You must propose to come for I said
I would shew the night flowers their Queen
Nay turn not away thy sweet head
'Tis the loveliest ever was seen . . .

"Mason, do you hear that?" Both Mason and Sherry stopped to listen. "Why, it's coming from our barn!" Mason slanted his arm across Sherry to stop her and said, "You stay here and I'll see what's going on. Better yet, go in the house. I'll be back in a minute."

"Mister, who are you and why are you milking our cow? What's going on?"

"Oh, hello! Name's Cullen Westover and I'm responding to your notice for employment down at the pier. Miss Edith plumb forgot to milk Sadie here, and I offered to take care of it while I waited for you. I hope that was all right."

"Sadie doesn't look like she minds it and I thank you for helping Edith. We sometimes forget how much she has to get done in a day while we're gone fishing."

Cullen stood and shook hands with Mason. "Miss Edith was making me a cup of coffee and remembered Sadie when she offered me cream. I was more than glad to help. I like staying busy." Both men strolled to the kitchen door and Cullen set down the pail just inside the kitchen from the side porch.

"There you are, Miss Edith. Sadie is comfortable and munching on some hay. It was no trouble at all." Edith blushed again and then looked at her stepmother. "Sherry, this is Mr. Cullen Westover, and he's here to apply for the job you posted. I invited him in for coffee and it reminded me when I was about to offer him some cream that I forgot to milk Sadie today." Sherry nodded in acknowledgement and continued taking off her boots. "Will you join us for dinner, Mr. Westover? We can discuss the details over coffee after the meal. Where's Caleb?" she asked Edith. "He's over at the Pritchard's playing with Samuel. I'll go get him." But Mason said, "I'll go get him. You just finish dinner. I'm starving."

Cullen sat at the table and looked at this family, each in turn. Mason was a strapping young lad of well over six feet and built as solid as an oak. He didn't try to pummel Cullen when he found him in their barn, so he must have an even temperament. Edith was petite and frail in appearance though he imagined she was the one who managed the household. *Sherry*... Sherry was striking, to say the least. He couldn't see much of her figure under the loose shirt and canvas pants, but her face was that of an angel. Deep russet hair and clear, light brown eyes rimmed with thick long lashes. Her cheeks were rosy and a bit chapped from the wind but, all in all, she made a beautiful picture. She was young, too. Even though she was tallish and appeared slight in build, she must be strong if she worked the trawler every day. It had to be brutal for a woman. Feeling he might be a bit obvious in his observations, Cullen lowered his eyes and continued to sip his coffee.

Sherry set her boots on the side porch and took the opportunity to give Cullen a once over. From the back, he appeared broad shouldered and had scruffy hair which was badly in need of a trim. Moving around to the stove to pour herself a cup of coffee, she noticed that his beard was just as scruffy as his hair and his skin was tanned by the sun just as his hair had been bleached by it. He had the overall appearance of a bum. In the next instant, he lifted his gaze to hers and she was instantly taken by his crystal blue eyes. Then he grinned at her, showing even white teeth. The grin reached his eyes and she was lost. How could she be attracted to a bum? What nonsense. It had been far too long since she even had thoughts like these or even been with a man. That must be the reason. Still, her heart fluttered and she felt like an enamored school girl, all the same.

"You best put your horse in the barn, Mr. Westover. It's not the biggest barn but there's an extra stall. Mason will show you where the grain bin is. You can give him some hay too."

"Thank you, Mrs. Newcomb. Honor will surely appreciate it." Cullen made for the door and Mason stopped him with a question; "What kind of horse is that, anyway? I've never seen one like him before."

"He's what you call a Percheron. A French breed that's related to the Draft horse. Don't let his size fool you. He's as gentle as a lamb." When Cullen reached in his coat pocket for a peppermint stick, Mason wondered why the man would ruin his appetite for dinner with such a treat. "Mister, you don't want to eat that before dinner, do you?" Cullen offered a big grin and replied, "This isn't for me. It's for Honor. He loves them." Mason grinned, too, and said, "This I've got to see!"

The two men walked side by side to the barn laughing and joking over such a thing and Sherry watched them with a smile of her own. It certainly wouldn't hurt to have a man around for Mason's sake, but she would just have to be careful to keep an eye on what sort of affect he had on the young man.

Cullen wondered at the lack of meat at the table but enjoyed the vegetables and yeast rolls; the yeast rolls especially. Patting his stomach, he sighed and complemented Edith on the meal. "That was purely divine, Miss Edith. I haven't enjoyed a meal this much in a very long time." Edith looked at Sherry and then blushed. "Mr. Westover, I'm so sorry for the lack of meat at the table. Times are a bit hard right now and we're cutting back on everything possible. We usually have fish but we get mighty sick of it sometimes. I hope you understand, sir."

Cullen thought she might cry by the sad look on her face. "But we have plenty of coffee and I made an apple cobbler for dessert. The apples are canned but I'm sure it will be tasty."

Sherry put her hand over Edith's on the table and patted it several times. "My dearest Edith. What would we do without you?" Then looking at Cullen, she said, "We might as well start our discussion while Edith serves the cobbler and coffee."

Sherry started the interview, such as it was. "Mr. Westover, do you have any experience in the fishing trade?"

"First of all, please, everyone call me Cullen. And yes, I have a bit of experience and have also read three books on the subject of trawling. The owner of a trawling business in the Chesapeake Bay gave them to me when I left his home. I have to admit to being fascinated by it all."

"Where are you from, Cullen?"

"Originally, I'm from Virginia. I was born and raised there. When I turned sixteen I left and have been traveling ever since. I was sorely tired of the hot weather where I had traveled for the last few years and thought I might like to see the ocean. I had never seen it even though I had been raised in a coastal state."

"So you just decided to travel to the Northeast for a change of pace?"

"No, it wasn't like that. Yes, I wanted to move to a cooler climate, that's true, but when I arrived at what I thought was the ocean, I met a man who ran his own trawling business in the Chesapeake Bay. He invited me into his home and I stayed there for a few weeks with his family. I worked with him on one of his boats and he taught me everything he thought I needed to know to get started. I had no idea I would be so taken with it. He mentioned that he has a cousin in Castine who had written of the good life he has made for himself trawlin'. And here I am. Oh, and I have a letter of reference from him." He reached into his back pocket and withdrew it for her perusal.

"What's his cousin's name? Perhaps we know him."

"His last name is Cummings. I don't remember if Brad ever told me his first name."

Mason and Sherry shared a look of recognition. Duncan Cummings was an independent outfit like Sherry's except he had two boats to her one, and he had described it as "a good life." Maybe that's what Sherry needed; another boat. Sherry read the glowing reference from Bradley Cummings and wondered what it was about this scruffy looking man that people were drawn to.

"Mason and I have thought about this for a long while. What we would like to do is have you on the boat for three months to see how you work out. The pay won't be much during that time, maybe ten dollars a month. After that time, if we believe you will be an asset and help us bring in more of a catch, we'll renegotiate the pay. Will that be agreeable, Cullen?"

Cullen scratched his beard and acted like he was giving it grave consideration. "Will we work on Saturdays and Sundays?"

"We work six days a week. However, we always try to come in early on Saturdays, unless we're having an exceptional catch."

Cullen had hoped for Saturday nights off and decided he could manage the issue. As was his usual habit, he had memorized where all of the gambling establishments were located around the bay. Now he had to find out if there were Blue Laws in and around Castine.

"Also," Sherry added, "I will expect you to join us in Church on Sunday mornings. There's an extra bedroom next to Mason's you can use. Meals will be free of charge. I hope that makes up for the pay you will receive for the first three months. Do we have a deal?"

Cullen was stuck on the church issue and had to think about it a bit more. Edith served the cobbler and they all dug in, giving him a chance to delay giving his answer. *Church?* When was the last time he'd been in one? His ma's funeral? But suddenly the image of weighing scales popped into his head. Gambling on Saturday nights, and church on Sunday. He wondered if everything would even out in God's mind if he decided to accept.

The cobbler was delicious and everyone thanked Edith for the surprising treat. Even little Caleb licked all around the outside of his mouth trying to get the last crumb.

"Well, Cullen?" Sherry's eyebrows shot up in question and Cullen knew he might as well get it over with.

"Well, Mrs. Newcomb, I'd be happy to work with you under your conditions as long as the pay is renegotiated according to how much of a catch I help you bring in. If it's a good bit more than what you're bringing in now, I would hope for a salary of at least twenty dollars a month."

Sherry nodded affirmatively and held out her hand to shake Cullen's. "Call me Sherry. My real name is Colleen, but my departed husband called me Sherry for the color of my eyes. Welcome, and I hope everything works out well for all of us."

Edith couldn't help herself from blurting, "And maybe I won't have to work at the cannery?" Cullen couldn't help recognizing the pleading tone of her voice. The cannery must not be a very nice place to work. He would have to visit and see for himself what the operation was like. He would learn all he could during the time he stayed with the Newcombs, his ultimate goal being to have a boat of his own some day.

"Edith, I know you hate the thought but we'll just have to wait and see how things go. Lord knows I don't want it to happen but I just can't see that far into the future."

Cullen distracted them from the issue by saying, "One more thing, Miss Sherry, I need a day to get some business taken care of. I need to open an account at the bank, and I need to send a telegram to my hometown inquiring as to my father's health and about any outstanding taxes on our farm that may be due. Will that be all right with you?"

A bank account? A farm? He had money? "That will be fine, Cullen, as long as when you're in town you get a haircut and your beard trimmed. No offense, but we can't have you in church looking like a caveman." Cullen burst out laughing and then Mason joined in. Edith blushed and giggled. Sherry smiled in spite of her ambivalent feelings about the man. It sure sounded good to hear laughter in the house once again.

"I'd be happy to get a haircut, Miss Sherry. Perhaps in the summer I'll even shave off my beard, but for the winter I think it best that it stays."

Chapter Six

The next morning after Sherry and Mason headed down to the Mermaid, Cullen took a good look around the house and grounds, including all of the outbuildings. He checked the woodpile to see if there was a good supply, and he thoroughly looked at the inside and outside of the barn. After all, it was to be Honor's new home. He could see a bit of daylight through the roof and added it to his list of things to do. He checked on the supplies in the barn, such as how many buckets, pitch forks, the supply of hay and grain. Then he looked for the water pump and remembered to ask Mason how deep it ran. He could imagine it freezing during a nor'easter, if they were as bad as Brad had told him they could be. He even checked out the chicken coop to see if it needed any repairs. All in all, things were in pretty good shape. He would have to remember to ask Edith if there was anything in the house that needed fixing.

As he rode into town to run his errands, the thought struck him that he was acting like this was *his home. His* family, and wondered what the heck had compelled him to check on the state of the property. Maybe he would just keep the list and do one thing every once in a while. That way it wouldn't be so obvious. But these people needed help. Sure, Mason was a big strapping boy, but had his father ever taught him anything else besides fishing? Then he felt like a fool on several levels. This *wasn't* his family, and he was staying in the house by the good graces of the *owner.* He didn't even know whether the "deal" would work out and yet he was mentally installing himself right in the middle of it. Was he so anxious to be part of a family that his mind shot immediately to that conclusion? He would have to keep himself in check. He never wanted to encroach on the Newcomb family. The thought made him sad.

After opening a bank account and sending his telegram, Cullen walked to the mercantile and bought some supplies. He made sure he had plenty of stationery and envelopes. He was planning on writing to Charlie and Ken, and the Cummings frequently over the next few months. Maybe he would even write to his father. He stocked up on peppermint sticks and a bag of penny candies for Caleb. When he finished paying for his order, he asked the boy behind the counter where he could get a haircut and where the post office might be.

While sitting in the barber's chair, he asked where a man might partake of a little nip of whiskey and if there might be games of chance in town. "Are they open on Sundays?" he asked, hoping for the answer he desired. "Ayuh, they ah. Men 'round heah work six days a week and wanted time to blow off some steam, if ya know what I'm sayin'. The hue and cry was so strong and loud that the officials had ta strike the Blue Law down in Castine. Nevah thought I'd see the day, no suh."

Well, that would work out just fine and dandy…*if* he needed the extra money. To familiarize himself with such establishments, he decided to visit them to check out the action. Sitting at the bar at the Crooked Crab, he was approached by a man in a suit, slicked back hair, and a smarmy grin. "You new around here?" Cullen replied, "Ayuh," and took another sip of whiskey from his shot glass. The man who reminded Cullen of a snake oil salesman wouldn't let it rest. "I thought so. What's your business in Castine?"

"It's none of your business, mister. I'm just here havin' a nip. Never thought I would be given the third degree. Nice meetin' ya. I think I'll be going now." He slammed back the rest of the shot, put his two bits on the bar, and walked out.

Cullen knocked on the kitchen door and waited for Edith to open it. "Cullen, you don't have to knock. You live here now. Come on in and warm yourself by the stove. I was just fixing Caleb some soup and leftover rolls for lunch. Would you like some?" The soup stewing in the pot smelled delicious and Cullen was more than eager to have some. "That would be kindly of you, Miss Edith. I'd love some."

When he had finished eating and helped Edith with the dishes, he went to the barn and gave Honor a peppermint stick and a good rubdown. "I bet you're anxious for a good run, aren't ya boy? I think you've rested enough from our travels. Let's get you saddled up and go for a ride. You'd like that wouldn't you?" Cullen saddled Honor and found a stool to help him mount. It was a lot easier than finding a stump or some wooden steps. He could mount the beast with no help at all but always took the easier way when it was available.

Sherry nudged Mason in the ribs as they walked up the hill from the dock.

"Would you look at that?" Cullen and his chestnut beast were running fast toward the house from an opposite field, Cullen whooping and hollering like an Indian. "What the devil is he doing? I hope the neighbors aren't watching." Mason just grinned. "I like him, Sherry. I really like him. He might be the answer to our prayers."

Sherry was pulling off her boots when Cullen walked through the kitchen door. As always, he had been in the barn babying Honor for a bit. When Sherry looked up she did a double-take. His hair was neat and layered even though it still reached the collar of his coat, and his beard was trimmed just right; long enough to keep his face warm but nicely shaped. *My Gosh, the man is actually handsome!*

Getting up from her chair, Sherry tripped over her boot laces and almost fell to the floor, except that Cullen caught her just in time. "Whoa there, Missy!" he grinned as he held her tight. She felt warm and luscious in his arms despite the panicked look on her face. He suddenly let go of her and Sherry swayed backward, catching herself before she appeared to be an ass for the second time.

"Why, Cullen you look quite handsome after your haircut," Edith gushed.

"Now that the barber has cut it, I can keep it trimmed for you." It was Cullen's turn to blush as he removed his coat and hung it on a peg on the side porch. Mason listened with amusement as Sherry and his sister struggled with their nervous chatter. He would have to keep an eye on Cullen for Edith's sake. But, Sherry? Now that was an interesting thought. He would let some time pass before making a judgment, but it was kind of exciting to envision him as part of the family. Time would tell.

Chapter Seven

This day felt like the very first day on the boat for Sherry. She tried to discount the feeling that it was because of Cullen. That would be ridiculous. It was only that there was something new instead of the same old grind, she told herself. She enjoyed watching Mason's face light up when Cullen went about doing things on his own that needed to be done. The man knew a fair bit about sailing and was a tremendous help.

Sherry's intuition about fishing spots was sharper than usual and they shouted with glee over their bountiful catch. Mason even did a little jig when the nets were hauled in. Yes, today was a good day, Cullen being with them, or not.

"What do you say, Miss Sherry? Shall we try our luck again or go back for the day?"

"Well, Mr. Westover, I tink we'll jest take'er out again and see what's what, eh?" she answered in an Irish accent. She was certainly being playful today. She was beautiful at the ship's wheel, more beautiful than any figurehead he had ever seen. It was *her* face that should launch a thousand ships. Today she was happy and laughing and it made Cullen's heart skip a beat. It began to rain and she lifted her face to the sky and shouted, "Thank you, God!" That puzzled Cullen. Thanking God for rain when she was in an ocean of water?

They found another fishing spot that tickled Sherry's fancy and cast out the nets. It was time for lunch and they grabbed their sacks and dug in with gusto. Edith sure could pack a good lunch and with Cullen's hunger today, it was worth its weight in gold. She would make a man a good wife some day, no doubt about it. Mason brought out a jug, pulled out the cork, and passed it around. "I just thought it was a day to celebrate a bit," he said as he passed the jug. It was ale and it tasted better than anything Cullen had ever put in his mouth.

After the second catch, the nets were full of fish with a few flopping off the top onto the deck. What a catch! What a day! "We've got to hurry back now. I don't want a high number of die offs," Sherry announced against the wind. Mason passed the jug around one more time as they neared home. A solitary figure stood on the dock, bracing himself against the wind and rain and it wasn't long before Sherry saw who it was. Dirk Jamison. What in the world did he want now?

Dirk was hard pressed to keep a smile on his face as The Mermaid glided toward shore. It stung his pride when they each ignored him while setting the boat to rights for the day. No one ignored him, *no one.* He couldn't remember the last time someone made him wait like this.

Sherry smiled and nodded in greeting as she passed him on her way up the hill. "Wait a minute, Sherry. I'd like to talk to you…in private." Sherry looked back at Mason and Cullen and then turned her attention back to Dirk. "Whatever you have to say, you can say it in front of them." Dirk's face turned red but he still smiled. "All right, I've come to ask you out for a nice dinner at the hotel in town. What do you say? We'll get a table near the fireplace, order some wine, and enjoy ourselves." Sherry's face was totally blank for a few seconds, and then she started to laugh. "*Come into my parlor said the spider to the fly!* You must be kidding, Dirk. I know what you want and I suggest you get the notion right out of your hard head. I'm not selling to you and that's that. Now excuse us. I'm sure Edith is close to having dinner ready." Then she almost sprinted up the hill.

Mason followed, his head bent toward the ground. Cullen took the opportunity to "reacquaint" himself with Dirk. "You know, I'd say the lady is plumb done with your attentions, Mr. Jamison. Why not just let her be to enjoy her life. You've been nothing but a headache to her. Just let her go. She's said her piece and I was witness to it. Good day, Mr. Jamison."

Dirk was enraged. Who the hell was this redneck from God knew where, daring to speak to him in such a manner? Didn't he know that Dirk practically owned Castine? Didn't he know how much power he wielded over its people? Well, he would soon find out. Dirk could not and would not let this pass. The man would pay dearly; so dearly that he would want to leave Castine and never look back. He gathered himself and walked back down the dock, passing men who he realized had been staring and listening to every word they could pick up from his conversation with the redneck. It had been a very long time since Dirk felt anything close to embarrassment and fumed over the fact that he felt it now. How could Sherry hire this man? He figured Westover was up to no good when he met him at the Cracked Crab. He needed an outlet for his anger and knew just where to go for relief.

Cullen couldn't get the confrontation out of his mind. He knew there must be a long history of trouble with Jamison, that Sherry had endured. He would find out this evening whether he had been truthful with the man about him being a headache for Sherry.

Everyone washed up and sat down to the table as Edith served dinner. Fresh cod, green beans, and boiled potatoes. Not Cullen's favorite but it filled his stomach. He wondered when Northerners slaughtered their hogs. It sure would be nice to have some tender pork with gravy. Perhaps when the meat became available, he would offer to cook a meal for the family. Something down-home delicious. He had spent many afternoons in the kitchen with Charlie and had picked up quite a bit as far as cooking was concerned. He'd never be able to make her biscuits but Edith's yeast rolls were heavenly, just the same.

When Edith brought out a pan of sticky buns for dessert, Cullen thought he would take the opportunity to ask some questions. He wasn't sure it would be a conversation Caleb should hear but the boy seemed totally engrossed with munching on his bun and licking his fingers.

"Sherry, Mason, I'd like to talk about what happened today. I'd like to know how much of a threat Jamison is to this family." Mason looked at Sherry and she gave him a distinct look that said, *"Keep your mouth shut."* Mason raised his eyebrows and threw up his hands. "Sherry, he has a right to know! He could be a big help in dealing with the bastard." Sherry gasped at Mason's language but it didn't deter him from speaking his mind.

"Jamison started harassing my father before he died. He wanted Pa's boat and never let up. Sometimes I think that's why Pa just let himself be washed overboard the day we lost him. It was constant, Cullen!" Mason dragged his hand across his face and then through his hair. "Now that Pa is gone, he's increased the pressure to have not only the boat, but Sherry, too!" Giving Sherry a pleading look, he continued, "Sherry, he's a dangerous man! We've always known that. Just how long do you think we can keep putting him off? Do you remember what happened to Kyle Jenner? He refused Jamison's offer and was found dead not long after. Then Jenner's family was forced to sell. The only reason we're still safe is that he also wants you."

Edith sat stoically, fighting tears that pooled in her doe eyes. Cullen felt bad for her. She was such a delicate girl with sensitive feelings. "Edith, what do you have to say about it all?" Cullen could have never anticipated her answer. "I want him dead. It's the only way out of this." Then she got up to refresh everyone's coffee cups.

Sherry started to cry, wondering how long Edith had felt this way. "Surely you don't mean that, Edith. I understand your frustration but I know you really don't want anyone's death, do you?" Edith grimaced and Cullen thought it was from the shame of her statement. He was wrong. She sat back down at her place at the table and her body began to shake. She was breathing shallow and fast as she admitted, "One day in town, I was in the mercantile and it was crowded. So I decided to come back later. There were people behind me making for the door, too, and just when I turned the door knob to leave, Dirk was coming in. There was a press at the door and…and…he, uh…he grabbed my…oh God, he…grabbed my breast. No one saw it so I had no proof. I was sandwiched between Dirk and the people behind me. I hate him, Sherry. I hate him deeply. I just want him gone and death seems the only way it will be final."

Mason abruptly stood from the table and made for his coat. Cullen knew what would happen if Mason confronted Jamison, and he stood up to stop the boy. "No, Mason. Not this way. Trust me, I know. You'll only end up dead if you go off half cocked. There are better ways, intelligent ways to go about this. We just have to think on it and come up with a plan. Come on, sit down and try to relax." Looking totally dejected, Mason plopped back down in his seat. "It better be soon, Cullen. We can't take much more of this. And if you think you aren't in danger, think again. You're now the biggest fly in his ointment. With you gone, it will be easier to go after Sherry and win."

Chapter Eight

Sherry hated winter. The glorious colors of autumn held no attraction for her as it signaled the coming of death, which was how she felt about the season. The nude branches of trees looked like tentacles beseeching the Almighty to let them live another day. Jacob had drowned in the winter. For Sherry, it was a depressing time and she wondered each year whether she could make it to spring when she would once again come alive and look forward. Right now, she just wanted to crawl under the covers of her bed and not come out. She was tired of this life. She dreamed of something new, something away from Penobscot Bay. Sometimes she wondered whether she would ever get the smell of fish off her hands. Even with Cullen's help, she was tired of it. For some reason, her negative thoughts always ended with daydreams of Cullen, and it made her feel even worse. She was strongly attracted to the man and he had shown no interest in her at all. She daydreamed of them being married and wondered if he could bring out the passion she had tamped down for so many years. Actually, she had never known passion so it was difficult for her to imagine what it would be like, but she knew there had to be something more.

Jacob had never ignited sexual or loving passion in her, his fumbling attempts on those nights he turned to her were tolerated but never enjoyed. Still, Jacob tried to be a good husband. It just wasn't a match made in heaven, to say the very least. And, oh, how she wanted passion in her life. She was still a young woman and wanted more children of her own. Children who had azure eyes and a smile that could melt butter. Children who looked just like Cullen Westover.

***

Dearest Ken and Charlie,

I've been thinking about you both a lot lately, and felt I had to write for some advice. You see, I've never been in love. The only love I ever had from a woman, I had to pay for. Sherry Newcomb is like no other woman I've ever met and I want her. Ken, stop thinking with your johnson. I mean, I think I want her for my wife. Aw, hell, I have no idea what I'm doing and I need help, dammit! How do I go about approaching her? How can I woo her and find out if she feels the same for me? How do I know the difference between wanting her and just wanting a family of my own?

Write back soon as I'm at my wits end over the matter.

Love,
Cullen
PS: Honor says hello. Sends a big sloppy kiss and says SEND PEPPERMINT STICKS!

Cullen had written the letter at the kitchen table under the light of a hurricane lamp. Just as he was folding it to put in an envelope, Sherry came padding into the kitchen in her nightgown and robe, her slippers scuffling across the wooden floor.

"I see you can't sleep, either," she said on her way across the kitchen. "I guess I'd better throw more wood in the stove." Cullen was silent as he watched her head for the side porch to pick up two chunks of wood. As she opened the front of the stove and bent down to throw them in, Cullen's mouth went dry. With her back to him, he could only see her perfectly rounded bottom and could feel a straining against his denim pants. Funny, he had just told

Ken in his letter to not think with his johnson and here he was about to burst his buttons.

"Would you like some coffee? I'll make some if you like."

"Nah, I was just writing a letter to my friends but I'm finished. I'll be going up to bed now."

"Yes, I should probably try and get back to sleep. Morning comes early for us, doesn't it?"

"It surely does, Miss Sherry. It surely does."

Before Cullen could even think twice, he gently grabbed her hand as she would walk past the table to climb the stairs to her room. She looked down at him with questioning eyes and stood waiting for his intent. Taking her reaction as a good sign, he pulled her down into his lap, wrapped his muscled arms around her, and took her mouth right there in the kitchen.

Her lips were warm and inviting so he deepened the kiss until they were both lost in the moment. She reached her arms around his neck and pulled him even closer, her bottom beginning to move of its own accord. The movement inflamed Cullen, and he knew they had to stop. Pulling away from her, he said, "Sherry, not like this. I'm so sorry. I hope you don't think I'm disrespecting you. But, God, I've wanted you ever since I first met you. Will you forgive me?"

Forgive him? "Of course, Cullen. But in case you didn't notice, I was enjoying it, too." She stood from his lap, brought the lapels of her robe back together, and stood smiling at him for a few moments. Then she ran her hand through his hair and kissed him on the forehead. "Goodnight." And she was gone, leaving Cullen alone with a miserable throbbing he had no way of relieving. For both of them, the rest of the night would be full of questions. *What did it mean? Was it wrong to enjoy it so much? Will I let it happen again? Should we talk about it?* Before Cullen finally drifted off to sleep, he thought, *why does this have to be so difficult?* He prayed for a return letter from Charlie and Ken very soon.

The next morning before breakfast, Mason was sitting at the table enjoying his first cup of coffee of the day when Cullen came down and poured himself a cup. Sherry came in not long after and made sure they didn't touch as they maneuvered around the kitchen.

"Good morning, Mr. Westover."

"Good morning, Miss Sherry."

"Did you sleep well?"

"Like a baby. You?"

"I had a lot on my mind but I finally drifted off."

Mason watched all of this with interest. Damned if they hadn't kissed or *something*, he thought.

"I thought I heard you two coming upstairs late last night. You woke me up. Of course, *I* had no trouble getting back to sleep. Maybe you shouldn't have coffee after dinner from now on." Mason gave them both a grin and continued sipping his coffee. Cullen immediately glanced at Sherry and she was blushing with embarrassment.

Was it Sherry's imagination or was Cullen wearing a shirt that was particularly tight this morning? She didn't remember ever seeing the shirt before. Did his pants always fit that snug? Was he taunting her or was it only because she was noticing it all because of what they shared last night? Whatever the reason, she had to get herself together and ignore the feelings. Any more of such shenanigans like last night and she would be in a terrible way. Yes, it was best to ignore what happened and carry on like usual. She had a family to take care of and who knew how long Cullen would be around? Perhaps he would get tired of the life and decide to move on. The thought caused her stomach to drop and her heart to flutter. Now that Cullen had joined their family, so to speak, how would it be to live without him?

Mason took to Cullen the moment they met and little Caleb called him Uncle Cullen. Edith's response to his presence was a mystery. It was hard to ever tell what was on her mind. Sherry only knew that she was accustomed to his being there and found herself wanting more of his attention. The memory of his lips last night would be enough to fuel her imagination for weeks. She had never known true desire so never realized it could actually hurt if left unfulfilled.

As Cullen walked to the post office, he sent up a little prayer that the Hutchinson's would write back immediately upon receipt of his letter. He was more confused than ever. It wasn't like he could slap five dollars down and say, "Giddy up, little lady, let's ride!" It was times like this he regretted his nomadic lifestyle. He had never set down roots and was woefully unprepared in the ways of courting and romance. He wondered if he should give her flowers and candy, or if he should just wait and see how things evolved. Should he ask her out for supper? Or should he just act like nothing happened between them? *Shit!* He knew he would be counting the days until he received a reply from Charlie and Ken. It would be frustrating as hell.

Dearest Cullen,

As always, we so enjoyed receiving your letter and were relieved to find that your biggest problems were love related. In answer, I have only this to offer...be respectful and attentive. Speak to her from your heart, not your head. If you feel she is receptive, let her know your feelings and tell her that you will wait until she has had time to discover her own feelings for you. Be kind and considerate. Be bold in your protection of her and the family but do not be controlling in your efforts. Make sure there is plenty of laughter in the home. Let them see who you really are and that you can be trusted. If you can accomplish all of that, how could she not fall madly in love with you? And now I will give the pen to Ken, so he can advise you, also.

Dear Cullen, I agree with all of the above and if I find out you've screwed this up, I swear I'll come up there and tan your hide, but good. If she takes too long in giving you an answer, try grabbing her like I did Charlie, kiss the daylights out of her, and just tell her what's what. She'll marry you now or never. It worked with Charlie.

Oh, Cullen. Don't pay any attention to my old coot. He never did that. It was actually me who grabbed HIM by the shirt front and said those words. He's a big talker, isn't he?

We both love you and hope for the best. I would love to be an aunt or even a grandma! (hint hint) Write soon!

Charlie and Ken

God, how he missed them! He shut his eyes and went immediately back in his mind to Charlie's kitchen where they had talked about all manner of things. Food cooking, a soft presence in his life, and lots of good advice. He had never felt as loved as he had during his time with them.

The thought occurred to him that if he treated Sherry like Ken treated Charlie, it certainly wouldn't hurt his cause. Anyway, he promised himself to read their letter several times until the words completely sank in. Teaching his heart how to truly love was certainly going to be time consuming, but hopefully worth every minute.

Chapter Nine

Thanksgiving was in a few weeks. Sherry started to panic because after Thanksgiving came the annual Christmas Ball. She usually accompanied Mason and Edith to the ball and remained a wallflower the entire night, refusing to dance when invited, and avoiding Dirk Jamison whenever possible. But this year she wanted to look beautiful and feel feminine for the first time since she had left Ireland. She wished for the presence of her dear Ma, so she could advise Sherry on things like the purchase of a new dress, how to style her hair, and how to encourage Cullen's attention. She started to cry as she sat at the kitchen table, brooding over her feelings of loneliness for her family. She had promised to bring them over from Ireland, and now it may never happen. They probably felt abandoned as the letters back and forth across the ocean dwindled to perhaps two a year.

It was the perfect time for a pity party as Mason, Edith, and Caleb had walked to Mrs. Ringwald's to purchase their monthly ration of bacon they allowed themselves. It was a luxury they just wouldn't deny. Cullen was in the barn with his horse. She'd swear he loved that horse more than most humans, and that just added to her self pity. Crying harder now, she lay her head in the crook of an arm and let it all out. She would later scold herself for wasting precious time on such foolishness.

Cullen walked in at that moment and instantly went to her side, lifting her from the chair and holding her head against his shoulder as her tears fell like gentle rain. "Sherry, what's wrong? Is there anything I can do? Tell me. Tell me what's wrong and I'll make it right for you." They stood thus until the tears stopped and the hiccoughs subsided.

"Oh, Cullen, I'm just being a fool. I was missing my family in Ireland, and feeling guilty because I promised them passage to America as soon as I could afford it. That was six years ago. I miss them terribly and need my ma something fierce." Lifting her head from his shoulder, she gazed at him through red rimmed eyes and said, "The Christmas Ball is in the middle of December, and I haven't a thing to wear. I want to look lovely this year instead of homely and undesirable. I want to feel like a woman and not a trawler. I need my mother's advice. I need…" and then she began crying again, holding Cullen tight, not in the least embarrassed by her racking sobs.

It wasn't until the next morning that Cullen was able to speak alone with Edith. He came downstairs early hoping to find her ready to prepare breakfast.

"Edith, can you help me with something?"

"Of course, Cullen, what can I do for you?"

"Does Sherry have any dresses that fit her?"

"I think so. Why?"

"I need to take it into town and have a dress made for the Christmas Ball. I'm not much good at things like this but I figured if she had a dress that fit her, the dressmaker might be able to make one her size. I want it to be a surprise. I'd like you to take the dress into town after we leave for the Mermaid, and also have yourself fitted for one. The dresses will be my Christmas presents for you and Sherry."

Edith's face lit up like the noonday sun as she threw her arms around Cullen and exclaimed, "For me? I can have a new dress, too?

Cullen laughed and said, "You didn't think I'd let you go to the ball without a frilly new dress, did you? From what I've seen in town, you and Sherry are the most beautiful women in Castine, and you should flaunt your beauty with new dresses. It will drive all the men crazy. They'll be buzzin' like bees around honeysuckle."

As Edith was gathering herself once again to the task of making breakfast, a thought struck her and she just had to ask, "Cullen, you don't really want other men buzzing around Sherry, do you?" Cullen blushed, gave her a sincere smile and said, "No, Edith. I don't. I'm not sure what to do about it yet, but you're right. I don't want other men buzzing around Miss Sherry. Can this be our secret, please?"

Edith hugged Cullen and told him of course she would keep his secret. Then she looked him straight in the eye and asked, "You're never going to leave us, are you? Promise?" Cullen patted her back and replied, "Barring any unforeseen circumstances, I'll be staying for as long as y'all want me here."

Edith squealed with glee and ran to the bottom of the stairs. "Mason, get your lazy behind up. I'm making pancakes for breakfast. For real this time!" Edith hated to go into her supply of maple syrup. She used it for a sweetener when they ran out of sugar, but this was a special occasion and she wouldn't worry about it right then.

Cullen watched Edith contemplate the use of her syrup and wondered what else the Newcombs did without. The next time he could find himself alone in the kitchen, he would check the pantry and cabinets. His *family* would *not* go without ever again if he could help it. Anyway, he was getting tired of this bland Northern food and wanted some Southern dishes. He would have to write to Charlie for more advice. He had to chuckle to himself; he could just see the excitement on her face at being needed from so far away. This evening when everything had settled down, he would write his letters of request.

Dearest Charlie,

HELP! These Northerners can't cook worth a poot! I'm dying for some of your biscuits and cornbread, some mashed potatoes instead of always boiled, and I'd give my right arm for some crispy fried chicken! I need recipes for all the dishes you know I love. Goodness, a man could starve up here. Oh, and instructions for making fried potatoes, onions and a mess of pinto beans. My mouth is watering just thinking about it.

Love Cullen
PS: Tell the old coot I said hello. I wouldn't want him thinking that I'm trying to steal his gal with a personal letter.

Dear Mrs. Cummings,

I'm writing today to ask a favor of you. I was wondering if you might send me the recipes for your batter for fried clams, oysters, and those little cornbread balls you make. Also the sauce you make for the fried clams and oysters. I don't much like Northern cooking, you see, and I'm having some terrible cravings for some Virginia food!

Tell Bradley and the children I said hello.

Sincerely,

Cullen

There, that should do it. He had never been one for plans or agendas and such, but he found himself increasingly motivated to keep lists going of things to be done or to be bought. He found it fulfilling now that he had other people to care for; *people he loved.* He looked at his list again and saw that sending a telegram to his hometown to check on his father was next on his list.

Plans were formulating in the back of Cullen's mind and he wanted to begin adding to his bank account. He figured if push came to shove, they might have to leave Castine, if he couldn't get Jamison to back off. He didn't trust the man as far as he could throw him and decided to start wearing his guns when he went into town. He was wearing them one such night as he walked into the Cracked Crab, looking for a poker game.

First he went to the bar and ordered a whiskey. While he sipped it, he looked around the saloon gauging the tables for a good game. No one looked up or even noticed him…until Jamison walked in. Apparently, word was going around that Jamison wasn't too happy with Cullen, and that suited him just fine. Men stopped what they were doing and looked back and forth between himself and Jamison, waiting to see what might happen.

Dirk sauntered up to the bar and touched his finger to his hat.

"Westover."

"Jamison."

"Just having another nip, are you?"

"That's right, and hoping to find a poker game in progress."

"You're a gambler, I see."

"Nope, just want to have some fun is all. Take my mind off the pressures of the day."

"Can I buy you another whiskey?"

"No thanks. I'm really not much of a drinker. One is fine."

"How about you and me find a table and start a game."

"Suits me. Lead the way."

The saloon went deadly quiet. Not even a breath of a whisper could be heard.

"This is my lucky table. You don't mind, do you?" Jamison was grinning like an ape but it didn't matter to Cullen where they played.

"Sure, why not? We'll just have to see whose table it is when it's all said and done."

Cullen noticed Jamison giving the owner of the saloon a pointed look. It didn't sit right with him, and felt a fix was underway. Sure enough, the owner came over to the table and asked if they needed a dealer. No way, no how, was that going to happen.

"I don't think so, but thanks for askin'."

Jamison grinned, "What's the matter, don't trust me?"

"Not as far as I can throw you, Jamison. I'll deal so there won't be any underhanded, funny business. You wanna play or not? Those are my conditions seein' as how I'm new in town and all."

Jamison laughed heartily which gave the rest of the men in the saloon permission to do the same. Cullen was definitely seeing which way the wind blew in Castine. Folks were scared senseless of the man.

Cullen shuffled and cut the cards several times, looking for bent corners and such, making a show of how clean a deal he wanted. Silently, he thought, *"God, it's for a good cause. Please remember that."*

According to his plan, Cullen let Jamison win four hands before settling in to do his damage. The fifth hand put into motion the second part of his act. Frustrated, Jamison said, "Are you going to call or sit there all night looking like a damned dummy?"

Cullen acted like he was seriously contemplating his hand and said, "Just wait a minute. I have to think about this." Scratching his beard, he shrugged his shoulders and said, "Shit, in for a penny, in for a pound," and called the bet on the table. Jamison chuckled and said, "Nice strategy," as he spread his cards down face up on the table. Two aces were staring at Cullen and he just gazed at them for a few moments. Then he spread his own hand out upside down so Jamison could clearly see it. A full house, jacks over eights.

The hand flustered Jamison, Cullen could tell. Then he got snitty and said, "Westover, I'm getting bored. How about we make this more interesting?" as he doubled the ante. Cullen wore a frightened look and said, "I don't know, Dirk. I can't lose very much or I'll have to stop playing."

Jamison laughed and called Cullen chicken shit.

"Maybe I am. Maybe I'm not loose with my money. Maybe I know when to quit before I'm skinned alive. But I'll play a few hands now that you've upped the ante. Let's see how it goes." Seven hands later, Jamison was down to two bucks and Cullen was stacking coins and paper money.

Mason came in to town that night looking for his best friends to hang around with for the evening. As he walked past the Cracked Crab, he noticed it was silent. He couldn't hear the tinny piano playing behind the closed doors, and everyone's eyes were glued to one table. Looking through the front glass window, he could see Cullen playing cards with Dirk Jamison, and started to panic. Before thinking twice, he burst through the closed doors and yelled, "Cullen, you've got to come quick! There are strangers on the Mermaid and I need your help. Come quick!" Cullen scooped up his winnings in his hat and ran for the door. "Sorry to leave in a hurry." Jamison's face turned red as a beet as he looked at the other men around the saloon. "What the hell are you all staring at! Mind your own damned business," and with that he stood up and stomped out of the Cracked Crab.

Chapter Ten

"What in the world are doing in a saloon playing cards with Dirk Jamison? Did you think poking a stick at the bear might be fun for a change? Tell me! What the hell, Cullen?"

"Take it easy, Mason. It's all for a good cause. Believe it or not, I'm stashing money away for…for a rainy day. Let's just leave it at that. And don't tell Sherry, okay?"

"No, I'm not going to leave it alone. You don't know who you're messing with! Jamison has the power to do most anything in this town and you just poked him real hard. He's not going to forget it."

"I know, and that's just how I want it. I want him flustered. I want him mad. I want him to come after me."

"Are you crazy? Do you have a wish to die?"

"No, I don't. As a matter of fact, I find I have more to look forward to than ever before. I realize you know I'm sweet on Sherry. Do you have any objections to my courting her?"

"Of course not. We all think very highly of you and in case you haven't noticed, Sherry looks like a lovelorn hound dog waiting for you to make a move. Why don't you tell her how you feel?"

"I can't. Not yet. I don't have enough to offer her. I won't come to a relationship empty handed. Now, that's all I have to say on the matter."

The two men walked another fifty feet in silence until they noticed a bright light coming from the dock. "I'll be damned. Jamison thought to destroy the Mermaid while we were playing cards." Both of them took off running in the direction of the dock and when they had almost reached their destination, they saw that it was the boat next to the Mermaid that was on fire. "Help! Everyone, help! FIRE!

FIRE!" Mason rang the distress bell halfway down the dock and doors opened and men came running with buckets and blankets.

Cullen and Mason worked on the side where the Mermaid was moored so they could keep an eye on stray embers that might catch her sails. Before it was all over, the smoking vessel next to them had lost part of her foredeck and main mast, the sails merely flying embers in the night sky. Mason and Cullen decided to stay on board for another hour or so until they determined it was safe to leave. When they left the boat and headed down the pier toward shore, Dirk Jamison was standing there smoking a cigar, the tip of which glowed bright orange in the dark as he took a long drag.

"Terrible thing, isn't it? You just never know what's going to happen from one minute to the next. Better be careful. The next fire could be on your boat." Dropping his cigar and stubbing it out, Jamison walked away, chuckling to himself.

"That son of a bitch! He set the fire! I told you, Cullen, he's dangerous and meaner than a snake. He'll stop at nothing to get his way."

"It was a warning, Mason. He would never destroy Sherry's boat because it's part of the whole package that is Sherry and the Mermaid. I'll talk to her about this and then we'll sit down and make some plans. I'm hoping the entire community will pitch in any way they can to help fix the burned boat. Who owns that one, anyway?"

"Henry Portman. He's just like us. Works like a dog to bring in a good catch and still ends up living on a prayer. I'm so tired of this. It's always something…if it's not a bad catch, it's repairs that are needed to the boat. One boat just can't get ahead. It's too much. I'm tired of the cold, I'm tired of the snow and ice. I just want out."

The next evening after Caleb was put to bed, they all sat down as a family in front of a roaring fire to discuss what had happened to the Portmans, and what Jamison had said. Sherry was devastated and weary of continuing on with the business. "He'll never stop. He's making my life a misery. He's like a constant black cloud hovering over my head and the burden of it gets heavier all the time."

Cullen wanted to gather her up in his arms and murmur loving reassurances that he would always protect her, but now was not the time. "I think I'll go into town tomorrow evening and talk with the sheriff. If I get nowhere with him I'll go to the closest judge and ask what can be done about him, although I have a sneaking suspicion they are both on Jamison's payroll. You can't have that much power without having to buy some of it."

Mason was looking mighty down in the mouth. "Sherry, why don't we just sell to Jamison. Sell the house and everything in it and just leave to start over far away from this damned bay. I feel like we never do more than tread water here in Castine."

"Mason, there was a day I would have said definitely not. A time when I would never give up the house, the Mermaid, everything. But I'm getting closer to changing my mind. Now I'm just as tired as you are." Rubbing her eyes, she continued, "Let's take a vote. How much longer are we truly willing to put up with Jamison and his plotting and planning?"

"Now wait a minute. Are you both just willing to give in to that animal?" Everyone turned to Edith, surprised she was taking a tougher stance. "There is a pall over this entire town. Everyone feels it yet no one does anything about it. There must be *something* that can be done. Everyone knows who set that fire. It's no secret and Jamison just loves that they know and that he's untouchable. It depresses the mind and body living like timid mice. Everyone in town would love it if Jamison just dropped dead." Those were Cullen's thoughts, exactly.

Cullen decided against wearing his guns to his visit with the sheriff the next evening. It wouldn't pay to get the man's hackles up when he just wanted some information. As he walked down the sidewalk toward the jailhouse, it seemed everyone was talking about the fire. He kept his head down, hoping to catch more snippets of conversation as he walked by. When he walked through the door and saw the sheriff, he thought, *Oh Lord*, as the man was a slovenly and rather odoriferous fella, reeking of the sour smell of whiskey that stays on one's breath after a bender.

"Evenin' Sherrif, the name's Cullen Westover."

"I know who you are."

"Is that right?"

"Everyone knows you're the new entry on Jamison's shitlist."

"Well, I'll be. Makes me feel pretty important. Does it take a special person to get on that list or just anyone who gets in his way?"

"The later."

"Are *you* on his list?"

"Hell, who isn't?"

"What are you going to do about it?"

"Nothing."

"Why not?"

"Because I like breathing. I advise you do the same…nothing."

"How long have the people of Castine lived like scared rabbits?"

"Long enough to get used to it, I reckon. Go along to get along, that's everyone's motto."

"Have you ever tried to do something about it?"

"Hell yes! What do you take me for?"

"Well, I didn't know. By your appearance you seem to be a defeated man. What happened?"

The sheriff got up from his chair behind an oak desk that was just as beaten and battered as he was. Instead of going for the coffee pot, he reached inside a cabinet that was in front of the picture window and took out a bottle of whiskey which he held up to Cullen as if asking if he would like a drink. Cullen answered, "No, I'm all right."

"Sit down, Mister, and I'll tell you a story." After two long swigs of liquor, he settled back in his chair and began his tale.

"I left this God forsaken place when I was just eighteen, leaving my mother and sister behind and sending money back home when I made any. Over the years, I became well practiced with pistols, shooting straight and hitting my targets most of the time. A marshal in Oklahoma hired me as his deputy. I was twenty years old.

"After a couple of years, I got a letter from my sister, Ruby, that our mother had died and I decided to come home and take care of her. Because of my experience in law, the sheriff here made me his deputy. When the old man died I became the full time sheriff." Taking another swig of whiskey, he continued, "Anyway, it wasn't long before I encountered Jamison's pa, Walter. Walter Jamison was nothing if not worse than Dirk; the corruption and intimidation, the ruthlessness and greed. It was their way of life.

"I tried to do what I could to limit his influence, pointing out the law, threatening to arrest him, and so forth. Trouble was I could never quite catch him breaking the law. He had paid men to protect him and his interests and, as we both know, money equals power. Those paid men were vipers of the first order, I tell ya. Evil, is more like it.

"When Dirk was nineteen, he raped my sister. It was brutal and Dirk thought it was a badge of pride to his manhood. He dragged her out into the street, holding her by her hair, where everyone could see what a bloody mess she was. Not only had he raped her, he beat her mercilessly. He told anyone who would listen what he did to Ruby, in stark detail, warning people that he had no trouble doing whatever was necessary to get his way.

"I went on a rampage, determined to rid the bay of the Jamisons, but Dirk told me he would kill my sister, and I believed him. It was bad enough that he had installed her upstairs at the Cracked Crab as his whore. I knew he would kill her. Whenever he gets frustrated or thwarted in any way, he takes it out on Ruby, sexually and physically.

"I know what you're thinking. I saw it on your face when you walked in here. Yes, I'm a total failure as sheriff. I'm a beaten man and even though I still have enough pride to be ashamed of it, it's just the way it is. The same is going to happen to you. Mark my words. Jamison always wins."

Cullen gave the man a few moments to collect himself before saying, "Why don't you post a reward for his arrest, dead or alive? You know all the laws he's broken and you know he started the fire on the Portman's boat night before last. Arson, the last time I checked, is a crime. I know, I know, you can't prove it, but he told me and Mason Newcomb, in so many words, that it would happen to us next. We both know he wants Sherry Newcomb's boat for his fleet, and he wants Sherry, herself. He won't stop until he gets what he wants and I've become a new hindrance to his achieving those goals. You post the reward and I'll bring him in."

The sheriff started laughing, "Have you lost your mind, mister? Plain and simple, that's just another way of committing murder. Everyone knows he can't be caught doing his crimes."

Cullen knew it was true. "How would the people of Castine feel about Dirk's death?"

"Hell, there'd be a party that wouldn't stop for days. The cheering would be so loud, you couldn't hear yourself think."

"What if I could get him in a position to come after me. What if I could make him so mad that he'd try to shoot me himself just for the joy of it? That would make it self defense, right? You wouldn't investigate such an occurrence, would you? You'd see it plain as day for what it was."

"All right, I tell you what. If you can make it happen, *and* if you have enough witnesses to say it was self defense, I won't push the issue. I'll accept it and move on."

Cullen shook the man's hand and said, "Hopefully, Castine can get its life back."

On the way home, he wondered at the power of his desire to rid the world of Dirk Jamison. He had never wished someone dead before and although it was the only answer for this town, it weighed heavy on his mind and soul. Nevertheless, he began running through certain scenarios and settled on the one he felt would do the trick. The question was how long it would take to make Jamison lose his mind.

Chapter Eleven

Sherry reached for the wooden box she kept on the top shelf in the pantry. It was too dangerous to keep their money in the Castine bank as Dirk Jamison had the controlling interest, and God only knew what he might do with their funds, if he had a mind to.

It was late in the evening and everyone had gone to bed. She sat at the kitchen table counting their income when Cullen came downstairs. "So, are you rich yet?"

"Cullen, you must be joking, although we *are* making more than before you joined us, and for that I am thankful." On a scrap of paper, she wrote down all their expenses against the income and found there were four dollars left over after saving an amount she set aside for paying taxes on the house and land; a big change from lacking enough to pay all their bills.

"I was just going out to check on Honor. I'll be right back." He did see to Honor, but also rummaged in his saddlebag that was hidden behind several bales of hay, for some cash. Taking ten dollars from the wad of bills, he patted Honor on the neck, gave him a peppermint stick, and made for the kitchen once again. When he walked through the kitchen door, he handed her the money. "What is this for?"

"Please, just take it. It would make me feel a whole lot better if you did. Plus, I have a hankerin' for some meat. Charlie just sent me some recipes for foods she made that I thought were delicious. I thought I might cook supper one night."

Sherry blushed and felt a bit ashamed. Here the man was, working like a dog and they hadn't been feeding him enough. When she felt the shame, she suddenly blurted out to change the subject, "Cullen, where do you go at night? Do you have a lady friend?"

Cullen was expecting this question at some point. "No, I don't have a lady friend, Sherry. Sometimes I like to go to town for a nip of whiskey and a game of cards, is all. It's a habit I formed a long time ago and I guess it's hard to break. Trust me when I say there is nothing untoward going on. I'm meeting some other trawlers and relaxing after a long day on the Mermaid. There's nothing to worry about."

Sherry nodded that she accepted his answer. "Oh, I forgot to tell you that a package came for you today. It's in the drawing room."

Cullen hoped it was what he guessed and went to retrieve it. A large parcel wrapped in brown paper with only his name on it, just as he instructed. Carrying it back to the kitchen, he said, "It's really not for me. It's for you and Edith."

Sherry cautiously untied the string and pulled back the paper to gaze at the lovely emerald green satin. It was truly beautiful. "Cullen, I never learned to sew." Then tears appeared in her eyes. Cullen walked over, picked up the first dress, shook it out, and held it up for her to see. The dress had been folded so what it truly was, was hidden. "Is this for me?" Cullen smiled and pulled her out of her chair, holding the dress up to see if it looked like a good fit.

"Yes, it's yours, Sherry. It's for the Christmas Ball."

"And what's the second one for?"

"It's for Edith to wear to the ball."

Fingering the emerald satin, he knew it had been the right choice of color. It would be beautiful with her auburn hair and milky complexion. Yes, she would be the belle of the ball, no doubt about it.

Sherry stood from the table and approached Cullen slowly. She then raised her arms around his neck and pulled him close. "Thank you, Cullen. It's a wonderful gift." Looking at his full mouth, she moved closer still until their lips were almost touching. She hoped Cullen would take the opportunity to kiss her like he had that night a while back.

Cullen could hardly breathe. When he felt he was beyond his endurance, he grabbed her tightly against his chest and bent down to ravish her lips like he wanted to do to the rest of her sweet body. There was no pretense in the kiss, it told her exactly what he wanted and that he wanted it *now*.

"Ahem." Mason coughed a few times to get their attention. "Am I interrupting anything?"

As much as he thought of Mason, Cullen wanted to throttle him that very instant. Sherry pulled away and turned crimson, knowing that Mason had witnessed their passion. And it *was* passionate. Very. She wanted nothing more than for the rest of the world to disappear, leaving only herself and Cullen to revel in the heat of the sensations that flowed through their primed bodies. And she knew Cullen was feeling the same as evidenced by the hardness pressing against her abdomen.

"Why don't you two just get married and save yourselves the embarrassment of being caught in each other's arms? Seems like the logical thing to do, don't you think?" Then Mason walked away, whistling a little tune as he got himself a glass of water, drank it, and returned to his room. "Goodnight, you lovebirds."

Cullen sat down at the table, wringing his hands and looking like the little boy who was caught with his hand in the cookie jar. "You know, it's not a bad idea, Sherry. It would keep Jamison away from you in at least one respect."

Sherry was instantly enraged. "Well, I've never received such a romantic proposal of marriage as this! I'm quite bowled over!" Her face reflected the exact opposite and Cullen knew what a tangle he made of the issue. "I don't need the cover of marriage to keep myself safe from Dirk Jamison. I've been doing it quite well by myself, thank you." She gazed at the dress with a look of regret, knowing she wouldn't accept it now. She felt like a fool, a worthless fool that no man would want except under bogus pretenses. Head hanging and feet dragging, she made her way to the steps upstairs and began to slowly climb, hoping the tears wouldn't come until after her bedroom door was closed.

Cullen couldn't believe his stupidity. He was a jackass of the first order and deserved to be spurned for such a lack of the romantic. He couldn't help that the first thought after Mason's remark was to suggest it wasn't such a bad idea to keep her safe from Jamison's attentions because it was what he truly wanted. But to put the idea forth for reasons other than love? He might as well bend over and let Honor cow kick him for being so insensitive and stupid. *Was he afraid Sherry would reject him if he got down on bended knee and asked with romantic flourish?* But he already knew he didn't have enough to offer her in the way of money or possessions, and made the decision to wait, anyway. *Damn!*

The next morning after a sleepless night, Cullen came down to the kitchen and found Mason at the kitchen table, stirring cream into his coffee. "Mason, I've botched everything. You won't believe what I did last night after you went back to bed."

"I'd believe it if it's about your loving Sherry. Go on, tell me how you messed things up."

"I said our getting married wasn't such a bad idea because it would protect her from Jamison in at least that respect."

"Very smooth, Cullen."

"I know. I feel awful about it."

"Well, what are you going to do? Just let her fume and try to kill her feelings for you?"

"That's just it. I don't know what the heck to do. You know my history with women. We've discussed it before. I feel like such a dolt."

"Don't worry. I'll talk to her for you." Mason replied. "I'll try to explain it was merely a knee-jerk reaction to getting what you really want, which is Sherry's love and a lifetime partnership…maybe with a couple more children, and maybe moving away from here; someplace warmer, and maybe farming or raising cattle as a change of pace from trawling. Maybe a place where I can find a pretty little thing to marry, myself. Yeah, that's what I'll tell her. Don't fret. I think I've got it handled."

"Who's the jackass now? What the heck, Mason! You're no help at all!"

Mason laughed like hell and almost choked on his coffee. "Why don't you just tell her the truth? Women like that."

Sherry heard Mason and Cullen talking when she reached the top of the stairs. Instead of going down, she stood at the top, out of their sight, and listened. When they were finished with their conversation, she tiptoed back to her room and briskly slammed the door so they would think she was just coming down. Descending the stairs, she noticed Edith wasn't in the kitchen.

"Where's Edith? She's late this morning." So saying, she turned and headed back up the stairs toward Edith's room. Gently knocking, Edith bade her to come in. "What's wrong, sweetheart? Are you not feeling well this morning?"

"Oh, Sherry. It's my time and I've got horrible cramping. Do we have any laudanum left in the pantry? You know, the bottle Doc Chambers gave us when Mason was hurt last summer? I think it would help."

Sherry yelled downstairs, "Mason! Would you bring the bottle of laudanum that's in the pantry upstairs, to Edith?"

Glancing back at Edith, she said, "Sweetie, don't take much. Just a little sip, all right?"

Mason and Sherry passed each other on the steps and Sherry continued on down to the kitchen to cook breakfast. Cullen eyed her with puppy dog eyes and she knew he felt horrible about last night. Nevertheless, she would give him something to think about. She would cook him an overdone and tasteless breakfast and give him something to really chew on.

Banging around the kitchen, Cullen knew Sherry was upset and had absolutely no idea how to make amends. Mason said to be honest and he thought it was worth a shot.

"Sherry?"

"What, Cullen."

"I love you."

"Sure you do, and I'm the Queen of England."

"No, Sherry, I've loved you since almost the beginning. I don't have much experience with courting and romantic gestures because I've never been in love. Please, forgive me for being insensitive last night. I just thought I could get what I want under the pretense of keeping you safe. It was stupid, I know, and I feel like a total ass. But one thing is God's honest truth…I love you with all my heart and soul."

Without turning around to face him, Sherry asked, "Exactly what *do* you want, Cullen?"

"I want what my heart and soul are crying out for. I want you for my wife. I thought it might be too soon to ask and then I told myself I didn't have enough to offer you as a husband. I guess what I said last night was for my own benefit. It gave me a reason not to wait until I was sure I had something more to offer you. It let me off the hook for my own decision to wait. If I don't have you soon, I'm afraid I'll lose my mind, Sherry. I want you that much…as a wife, as a lover, a partner and, hopefully, as the mother of my children."

Tears fell from Sherry's eyes. She wanted so badly to believe him. She wanted to sing from the rooftops that she loved Cullen Westover, no matter that they hadn't actually been "courting." Hadn't she known from the very beginning that she was attracted to him? Perhaps it was love at first sight for them both. And then she remembered Jacob's pleading with her to become his wife and also remembered the disappointment after accepting his promises and flowery words. Could she trust Cullen to not disappoint her like Jacob did? Cullen had seemed honest with his feelings so she would return the favor.

"Cullen, when I met Jacob, I was fresh off the boat from Ireland. He noticed me and began pursuing me with what seemed like a vengeance. He made me promises and spoke like a poet until I agreed. The day after the wedding I knew it was a mistake. There was no love in my marriage. No passion. I might as well have been his maid or nanny.

"When he died, I vowed to never again be married. I thought living alone as a woman would be better than what I had tolerated with Jacob. I'm not saying Jacob didn't treat me well, I'm just saying that as a young woman, I did without passion and affection. I felt worthless and it was awful. Then Caleb came along and I felt chained to my situation. Do you understand what I'm saying? I've heard beautiful words before. What are you going to do to make me know that you're sincere?"

"Sherry, send Mason, Edith and Caleb on some errand tonight. Make it so they are gone for at least two hours. I'll show you that I am not Jacob Newcomb. I'll show what's in my heart." And then he got up and walked out the kitchen door. Maybe Honor would help him get his head on straight. The horse was usually good for that.

Chapter Twelve

That day on the Mermaid was difficult for Cullen and Sherry. They remained silent most of the day and kept to themselves as much as possible. Mason knew what was going on and just let them be.

It was a gloomy day and the sky looked like it was about to dump a foot of snow. The water was choppy and the swells were high. A bad day for not having your mind on your work. They had already brought up one net with a good catch and were dropping the second for another when a menacing wave broke over the rail and knocked Sherry off her feet. Cullen was standing nearby and rushed to her side to keep her from washing to the other side of the deck.

"Sherry! Grab my hand!" The boat began pitching from side to side as the bay roiled with new vigor. "Mason! Let's bring up the second net and head for home! I don't like the looks of this weather!" Mason nodded and went about pulling it in. Cullen set Sherry in a corner he felt would be safe and helped Mason get the boat ready to sail for shore.

Sherry was soaking wet and shivering. Her lips were blue and her teeth were chattering like the staccato beat of a woodpecker at work.

"Cullen!" Mason yelled across the deck. "There's a flask of whiskey down in the hold! Get it and give some to Sherry!"

To hell with that. Cullen picked Sherry up and took her down to the hold where he knew there were blankets, and deposited her on a pile of netting. "I'll be back to check on you soon. Why don't you take off those wet clothes and draw a couple of blankets around you to stay warm. We'll be home before you know it."

When Cullen raced back on deck to help Mason, there was a sudden crack of thunder and lightening split the sky.

What the hell? Cullen had never witnessed a thunderstorm during winter. It was a bizarre occurrence as far as he was concerned, and he admitted to a certain amount of trepidation because of it. Bradley Cummings had warned him to have respect for the ocean, the Chesapeake Bay having swallowed many a sailor because of storms that came upon them out of nowhere. The Chesapeake was famous for it.

Mason stood at the wheel like a Norse god, his blond hair flying in the wind and his square jaw jutted against the strength of it. Cullen was mighty proud in that moment. Mason was one hell of a young man and extremely capable to boot. Looking at him made Cullen feel like a greenhorn. It was likely he would never have the same knowledge and ability as Mason, and that was fine with him. The boy knew enough for them both.

As they navigated the waves home, Cullen wondered whether or not Sherry would follow his plan for the evening. Perhaps she would be too exhausted and he could certainly understand that. Maybe Mason and Sherry considered what happened that day as something of the norm, but Cullen was shaken by it. Even as they headed for shore, he was already thinking of making some sort of harness for her to wear so she would never be swept overboard. The thought of such a possibility sent icy chills down his spine.

Sherry's behind and left elbow were bruised and it wasn't the first time, nor would it be the last. Countless times she had suffered little mishaps on the boat and always weathered them just fine. Why Cullen was making such a fuss, she didn't know. He looked petrified and wouldn't stop clucking around her like a mother hen. "Cullen, stop! I'm all right! This isn't my first time, you know, and it won't be the last."

"I'm sorry, Sherry. I can't help it. I keep seeing over and over in my mind the sight of you being swept off your feet and washing across the deck. I don't think I'll ever forget it."

"My feet are half frozen," she said as she lifted her robe, crossed her legs at the knee, and rubbed one of them between her hands.

"Here, let me do that," Cullen sighed with a mix of fear and desire.

Sherry sat back in the kitchen chair and let Cullen rub the life back into her feet with his own warmth. What would it be like to have a husband who was so solicitous, and would it last after the honeymoon? She was tired of thinking about the "what if's" and decided to just enjoy the foot rub. She closed her eyes and concentrated on the feeling of his hands on her feet. It was delicious and she relaxed into the sensations and took them for what they were…Cullen cared. She could feel the love in his touch and no longer wanted to doubt him.

"Mason!" Sherry shouted into the drawing room. "I need you to take Edith and Caleb to the lending library this evening. Caleb needs some new stories and I'd like a new novel to read. Don't just pick one willy-nilly, either. Take your time to choose something that I can get lost in."

Mason came into the kitchen and witnessed the foot rub. *Books my arse,* he thought. However, giving them time alone fit in with his desire to see the couple married, so he would take Edith and Caleb away from the house for a spell. "Give me a few dollars and we'll stop for dinner. Maybe some ice cream, too. You know how Caleb loves his ice cream."

Looking pointedly at Cullen, he saw his friend mouth the words, *two hours, okay?* Mason winked and walked away thinking perhaps he was a bit conflicted. Sherry, *was* his stepmother, after all. Although he was old enough to understand, there was still a hint of protectiveness he felt at the thought of another man being intimate with her. Shaking his head to clear the thought, he gathered Edith and Caleb and walked them into town.

Once the kitchen door was closed and they were alone, Cullen moved his hands from her feet to her calves, kneading the muscles until Sherry moaned with pleasure. He tried to maintain normal breathing but it was damn difficult. Deciding to go for broke, he raised his hands even higher and massaged her inner thighs. This time, Sherry groaned and her hips went slack in invitation. It's all Cullen needed to know that she would consent to make love with him.

Suddenly, he stood with enough force to topple his chair back onto the floor, scooped Sherry up, and headed quickly for the stairs. Finding her room was easy; he always stared a hole through it each morning and evening, wondering if she was lying in her bed, all soft and warm. The images always brought a quick response he had to quell before entering the kitchen. At night, he allowed the sensations to go unabated, enjoying the feel of the strain and the accompanying fantasies. And Cullen *did* fantasize about Sherry. It was a constant pastime and he often wondered how he got as much work done as he did in a day.

He pushed her bedroom door open with his foot, walked to the bed, and gently deposited her on the covers. "Sherry, are you sure?" Sherry smiled and opened her arms to him, "Oh yes, I'm sure, Cullen. Come to me."

Their lovemaking was slow and gentle at first, their hands exploring and caressing, acquainting themselves with each other's fevered flesh. Cullen had learned over the years how to please a woman and it gave him immense pleasure watching his lover's enjoyment and physical reactions to his tender ministrations. Sherry was enjoying the attention and he made sure no stone was left unturned in helping her reach her ultimate pinnacle.

When Sherry could hold it back no more, Cullen waited for her to ride the wave and knew the power and depth of her experience. When it ended and Sherry was replete, he entered her swollen flesh and began his second assault. Together they spiraled into their own private world where one body was no longer separate from the other. Their kisses were deep and soulful, and their bodies full of purpose in a dance that was as old as time.

Cullen was overwhelmed by the depth of his feelings. He had no idea sex could hold so much meaning. He loved this woman; loved her deeply and with all his heart. He hoped it was the same for Sherry. He wanted her to feel the depth of his intentions, leaving no doubt as to how much he cherished her.

As they lay in each others' arms, drenched in perspiration from the wondrous act they had just completed, Cullen was the first to speak.

"Darlin', are you all right?"

"No, I'm not."

Leaning up on an elbow he asked, "Did I hurt you?"

"No."

"Then why are you not all right? Do you regret it?"

"No."

"Then, what? Tell me, please!"

"I want more, that's all, and we don't have the time."

Cullen laughed, pulling her on top of his chest and roundly kissed her rosy lips.

"Marry me and I promise to give it to you all the time."

With Sherry on top of him, he became aroused once again but knew their time of privacy was almost over. Mason would be coming through the door any time now and they had to slam back into reality and daily routine. He kissed the tip of her nose and said, "Sweetheart, we have to get up and dressed before Mason gets back. C'mon, now. Up you go."

They ended up downstairs, each sitting in a chair by the fire, Cullen reading the local newspaper and Sherry crocheting what looked to be a little ball of threads, both looking as innocent as two babes in the woods. It was only minutes later that Mason, Edith and Caleb, came through the kitchen door. Mason yelled, "Hello! We're home!" hoping to give them fair warning.

Sherry winked at Cullen and yelled back, "We're in here by the fire. Come join us."

Mason looked at Cullen and then at Sherry, and thought they must be the best actors this side of London. "We brought you some sandwiches. I didn't know if you had eaten or not." Cullen grabbed the paper sack, gave Sherry one of the sandwiches and then unwrapped his, practically inhaling it. Sherry was doing justice to hers, too, and Mason started howling in laughter. "You weren't hungry, were you? You must have worked up quite an appetite *today.*" Sherry blushed but never let on to his meaning.

"I was too tired to cook anything, Mason. Thanks for thinking of us."

"Yeah, me too. Did you bring anything else? Some dessert, maybe?"

Mason chortled and handed Sherry the book he had selected for her at the lending library. It was a copy of Jane Eyre, apparently never having been read before. It looked brand new. Handing Cullen another sack, he said, "You can have the rest of these, I've had enough." The bag was still half full of chocolate bonbons which Cullen chewed happily. "Mmm, these are so good! Here, Sherry, try one!"

Mason was tired of the charade, left them to their theatrics, and headed for his bed.

Chapter Thirteen

A few days later, Dirk Jamison was meeting with his two top henchmen.

"I want Westover roughed up badly. Make him understand what it's like to cross a Jamison. Don't kill him or Sherry Newcomb will never give me what I want. I'd hate to have to kill such a tasty piece as she is. It would be such a waste."

Jamison's top man, Cory Pullen, didn't like the idea but was damn sure not going to cross Dirk. "I hear ya, boss. Might take us a while, though. I gotta study his habits, ye see."

The other man, Johnny Culp, grinned and added, "Don't you worry, boss. We'll get'er done, ayuh. He'll never be able to take on both me and Cory, no suh."

Dirk wished he could count on them to get it done but knew they were both ignorant knuckleheads. God, what he wouldn't pay for some decent help.

***

Cullen sat at the kitchen table, cleaning his guns and sharpening his eight inch hunting knife. It was always a peaceful and calming chore, one he liked to do alone. However, as he was realizing more and more these days, having a family sometimes didn't allow for much solitude.

"I heard the chamber of your gun spinning and thought I'd come down and see if I could help," Mason said shyly. The only gun in their house was an old shotgun that had been passed down through a few generations, and Jacob never allowed him to touch it. Now he felt at a total loss to help Cullen with whatever it was he was planning. And he *knew* Cullen was planning something. It had been written all over the man's face for days."

"You know how to shoot a gun, Mason?"

"No, I'm ashamed to say I can't…or never have, at least."

"Well, I think it's time for you to learn. I also think it's time you had your own gun. Which do you think you'd prefer? A pistol or rifle?"

"Hell, Cullen, how would I know?"

Cullen explained the intricacies of both and then said, "Bring me you're pa's shotgun and I'll clean it. Tomorrow after church, we'll go for some target practice. I'm not sure whether we should tell Sherry or not, but that's your call."

"She can't keep me a child forever, you know. I'm almost twenty and work like a man. I think I should be treated like one. So, there's your answer. Sherry has nothing to say about it."

Cullen grinned and agreed, "You certainly are a man, Mason. I'll give you that. I've met men who are twice your age that couldn't hold a candle to you. See if Edith has any tin cans in the garbage. We'll use them as targets."

"So, are you going to tell me or not? What's your plan, Cullen?"

"Don't really have one, Mason. All I know is that Jamison has got to go, no matter how it's done. I won't allow him to accost our women again, whether it be physically *or* verbally. I've talked with the Sheriff, and I think I know what I'm going to do. There's a lot of 'if's' about it and things will have to fall into place like dominos. I just don't know when the opportunity will present itself.

"Let's get you some practice shooting a gun first. That will be a tremendous help. If you're good with a pistol, we'll get you one with a gun belt. I want to know you can shoot from the hip and hit your targets."

Unfortunately, Mason wouldn't have a chance to practice shooting the next day.

After sharpening his hunting knife the night before, Cullen decided to run down to the Mermaid before church, and get all the knives on board to sharpen them; maybe teach Mason how to use a sharpening stone to its full advantage. There were four, all totaled, if he remembered correctly.

He hopped aboard and looked in all the usual places the knives were kept, stuck them inside his belt, and was ready to climb back on the pier when he was blindsided by the punch of a ham fisted, hulk of a man.

"This is from Dirk Jamison. He says to tell you that your sorry ass better be gone this time tomorrow, or else." And then *WHAM,* another hit to Cullen's gut that knocked him off his feet and flat on his back on the deck of the boat. He'd been in bar fights before but had never experienced such a blow. The man must have arms like three trunks with the power of a locomotive behind them. He could hardly breathe.

He was able to scramble away from the two for just enough time to pull two knives out of his belt. He stood with legs spread, embracing the deck as he might have dug his boots in dirt under different circumstances, a knife in each hand, and swaying menacingly as he tried to intimidate the two men.

"Look at'im, Cory, he thinks he can take us both on. Wanna go first? I can wait. See'n yuns fight makes my blood boil and I'll give him the finishing touches to get the message across. Go on, take your pleasure."

Cory didn't like the odds of approaching a man with two knives, arms flailing. Jamison had forbid killing the man, which diminished his odds greatly. "Nah, you go first Johnny. I like to watch, too. You can go second the next time."

While the idiots were jabbering, Cullen noticed a family out in their yard, watching with alarm and morbid fascination. Good. At least he would have witnesses.

"Come and get it, Johnny. Come on and taste the lick of these blades, if you're man enough." Cullen still swayed from side to side, and worked the knives in an almost trance inducing dance.

Johnny was game. He always was because he never took the time to contemplate the consequences of his actions. "Let's do it, Redneck," he said, moving in on Cullen.

Being almost as ungainly as a buffalo, it was easy to feint this way and that until Cullen could find the exact moment for a stab in the gut. If he could get the chance, he'd stick him in the abdomen and jerk the blade up, making sure it would stop the man. It was a deadly cut and Cullen just had to keep moving until he saw his opportunity.

In the meantime, Cory gazed with glee at the two going at it, saliva dripping down his chin. Death always aroused him. Being able to watch instead of doing the deed was the best part. Even though Jamison said not to kill Westover, he would take the opportunity to fantasize about the outcome. However, in just about thirty seconds or so, Cory watched in shocked amazement as Johnny's body lurched from the waist forward, arms holding his gut and then looking at his bloodied hands. "Cory? CORY! Where are you? Kill this bastard!" In the next moment he was merely a pile of flesh lying on deck.

"Come on, Cory. You're next," Cullen taunted, hands dripping blood and regaining the stance of a knife fighter.

"You're damned right, Westover. You're a dead man!" Cory screamed a war cry and moved in for the kill, emotion driving him instead of concentration on the technique he would use to bring Westover down. It was a fatal mistake as Cullen used the same maneuver that took Johnny's life, on Cory. Cory fell in a heap and gurgled his last breath as

Cullen stepped over him to make his way to the family who had been watching.

"Howdy. If you would be so kind," he said huffing huge breaths of air, "would you please follow me to the sheriff's office and give him your statement of what you saw?"

Silence. Total silence. Finally, the man of the house stepped forward and pleaded, "Suh, don't ask me to do that. I got a family ta feed and a house to pay fer. Jamison will kill me sure as hell if I do what yer askin'."

"No, he won't. Jamison's time of ruling Castine is coming to an end, I promise you."

Moving closer, Cullen held out his bloodied hand for the man to shake. Looking from his wife to all his children, the man's wife said to her husband, "Go on. You go on and make our statement of what we saw. We can't live under that devil's thumb no more." She then looked Cullen square in the eye and warned, "Mistuh, if you go back on your promise, we'll all be dead. You know that don'tcha?"

"Yes, ma'am, I do." Cullen would make good on that promise if it was the last thing he ever did on God's green earth.

As luck would have it, the man had his wagon ready to carry the family to church that morning. Instead, it would be a trip he would never forget, and he gained courage with every beat of his heart as they made their way down Main Street.

The sheriff was outside on the porch of the jailhouse, getting a stack of wood to bring inside for the wood stove. Out of the corner of his eye, he noticed the wagon pulling to a stop before him. "Mornin'. What can I do...*Westover*? What the hell have you done?"

"Sheriff, this man," Cullen hadn't even gotten his name, "this man and his family witnessed two of Jamison's henchmen try to kill me while I was on the Mermaid. They saw everything and he's here to give you his statement."

Cullen was weak as a kitten, the adrenaline rush having left him tired and shaky.

"Well, for pity's sake. Come on in here, Clyde, and we'll get it done." The sheriff was elated and suddenly felt, for the first time in years, that there might be hope for Castine, after all.

***

Jamison watched the proceedings from across the street at the mercantile. What the hell had happened? Westover was a bloody mess. If he died, Dirk would kill those two ingrates he sent to pay Westover a visit. He paid them enough to follow easy damned instructions.

Not being able to help himself, he walked over to the sheriff's office and opened the door. "What's going on here, sheriff? Mr. Westover looks plumb done in."

Cullen shot out of his chair, got within three inches of Jamison's face and spat, "I just killed two of your henchmen, Jamison. Have you come to witness the carnage you wrought? Did you think that *I* would be the loser? Well think again…and I'm telling you this in front of Clyde and the sheriff, if you *ever* come after me or my family again, I'll kill you, do you understand?"

"Sheriff, are you going to let this man threaten me in this manner? There is absolutely no proof that Cory and Johnny were acting on my orders."

"How did you know it was Pullen and Culp?" the sheriff asked. "I don't recall Mr. Westover giving their names yet. You interrupted us in the process of getting to that point." Then he smiled at Jamison and sat back down, picking up pen and paper to begin taking the statement.

Jamison turned a grayish pallor, turned on his heel, and walked out the door. *DAMMIT! Couldn't those yahoos do anything right?* Well, they were gone but were also replaceable. Given another couple of days, he was sure he could find someone looking for a certain type of work; *his type of work*. Money talked and he'd pay well for a job well done. Then he pondered the fact that he was stupid enough, himself, to use the names of the men he had ordered to accomplish the deed. He would have to tighten up and keep his mind sharp. *What was it about Westover that got to him, anyway?*

As Clyde Balderson pulled his wagon up to the kitchen door, Sherry witnessed a bloody Cullen through the window and flew down the stairs, running outside and yelling, "Cullen, oh my God, Cullen! What happened? Are you all right?" Then it was Mason and Edith rushing out the door, little Caleb following behind.

Cullen looked at Mason, and the boy came rushing to his side to help him out of the wagon and to the ground. "Did you get him?" Mason whispered.

"No, but I got two of his bullies. They're dead."

"Holy Moses!" Mason cried. "When? Where? I thought you were still in bed!"

"Not now, son. Let me go inside and get cleaned up." Then looking at Sherry, he apologized, "I'm sorry, Sherry. But I don't think I can make it to church this morning," at which point he fell to his knees.

Mason picked him up and turned to bring him inside, but stopped and turned back around. "Clyde, you have my sincere thanks for helping Cullen. I owe you one, my friend." Clyde nodded and clicked his horses to walk on, feeling like a better man.

Sherry was beside herself, cutting Cullen's shirt off to look at any wounds there may be. He kept holding his arm over his side so there must be something wrong.

"Quit cutting my shirt! I only have two, you know," he chastised between gritted teeth. "I think it's my rib. I think it's broken, and it's hard to breath."

"Mason, go get Doc, quick! And don't take no for an answer!" She ignored Cullen's plea to not cut his shirt and promised to buy him two new ones to take its place.

"What happened, Cullen? Tell me!"

"I'll wait for Mason to get back. I want him to hear it. Just let me lie here for a minute and try to catch my breath."

Mason returned with Doc Chambers in toe and the old man was madder than a wet hen. "Mason Newcomb, what right do you have literally picking me up and throwing me in a wagon? I told you I had a patient and did that stop you? Hell no, it didn't! You'll rue the day, I tell ya, rue the day you let yourself lose control like that!"

Mason looked at the old man as he was mid tirade and just smiled. Then, when he could take no more, he said, "Doc, shut the hell up and do your job. This man is in much worse shape than Prissy Talbert, who we all know acts like hangnail is going to kill her. Now, please, take a look at Cullen. He's in bad shape."

All the starch went out of Doc, and he looked like a rag doll. "All right. Where's the patient." Walking into the kitchen, they found Cullen lying flat on the kitchen table, wheezing for air. "Let me guess. Dirk Jamison's work, am I right?" Cullen nodded, and Sherry started to wail, "Saint's preserve us! That man will be the death of us all! I cannot believe he has the gall to touch one of mine! He'll pay for this, you wait and see!"

Caleb was sitting in the corner silently crying, tears running down his little cheeks as he shook with fear and misery. "Uncle Cullen gonna die?" he asked between sobs. Mason picked the child up and held him close. "See? He's still with us and will be forever and always. Isn't that right, Uncle Cullen?"

Cullen grinned at the boy and held out his hand to stroke his little brown curls. "Hey, son, I'm fine. Really, I'm fine.

Doc here is going to fix me right up in no time, isn't that right, Doc?" Doc grunted and proceeded to poke and prod Cullen in every possible place on his body. Looking at the frightened child, Doc said, "He's going to be fine. He's got two broken ribs, is all. He'll be right as rain soon, just you wait and see little fella."

Looking at Sherry, he told her, "He needs to stay in bed for at least two weeks, Mrs. Newcomb. I mean it, now! If he tries to move before those ribs have healed, he could poke himself in a lung. The reason he's breathing so hard is that someone, he who is thus far nameless, gut punched him so hard it knocked the breath right out of him. Give him another hour or two and it should return to normal."

Cullen wheezed, "Thanks Doc. Please send me your bill for services as soon as possible. I'll make sure you're paid right away."

As the doctor was walking toward the door, Sherry asked, "Uh, how are we going to get him upstairs, Doc?" The old man smiled and said, "Very carefully."

When the door closed behind him, Mason, Sherry and Edith stood silent, just looking at each other with no idea of how to proceed. Suddenly Edith said loudly, "I'll make him some chicken broth. Mason, go kill me a chicken. Sherry, go upstairs and make sure Cullen's linens are clean. If not, change his bed. Go on, both of you. In just a bit we'll all three help him upstairs when all is ready."

Sherry and Mason looked at each other and couldn't help smiling. "Yes, Edith is right. Let's move, shall we?"

Cullen had to chuckle, never having seen Edith in such a take charge mood. Yep, they would have to find her a good husband. She'd be just the ticket for some lucky man. "Edith, you are some good woman, you know that?" Cullen said between breaths. "I admire you so much. You've a good heart and a fine mind."

Edith blushed and replied, "Cullen Westover, Sherry is one lucky woman because you're some kinda man. You've a good heart and soul and I love and respect you."

Cullen held out his hand to her and when she placed hers in his big calloused one, he brought it toward his mouth and kissed it tenderly. Both had pools of tears in their eyes and no further words of affection would ever again be necessary between them. They were family and would always be so.

When all preparations for Cullen's recovery were finished, and Edith's chicken broth simmered to perfection in the pot, they crowded around the injured man, trying to figure out how to get him upstairs and in bed. One would pull this way, the other that way, and they were hurting him terribly.

"Wait! Just wait a minute, please. I'm going to hold my arms to my sides, bent at the elbows like a chair arm. Sherry, you take one side and Mason, you take the other. Edith, if I start to fall backward, you just push me in the butt until I'm right again. Now let's go."

All in all, with little breaks for Cullen to catch his breath, it took thirty minutes to get him off the table and up the stairs. Getting him into the bed was painful for him, the broken ribs moving in wrong directions as he sat and then tried to lie down. At that point, Cullen just wanted to be left alone.

"Why don't y'all go downstairs and eat supper. I need to rest a bit. Go on, go about your business and leave me to mine. I'll see you after you eat." He hated to sound ungrateful but the pain was making him cranky.

Dinner was a quiet affair that night, Sherry and Mason exchanging looks as if to say, *"What should we do?"* Edith looked at Sherry and Mason looking at each other and huffed, "For gosh sakes! Why would we even have to ask each other what to do about this? I say we kill Jamison. That will be the end of it all. No more misery and fear."

"Edith, does it make you feel better to talk like that?" Mason asked.

"Yes, it does. It makes me feel stronger than sitting around wringing my hands."

"I hear you, Sis. I hear you. I wish I had the gumption to do the deed myself but I would need Cullen to help me." Then they all laughed at such nonsense, knowing Cullen was out of commission for the foreseeable future.

Chapter Fourteen

Later that evening, after all the chores were done and Cullen was fed, it was time to ask him what happened. He lay there miserable in the bed, his pants still bloody and dried blood caked on his upper chest and neck. Sherry would bathe him after everyone was down for the night.

"I was in the kitchen last evening cleaning my guns and sharpening my hunting knife, and this morning decided to go get the knives off the Mermaid while my sharpening stone was still out and oiled. I remembered four knives and where they were usually kept and went about gathering them, sliding them into the inside of my belt.

"When I was ready to jump back on the pier, this huge son of a bitch, pardon ladies, gut punched me out of nowhere. Then he punched me again, twice as hard. I was able to scatter away from him and pulled two of the knives out of my belt, dancing around the deck like a mad man.

"I could hear them talking to each other about the fun they were going to have beating me to a pulp, and deciding which one would go first and such, when I recognized their names as being Jamison's top henchmen. The sheriff had told me who they were and to watch out for them. I thought for sure they were going to kill me so I waited until I could stab the first one in the gut. He went down like a mountain. That really angered the other one and he screamed like a banshee, charging after me to finish me off.

"I don't think either of them were very smart. Brawny, without a brain between them, I'd say. Anyway, I used the same maneuver to cut him like I did the first one and, to my knowledge, they are still lying dead on the deck of the Mermaid.

"Fortunately, during all their deliberations on who would be first to do me damage and so forth, I was able to see a family standing in their yard watching the whole thing happening. After I was able to get away, I walked up and asked if they would be willing to give the sheriff a statement as to what they witnessed. At first the man, Clyde, didn't want to. Then his wife told him to do it, hoping it was a good first step in taking care of the Jamison issue for good. There you have it, and here we are, only a little worse for the wear."

Mason was loaded for bear. "Cullen, we're going to finally take care of this, right? It's time." Cullen nodded that he agreed and everyone but Sherry left the room for their own beds.

"I'll be right back. I need some warm water to clean you up. Try not to move, all right?" Sherry was trying to hold herself together and not show Cullen how upset she was. Returning with warm water and soap, she began peeling the covers back to undress him. She slowly pulled his pants off and found there was blood on his under drawers, too. What a mess.

Even though they had already made love, she found herself blushing and embarrassed. "Cullen, I'm going to have to remove your under drawers. They have blood on them." Cullen merely grunted and let her do what she would. He lay there in the altogether without shame or embarrassment. She was his woman and she could do what she needed or wanted to do.

The novelty of having all his needs cared for by the entire family wore off after about the fourth day of being confined to his bed. He missed Sherry and Mason when they were on the boat during the day, and also missed sitting with everyone around the dinner table in the evening, sharing food and laughter.

Edith cooked some of his favorite foods from the recipes he had received from Charlie and Mrs. Cummings, and did a pretty good job of it, he had to admit. The rest of the family took to the Southern food like a duck takes to water, Mason having consumed almost a whole fried chicken by himself and Caleb eating enough mashed potatoes to fill an adult, let alone a little boy. Sherry was leery of the corn pudding at first but then swooned over the sweetness and consistency.

It was lonely upstairs. He worried about Honor; if his horse was getting the attention and treatment he needed. He found himself thinking a lot about his father, wondering if he was on the mend or dwindling down to his final days. The sheriff promised to contact him if that were the case but Cullen had received no telegrams to that effect. When the boredom became unbearable, he would close his eyes and picture every square inch of the farm, remembering his love of the place and all that was required to keep it going. Even though he and his father hadn't gotten along for several years until Cullen finally left home, he had enjoyed farm life.

He envisioned the family moving down to Virginia, restoring the old farmhouse, and working the land together. He wondered if Mason and Sherry would take to it like he had as a child. Edith would fit just about anywhere you put her...unless it was a fish cannery. Then his mind would meander to the Mermaid, the salt water and feel of the boat swaying to and fro in the waves of the Penobscot Bay. He was conflicted, all right, and that's when he'd give up all the mental gymnastics and just take a nap. He would feel himself drifting into sleep, the picture of Sherry naked under his body clear as day. Upon entering his room one time and witnessing a smile on his face and a bulge in the covers below his belt line, Sherry had later asked him what he was dreaming of and he blushed and simply winked at her in reply.

Sherry knew Cullen was bored. A man like him was a man of action and she took pity on him each evening by reading to him. Cullen didn't care much for Jane Eyre, and would have preferred a penny dreadful over such romantic fluff.

When Cullen complained of being stiff from lying in bed so long, Sherry massaged his back and legs, carefully turning him on his side, trying whatever she could to keep him comfortable so lying flat all day wasn't so trying. It was a tough job and it was sometimes exhausting after a day on the Mermaid, but it would soon be over.

One afternoon Cullen awoke from a nap and looking out the window, saw it was snowing so hard he couldn't see the limbs of the old oak tree several yards away. Cullen used that old tree as a daily indicator of the weather outside. Then, looking at the clock on the dresser across the room, he saw that it was almost time for Sherry and Mason to be sailing for home and wondered if they were safe sailing in the storm. "Edith! Edith, will you please come up here for a minute?"

Edith came running, images of him falling out of bed or some such, but when she entered his room he just smiled. "Sweet Edith, will you please look out the window and tell me what you see? It's snowing like crazy out there and I'm worried about Sherry and Mason."

Edith softly laughed, "Cullen this is nothing compared to some types of weather we have to endure. Sherry and Mason are just fine, trust me. They might be a bit late today, but they'll manage just fine." Cullen didn't look relieved by her words. "Trust me, Cullen, all is well. Is there anything I can get for you? Fluff your pillow? Get you a drink of water?"

"Get me up out of this bed? PLEASE? I'm going crazy up here! How many days has it been so far, anyway? Thirty? Sixty? I'm going nuts!"

"It's been ten days and that means four more *if* Doc feels like those ribs have mended. So you might as well relax.

I'm not helping you get up. Sherry would have my hide and you know it."

"Will you send Mason upstairs this evening? I'd like to talk to him after dinner." Edith nodded that she would.

Edith turned and started for the door when Cullen broke into song, making up the words as he went along. He was loud and obnoxious, which Edith figured was payment in kind for her lack of cooperation in setting him free. Giggling, she continued down the stairs to start their dinner.

The evening meal was over. Cullen ate clam chowder and yeast rolls. After having fixed some of the recipes he had given Edith from Charlie and Mrs. Cummings, she had started experimenting with different spices, and the chowder that night had been more flavorful than usual.

He listened to the bustle downstairs in the kitchen. Thank God, there were two sets of steps in the house to the upstairs. They always used the back stairs near the kitchen, the ones in the front of the house going down to the parlor. Cullen smiled. It felt good to *not* be company. It felt good to be family. Soon he heard heavy footsteps treading those stairs and knew Mason was coming to see him.

"Mason, how's it going? You look like something the cat dragged in. You feeling all right?"

"I'm fine. Just dog tired, is all. It took your being absent from the boat for a while to make me truly see how much work you get done in a day. I miss you, buddy."

"Pull up a chair and sit awhile."

"Don't mind if I do, Cullen." The young man practically fell into the chair, he was so tired.

"So tell me, have you been ruminating over our 'problem' lately?"

"It's all I can think about. You've got to get better, Cullen. We've got to make some plans."

"Well, I think I've come up with one. I hate the thought of ruining the Christmas Ball, but I think it's our best chance to get Jamison's goat."

"To hell with the ball, tell me your plan."

And so the two men sat and looked at the issue from all angles, chewed on them a bit, and finally decided on what to do.

Chapter Fifteen

Thanksgiving had come and gone without fanfare this year. Cullen was still laid up in bed and Jamison was still Jamison. They never knew what the man would do next.

Now it was time for the Christmas Ball, and Sherry was so looking forward to it. She couldn't wait to dress in her new gown and walk into the ball on Cullen's arm.

The entire week before the ball, Sherry fantasized about how to fix her hair and whether or not to wear a corset. She hadn't worn one for so long, she didn't know whether she'd be able to breathe through the unfamiliar stricture. She stood in front of her full length mirror, pushing her breasts up to see how much cleavage she should allow and whether she could affect a nice plumpness without a corset. She would have to try the dress on both ways to judge which way to choose. Maybe she'd go to the mercantile to buy some lip rouge. Maybe some face powder. She wondered if Cullen would think her too gaudy looking with makeup. Augh! It was all driving her crazy! She shouldn't be so overly concerned with her appearance. It was unseemly for a woman to be so vain.

***

Cullen was no longer bed ridden, but was taking it easy and merely doing little chores here and there. He spent a good deal of time in the barn with Honor, having missed him terribly during his two weeks in bed. He bundled up in the afternoons and took short walks through the snow, gaining his strength back. His stomach was still bruised but it felt like the ribs had mended, as far as he could tell.

One day he took his pistols and some tin cans and rode Honor across the pasture and near the tree line of some woods. He shot enough targets to know that he was still as sharp as ever, hitting nearly one hundred percent of them square in the middle.

The next day he trudged through the snow into town to talk with the sheriff.

"Sheriff, howdy do! I've come with a couple of questions for you."

"What can I do for you, Westover? I heard about your injuries and meant to drop by and see how you were doing, but…you know how it is. Ladies don't like inebriated men in their homes."

"Not a problem, and I'm doing much better, thank you. I'm pretty sure my ribs are fully mended. Doc's coming out tomorrow to give me the final once over."

The sheriff went to his special cupboard and took out his bottle. He didn't take a drink but had it close by just in case. To Cullen, it was almost like the man had a hold of the demon liquor by the neck and would look it straight in the eye to keep from indulging. If that was so, he was mighty glad to see it.

"I need to know what kind of shot Jamison is. Did he always wear his guns or is that something he's taken to doing just lately?"

The sheriff grinned. "He couldn't hit a barrel of cow dung that was right in front of him. He wears them to be intimidating, and it works." The man stared at the bottle and then back at Cullen. "The question is, are *you* a good shot? What's *your* accuracy? That's what I want to know."

"I've never been a hired gunman, if that's what you're asking. But I do have a natural ability that I've had since I was a lad. An instinct, you might say. If you want to know if I can hit a bumblebee in mid flight, the answer is yes."

"Well, now. That's an interesting fact I'll just tuck in the back of my mind, somewhere it can't be found. I sense a plan is in the works?"

"You would be correct. Me and Mason, at the Christmas Ball. And we need your help, sheriff. How good an actor are you?"

The sheriff laughed heartily. "Me? An actor? Well, I've done any number of things in my life and I guess I might as well add acting to the list. What do you have in mind?

Cullen sat forward in his chair. "Well, it'll go like this . . ."

***

"Hey Mason, we need to go to town and get some new duds to wear to the ball. We don't want to look unworthy of our women, do we?"

Mason laughed, "And just what will we use to pay for these 'duds'? Will we get them with only our good looks?"

"Hell, Mason, you're about the handsomest young man in Castine. Surely, you haven't missed all the young ladies following you with their eyes and twittering to each other as you pass by? Damned if I don't believe you *could* get them with your looks alone."

"Why, Cullen, do you have a crush on me?"

"How about the crush of my boot up your butt?"

They laughed as Cullen put his arm around Mason's shoulders and led him into town. Sure enough, all the ladies ogled and twittered as they passed.

"See? I told you. You can have the pick of the litter any time you want. I'm jealous." Mason burst out laughing and then tried to become more serious about their mission to find suitable clothing for the dance.

Jamison was walking out of the Cracked Crab, having had a distasteful encounter with Ruby. She had the audacity to ask him for something she knew she couldn't have.

"Dirk, will you take me to the Christmas Ball?"

Jamison laughed and spit in her face. "How dare you ask me to take you out, you used and worthless sow. You are for screwing only…and some occasional other pleasures that I pay you for when I deign to even pay you."

Before Ruby could move, Jamison slapped her hard across the face. As she fell to the floor, he kicked her repeatedly in the gut and then stepped over her body to exit the room where he kept her prisoner. He was Ruby's only client. He was her master, she his slave.

Ruby cried pitifully and swore she would escape her prison soon. She would either escape or kill him. Everyone in town knew her situation and no one had the guts to interfere. And she didn't believe anyone would blame her for it. The man was evil to the core.

When she tried to get up from the floor, she cried out in pain as blood ran from the back of her throat and out of her mouth. She made it to the window which faced the back alley, and managed to open it. "Help! Somebody, please help me! I need the doctor!" Looking up and down the alley, she spied her brother relieving himself on the grass behind the jailhouse.

"Darrell! Darrell, help me! Come get me, brother!"

Darrell looked up when he heard the screams. It was Ruby and she was in trouble. He buttoned his fly and ran as fast as he could to see if she was hurt. Entering the back door of the Cracked Crab, he ran up the back steps and reached her room in a flash. He tried opening her door but it was locked.

"Ruby, unlock the door, darlin'! Unlock it!"

"I can't, Darrell! He keeps me locked in," she cried.

Darrel backed up to the opposite wall in the hallway and charged into the door, busting it off its hinges. There he found his precious sister, clothes ripped, and blood running out of her mouth.

"Darrell, I think he's killed me this time. I think the blood is coming from my stomach."

Darrell wrapped a quilt around her and put slippers on her feet. "Come on, Ruby. I'll take you to Doc's office. I know you're going to be all right and rest assured he'll never touch you again. It's time to stop giving in to his threats."

As they walked down the alley, Darrell told her that Jamison had threatened to kill her if he ever interfered. He told her he just couldn't take that chance with her life. He apologized over and over again and held her tighter.

Knocking on Doc's back door, his wife answered and showed them into an examining room. "Doc will be right with you. Darrell, lay her down on that table and cover her with the quilt. I'll be right back."

At the moment, Jamison was walking toward the barber shop when he saw Mason and Cullen approaching the mercantile. They were laughing and joking like brothers, and for some reason it made him angry, royally. Seeing them happy was like a knife in his chest. That bastard Westover was going to meet with some nasty business, and soon. Jamison felt as though he was losing control and that could never happen. Once Westover was gone for good, things would return to normal. He rested his hand on the pistol he was now carrying with him everywhere. The pleasure of killing Westover shouldn't be handed over to anyone else. He deserved the pleasure he would feel from doing the man in, himself. And then he would celebrate with Ruby.

Chapter Sixteen

It was the day of the Christmas Ball, and Sherry and Edith were running around like little hens, trying to remember all that had to be done. The men could take care of themselves. They were sure Mason and Cullen would look fine, but *they* wanted to show Castine how the Newcomb women cleaned up.

Cullen and Mason were in the barn brushing Honor, and going over their plans. It was simple, really, and Cullen told his buddy to just follow along with whatever he felt would work, depending on the situation as it unfolded.

Jamison was at the barber, getting a clean shave and a haircut. This was the night he planned on finally wooing Sherry into his arms. He ruminated over the plans for days, feeling certain she would capitulate and agree to be his. He was so sure of himself that he tipped the barber a whole dollar and walked out of the shop whistling a jaunty little tune. Yes sir, Dirk Jamison always got what he wanted and tonight would be no different.

Sherry gave herself a last look in the mirror and smiled at the transformation from trawler to belle of the ball. At least she hoped that's what she would be, if only in Cullen's eyes. The gown was magnificent. The dressmaker had woven golden threads into the lace collar and cuffs and she was dazzled by the reflection of sparkles as she moved this way and that. She just hoped they would have enough time at the ball to really enjoy the way it made her feel. She wanted Cullen to be proud of her. She wanted to be Cullen's fairy princess before hopefully becoming his queen.

When she descended the stairs, Cullen could only stare in amazement. His woman was breathtakingly gorgeous. He finally gathered himself and handed her a wrapped package.

"For me? Oh, Cullen, you shouldn't have."

"Nonsense. Open it. I hope you like it."

Sherry opened the brown paper and touched the softest white rabbit fur muff for her hands. "Oh, Cullen, it's beautiful!" She closed her eyes and rubbed the soft fur over her face. "It's so elegant. I've never had something so nice. Thank you. It means the world to me."

Cullen kissed her forehead and helped her into her coat. Mason was helping Edith with hers and it wasn't long before they were all in the wagon and heading for town. As the wagon rolled on, Edith took the opportunity to have a chat with her brother.

"Mason?"

"Yes, sis?"

"Do you think any of the boys at the dance will find me beautiful? Do you think any of them will be interested in me?"

"Edith, have you looked in a mirror lately? I've watched you grow from a skinny little girl into a ravishing young woman. How could you even ask such a thing?"

"I sometimes feel so alone, brother. I feel like I'm on the outside looking in and that there will be no fairytale romance in my life. Oh, Mason, I just want to be married and have children of my own. I want to leave Castine and never look back. I want to be a farmer's wife. I'm tired of the water. I want to work the land."

Mason put his arm around his sister's shoulders, hugged her close, and thought how much alike they were and how they shared similar dreams. Hearing her thoughts and feelings merely reminded him once again that he was ready to leave Castine behind.

***

The sheriff noted immediately that Jamison was wearing his gun and made no move to stop him from entering the ball.

"Evening, Sheriff."

Darrell gave him a slight nod and stood aside as the man stepped through the front door, looking full of himself, as usual. It was hard to keep from shooting him square in the forehead after what he'd done to Ruby, but he had to play his part tonight, whatever the end result.

Soon he saw Westover and the Newcombs approaching in their wagon, and noticed the glint of gun metal in the moonlight as they passed. As previously agreed upon, the sheriff nodded and touched the side of his nose as a signal that Jamison had already arrived.

After the wagon was parked, the group made their way to the dance hall where they could hear music already playing.

"I'm so excited!" Edith exclaimed. "I haven't had a new dress in years!"

"You look devastating in that dress, Sis. I'll have to keep my eye on you every minute. Every man here will want to dance with you," Mason beamed as he led her safely through the door.

Cullen bent down to whisper in Sherry's ear, "Save every dance for me, will you?" Sherry blushed, batted her eyelashes, and said, "Why, it would be impolite to shun every man here just for your benefit, Cullen. I mean, shouldn't all the gents get to be seen with me tonight?" Playing the coquette, she glided through the door in a swish of skirts and made for a clutch of ladies by the refreshment table. Cullen thought she would make a great Southern belle with that act and found himself grinning at the thought.

"Come on, Cullen. Let me introduce you to some of my friends," Mason said as he patted his best friend on the shoulder. "I've told them a lot about you."

Cullen smiled through the introductions and shook every man's hand, listening to their banter for a few minutes and then excusing himself. He spied the sheriff on the other side of the room and made his way through the crowd to speak with him. "Sheriff, how's it goin'?"

"Jamison is over at the punch table, staring a hole through Sherry. I guess it's time for the act to begin."

Cullen nodded and made his way to Sherry, who far outshined any woman at the ball.

"Sweetheart, may I have this dance?" Sherry gave a slight curtsy and followed Cullen onto the dance floor. Gathering her in his arms as close as was respectable, he fairly swept her off her feet and into a waltz.

"Sherry, darling, look into my eyes and let me see your love there. Come closer so I can feel your luscious body."

Sherry was taken aback at first but then became lost in her lover's eyes. "Sir, what will people think?" she breathed close to his mouth. "My reputation is at stake, after all."

With that, Cullen pulled her closer still and as they whirled across the dance floor, he noticed daggers flying from Jamison's eyes. When he knew the man was watching, he really laid the act on thick, not that it was a burden. He was enjoying every second she was in his arms. When the music stopped, he kissed her lightly on the lips and led her off the dance floor, holding her hand.

Jamison made another trip to the punch bowl and inconspicuously poured a good amount of whiskey into his cup. Good, that made two cups so far. Cullen would count them until he felt Jamison was ripe for the *coup de grace*.

The band played a faster tune and people gathered for a contra dance. Cullen watched the dancers for a few moments and figured it looked much like square dancing in the south, except in lines instead of squares. Once again, he led Sherry to the dance floor and joyfully participated, giving Sherry a quick kiss on the cheek every time she twirled past him. Again, Jamison looked livid. Again he made his way to the punch bowl in the corner to pour whiskey into his cup. That made three.

"Good Lord, I'm in need of some fresh air after all that dancing!" Sherry agreed and suggested Cullen go outside for the brisk evening air. He smiled and made his way toward Mason and his friends, suggesting they join him outside for a little nip of whiskey. They gladly joined him, game for anything that would take them away from the embarrassment of being wall flowers.

Outside, they chatted about this or that as Cullen kept his eye on the door. Almost as if Jamison knew his own part in the play, the man came outside for a cigar at which time Cullen started speaking in a louder voice, "Thanks for joining me, gentlemen. I have some news I'd like to share. I'm fairly busting my buttons waiting to tell someone." He cleared this throat and proceeded, "You see, Miss Sherry has agreed to become my wife. I asked her this morning and she seemed as excited as I am to tie the knot. I'd like all of you to stand with me at the wedding, Mason being my best man, which will be held on Christmas Eve." Everyone cheered loudly and pounded Cullen on the back until he felt he might fall over. Looking toward the dance hall door, Cullen saw Jamison making his way over to their group, looking as if he were going to explode.

"Couldn't help but overhear you, Westover. I guess congratulations would be in order."

"Why thank you, Jamison. I wouldn't have thought you believed in the institution of marriage."

"To the contrary, Westover. I believe in it whole heartedly; so much so that I'm going to take Sherry away from you this very night. Sherry and I have had an understanding for a very long time and I'm going to make sure she honors it. Now good evening, gentleman. I hope you enjoy the dance."

The boys were slack jawed and silent as Jamison walked away. Then they looked at Cullen as if to ask, *"Are you going to let him get away with that?"*

Mason grabbed Cullen's arm and dragged him back into the dance hall.

"Go get Sherry and get her out of here now or Jamison is going to do something he's going to be very sorry for."

"That's the point, Mason. We're goading him, remember?"

"Yeah, but I guess I never thought Sherry might get hurt as a consequence."

"Don't worry, I'm going to stick to Sherry like glue for the rest of the night."

"You better or I'll have your head if anything happens to her."

Jamison wasted no time in finding Sherry and getting her on the dance floor. "You look like such a lady tonight, Sherry."

"I *am* a lady, Dirk."

"No, a lady never goes back on her promises."

"What promises? I've never made a promise to you for as long as I've known you. What in the world are you talking about?"

"You've known for quite a while that I want you to marry me. Now you've gone and promised yourself to Westover. What the hell do you see in that redneck?"

"I see the man who I love with all my heart and soul. I see a man who is good and honorable; a man who has agreed to love and honor me for the rest of my life. How could you possibly think I would ever marry you? You're the very opposite of all that is good in Cullen. You are an ugly and evil man, Dirk, and I pity you."

Sherry broke out of his arms in time to fall into Cullen's, he being right behind her as if by magic.

"Jamison, I'd appreciate your leaving my fiancé alone. Please don't touch her again." He put his arm around Sherry's shoulder and moved her across the room, out of Jamison's reach.

Jamison yelled after them, "We'll just wait and see who Sherry chooses. I'll have her one way or another and you can go to hell, you ignorant cracker!"

The music stopped and every head was turned in his direction. The crowd looked from Jamison to Cullen and back, as if there were a game of horse shoes in progress. As if as one, the crowd started stepping back against the walls and out of their way.

"What's the matter, folks? Why'd the band stop playing? C'mon, let's dance!" Cullen yelled. Still, the crowd stood like statues waiting for Jamison's next move.

Waiting for his cue, Darrell had taken a swig of whiskey, washed it around in his mouth and spit it out the door, ready to enter the fray. After what happened to Ruby, he swore to give up the demon liquor. Wobbling over to the two men, he announced two feet from Jamison's face, "Won't be any shootin' here t'night, gents. Won't allow it. Jush go on peaceful like. Go on." Jamison laughed and pushed Darrell out of the way. "And just what are you going to do about it you dirty drunk?"

Darrell backed off and sulked toward the doors, thinking he didn't much like being an actor.

"Aw hell, let's take this outside, Jamison. Let the people go on having a good time." Jamison walked up to Cullen and stood not six inches away from his face. "Another time, Westover. Another time when you won't see me coming."

Well, damn! Cullen should have known Jamison would be too much of a coward to act on his own behalf. He'd wait until he could hire someone to do his dirty work for him.

"That's the point, Jamison. Outside, right now. I won't let you be a coward after your big threats. Be a man for once in your pathetic life. Take care of your owned damned business."

"Go to hell, Westover," Jamison said as he headed toward Sherry. He roughly grabbed her by the arm and started dragging her toward the door when Cullen and Mason blocked his way.

"Let us pass, Westover, or you'll be very sorry."

"Let go of me this instant, Dirk! Who in the world do you think you are?" Sherry growled.

"I think I'm your future husband and I mean to make it happen soon."

Cullen was incensed. Jamison was crazier than he ever imagined.

Quick as a flash of lightening, Cullen grabbed Jamison's throat and squeezed with all his might until he let go of Sherry.

Mason wanted so badly to beat the tar out of the man but Cullen had made him promise to just stand by in case he needed some assistance. He *did* grab Sherry and move her aside where a few Castine men crowded around her in a wall of protection. Then he returned to Cullen in case he was needed.

Cullen and Jamison were squared off in front of each other, Jamison holding his own throat and Cullen enraged beyond belief. "Take off your gun, Jamison, and I'll take off mine. C'mon, just you and me will fight it out like men. You *are* a man, aren't you?"

Jamison looked hesitant but threw the first punch, not wanting to appear weak in people's eyes. He'd never been in a fist fight with a man in his life, choosing to beat women instead. They made much easier targets.

Cullen ducked the punch and went in for the kill. The mere thought of Jamison even touching Sherry at all made him see red. His first punch hit Jamison in the face and the man went down like a stone. Then something truly fascinating happened. Every man and woman in the dance hall came running to kick Jamison while he was down. There were so many of them that Jamison couldn't get up and away, so he curled himself into a ball and tried to weather the assault.

Cullen looked around for the sheriff and saw the man standing against the front door jam, wearing a wicked smile. He had no intention of stopping the crowd and hoped they killed the son of a bitch. Cullen and Mason exchanged glances and then smiled, backing away to allow the crowd all the room they needed to punish Jamison for his reign of terror in Castine.

Mason laughed when he saw old Mrs. Prescott hitting Jamison over the head with an empty pie plate. Even Mrs. Waller got her kicks in, making sure they were heel first, doing the most damage possible. When Cullen felt the brawl had gone on long enough, he yelled above the fray, "Okay, everyone! Stop! Stop before you kill him!"

An elderly man answered, "That's what we want! We *want* to kill him, the no good son of the devil! Leave us be until the job is done!"

Cullen understood the rage. He understood how long people had lived under Jamison's thumb, but he wouldn't allow them to live with the guilt over their actions after they killed him. He knew what it was like to take a man's life and live with the guilt and shame afterward. A day didn't go by that he didn't think of the men he had killed in the desert that day, even though it was in self defense.

Cullen motioned for Mason and Darrell's help and all three began pulling people away from Jamison's body. He was a crumpled mess, bleeding from his nose, his eyes swollen shut. Enough was enough...*for now*.

Mason likened the scene to a pack of wolves attacking a calf, and found he had no taste for it even though he hated Jamison just as much as the next man in Castine.

Darrell had watched, trying to count every kick and punch, each one for Ruby. He wished she was here to see this. But in the end, he knew he was the sheriff and couldn't allow the brutality to continue.

When everyone had backed off, Cullen picked Jamison up from the floor, stood him straight, and drew his fist back as if to strike one last blow. His fist remained in the air while he shook with rage and indignation, knowing he shouldn't strike but wanting to so badly.

Mason stepped in to take one of Jamison's arms while Darrell took the other, and they dragged him from the premises to the cheers and whistles of the crowd. The band started playing again and people took the closest partner to them and danced jigs all around the floor. It had been an incredible release of emotion for the people to see Jamison so low and the atmosphere fairly crackled with the intention that his reign was now over. No matter what happened tomorrow, they wouldn't allow it to go on for one more second.

When the cold air hit Jamison's face, he tried to lift his head and instead mumbled, "You're a dead man, Westover. Dead, do you hear me?"

Darrell said, "Sounds like a threat to me. Well, you'll do no more damage this night. You can sleep it off in a jail cell. Tomorrow I'll decide what to do with your sorry ass." Looking back at Cullen, he asked, "Do you think Sherry will want to press charges against him?"

Cullen thought for a second and replied, "I'll ask her. Right now I just want to go back in to the ball and dance with my woman. Mason? You up for it?"

"I don't dress up like this for nothing. Might as well make the most of it. Night's young."

The two men watched as the sheriff dragged a beaten and bloody Dirk Jamison toward the jailhouse. "Damn, it didn't work. I thought for sure I could goad him in to drawing his gun."

Mason felt likewise deflated at the end result. Now what would they do? Jamison would be insane with rage and God only knew what havoc he would wreak upon them next. As if on cue, both men let out a slow, *well sheeeit.*

Sherry was dancing with the widowed preacher when Cullen returned to the dance. It was like all he could see was emerald green floating around the room above all else. Just her. Just the woman of his dreams. Walking onto the dance floor, he cut in on the preacher and held Sherry tight.

"I'm sorry your plan didn't work, Cullen."

"Me, too. I really hadn't planned on what a coward Jamison truly is."

"Oh well, it was nice to be your fiancé for a night," she smiled.

Oh, how Cullen wanted to drop to his knees right there for all to see, and propose that very moment. He wanted nothing more. He closed his eyes as they danced another waltz and could see her in his mind's eye…a wedding dress…then her rounded belly carrying his child…sitting on the porch in rocking chairs, listening to the cattle low…*what?* He really shouldn't have been surprised by the thought. Going home and rebuilding the homestead was close in his mind these days. From what he could surmise from their -frequent comments, the Newcombs were ready to leave Castine, anyway.

I love you, Sherry . . .

Chapter Seventeen

Mason was listless and disinterested in life lately. Everyone in the family noticed but didn't comment. Edith tried engaging him in conversation and he made little effort to reply. He was lost to them for some reason, deep within himself where his personal demons seemed to be thriving. It appeared they were going to overtake the young man unless the family could get through to him.

"Mason, Stern's chasing a bear outside the kitchen door, and the house is on fire."

"That's nice."

"Not only that, President Johnson has proposed and I think I'm going to marry him."

"Uh huh."

"MASON!!!!"

"Hmm?"

Edith marched over to Mason and slapped his face smartly, trying to wake him from his stupor.

"What'd you do that for?" he yelled. Edith gave up and returned to the kitchen sink where she was washing dishes, flinging pots and pans, and generally in a snit.

Cullen came in from the barn and immediately noticed Edith was furious. Then he looked at Mason drooping over the kitchen table and knew the reason why.

"Mason, I need you to come outside with me."

"Okay." Mason slowly stood from his chair, head hanging, and followed Cullen outside.

"What the hell is the matter with you, boy? We're worried sick about you and can't get through that thick skull of yours. You're going to tell me right now what's going on or I'm going to kick your ass all over this yard."

Mason looked up and smirked. "Go to hell, Cullen."

Cullen pushed against Mason's shoulder, knocking him back a few steps. Nothing. So he pushed again. Still nothing. So he cold-cocked him…knocked him down flat. Mason flew off the ground, head down and aiming at Cullen's gut. "What's the matter, boy? Cat got your tongue lately?"

Mason's head-butt knocked Cullen to the ground and they began wrestling. He was livid and Cullen kept hurling insults, goading him along.

"Is that all you got, huh? Is that all you can manage, *boy?* C'mon, c'mon, show me what you've got." Around and around they rolled, trading punches to the face and kidneys, spitting blood at each other and grinding out their frustrations.

Suddenly, Mason had Cullen on his back and used the advantage to put his hands around the man's throat. He shook with rage and worked mightily to keep from squeezing the life out of…*his best friend in the world.* It was then Mason let go and cried his rage to the heavens. "Oh my God! How can I ever be married!?"

What? That was the least likely response Cullen could have ever imagined but let him go on with it. It needed to come out and he would remain silent as the flames of whatever torture beset his friend raged and hopefully expired.

"I can't do it! I can't protect them! I have no plan, I haven't the wherewithal, and I…I *failed them!* He's coming and there's not a damned thing I can do about it! I'm worthless! I don't deserve a woman and family of my own because I'm weak! I'm weak and useless! Oh God…help me…" He rolled off of Cullen and lay down in the snow, wailing to the skies. His sobs broke Cullen's heart.

Standing beside Mason, he reached down for his hand and lifted him up into his arms like a father or big brother would do. He patted his back and whispered, "It's going to be all right, Mason. I'm here and I'll always be behind you. Together we'll see this through. I'm going to teach you all you need to know about protecting your loved ones. I swear to God, I will."

He held Mason tight while tears and misery flowed from the boy. *Boy?* Mason was a man. The fact that he worried about what kind of man he was, told Cullen he was well on his way to becoming the man he dreamed of being.

"I respect you more than any man I've ever known. You're going to be a fine husband and father. Don't be so hard on yourself. This is the first real trouble you've ever had in your life and Jamison is more than most men can handle. But, we will. We'll be the ones to take him down. Me *and* you."

He guided Mason toward the barn after he was spent with emotion. He handed him a brush and took him to stand in front of Honor. Mason started stroking the brush over the horse's back as if in a daze. Cullen opened his hidden saddle bag and brought out a flask which he offered to him. "Here, take a couple of good swigs of this and you'll feel better." Luckily, the flask was only half full because Mason drank it dry. Then he went back to brushing Honor.

Cullen's attention was drawn to the barn doors where he found Edith and Sherry peeking around the corner, smiles on their faces and tears in their eyes. Sherry mouthed, *"Thank you."* Cullen kissed his fingers and blew it in her direction.

***

Things were pretty quiet for a while. Ice had covered the bay and it gave the men a chance to do some much needed repairs to the house and barn.

Jamison hadn't shown himself in other than the usual ways, but Cullen knew they hadn't yet experienced one tenth of the man's wrath. He was biding his time, setting traps, so to speak, and lining up his lieutenants. In the meantime, Mason had posted their property, warning trespassers would be shot on sight.

Also during this time, several townsmen came to visit, asking if there was a plan regarding Jamison, and if they could take part in it. The Christmas Ball had started the wheels of discontent in motion and people were impatient for action in that regard.

Cullen had been going to town more often in the evenings, for two reasons. First, he needed more money. He had a big family now and needed the funds to do whatever became necessary, including getting them out of Castine, if need be.

Second, he wanted to run into Jamison in one of the saloons. He planned to be a thorn in the man's side as long as it took to make him flinch during their silent war. It was times such as these Cullen wished to have some military experience under his belt. He had been too far west by the time the War of Northern Aggression started, and wondered sometimes how his father had managed to stay afloat, having heard horror stories of how the Yankees came through like locusts, taking everything that could be carried or what could be walked away with them. He felt guilt and shame when he looked back, knowing he should have come home to help his father. He would probably have been conscripted if he had. It was now a moot point, anyway.

Cullen noticed that on Friday evenings, there was a pretty young lady who worked at Stewart's Apothecary across from the Cracked Crab. It must have been her regular shift because he always saw her behind the counter on those evenings. She had a bright smile and winning mannerisms, always pleasant with her customers and, mostly, every time Mason was in town, the girl made herself as conspicuous as possible. She was tallish, probably five feet, nine inches, or so. A great height for Mason. She was already curvy and could really wear a dress well. So . . .

The next Friday evening, Cullen coaxed Mason into going into town with him. On their way, Cullen asked Mason to stop in the apothecary and get some liniment for his shoulder. It apparently had been bothering him without anyone's knowledge. He was very specific on what kind of liniment he wanted and asked that Mason consult the lady behind the counter for information on same before he bought any straight off the shelf.

"I'll be at the Cracked Crab. Please go to the apothecary before it closes, okay? Come on back over to the Crab and I'll buy you a beer when you're done. And don't tell Sherry!"

Mason laughed and walked across the street, dodging ice and mud puddles, and noticed, for the very first time, the girl behind the counter. She looked somewhat familiar but he couldn't place where they might have met. She must have been at the Christmas Ball, but he didn't remember seeing her.

The bell above the door jingled and Beth Stewart looked up. *Oh, my gosh! It's Mason Newcomb!* She patted her hair, pressed her lips tightly to bring them color, and brushed off her skirts. "May I help you, sir?"

Mason made his way to the back counter and forgot what he was there for.

"Uh, yes, I need . . . "

"You need what?"

"Well, I . . . uh . . ."

"My name is Beth, and if you could give me one word to describe what…."

"Bethy Stewart?"

"Yes, I'm Beth Stewart."

"We went to school together, right?"

"Well, I don't know. What is your name?"

"Oh, yeah, I'm Mason Newcomb," he stammered as he reached across the counter to shake her hand. Shake her hand? She wasn't a man! Augh!

Beth felt his awkwardness and seeming discomfort were good signs that she had at least captured *some* part of his interest.

"I'm here to get some liniment for my friend, Cullen. Uh, Cullen Westover. You may know him. He works with us on the Mermaid. Uh, it's a trawler. We fish for a living. Anyway, Cullen hurt his shoulder and needs some, um, relief. I thought you might have something special in the back that would be best looking…I mean, best suited…that is, best feeling…" It was no use. He had humiliated himself enough.

Beth took pity on him and said, "I think I might have something in the back, if you'll just follow me," despite the sign above the door to the store room that read, "No Patrons Allowed."

Mason pulled on his collar, thinking it was certainly warm in the store, and followed behind her, noticing full well how good she looked from that angle.

Oh Lord.

The back of the store was a cramped space and between the two of them looking through the stocked shelves, it was tight. Beth made sure she had to pass him at least twice which gave her a chance to brush close by his chest.

"Oh, here it is. Made special by a German fella. Customers say it works really well. Would you like to buy this brand?"

Mason wasn't looking at the liniment. He stood stock still, hat in hand, looking at her like she might disappear. He stared at her lips so long that Beth became a bit uncomfortable. *Is he going to kiss me, or not!* It certainly would fulfill one of her fondest fantasies about the man.

"Yes, I'll take that one. Would you wrap it for me? I wouldn't want to lose it on the way home." Beth smiled and reached beneath the counter for a box, some paper, and string. It would buy him at least a few more minutes to look at her, and Beth was certainly in no hurry to get the package wrapped.

When she couldn't wrap any slower, it was finally done and Mason paid her.

"Well, I guess I'll see you around sometime. It was nice seeing you again," he said as he backed into a display of boxed bandages. They fell all over the floor and he stooped to pick them up. Beth ran around the counter and bent down to help him. "It's okay. It's slow tonight and it will give me something to do when you're gone. I mean, it will keep me busy."

Again, Mason stared a hole through her. Enough was enough! "Mason Newcomb, are you going to ask me to go out with you or not?" Mason blushed to the roots of his hair but smiled a winsome grin and replied, "I thought you'd never ask!" They both started laughing and the ice was finally broken. Why hadn't he noticed her around town before? It didn't matter. He was going to see her a lot more, if her father would allow it.

Cullen sat a table close to the front window and looked over through the apothecary window between poker hands. It seemed to be going well. He could see Mason blushing clear across the street. By his accounting, they had been in there together for about a half hour. Plenty of time to strike up a conversation and perhaps make plans for some courting. He sipped his shot of whiskey and got his head back in the game.

Mason came bolting through the doors of the saloon like a bull in a china closet. He rushed over to the bar and ordered a beer and put it on Cullen's tab, swallowing it down in only a few gulps. He ordered another and then pulled up a chair to watch Cullen's game. "Where's my liniment?" Mason just smiled and said, "I'm getting married, Cullen."

Chapter Eighteen

"Well, that was fast. Does your *fiancé* know about this?"

"Not yet, but mark my words, she'll be mine."

Another hand was dealt and Mason took the time to look at the money in front of each player, gauging who was winning…or not. As usual, Cullen was ahead. Mason was perplexed by the fascination in games of chance. Money was too precious to gamble away but it never seemed to bother Cullen. Of course, Cullen won most of the time which was why he did it, he supposed. Maybe he should learn how to play. It might be a good skill, after all.

Another two hours went by and Mason felt he was getting the gist of the game, but was feeling tired after three beers. "Cullen, how about we call it a night. I'm tired and we have to work on the Mermaid tomorrow while she's moored in the ice."

Cullen nodded, and after winning that hand, said goodnight to his fellow players. "As always, gentlemen, it's been a real pleasure. See you next weekend?"

"Westover, it's a good damned thing you're so funny and entertaining. At least we're getting something for the money we lose to your sorry ass!" the man sitting next to him exclaimed, and everyone laughed. Cullen stood, giving the man a pat on the back, and said in an exaggerated Southern accent, "Glad to be of service, Dilly. Y'all have a good night now, heah?" Giving them a mock bow, he and Mason made for the door.

"Cullen, may I ask how much you won tonight?"

"Sure…you can ask."

"Okay, I'm sorry. It's none of my business."

"Nah, I'm just joshin' ya. I haven't counted it yet but I imagine there's more than fifty dollars in winnings."

"Teach me how to play?"

Cullen was instantly reminded of the cattle driver who taught him his own poker skills, and remembered how many times the turn of a friendly card had meant the difference between eating and starving. Perhaps teaching Mason the skill was a good idea.

"All right, but not in front of Sherry. She'd have my hide, for sure."

"Cullen, I'm a man now. She has nothing to do with it."

"I know, but maybe we could let her hang on to her illusions for a while. She still feels protective of you and Edith, even though you're basically adults. I understand how she feels because I feel the same way. You're the little brother and sister I never had."

Cullen tuned his head and looked at Mason as they walked home. "Well, you're not little but you know what I mean." They laughed and walked on.

When they were almost home, two men with kerchiefs over their faces stepped out in front of their path. "Hold up, ye damned troublemakahs! We need to have a chat with yuns, friendly-like."

"Let me guess, Dirk Jamison sent you. And there's really nothing to talk about so let us pass." Cullen slowly unbuttoned his coat in the moonlight, and pushed it open with hands on hips. He started walking forward again but the two masked men threw their arms out to stop him.

Cullen stood menacingly and said, "I'm feeling quite threatened, aren't you, Mason? I'm pretty sure I should defend myself."
"Big words and fancy talk aren't going to help you now, Westovah." *Big words and fancy talk?* Now Cullen knew the intellect with which he was dealing.

"All right, gentlemen, say your piece and move out of our way." Cullen backed up several paces and waited for them to step aside.

One of the men started chuckling which infected the other into doing the same.

"Mister, I know you ain't from 'round heah, but we mainly do this kind of communicating with ah fists. You need a lesson in leavin' things be as they ah. Who the hell do you think you ah comin' to Castine, and tryin' to change the way things have been fah yeahs? Mr. Jamison don't like it none, no he don't."

"I don't think I'm anyone special, so if you're done we'd like to walk on."

Cullen was biding his time, waiting for the signal that it was okay to shoot in self defense. *One . . . two . . . three . . .* Mr. Verbally Eloquent, pulled out a knife just one second before Mr. Imtoostupid Tospeak, pulled his. It was all the signal Cullen needed.

Mason never saw it coming. He heard the loud report of pistols before he even recognized that Cullen had moved. It was utterly amazing, so much so that he didn't pay one bit of attention to the two brawny morons falling like anchors to the ground, moaning and holding their wounds.

"Holy cow, Cullen! I barely saw you move! That was amazing!"

"It's nothing to be proud of. Go tell Sherry I'll be a bit late getting home tonight. I've got to get to the sheriff and report this."

"No way, I'm going with you as a witness. Besides, Beth might still be in the store and I want to get another look at her before I sleep tonight."

Both men relaxed a bit before walking back into town. "You know, I'm tired of this walk. It's getting old."

"I know, but I needed the exercise after my injuries. Tell you what, let's look for a horse that will fit you. Not any old horse will do. You need something . . ." They talked about anything and everything along the way besides the two wounded men they left along the road. Despite the light banter between the two, Cullen once again felt the weight of wounding a man. If they were able to stop Jamison and free the town of his reign of terror, he would never again lift a gun to take a man's life. He'd continue to wear his guns, but he doubted seriously if he would ever shoot at another human being as long as he lived unless it was absolutely necessary to protect his family.

Cullen opened the door of the sheriff's office and grinned at Darrell. Darrell grinned back and said, "Evenin' gents. What can I do for you this evening?"

"There's a pile of trash, oh, about the size of two men, along the road to Sherry's place. Jamison sent them to try and scare me. Once they pulled their knives, I shot'em both. It was self defense, to which Mason can attest. Last we heard from them was moaning and groaning."

"That's right, Sheriff. I saw the whole thing. Cullen gave them plenty of opportunity to back off and leave us alone but they just kept coming. When they pulled their knives, Cullen did the only thing he could in order to protect us both, God's honest truth."

Darrell nodded and replied, "I guess the war is back on. Keep up the good work, even if you have to do it one by one. I suggest, for affect, you check and see if they're still laying there come morning, and then load them in a wagon and dump them on Jamison's front lawn. It will make one hell of a statement. I'll turn a blind eye, of course."

"Thanks, Darrell." Before leaving, Cullen looked both men in the eyes and said, "You know, I don't find this task pleasant. I told you before that I was never a gunslinger and I'm not used to wounding men or taking a man's life. However, I have family now and I'll do anything necessary to protect them and theirs. I just wanted to be clear on the issue."

***

Later that night, after everyone had gone to their bedrooms, Cullen waited until he thought they had all fallen asleep, and quietly opened Sherry's door.

Walking softly across the floor, he turned up the lamp on her bedside table and watched her sleep. The auburn nimbus of her hair against the white pillow took his breath away. Her long eyelashes lay against her rosy cheeks, and she had pushed the quilts down below her chest in her sleep. He watched her breathe, the slow rise and fall of her chest, and couldn't resist touching her.

Bending down over her body, he kissed her lips and gently grasped a firm, ripe breast in his hand, softly kneading it. Sherry moaned in her sleep and instinctively raised her arms around Cullen's neck and pulled him close.

Cullen thought to himself, *not like this. Not anymore.*

"Sherry? Sherry, wake up."

"Cullen, I'm so glad you came," she whispered.

"Come on, wake up, we need to talk."

Sherry sat up against the headboard and gazed at Cullen with an amorous smile.

"What's more important than making love?" she asked, still feeling lethargic.

"I won't take you anymore under these circumstances. It's too risky. What if I got you with child? I'll not have anyone saying that I had to marry you." Sitting on the edge of the bed, he continued, "Colleen Newcomb, will you do me the honor of becoming my wife?

"I was going to wait until I had more to offer you but I just can't wait any longer. I'm tired of trying to keep my hands off of you. I'm tired of trying to stay away from you so I won't be tempted. But, mostly, I'm tired of not having what's more important than any of that. My soul aches to join with yours, Sherry. I don't want to pretend anymore. I love you with every beat of my heart and it's time for us to act on what we both want. At least I hope it's what you want, too.

"At the Christmas Ball, when we were trying to goad Jamison into fighting back, it almost broke my heart to tell those boys that I had asked you to be my wife and that you accepted my proposal. I wanted it to be real. But instead, I gave in to my pride by trying to put it off until I felt I was more ready to provide for a family. I'm done with such thinking. Please, be mine?"

Sherry wanted to shout *YES* immediately but was once again taken back in time to when Jacob and made her flowery promises that he never kept.

"I love you, Cullen, but I need to be convinced that you won't change after I say, 'I do.' I need to know that your love for me will continue through the years, and that our marriage will never become stale and lifeless. I hope you understand how I feel. I've told you about Jacob and our marriage. You know how miserable I was."

Cullen did know, and it made him angry that a man would make promises to a woman that he had no intention of keeping. "I'm a young man, Sherry. I'm only twenty-nine."

Sherry's eyes showed her surprise. Why hadn't they ever talked about their ages before now? "I'm twenty-six next month. Am I too old for you? Were you expecting a younger woman to take to wife?"

"Hell no! I want an experienced woman," he said as he waggled his eyebrows. Standing back as if he were examining her attributes like a horse at sale, he continued, "You've already had a child so I know you're fertile and good in that area. You'll do."

Sherry smacked his shoulder and pulled him down on the bed. They kissed passionately and let their hands roam along each other's wanting bodies. "Let me go to my bed before we can't stop. Like I said, you'll not be pregnant when we marry. Uh, we *are* going to marry, right?"

"There is something I want to do before I give you my answer, Cullen. It will only take a couple more days. Are you agreeable to that?"

"If that's what you need, my love. But, please, don't take too long? I'm nearly crazy with desire for you. Oh, one more thing…I'd like to adopt Caleb. I already feel like he's my own and, if you have no objections, I'd like to make it legal."

"In a couple of days, darling. It won't take longer than that."

Chapter Nineteen

Sherry was anxious to give Cullen her answer but felt compelled to follow through with her decision to consult Mason and Edith, first.

"Caleb is down for the evening and Mason, Edith, and I need to run some errands in town. We'll only be an hour, or so. Will you stay and keep an eye on Caleb?" she asked Cullen.

"Of course! Y'all have a good time."

She went in the pantry to get some money out of the box, thinking she would treat them to some ice cream. At least at the café they would be able to sit down when they talked.

Sherry blew Cullen a kiss and the trio exited the kitchen and made their way to the wagon that Mason had hitched to their ancient mare, Daisy.

Mason was dubious about leaving Cullen behind and wondered what the heck Sherry had in mind making this trip to town. "Sherry, what's this all about? Are you ill? Is something wrong?"

Sherry smiled and patted his arm. "Nothing is wrong. I just have something that I need to talk with you and Edith about, that's all. Family business, you might say."

When they arrived in front of the café where the only ice cream in town was made, Mason wrapped Daisy's reins to the hitching post, and they made their way inside.

When they were seated and their orders for ice cream given, Sherry smiled at Mason and Edith, and began what she hoped would be a favorable conversation between them.

"Cullen has asked me to marry him and I wanted to talk it over with you two before giving him my answer."

Both Mason and Edith looked thrilled but she continued on, "He wants to legally adopt Caleb, too. He says his love for me is deep and true and that it will always be that way. We never even asked Cullen how old he is, but he's twenty-nine. As you both know, I'll be twenty-six next month. I think being so close in age is a benefit.

"There is one thing of importance we still need to discuss, though. I'm not sure Cullen will want to stay in Castine, much longer. I've noticed how much this weather gets to him. I think the romance of trawling might also be fading. If we do get married, I have to know that if we ever leave Castine, you both will come with us. I won't marry him otherwise. You are my family, and I love you both more than blood could ever tell." Then she laughed softly, "We all know I was always too young to be your mother, and I feel more like you are my dearest siblings. I want you in my life and when the time comes for you to marry and leave the house, I want you both to be at least close by. I can't imagine my life without you, ever."

Edith's eyes held unshed tears, and Mason nodded his head, recognizing the gravity of the issue in Sherry's heart. "Sherry, I can't speak for Edith, but I will follow you and Cullen wherever you want to go. I've mostly kept it to myself for a long time now, but I'm sick and tired of trawling. I'm sick of this wretched cold weather. I'm sick of Dirk Jamison, and I'm sick of the smell of fish. I want to get married and have a family of my own and I feel sure that with another few years of Cullen's teaching me what I need to know, I'll be ready to handle anything that comes along. And yes, I also want us all to stick together. Edith? How about you?"

Edith looked from Mason to Sherry and back, and said, "When do we leave?"

Dear Edith, she was always game for most anything. Appearances could truly be deceiving. One would think her the most reticent of young women, shy and rarely sharing her opinion. What people didn't know was that Edith was a very complex girl with deep thoughts and desires. At almost eighteen, she could hold her own with anyone, given the chance.

Their ice cream was served and they dove in with gusto, the cold cream melting in their mouths, making them moan with pleasure.

Mason finished his first, pushed his bowl away, and said, "So, when is the wedding? I'm surprised it took you two this long to come to terms with your feelings. I knew from the start that you were made for each other. So my answer is yes, without a doubt, I want you to make it legal so he'll be part of our family forever. I do want to warn you, though, if he ever hurts you, I'll have to kill him." Now it was Sherry's turn to shed tears of love and happiness.

Edith smiled and took Sherry's hand across the table, "Dear, dear Sherry. What would we have done without you in our lives? Why wouldn't we want your happiness? I love Cullen just like I do Mason. He's a fine man. He has a heart of gold and the strength of ten men in all the ways that matter. He'll make you a fine husband, never doubt it. So I say yes, also. Yes to our family finally being brought together, bound by the bonds of marriage."

***

Jamison had been standing in the cold, wearing a heavy coat, scarf wrapped around his neck, and smoking a cigar while waiting for Sherry to finish whatever was taking her and her children so long at the café. From what he could tell, Westover wasn't anywhere to be seen tonight, and that meant he could finally have a few words with her alone.

When he saw that they were getting up from their table, he started across the street to meet them as soon as they left the café. All three of them were laughing and hugging each other. One would think they were celebrating something. He sure hoped not.

"Sherry, how nice to run into you like this. Out for an evening with the family?"

Sherry stopped dead in her tracks, fear skittering down her spine at the sound of Jamison's voice. "Hello, Dirk. We were just having some ice cream but need to head on home now." She put an arm through Mason's and started for the wagon.

"What's your hurry? I thought perhaps we could enjoy a cup of hot coffee while the children take a walk."
Children?

"Mason and Edith are *not* children, in case you haven't noticed these past few years. And we must be going. Thank you for the invitation but I must decline."

As they walked past him, Jamison added, "Don't fight it anymore, Sherry. We both know you can't win. Why not just agree to be my wife now and save yourself the trouble of eluding me further?"

"Not that it is any of your business, but Mason, Edith and I are in town to celebrate and talk about my wedding plans. There's a lot to be done, you see. I'm marrying Cullen Westover, and there is nothing you can do about it. We were supposed to be married on Christmas Eve, but your theatrics at the ball rather ruined it for us.

"It is *you* who should give up and move on with your life, Dirk. I will never agree to marry you and I will not sell you the Mermaid."

Jamison squeezed her arm tightly trying to drag her close when Mason grabbed the lapels of his coat and hit him squarely in the jaw, knocking him to the sidewalk. "If you *ever* touch Sherry again, I will kill you, understand?"

Within seconds, three men ran out of the Cracked Crab and came to Jamison's rescue. "Do you think you and Westover can deter me from what I want? Think again,

Sherry. I'll find Ruby, *and* I'll have you and your boat. No one takes *anything* away from Dirk Jamison, no one! Westover is going to die, count on it."

His men picked him up off the sidewalk and brushed him off. Jamison righted himself and returned to the Cracked Crab, infuriated over the fact that he had nowhere to go with his anger and frustration. He had his men combing Castine looking for Ruby, but so far she hadn't been found. He was sure Darrell and the doctor in town knew where she was but he still had at least an ounce of respect left for the law, and wouldn't push the issue.

Sherry watched Jamison go and felt nothing but revulsion. The situation was now completely out of hand and the family would have to move fast to halt his plans to do away with Cullen. She would absolutely not let that happen. Now that she allowed her love for Cullen to flow free of the past, she would not allow a lowlife like Jamison to take him away from her.

"Come on, let's get home. It's colder than Jamison's heart out here."

The ride home was silent, each of them lost in their own thoughts and fears. Mason thought it was time for a family meeting *tonight*. There was no time to lose. Decisions had to be made, not just talked about. The time to act was now.

Chapter Twenty

Cullen had fallen asleep in front of a roaring fire in the parlor, dreaming of Bradley Cummings. It seemed Cullen was sailing the Mermaid down the coast toward the Chesapeake Bay, delivering her to Bradley. In the dream, he felt fear of letting go and of facing an uncertain future. He looked behind him and saw his family, stone faced and resolute. Caleb was holding on to his leg and when he looked down upon the little blond head, he saw the boy smiling as if that day were like any other, and thought, *"At least the boy is with me."* Then he felt a tapping on his shoulder and hoped it was Sherry, finally showing him a sign of her acceptance of the decision he had obviously made to leave their home. He turned to face her and . . .

"Cullen, wake up. We're home." Sherry was nudging his shoulder, trying to wake him. "Come on, Cullen. We need to have a family meeting. It's important," she said as Cullen pulled himself out of his favorite chair.

The rest of the evening was spent talking about all of the precautions they would take until Jamison showed his hand once again. If they hadn't been so scared, they would have been bored because they were sick of the topic of what Jamison would do next.

The next morning there was a loud rapping on the front door. Mason quickly pulled his drawers on and ran down the stairs. When he opened the door, he found Edward "Tellie" Sharp, from the telegraph office. "Sorry to wake ya so early Mason, but looks like Mr. Westover better see this one right away. Tell him I'm sorry for the sad news. Good day to ya," he said as he mounted his bay gelding.

Mason dreaded bad news and was loath to wake Cullen to deliver the telegram. It was Sunday morning and the weather outside was atrocious; snow mixed with sleet, and although it was beautiful with ice covering tree branches, it would be a dangerous ride to church. Hopefully he could convince Sherry to stay home this week.

Just as Mason would climb the stairs to Cullen's room, they met on the stairs going into the kitchen. "Morning, Mason. Looks like church is out this week, huh?" Mason merely stared up at Cullen, and silently passed him the telegram.

YOUR FATHER HAS PASSED. FUNERAL TO BE HELD TOMORROW. AWAITING INSTRUCTIONS REGARDING FARM AND TAXES.

SHERIFF
DINWIDDIE COUNTY, VIRGINIA

"Mason, I've got to go to the telegraph office. Tell Sherry to go back to bed when she wakes up, and I'll be back as soon as I can. Maybe I'll stop at the bakery and bring home some breakfast. Coffee and pastries sure sound good." Mason nodded and asked, "I know it's none of my business, but what did the telegram say?"

"My father died and I need to send a return telegram giving instructions regarding what I intend to do about the farm. You can *always* ask me anything you want, Mason. We're family and we shouldn't have any secrets. I'm going to saddle Honor. I'll be back soon."

Before Cullen left for the telegraph office, he had looked once again at his bank book for the balance. He had no idea how much his father's funeral would cost, nor did he know if there were any taxes due on the farm. He just hoped he had enough to cover the expenses without totally depleting his bank account. Thinking of depleting bank accounts, it reminded Cullen that he really should withdraw his money for fear that Jamison might try to swindle him in some manner. To his mind, there wasn't anything Jamison wouldn't do to get his way. He was tired of worrying about the man.

"Mornin' Tellie. I need to answer the telegram you delivered this morning." Tellie nodded and offered his condolences. Licking the point of his pencil he wrote down Cullen's message.

"Sheriff, Dinwiddie County, Virginia, Please advise costs of funeral and any taxes due. Am keeping the farm. Please keep an eye on the place if you will. Charles Maklin."

Smiling at Tellie and offering the man his hand, he said, "Tellie, I want you to know how much I appreciate your keeping my secret. I'm not a wanted man. I just wanted a new start so I could make a new reputation for myself. You've been a real friend in helping me do that. I'm in your debt."

The two men shook hands and Tellie said, "Mr. Westover, I'm glad to do it and I want you to know how much we here in Castine appreciate your help with Dirk Jamison. Seems like the town is coming alive again with the hope you'll finally put him in his place." Cullen grinned and replied, "I'll give it my best, Tellie. You can count it." After sending one more telegram, Cullen left feeling much relieved that the wheels of progress were about to start moving toward his future.

Honor lost his footing only a couple of times on the trip home. Fortunately, the horse was so heavy he broke through most of the ice along the way. Holding the box of pastries under his coat so they might stay warm, Cullen dismounted and left Honor ground tied so he could get the breakfast treats into the kitchen. "I'm home! Breakfast is ready!" Then he went back out to get Honor settled in the barn, snug and warm. A good bit of hay, a little grain, and a warm mash for his dinner that evening, and the animal would be in horse heaven. Cullen couldn't wait for spring to arrive so he and his best pal could go riding across the countryside.

The aroma of perfectly brewed coffee made Cullen's mouth water as he entered the kitchen. Caleb was sipping hot chocolate and waiting for a warm pastry. Everyone else sat at the table staring at Cullen with uncertain expressions on their faces.

"Pour me a cup of that heaven you call coffee, Edith. I've been craving some of this apple strudel ever since I bought it this morning." Cullen shook off his coat and hung it on the side porch. "Why all the long faces?" Sherry was the first to speak, "Oh, Cullen, I'm so sorry to hear of your father's passing. We want you to know that we'll do everything possible to help ease your grief."

"What grief? I've seen my father once in the past thirteen years and we had nothing to say to each other worth mentioning. Truth be told, I'm glad he's gone Home to be with my mother and sister. He never really stopped grieving for them, ever. He's been a lost soul all the years since Ma's death. I'm glad he's happy again.

"So, let's enjoy this breakfast. It sure is a treat, eh? Edith doesn't have to cook and Caleb looks like he'll sure enjoy it. Won't ya, Caleb?" The boy's chocolaty grin was answer enough.

Once they were through eating and another pot of coffee was brewing on the stove, Cullen decided to bring up his feelings about what their future might look like. Taking a deep breath, he just let it spill from his lips without worry of how they would take it.

"Now that my pa is gone, there's three hundred and fifty acres of land lying fallow, and just a few cattle left. The farmhouse is in a shambles, and the barn is practically falling down, if I remember correctly. It's in Dinwiddie County, Virginia. It's mine now. All of it.

"The weather in Virginia is rarely extreme. Spring starts at the end of March, with forsythia blooming by the fifteenth." Cullen closed his eyes and continued, "My ma's daffodils bloom right after the forsythia. The honeysuckle grows in thick bushes near the creek in the back yard, and their sweet fragrance floats through the bedroom windows at night. If you walk about a hundred yards or so farther up the creek, there's a fishing hole I damned up when I was just a boy.

"I don't know about now, but when I was a young, the people of McKenney were good, honest people. They came together in times of trouble and made sure their neighbors had all the help they needed, no matter the circumstance." He snuffled a bit and continued, "Miss Letty Wetherby's café was the source of all kinds of delicious aromas. Her biscuits couldn't be beat, no sir. Twice a month, the three of us would go into town for a big breakfast at Letty's. Pa wanted to give my mother the treat of not having to cook before church.

"Anyway, this has been my thinking of late…Sherry and I get married soon, and by that I mean, *very soon*. Well, if she'll have me.

"I'll send a telegram to Bradley Cummings and," he said while looking at Mason and Sherry, "we'll see how much Brad will offer for the Mermaid. I'm sure he could use another trawler in his fleet.

"Of course, this is merely what *I've* been thinking during the last few days. Well, weeks, if truth be told. I really have no stomach for killing men. I'm tired of looking over my shoulder and worrying about my family where Jamison is concerned."

With that, he pushed his chair onto its back legs, folded his hands across his stomach, and waited for whatever storm might erupt. Everyone at the table looked at each other for a minute or so, and finally Edith spoke up. "If this is a democratic family where each of us gets their own vote, I am officially voting for Virginia."

Sherry looked to Mason for his response. "What if I get married? Will my wife be welcome?"

Sherry raised an eyebrow at Mason, as if to ask, *"What? You're getting married? This is certainly big news to me!"*

Cullen started laughing and pounded Mason on the back. "Why, of course! The more, the merrier, I always say!"

Sherry swallowed hard, trying to digest it all. "How will we make a living while we're getting the house and barn back in shape? Where is all the money going to come from for rebuilding and planting, and such?"

Cullen understood her worries. "I think with the money I have of my own, and the money you'll get from the Mermaid and the house, we should be good for at least a year, if we're careful.

"There is something else I need to tell y'all." Taking a deep breath, he began the most painful part of all. "My real name is Charles Maklin." Sherry's eyes got a big as saucers and she quickly stood up from the table and slapped him sharply across the face.

"What was that for?"

"You've been lying to us all this time! What else have you been lying about? *Why* did you change your name? Are you wanted by the law? Is someone looking for you?"

Her chest was heaving with her anger and distrust, and Cullen couldn't blame her for it. The truth was the only thing that could cut through those feelings and he knew it was the right thing to do.

"Sherry, when I was in the New Mexico Territory, I stopped in a small town for some rest and a game of cards. I was down to my last few dollars and needed supplies. Using the all of the money would have broke me.

"So I played, against my better judgment as I look back, with a slick card sharp who I thought I could easily beat.

Unfortunately, he was better at the game than I was and I lost five dollars to him before I caught the manner in which he was cheating.

"I decided then and there to get up and walk away. I mounted my horse and left town immediately. Me and Nocount, that was my horse, weren't making fast tracts by any means, and I guess we had been riding for about four hours when I heard horses riding up fast behind me.

"When I turned around, I just said hello and asked what I could do for them. One of the men pulled his pistol on me and announced that they were taking me back to town for hangin'. I asked what for? Long story short, they had shot the gambler I had been playing with earlier in the afternoon and were going to pin it on me; hang me for it. And no one in town would have dared say there were lying. They admitted to killing him and all four agreed that making me the scapegoat had been a mighty fine idea.

"Mason, I've told you I have an instinct for shooting. I'm fast and accurate. What was I going to do? Just let them hang me? God forgive me, before the thought really entered my mind, I pulled both my pistols and shot all four of them. I changed my name and worked my way east. I was thinking of making it to the coast because I had never seen the ocean and when I finally made it, me and Honor just basked in the hot sand for hours. That's when Bradley Cummings found me and you know the rest.

"Now before you go off half cocked, Sherry, just let me finish about the men I shot. When I fell in love with you, I sent a telegram to the marshal of that territory and asked if there had been any murders near the town I had gambled in. He sent back a message that not only were four dead men found, but there had been a hefty reward for their capture, dead or alive. So if I was to go back and visit that marshal, I would be given five hundred dollars in reward. That's the whole of it. That's the God's honest truth. Just let me know if you want me to pack my bags and leave. I'll understand. I knew the risk in telling you but if we made our way back to the farm, you'd find out anyway. There really was no choice but to tell you."

Sherry sank back down in her chair, speechless and teary. Cullen just let the tale sink in as he sat waiting for more questions. Sherry was first.

"Cullen, I mean, Charles, do you cheat people at cards?"

"I *can* cheat, yes. But only when I'm playing someone that I know also cheats. Then it's a game of who is better at it. I would never take money from an honest working man. Only card sharps like myself." Turning to look at Mason, he continued, "You've seen me play. Who are the people I play with? Jamison's men or other men who, shall we say, manipulate the cards to their benefit. Once in a while I'll play with the town's people but I never cheat them. I play straight as an arrow under those circumstances, I swear. But if I had the chance to cheat playing Jamison, you better believe I would."

For some reason, Mason wasn't fazed by Cullen's admission. *Charles, that is.* "I can't call you Charles, I'm sorry. You'll always be Cullen to me. All of what you just told us makes not one hill of beans to me. I know the man you are. I've seen into your heart. I say we head for Virginia. Maybe we can sail down the coast and meet with Mr. Cummings. Maybe he'll buy the Mermaid. I just want out of Castine."

Edith felt much the same. "Cullen, I don't give a hoot about any of what you just told us. I feel the same as Mason. Let's go."

Sherry was reticent. She wasn't ready to give Cullen blanket forgiveness. She got up from the table and went upstairs to her room.

Cullen was crestfallen. "Well, I guess we know where Sherry stands. I think I'm going to leave Castine for three or four days. Give her some time to think about things." He got up and went upstairs to gather some things for his trip.

When he returned to the kitchen, Edith had packed him a good supply of food. "You take care of yourself, Cullen, and come back as soon as you can. We'll miss you." She kissed him on the cheek and hugged him close. Just then, Mason remembered the episode from the night before and warned Cullen. "Make sure you don't stay away too long. With Jamison after Sherry again last night, it's going to be tense around here, to say the least. Just wanted you to keep that thought in mind as you ride along."

"Tell Sherry I love her. I'll see you soon." Then he was off to the barn to saddle his faithful companion.

Chapter Twenty-One

Sherry was terribly confused. She was having trouble distinguishing between the two men who were Cullen Westover and Charles Maklin. One man loved her deeply, she knew that. She had felt it deep in her soul. The other was a card cheating murderer who bore no resemblance to the man she loved. How could this be? How could a card cheating murderer have everyone so fooled? Surely it wasn't Cullen's intention to worm his way into their lives for nefarious reasons, was it? Why not choose someone who had a lot more to cheat them out of? They weren't dirt poor but they lived from day to day. A swindler would choose more prosperous prey, wouldn't they?

After Cullen had left, Sherry determined to go on as if nothing had happened. They would work and carry on like usual. The ice cover on the bay had broken and mostly dissipated so their brief holiday from trawling was over. It was time to get back into the routine she was coming to dread more and more with each passing day. Without Cullen, it would be especially dreadful. She missed him already, and only the Lord knew when he would return, if at all. She just didn't know what to think anymore.

All the things she had learned to tolerate on the trawler were bugging the living daylights out of her that day; the seagulls and their relentless squawking, the sea spray that froze on her eyelashes, and the responsibility of finding good pockets of cod in the bay, all tried her patience. She wanted to scream and jump overboard just to get away from the anxiety of having to further tolerate that way of life. Before Cullen arrived, she was merely an automaton, going through the motions to keep the family warm and fed. Now she knew what a different life might be like; a life of love and soulful contentment even if they wound end up having to continue trawling to make a living. Cullen made it all worth while.

She wondered where he was and what he was doing. Maybe she had pushed him over the edge with her reaction to his confessions. Maybe he didn't feel she was worth trying to convince that he was worthy of her love. Her day on the Mermaid was full of self recriminations for jumping to conclusions about what Cullen had admitted to the family. She felt bereft at the thought of possibly never seeing him again. She had messed things up badly and didn't know what to do about it.

Mason kept a close eye on her that day. He knew she must be feeling dispirited about Cullen's choice to leave for a few days and gave her time alone with her ruminations. *If* that was the real reason he left. It wasn't that Mason didn't trust the man, because he did. He just had a niggling feeling that Cullen was up to something more and it had to do with the future he had envisioned for their family. Whatever he was doing was more than all right with Mason. He just hoped Sherry would be ready to forgive the man by the time he returned.

Later that evening, Sherry barely touched her meal and made excuses to go upstairs early. Sleep was the only thing she wanted. It was a safe haven away from the loss she felt at Cullen's leaving, if she was able to sleep at all.

Edith and Mason commiserated with each other while Edith cleaned up the kitchen from dinner. There was plenty left over because she forgot Cullen wouldn't be there to share the meal with them. Both admitted they were willing to wait five days without worry to see if Cullen came back. Mason wanted to give him time to accomplish whatever it was he left to do.

It had been seven days and Cullen still hadn't returned, and that settled the issue for Sherry. He wasn't coming back and she would have to begin the healing process so the family wouldn't suffer watching her fall apart. She put on a happy face each morning and smiled at Cullen on the Mermaid, every time she saw him looking at her. In the evening she ate her dinner and chatted for a few minutes with the family, holding Caleb on her lap and sifting her fingers through his silken hair. It was all she could manage.

Some nights she felt she would scream before she could escape to her room where she was able to allow the tears and feelings to come that would hopefully cleanse her grief. But would it really ever end? Now that she knew what real love was like, how could she carry on without it?

She awoke the next morning, slogging through the process of washing and dressing, and tried to smile on her way down the stairs for breakfast. Another long and unendurable day was ahead. How she would make it, she had no idea. She lived moment by moment the past week and, fortunately, she had been able to hide her pain from the family. Caleb had no idea what was going on. He just knew Cullen had gone on a short trip but would return in a few days. Mason and Edith also wore smiles and pretended that everything was as it should be. What a farce for them all. Why were they hiding their feelings from one another?

Meanwhile, Dirk Jamison was watching them closely each day. He was dying to know what happened to Westover, and felt the passing of an entire week surely denoted the man's leaving for good. Maybe Sherry's announcement that they were to be married was a ruse. Maybe it was time to turn up the heat and force her hand. If he had been listening to the chatter in town, he would have known Westover's father had passed away, and he was gone for only enough time to bury him and return. But Jamison never kept his ear to the ground, feeling no one had anything of value to contribute to his world.

***

Cullen couldn't stop his mind from constant internal dialogs in which he had everything in hand. In his mind, nothing had changed and he felt Sherry would surely forgive him upon his return. However, he still had one important goal to accomplish, and that meant traveling around the bay and south of the Penobscot, trying to make money. He stopped at two saloons per day, at the very least, looking for men with money who were looking for the entertainment a game of poker might provide. Despite the fact he wasn't sleeping well, Cullen was still sharp as a tack, keeping a watchful eye on every player and their cards, and trying to determine his own odds of winning. So far, his pockets were heavier after each day at the tables. He didn't want to jinx himself by counting it. It was something he never did until he was back on the road and well away from the tables.

He knew he had been away longer than anticipated, but the streak of luck was too much to pass up. Every moment he wasn't playing, he was estimating costs in an effort to gauge how much would be enough to accomplish plans for his family.

So far, he had only encountered one card cheat. The man was a braggart who regaled his buddies with stories of how much money he had made working for a man named Jamison, in Castine. He was there that night trying to double the amount. It was all Cullen needed to hear. He turned his clasped fingers inside out and cracked his knuckles, just itching to fleece the bastard out of his entire pay. Pulling his hat lower over his forehead, he asked the man to join his table.

When all was said and done, Cullen had taken every penny the man had. He had seen men gamble away every bit of their money, hoping for a few hands that would bring them flush again. It never worked and it was a lousy strategy. Before the braggart got any ideas of taking his money back by force, Cullen rocked back in his chair and lay both hands on his pistols.

"Don't even think about it," he said. "You'll be dead before you even clear leather." Cullen then smiled, and continued, "Now I'm gonna take my winnings and clear out of here. I'm gonna back right out that door without one second of trouble from you, ya hear? If not, don't blame me for the holes I'll put in your forehead." Gathering every last bit of his winnings, he stuffed it in his pants pockets and got up from the table. "It's been a real pleasure. I hope to play with y'all again soon."

Taking the episode as perhaps an omen, Cullen decided it was time to go home. *Home.* The thought brought a flush of happiness rushing through his veins. It was time to go home to his woman. It was time to settle whatever remaining questions and hurt feelings were left from his confessions. He couldn't believe Sherry felt so little for him as to run because of changing his name. Of course, there was no accounting for how women felt about such things. He just hoped she would open her heart and see the truth of how things were in his own heart and mind.

Cullen figured he could make it home within two days if he didn't waste any time. He would stop only to eat and sleep. Honor would be glad to be back home in his stall, living the good life.

***

Sherry stepped onto the pier behind Mason, and walked with her head down against the rain and strong winds that had developed during the day on the Penobscot. It was the ninth day she made it through the listless depression that laid heavy on her mind and heart; the ninth day she wore a mask to hide that she was dying inside.

Mason gathered her close to his side to help break the wind that was whipping her hair into a cloud around her head, and headed up the hill. When he looked up toward the house, he saw Honor ground tied outside the kitchen door.

"Look Sherry! Cullen is back!"

"What? Are you sure?"

"Of course I'm sure, silly. Why would Honor be back without Cullen?"

Immediately, Sherry's leaden heart lifted and felt joy returning to her soul. Why did she care what his name was or had been? She had been a fool to walk away from her man when he had been truthful. She would never make that mistake again. He was home and it was all that mattered.

They both began running against the wind and rain, anxious to see Cullen's face again. When they were almost to the side yard, Cullen walked out of the kitchen and saw them running. A huge smile replaced his mien of worry and he opened his arms to catch Sherry as she ran full speed into his embrace. He hugged her tight as if she might disappear, and planted kisses all over her face. "Oh Sherry, my darling Sherry. Have you forgiven me?"

"There was never really anything to forgive, Cullen. I was shocked and acted poorly. I should have trusted you as you trust me. I'm so sorry, sweetheart. I promise to never doubt you again."

All was right again in their world.

***

Edith prepared a welcome home dinner, and they all ate with great appetite and relief. Cullen was honest with them about where he had been and what he had been doing. "I haven't counted the money yet. I was waiting until we were all together. After the table is cleared, we can see if my time away was fruitful or not."

Sherry didn't care that he won the money playing cards because she knew he did it with a purpose, and that purpose was to help the family. Whether they stayed in Castine, or not, he did it for them.

Edith served a lovely chocolate cake for dessert, and they enjoyed the sweetness that was equal to that in their hearts. Cullen's return answered their every prayer. It was so good to have him home again.

Cullen stood from the table and dug his hands in his pants pockets. When he pulled out the huge wads of paper money and then handfuls of coin, they all exclaimed they had never seen so much of it at one time. "Holy Moses, Cullen! You must have a thousand dollars there!" Mason exclaimed.

Each of them took a small pile and began counting, enjoying the feel of such wealth in their hands. When they were each finished, Sherry got a pencil and some paper and added the totals. "Nine hundred eighty-three dollars and fifty cents! Oh, Cullen! That's enough to do just about anything, isn't it?"

Cullen was grinning from ear to ear. "I've never gambled so much at one time in my entire life. I was on a mission, for sure, and Lady Luck was certainly with me. I figure, on my side of things, I have almost two thousand dollars after paying for my pa's funeral and the taxes on the farm. Add that to what you will make on the sale of the Mermaid and the house, and we'll be set." Stacking the money into one pile, he continued with a look of concern, "Sherry, have you given any more thought to what I proposed before I left? Is it time you and the family left Castine?"

Sherry smiled at him, and said, "First things, first. I'm going to be married by tomorrow evening. Then we'll discuss when we're leaving." Having said that, she jumped into Cullen's lap and planted a juicy kiss on his lips. Cullen looked to Mason and Edith, and said, "Well, how about that? Do we have your permission?"

Mason rolled his eyes. "Cullen you had it before you left. Now let's get moving and make some plans. Will you send Mr. Cummings a telegram tomorrow? Ask him if he wants the Mermaid?"

And so it went that evening. Love and excitement filled the air as they planned a new life where they would all be happy and away from Jamison. It was a dream come true for the family. Even Caleb was caught up in the excitement and asked, "Can I help, too?"

Chapter Twenty-Two

The next day was a Thursday, and by mutual decision they decided to not take the Mermaid out trawling. There was too much to do with the wedding and contacting Bradley Cummings. Telegrams needed to be sent and, hopefully, with quick replies if they were lucky.

After they arrived in town, Cullen riding Honor, and Mason manning the wagon. Sherry and Edith took Caleb and went shopping for wedding clothes and accoutrements while Cullen and Mason went to see Tellie.

"Mornin', Tellie! I've got a couple of telegrams to send. Sharpen your pencil."

"Sure thing, Mr. Westover. Whatcha need?"

"To Mr. and Mrs. Kenneth Hutchinson, Summerfield, Arkansas. 'Getting married today. Wish you were here. You will meet her and new family soon. Going home to Virginia. Love Cullen.'"

Tellie was tapping furiously, and when he was done, he asked, "Next?"

"To Mr. Bradley Cummings, Hampton, Virginia. 'Interested in another trawler for your fleet? Please advise. Cullen Westover.'"

Tellie was really on the money that day. "Next?"

"To the Sheriff, McKenney, Dinwiddie County, Virginia. 'Funeral and tax expenses paid. Will be coming home within next few months. Charles Maklin.' Tellie, do you have a map of where the trains run? And maybe a schedule? I'll need to know everything about traveling down the East Coast."

"Sure do. You can have mine. I get a new one every month."

Cullen folded the sheets of paper and placed them in his back pocket.

"That'll be all for today, Tellie. Thanks for the speedy service. How much do I owe you?"

Leaving the telegraph office, Cullen asked Mason, "Feel like eating a hearty breakfast? I didn't get enough this morning. I feel like I could eat a whole cow."

Mason was always game for a good meal. "Heck, yeah! But can we go to Stewart's first? Things are moving pretty fast and I need to stake a claim, so to speak, with Beth."

"You're serious about her, aren't you."

"Yes, I am. I told you I was going to marry her."

"Have you even taken her out yet?"

"No, and that's why I need to 'stake my claim,' you big oaf. I need to let her know my intentions and then sweet talk her father into letting us court."

"Okay, but I'm coming with you. I need to meet this young lady and see if she's good enough for you."

"Like you could ever keep me away from her," Mason grinned.

Both men laughed and headed for Stewart's Apothecary. As luck would have it, good or bad, Mr. Stewart was working with Beth that morning.

"Good morning, Mr. Stewart. Is Beth here, by any chance?"

"Yes, she's in the back. Whom may I say is asking?"

"Mason Newcomb, sir."

"And what, may I ask, is the reason?"

"Sir, I have come to ask if she would be agreeable to my courting her. And, of course, to ask your permission if she is interested."

Looking at Cullen, he told Mr. Stewart, "This is Cullen Westover. He and Miss Sherry are getting married today."

Cullen offered his hand to Mr. Stewart, and they shook in introduction.

"Mason is a mature and capable young man, sir. He's got a good head on his shoulders and has taken quite a fancy to your lovely daughter. I can vouch for him, if it would make you feel better about letting them court."

Mr. Stewart was dubious, but how could he refuse such gentlemanly behavior? "Beth? Beth, come out here, please."

"Yes, Pa?"

"This young man has come asking for permission to court you. What do you have to say?"

Beth blushed and tried to wait a few moments before shouting, YES! Clearing her throat, she finally murmured, "I guess that would be acceptable, Mr. Newcomb. I might enjoy that very much."

Everyone looked back at Mr. Stewart, to see if he would allow it. "I would have to ask at this point what your intentions are, Mr. Newcomb. That is, where do you expect this 'courting' will lead?"

Mason never missed a beat as he answered, "My intention is that Beth becomes my wife, sir. I knew it from the first time I saw her in your store. I've never felt anything so strong or right. I believe it's meant to be."

Beth thought she might faint right on the spot. "Really? You want to marry me?"

"Yes, Beth, I do. Like I said, it feels so right, and in my heart I believe you are the one for me. I hope you come to love me as much as I love you. I'm hoping our courtship will prove that you feel the same."

Looking back at Mr. Stewart, he continued, "Sir, would it be all right if Beth attends the wedding this afternoon? I want her to meet the rest of my family and it would be the perfect occasion."

This was all happening too fast for Mr. Stewart, but he couldn't very well refuse. After all, Beth was almost nineteen years old, and no one had shown any interest in her until now. Perhaps it would be good to let them do as they please for a while, within limits, of course.

"That will be fine, Mr. Newcomb." The three men shook hands in parting and the matter was settled. "But I'll be watching you, never doubt it."

Mason told Beth what time he would come for her, and he and Cullen left to find the girls.

***

Jamison saw that Westover was back in town, and his heart sank. Damn! Thinking the man was gone for good, he had been taking his time in planning his next move with Sherry. Now it might be too late.

What were they up to, now? Was someone sick? Is that what they were doing at Stewart's? Getting medicine? Was it Sherry who might be ill? He just hoped she stayed alive until after he married her. If not, all his plans would be blown to hell. He still hadn't found Ruby, and he was feeling more and more out of control lately. He now had severe headaches and started treating himself with laudanum. It was the only thing that could curb the pain in his head. It also made him feel more invincible that ever. Jamison's ego plus opium were not a good mix.

***

Mason looked for the girls while Cullen searched for the pastor. He found the man placing flowers in front of the pulpit while softly singing a hymn. *Onward Christian Soldiers, fighting as to war, with the cross of Jesus . . .*

"Oh, sorry, I didn't see you standing there. What can I do for you this fine day?"

"Sir, I've come to see if you can perform a wedding ceremony this afternoon. My name is Charles Macklin, and I've asked Sherry Newcomb to marry me. She's agreed and we'd like to get married this afternoon, your schedule permitting, of course."

"I know who you are, and I'll be more than happy to perform the ceremony. Have you gotten a license yet? If not, just go to the Justice of the Peace and he'll provide you with one. Both of you have to sign, so Miss Sherry better be with you when you go."

"Thank you, sir! What time would be convenient for you?"

"Would four o'clock suit?"

"Yes, sir, it sure would. See you then!"

Cullen couldn't believe it. It was really happening after all the weeks of yearning to make Sherry his bride.

Chapter Twenty-Three

Something was bothering Sherry, and she didn't know whether or not to bring it up. Even though she knew Cullen gambled to win money for the family, when she had the time to really think about it, it didn't truly sit well with her.

Upon finding the girls at the dress shop, Cullen noted Sherry's pensive mood and asked what was wrong. Sherry answered immediately, "Oh Cullen, do you think it would be all right to give some of the money you won to the church? I would feel so much better about it if you would."

He had never imagined something like that would be bothering Sherry, but understood her feelings. "Yes, I think that would be a fine idea, Sweetie. How about if I give them one hundred dollars? That should be enough for the church to accomplish some of its goals in the community, don't you think?"

"Yes, that would be fine, I think. Perhaps we can give it to the pastor this afternoon after the wedding."

"All right. Now tell me what else is bothering you. I can see it written all over your face."

"I'm just missing my folks, is all. I'm so very happy to be marrying you, dear heart, but I'd be lying if I didn't admit it would be so much better for me with them here. You understand, don't you?"

"Of course, I do. Let's write them a letter tonight, telling them all about it in detail. Maybe we can at least write them pictures for their imaginations."

Cullen hoped for much more than that but it would have to do for the time being.

***

The dress Sherry chose for her wedding was a satin of soft sage green with ivory lace at the collar and sleeves. She even indulged in a lovely ivory crocheted shawl to wear over it. She picked a hat that was a matching shade of green that had a bit of netting in the front that might serve as a veil. Some ivory gloves were the last touch to what was, in her mind, the perfect ensemble in which to be married.

Edith chose a hunter green dress of like material, with matching hat and gloves. She chose carefully, thinking the outfit might serve as her own wedding dress one day.

Now they must hurry home to fix each other's hair and iron out any wrinkles from their dresses that might have been mussed on the trip back home in the wagon.

Arriving home, Edith was so excited she could barely breathe, and Sherry was so nervous she could hardly stand. All the fussing and arranging began and the end result was stunning. "Oh, Sherry! You look gorgeous! Cullen won't believe his own eyes when he sees you!"

"Thank you, Edith. You look more beautiful than I've ever seen you. I'm so proud of you, you know. Only seventeen and already you're a beautiful and competent woman. I know Cullen and Mason feel the same."

Just then they heard the kitchen door open. Mason and Cullen were laughing and cutting up, acting like two boys who just learned there would be no more school for the summer. The joy in the house was palpable and Sherry wanted to remember each and every moment to savor for years to come.

Sherry and Edith gave each other one last inspection before going downstairs. Sherry so hoped Cullen would find her a beautiful bride. She wanted him to be proud of her. It was important to her that Cullen felt he had made a good choice in a wife. She was very much committed to being the very best wife possible. She loved him so deeply.

As the two women came downstairs, Cullen looked up and found he was speechless. He could only stare in astonishment at the beautiful vision that was to be his wife. "Sherry, you take my breath away," he finally managed to say. "A more beautiful bride there never was."

Mason was likewise surprised by Edith's transformation. "Sis, you're all grown up! Before the Christmas Ball, I never imagined there was a figure like that under your work dresses. My God, how will I keep the men away from you? Come here and turn around. Let me see every inch of you." Edith beamed with pleasure. "Oh, Mason, stop being silly." She was blushing fifty shades of red but was also savoring the compliment.

Sherry remained standing at the bottom of the stairs, her eyes never leaving Cullen's smiling face. The barber had shaved off his beard and it was the first time she was seeing him without one. He had dimples and a cleft chin! "My goodness, you are handsome, Cullen. Had I known what was underneath all that hair, I would have asked you to shave it off weeks ago." After looking her fill, she added, "You two better get ready. We only have an hour to get the license and show up at church."

Cullen was glad she appreciated the surprise of a smooth shaven face. "I want us to have a family picture taken after the wedding. I don't care how much it costs." Cullen was just as determined to remember every second of that day, forever capturing the look of their love and happiness in a photograph. "We'll have two taken. One of the family, and one with just me and Sherry. Does that sound all right?"

They all agreed pictures were a marvelous idea. The rest of them didn't know it but Mason would have Beth stand in the family picture, he was that sure of the fact they would soon be married.

The men dressed quickly and they all left the house by the kitchen door, finding a lovely carriage awaiting them and Honor wearing a white plume in his bridle. Sherry laughed at the sight but thought the carriage was the perfect final touch for the day.

They first went to the Justice for the license, then picked Beth up from the shop, and finally arrived at the church. Sherry wondered who Beth was and why she was attending their wedding but she imagined introductions would answer her questions shortly.

"Dearly beloved, we are gathered here . . ."

Sherry could see the pastor's mouth moving but didn't hear a word he said. She was as nervous as a virgin bride and just wanted to say I do, hopefully at the appropriate moment. Cullen was beaming with joy and wanted the world to know this gorgeous woman at his side would be his wife forever more.

When the pastor called for the rings, Mason nudged Caleb, and the boy took the rings out of his pocket. Everyone giggled as he took his part in the ceremony very seriously, and handed them each a ring.

"By the power vested in me, you are now man and wife. You may kiss the bride."

Cullen gave Sherry a chaste kiss, and then the rest of the family was clapping and cheering the bride and groom. Cullen shook the pastor's hand in gratitude, palming him the money he had promised Sherry he would, and then they left the church. "Be happy!" the pastor called after them.

Sherry didn't want to just go home and asked, "Where will we celebrate?"

"We're going to the 'Steak and Ale.' I hear they have the best meals around. Nothing but the best for my *wife*." Sherry grinned and added,

"Nothing but the best from my *husband*." Chances were good they would call each other by those words for the next month, just wanting to hear the sound of them. *Husband and wife.*

When everyone was settled in the carriage, Mason made the formal introductions where Beth was concerned.

"This is Beth Stewart, and she's going to be *my* wife one day soon."

Sherry looked at a blushing Beth and gently pulled her into a hug. "Oh, my goodness! You two certainly move fast, don't you?"

"It's not so fast if you know from the first second you meet someone that you want them in your life forever. I knew that from the first time I saw her in Stewart's. She's the woman for me."

Beth remained quiet, not wanting to have the attention on her at Sherry's own wedding but finally said, "We'll see," she said. "Truth be told, I've had my eye on Mason for years."

Mason turned to her in surprise and asked, "Really? Are you serious? I mean…truly?" Beth giggled, "I wouldn't lie to you Mason Newcomb. I've admired you since we were in school together. I thought you would never approach me. What did you want me to do? Wear a sign around my neck announcing it to the world?"

Everyone laughed at her reply, thinking she just might fit beautifully into their family. A good sense of humor went a long way in life and Beth Stewart appeared to have quite the wit.

Just as they would pass the sheriff's office, Dirk Jamison galloped quickly up behind them and pulled around to the front of the carriage, stopping his horse in front of Honor. "Get out of the carriage, Sherry. Get out and follow me to the Justice's office. I'm going to have your marriage license stricken from the records. You were a fool to think I'd ever let this happen. Come on, now. Get out and follow me."

Cullen had wondered if something like this might happen when he rented the open carriage, and wore his guns just in case. He wanted the entire town to see they were getting married and hoped Jamison would be the first one to notice.

"I don't think so, Jamison. We're married and there isn't a damned thing you can do about it. Just move along and let us be on our way. We're off to celebrate our nuptials. I'll remember to drink to you when we get there."

"No, you won't! I've let this nonsense go on long enough and what I say *goes* in this town. There's not one person living here that would bat an eye at my killing you right here and now, or they'd never live to tell it if they did. I *own* this town and everyone in it, including that worthless sheriff. Now do yourself a favor and listen to me. I'm sure Sherry doesn't want to see you dead."

Cullen was stone faced when he said, "You'll have to kill me first, Jamison."

Dirk just smiled and replied, "Have it your way, Westover."

Cullen stood and waited for Jamison to touch his pistol before pulling his own. In a split second, Jamison rolled off his horse and hit the ground.

The sheriff had watched and listened to the entire exchange. He sauntered over to Jamison's body and flipped him onto his back with the toe of his boot. Bending down and trying to find a pulse, he found none. Rising again, he looked at Cullen and Sherry, and said, "Congratulations on your wedding. Please, go on with your celebrations. I'll have this cleaned up in no time." Taking off his hat, he bowed to the ladies and grinned at Cullen. "Please, don't give this another thought. I'll take care of everything."

Everyone in the carriage was stunned and silent until the sheriff said he would take care of everything. Then Mason whooped and hollered, and yelled, "This wedding party is just starting! Let's go get some pictures taken!"

Sherry couldn't believe Mason remained in such a festive mood after witnessing a man's death, and worried that perhaps he was becoming inured to violence. Perhaps it was relief at finally being free of Dirk's threats. She had to admit to feeling a certain amount of relief at seeing him lying on the ground, not moving, not breathing, and wondered what was wrong with her that she had no respect for the man's passing. She would examine her feelings later when time permitted. Today was her wedding day and she didn't want to let Jamison ruin it.

Cullen sensed her disquiet and put his arm around her shoulders. Leaning close, he whispered in her ear, "Don't think about it. Strike it from your mind and enjoy your wedding day. I'm not a murderer, you know that. He went for his gun first, and I merely defended my family. It's over now. He'll never hurt you again. So smile, Lady Wife, and rejoice in our love that has united us until the day we die." He lightly kissed her cheek and clicked to Honor to take them to the photographer's studio on Cameron Street.

Lord, what a beautiful sight they all were. The owner of the studio provided a full length mirror for the ladies so they could primp and adjust themselves just right. There was a comb provided for the men to make sure every hair was in place. There were two sittings just as he had suggested. The first picture was taken of just Cullen and Sherry.

Mason grinned at the couple sitting stock still in front of the camera. "I want you two to smile. Don't listen to the photographer. Just think about how much you love each other and let it show. If the picture doesn't turn out, we'll just take it over until we get it right." Mason thought wedding pictures where the bride and groom looked like they were angry as hell were bad luck. Certainly, he and Beth would be smiling when theirs were taken.

Mason, Edith, and Beth placed themselves behind the camera and wore big grins trying to make the couple smile. It worked but when they all viewed the finished product, it would be very apparent what had been on both the bride and groom's minds. Sherry's delicate smile bespoke her deepest love, while Cullen's showed immense pride and not a little desire. It would be a most handsome picture.

The family picture, including Beth, turned out in much the same manner. All were smiling and their happiness fairly jumped out at the person viewing the image.

Chapter Twenty-Four

As soon as Cullen and Sherry had left the building with their marriage license, the clerk ran from behind his counter, out the door, and to the nearest person he knew would spread the word of the coming event.

"Westover is marrying Sherry Newcomb this afternoon! Land sakes! Dirk Jamison is gonna have a litter of kittens over this!"

The recipient of this piece of gossip then told the next person she saw, who happened to be the president of The Castine Club for Women, and she, in turn, told everyone she met on the street. It wasn't long before clutches of women met up and down the sidewalks, one being right in front of Stewart's Apothecary, clucking like hens over this latest juicy bit of gossip. Mrs. Stewart walked out to greet the ladies, and contributed her own side of the story.

"Yes, it's true. My Bethy is attending the wedding. Seems Mason Newcomb has taken a shine to my girl. The wedding is probably taking place even as we speak. I'm thinking it sure would be nice to provide the happy couple with something special, yeah? What do you ladies think?"

The women collectively gasped in excitement and immediately moved as a swarm to the town bakery to order a wedding cake. Then they dispersed, as if following a beacon, to their homes. Soon the town was filled with the delicious aromas of food cooking, each woman wanting to contribute her fair share to the celebration.

***

The Steak and Ale was certainly the finest restaurant Sherry had ever dined in. "Oh, Cullen, look at these prices! We can't afford this!"

"Don't worry about that, Mrs. West…Maklin. This is your day and I'll be darned if I'll allow money to interfere with your happiness. So, eat, drink, and enjoy, all of you!"

Mason was grinning from ear to ear, "You don't have to tell me twice, Cullen. I already know what I'm ordering. How about you, Beth? Have you ever eaten here before?"

"Yes, I've eaten here a few times for certain celebrations. The food is indeed good but I prefer to do the cooking. I enjoy preparing feasts at Thanksgiving and Christmas."

Sherry beamed, "So you're an accomplished cook, are you? How wonderful! Edith is also a talented cook. Me? I can't boil water."

Everyone laughed and continued to peruse the menus. Caleb spoke up and asked for mashed potatoes and fried chicken which made Cullen proud as punch. "Yes sir, I'll have him being a Southern boy in no time."

For some reason, Beth's mind went immediately to the possibility that the Newcombs would be leaving for the south, and blurted, "You're not leaving Castine, are you?" Sherry felt bad for the girl, and was able to read her thoughts. She took the girl's hand and said, "Yes, we are leaving, Beth. We're moving to Virginia, but I would appreciate your not telling anyone yet, all right?" Then she leaned over to whisper, "Don't look so stricken, dear. I think we both know that you will be going with us as Mrs. Mason Newcomb, am I right? Mason has already told us how he feels about you and what he wants. Do you think you would enjoy moving south? Or would you miss your family too much?"

Beth looked much relieved and wiped a tear from her eye before anyone noticed. She squeezed Sherry's hand and gave her a look that said, *We'll talk about this later.*

Cullen ordered a bottle of red wine and they all raised their glasses in a toast to his lovely wife. "To my wife, Colleen . . . what's your middle name, Sherry?" "Sinead," she replied. "To my wife, Colleen Sinead Maklin. May she always love me as much as she does today." They clinked glasses and drank freely, being swept up in feelings of love and family. "Mmmmm, quite delicious, Mr. Maklin," Beth giggled. "May I have a little more?"

"Of course, dear Beth. I'll just order another bottle…or two. Or maybe three!" Edith added, "Good, because I would like another full glass, please." They laughed heartily, taking their time in ordering so as to make the meal last.

Two hours later, when they were finished and the check was paid, Cullen got up from his chair and noticed that for the first time, he had no qualms about Sherry being out in public. There was no further threat from Jamison. She was free to go about her business without harassment or molestation. When they all stood in the sunshine outside of the restaurant, Cullen, Edith, Mason and Sherry looked at each other and stood in silence, knowing exactly what the other was feeling. Mason puffed up his chest with a deep inhalation of air and said on the exhale, "It's over. So be it." Then they each perked up as Cullen whistled for Honor to bring the carriage. It would take a while, but the name Dirk Jamison would one day be erased from their memories as if he had been only a bad dream.

The sheriff had done as he promised, and the only remaining evidence of Jamison's demise was a small pool of blood on the street. Durrell waved them down and said, "I'm so sorry to have to do this, but I need all of your statements as to what happened this afternoon. You'll have to come on in my office so we can begin."

The announcement put somewhat of a damper on the occasion but Cullen understood that Darrell was just doing his job. It took another hour before they were back in the carriage and on their way home. Sherry was tired and wondered if it was because of the wine she drank. Mason and Beth were cuddled up on one side of the carriage, holding hands and whispering to each other. Caleb was sound asleep, and Sherry knew what the look on Cullen's face meant. He couldn't wait to get his wife alone in their bedroom. She giggled at his expression and blushed even though she wasn't a virgin bride.

As the carriage rolled around the last bend toward the Newcomb place, they noticed horses and wagons parked in front of the house. "For goodness sakes!" cried Edith. "What's going on? Oh Lord, has something happened to the Mermaid?"

When they pulled up to the kitchen entrance, women started running out shouting, "Congratulations! Congratulations!" Sherry smiled and allowed the women to escort her into the kitchen where she witnessed the most sumptuous array of foods imaginable.

"We just wanted to let you know how happy we are you found such a good man." Old Mrs. Pritchard barked, "Been takin' bets, we have, ta see how long it took fer Westover ta ask fer yer hand. I won!" The ladies laughed and cackled, strutting around the kitchen, trying to place their dishes to the best advantage.

"Come on in the parlor for another surprise!" The ladies ushered her into the parlor where she found a beautiful wedding cake. It was three tiers and decorated exquisitely.

"Oh, my heavens! It's the most beautiful thing I've ever seen! How can I thank you all for everything you've done to make my day so happy and complete?" Then Sherry started crying in gratitude and hugged each and every woman who had worked so hard. "This is so generous of you all. Thank you from the bottom of my heart, ladies. I shall never forget this, ever!"

She wondered where Cullen had disappeared to and found him in the middle of a circle of men outside, each man slapping his back and thanking him for ridding Castine of Jamison's reign of terror. Cullen didn't look proud of the accolades, and tried to change the subject to that of the wedding.

Sherry was grateful for the love and attention from well-wishers, but felt, for some reason, that she wanted only her family at the moment. And so she searched for Mason and Edith, hoping that they were keeping an eye on Caleb.

Edith was chatting with a handsome young man who Sherry had seen only a few times in church. She was smiling and laughed when the young man said something funny, and suddenly Sherry knew that Edith would one day soon be married, herself. Mason and Edith were growing up and would leave the nest if Cullen didn't provide the land and homes necessary to keep them all together. Sherry felt a sense of panic and rushed through the crowd of men to reach Cullen's side.

As soon as Cullen saw her face, he knew something was wrong. "Excuse me, gentlemen, I believe my wife needs me for a second." The men guffawed and told him to get used to it. She had probably broken a fingernail and didn't know what to do. Apparently, flasks of whiskey had been passed back and forth. Otherwise, Sherry would have laid into them for such a stupid statement. Hellfire! They knew Sherry sailed her own boat!

"What is it, Mrs. Maklin," he whispered in her ear. "What's got you so upset?"

"Cullen, you must make me a promise this very minute. You must promise me that there will be enough land and money to build houses for Mason and Beth, and Edith and her husband. Promise me, please? We have to stay together!"

Cullen grabbed her in a bear hug and whispered, "Of course, darling. We are a clan now and one that will stay together through thick and thin. I promise. Now let's enjoy our party, all right? I see some men with instruments walking down the road so I guess there will be dancing. This is great, isn't it? Let's make some memories." Then he gently guided her back to the kitchen, accepted a plate of food the women had prepared for him and made his way back outside.

Mason started a bonfire which the men quickly gathered around with their own plates of food. Cullen stood back and felt the atmosphere was almost electric with the heightened level of joy and relief. Yes, Castine would recover from Jamison's reign of terror. The feeling was palpable. He just wished he could have accomplished it without taking the man's life.

As the sun went down on Castine, the party moved to the front yard of the Newcomb place, and the musical instruments were tuned. The snow from the last storm was gone, torches were set along the perimeter of the yard, and people started dancing in high spirits. When Cullen and Sherry approached, the dancers made way for the bride and groom, and the band played a softer tune to which the couple could dance close in each other's arms.

Then Mason and Beth joined them, Mason beaming, so proud he was of Beth Stewart, and so anxious to make her his wife.

Edith and her gentleman were next, and Sherry watched as her daughter and dearest friend gracefully glided across the frozen lawn. The people of Maine were a hearty bunch, as she could see no one shivering or trying to escape the cold. Would she miss them? Yes, the people she would miss, but the weather? Heavens no, she thought.

When Prissy, the president of the Castine Club for Women, deemed it was time to come in and cut the cake, everyone followed her lead into the parlor and kitchen, anywhere on the first floor of the house where there was space. People were crammed in like sardines, leaving a small space around the cake for the bride and groom.

Sherry took the knife Prissy offered, and made the first cut on the top tier. Cullen was next, and as tradition demanded, they fed each other bites of cake through entwined arms. The cheers that went up were deafening and Cullen thought he would never be happier than he was in that moment. His dreams were coming true just as Charlie said they would. Lord, how he wished Charlie and Ken were there to help them celebrate. He missed them fiercely.

The crowd was losing steam around nine o'clock that evening, and people were making their way home. Mason approached Sherry and said, "I'm going to walk Beth home. I'll be back soon." And as she watched her "son" walk down the road with the young woman on his arm, she reflected that today had been bittersweet in some ways. But now it was time to put those thoughts away and concentrate on her husband. *My husband . . .*

***

As the front door was closed on the last of the guests, Cullen reached out his hand to his wife and silently led her upstairs. No words were necessary as each knew the joy and anticipation of what would be theirs that night.

Their joining was not wild and passionate, no. It was a private celebration of their union in marriage. It was languid and sweet in an effort to feel each and every sensation of their new relationship. It was a spiritual feast in what God had intended for husbands and wives. It was a new beginning and it wasn't to be rushed. That night would forever be remembered in their hearts and minds as the pinnacle of love, true love, which God had intended for his children. They would now be bound, heart and soul, for the next step of their journey.

Even though they were exhausted from the days celebrations, when their lovemaking was over, neither could fall asleep. Both were loath to end the day and lay in each other's arms, touching one other in light loving strokes.

"I'm so tired but don't want to sleep, Mrs. Maklin."

"I know what you mean, Mr. Maklin. I don't want the bubble to burst just yet."

Cullen softly chortled, "Mrs. Maklin, it isn't a bubble. It's just the first day in a lifetime full of days that we will be blessed to share. We belong together and nothing will part us."

"I know, Cullen. I know that we have the rest of our lives but will it always be this special? Will time and responsibilities wear us down to the point of forgetting this day and night?"

"Never, my love. Never."

Silent and contemplative once again, they spent a few moments reflecting on what was just said.

"Mr. Maklin?"

"Yes, Mrs. Maklin?"

"You do want children, don't you?"

"You know the answer to that, Mrs. Maklin. I want as many as you will give me."

"Good. I mean, I'm glad because we take no precautions."

"Don't worry about it, my love. We'll leave it up to God, all right?"

Silence once again . . .

"Cullen?"

"Yes, dear?"

"I'm feeling a bit overwhelmed. There is so much to do to get ready to travel south. How will we manage it all?"

"Not tonight, sweetheart. Don't worry tonight. Things have a way of turning out for the best. Time is of no concern. Let's not rush it. Let's sleep now. Tomorrow is another day."

"Cullen?"

"Yes, Colleen?"

"I love you deeply, you know that, don't you? I'll always love you just as much as I do in this moment."

"I love you, too, my sweet. Forever, until my last dying breath."

Chapter Twenty-Five

The next morning Edith made an announcement. "No trawling today! We need to have a family meeting and get some things settled." Bringing paper and a pencil to the table, she wrote at the top, "Things to Do."

"I'm taking it upon myself to keep a list of things to do and dole out responsibilities until we are finally on the road to Virginia. So, I am the manager and you will all follow my directions, okay?"

Mason looked as if he would say something, and Edith held up a finger and shushed him immediately. "There is much to do, and after today, because today we are going to relax and enjoy ourselves, we will begin the process of moving. Are there any objections?"

Mason, Sherry and Cullen merely stared at her in surprise and a bit of confusion. They said nothing so Edith continued her directives. "First things, first. Cullen, you need to write a letter to Mr. Cummings, and ask how he would like to proceed with the sale of the Mermaid," which she wrote as her first entry on the list.

"Then we must decide which mode of travel is the most expedient and thrifty. We don't want to waste one dime if we don't have to," she said as she wrote it down on the list. 'For instance, will we move the furniture by train or in hold of the Mermaid? Who will sail her down the coast? Will we travel together or separately? Seems to me the best idea would be for Mason and me to sail on the Mermaid, and you, Cullen, take Sherry and Caleb on the train. Or visa versa. Maybe. What do you think?"

Cullen smiled and said softly, "Edith, I'm thankful you want to take on this task and there is no one better suited to the job. I'm just asking that you allow for contingencies and tasks done out of order, that's all. I'm asking that you be flexible, okay?"

Edith blushed red, and replied, "Why, of course I'll be flexible, Cullen! I'm not a tyrant, after all!" Mason couldn't help himself and burst out laughing which in turn made Sherry and Cullen laugh too. "It'll all get done, I promise," Cullen assured her. "Now, is there any food left over from yesterday that we might feast on? Where's the rest of the wedding cake?"

Poor Edith had lived under threat for so long that she finally wanted to take the bull by the horns and be in charge of her own destiny. Jamison was gone and his demise somehow gave her a sense of new-found power, which Cullen did not want to crush.

"Let's eat and lay around all day. When one of us comes up with an idea, we'll give it to Edith to record on her list. All in favor?" A resounding "Aye" was noted and they headed for the pantry to raid the leftovers from the previous night.

***

Later that evening, there was a knock on the front door. Stern barked because he knew only strangers used that door and so sounded the alarm. Sherry opened it to find their neighbor, Robert Payne, on the other side.

"Hello, Robert. Come in, come in." Sherry guided him to a chair in front of the fire and bade him to sit for a spell.

"Missus Sherry, I wonder if you might have a few minutes to talk with me."

"Of course, Robert. What's is it?"

"Well, I got ta thinkin' about whether yer gonna stay in Castine, ya see. If not, I'd like to make ya an offer on the Mermaid."

Sherry and Cullen looked at one another as if one of their largest problems might just be solved. "Well, we've already had an offer on the Mermaid, Robert. A man from the Chesapeake Bay has offered to buy her from us."

Robert frowned and said, "Might I ask the offering price? Maybe I can match or even raise it. I know the Mermaid is fit and that you've taken good care of her. I'm willing to work out a fair price."

Cullen scratched his chin as if in deep thought. "Well, the offer right now stands at four thousand dollars. I'd have to write to the man who offered to buy her and see if he still wants the Mermaid." Cullen had received a return telegram from Brad not long after he sent the initial offer to buy her and was shocked at the man's generosity. He felt sure Brad was being overly generous because of their friendship, but didn't know for sure what the boat was really worth.

"Hmm, I see," said Robert Payne. "Ayuh, it's a fair offer, it is, but I been savin' for a third boat for a long time, ya see, and I got a good bit put away. I'll offer ya five thousand and not a penny more. What say ya about that, ayuh?"

Husband and wife looked at each other and weighed the offer against the possible fissure in Cullen's relationship with Bradley Cummings. Cullen spoke up and said, "I'll have to send a telegram tomorrow and ask how the man feels about letting the Mermaid go. Will you give us a few days to get an answer? Also, you have five thousand in cash, right?"

Robert smiled, "Ayuh, cold and hard, it is." The man stood and made to shake Cullen and Sherry's hands. "I'll give ya a week, I will. Should be enough time, ayuh?"

When Robert was gone, Sherry and Cullen were dancing around the parlor like children, wondering at their good fortune. "I just hope Brad was only offering because of friendship. We'll see. I'll send a telegram tomorrow morning."

~

TO BRADLEY CUMMINGS
HAMPTON, CHESAPEAKE BAY, VIRGINIA

DID YOU REALLY WANT TO BUY MERMAID OR JUST BEING A FRIEND? HAVE ANOTHER OFFER BUT WILL SAY NO IF YOU REALLY WANT HER. PLEASE ADVISE. BEST REGARDS.

CULLEN WESTOVER

~

TO CULLEN WESTOVER
CASTINE, MAINE

WAS BEING A FRIEND. KNEW IT WOULD BE DIFFICULT TO TRANSPORT HER. TAKE LOCAL OFFER. BEST OF LUCK.

BRAD CUMMINGS

"Well, that settles it," Cullen said as he read the return telegram. Edith would be much relieved. The thought made him smile. Dearest Edith.

***

Cullen ruminated over his good luck too frequently these days, and was becoming a bit superstitious about it. He was sure he was being set up for some huge fall and started to feel anxious. How could one man enjoy such a long streak of luck? In his mind, it just wasn't probable. He felt the sky was about to fall each and every moment of the day and wanted desperately to talk with someone about it. He didn't want to worry the family since they were so excited to be on their way to Virginia, and he wasn't sure he would sound sane if he were to share such feelings with anyone else.

The pressure was building in him to verbalize his worries and one day, in the barn with Honor, he decided to talk to his horse. As he would say his first words, the inanity of expecting an animal, even one as beloved as Honor, to understand and commiserate felt foolish beyond measure. Then the thought struck him that the one place he might go with his problems had been there all the time.

"Dear Lord, I hope you can hear me. I've got a lot on my mind and I hope you will understand and give me some sort of counsel. You've been mighty good to me in the last several months and I can't help but feel that it's going to end abruptly. I hope you don't think I'm just being foolish . . . *Have faith . . .* and I want you to know how very much . . . *Trust in Me . . .* I appreciate your generosity." Cullen shook his head wondering why he was hearing voices in his head.

"Please remember that I now have a family to support and keep safe . . . *I will provide . . .* so I hope you will be my guide during the . . . *Have faith . . .* next year or so while I prepare a home for them. Will you stay with me, Lord? Will you look after us while we . . . *I love you, my son . . .* build our new home and tend to the land?" Cullen truly thought he was going crazy hearing this voice in his head, but it was a kind and benevolent voice and he somehow knew he could trust it.

He sat down next to Honor's stall and listened intently for the voice, hoping upon hope that it would continue. Instead of words, Cullen began seeing pictures of arriving safely to the homestead, everyone laughing and dancing upon their arrival. He looked around in his mind's eye at the land and saw that it was green and lush. Then he began seeing the house and out buildings after they were refurbished or rebuilt, and watched as Sherry walked across the yard to the water pump, her stomach growing heavy with his child. Everyone was there. Mason and Beth, Edith and Caleb.

The feeling in his heart was so joyous that he got up on his knees and began repeating, "Thank you. Thank you. Thank you," over and over again. And with each thank you, he realized that he meant it to the depths of his soul and finally understood that as a child of God, he deserved all the goodness He would provide. Most importantly, he was no longer afraid. His fear was replaced with profound gratitude and a strong faith that he and his family would always be provided for. Cullen didn't think it was possible to be so happy. Tears rushed down his cheeks and he was even glad for the tears, as they were evidence from his soul that what he had just experienced was very real.

Cullen wanted to kneel there on the barn floor forever, wanting the experience to last. He was afraid if he continued on with his chores, he might forget what happened. And then suddenly he felt very alone with what happened. Was this something else he couldn't share with anyone? Would Sherry believe him?

However, the longer he kneeled on the ground, the more secure he felt in the experience, and knew that it would forever remain a part of him. There was a bedrock certainty that he had just been touched by the grace of God, and he would keep it private. Yes, he would keep it between himself and his God. It felt so personal. Without feeling selfish, he decided to keep it private deep within his heart. So be it.

Part Two

Chapter Twenty-Six

It was the beginning of March before Edith's "To Do" list had been completely accomplished and in three days time the family would be on a train with all of their possessions, riding toward their new home in Virginia.

"C'mon, Cullen! We're going to be late! How will that look, huh? I swear, sometimes you move like you're standing in quicksand. Sherry! Are you ready yet?" Dithering with his necktie, Mason was a ball of nerves. He just wished this day was over so they could relax for a few of days before leaving Castine.

Edith felt sorry for Mason, as she had never seen him so distressed. "Here, let me do that. We'll never get out of here if you men don't get a move on. Goodness, one would think you're going before the judge for your own sentencing. Sherry? Where are you? Come on, let's go!"

Caleb was also a bit distressed at seeing Mason in such a state. "Mason, you can have a piece of my hard candy, okay? Don't worry." Mason ruffled Caleb's curls and smiled. "I won't, little brother."

Everyone gathered at the wagon and Cullen and Mason helped the women get situated before they left for town. As Honor pulled the wagon away from the house, Cullen began whistling a funeral dirge which really set Mason off. "Sure, make fun of me, why don't you? It's not funny, dammit! Haven't you ever been nervous before?"

"Sure, I have! Plenty of times," Cullen grinned...and resumed whistling the dirge. Sherry gave his shoulder a slap and they all began laughing. Except for Mason.

As they approached their destination, Mason gulped a few times, straightened his tie, and told himself to not be such a ninny. Cullen gave him a quick hug and escorted him to his position in the church, stood beside him, and whispered, "You'll be fine, brother. It'll be over before you know it."

Mason thought he must be insane for making this decision. Why, he had no business at all taking on this responsibility and felt so unprepared for it! The pianist began playing the wedding march and Mason literally jumped at the sound. Perspiration was running down his back in what felt like a river, and he tugged at his collar, thinking he was going to choke to death. Then…

Then he saw her. Dressed in white satin and wearing a beatific smile, her arm entwined with that of her father's who looked like he could chew nails. *Oh Lord . . .*

As the two marched down the isle, his heart slowed, he stopped perspiring, and suddenly felt like the luckiest man in the world. How could he have been so nervous? God had seen fit to guide him straight to this vision of loveliness, and he treasured her beyond measure. She was his queen, his soul mate, his helpmate, and companion, forever.

When Mr. Stewart finally gave her away, Mason took her hand as they turned to listen as the pastor pronounced the joyous but solemn meaning of marriage, and when he was through, asked them to share their vows. Mason placed the gold band on Beth's finger and the pastor proclaimed them man and wife. Cullen slapped him on the back in brotherly fashion and followed the bride and groom down the isle and out of the church.

"There, that wasn't so bad, was it?" asked Cullen

"Not at all. I can't believe she's actually mine!"

Beth was radiant as they made their way to the fellowship hall for the reception. Mason couldn't take his eyes off of her. Yes, he was a lucky man, all right. And he would be thankful for her for the rest of his life.

The Stewarts had prepared a fine reception for them. The Women's Club had prepared a veritable feast and the guests were having a grand old time. There was music and dancing and children running everywhere. There was delicious wine punch aplenty. It was quite a celebration…until Mr. Stewart pulled Mason away from the crowd.

If Mason wasn't missing his mark, the man was going to give him some dire warnings about how to treat his daughter, such as killing Mason if he ever hurt her.

"Son, I trust you to take good care of my daughter. You make sure she writes home at least twice a month, will you? Her mother is going to miss her sorely. Well, I will too, of course." Clearing his throat, Mr. Stewart reached into his pocket and withdrew a white envelope which he then placed in Mason's inside coat pocket. "This is just a little wedding present. I hope you use it wisely." Then he tentatively patted Mason's back and left him standing there. Mason had to admit it would be nice to get away from Mr. Stewart. The man was downright intimidating.

The guests were truly enjoying the occasion, knowing it would be the last bit of time they would share with the Newcomb family. Their leave-taking would be long and drawn out because of it, and Mason breathed a sigh of relief when it was finally time for he and Beth to leave for the hotel on Main Street. It was where they would spend their honeymoon, such as it was. At least they would have two days in which to get used to being married and also to get to know each other better. It had been a fast courtship but time had been of the essence if he was going to make her his bride. He wondered if she was nervous about leaving Castine, which had been her home since birth.

Alone in their hotel room, Mason asked, "Beth, do you really feel all right about leaving Castine?"

Beth laughed, "Are you joking? I've hated this blasted cold weather my whole life! Besides, I want to be wherever you are, darling." Then she raised her arms in welcome and Mason stepped into her embrace. "We only have two days, Mr. Newcomb. Let's make the most of it." Mason smiled and replied, "You bet, Mrs. Newcomb. Let's do."

Chapter Twenty-Seven

It was surprising just how little time it took to pack a lifetime of possessions. Sherry was amazed by how efficient the family was in deciding what to take and what to either sell or dispose of.

Cullen had rented a boxcar in which to pack everything, the boxcar being held at the station while it was being loaded. They had only one day to accomplish the herculean task and when Tellie had spread word of their dilemma, neighboring men showed up in wagons to help get it all moved in time.

When the last wagon pulled away from the house, Sherry stayed behind to say goodbye.

"Goodbye, Jacob. I hope you won't hold this against me, selling your family home, and all. But Mr. Stewart bought the place and you and the Stewart family have been friends a very long time. Maybe even for generations. Please be happy for me and the family. I'm afraid the trawling life just wasn't for us. If you remember, you never cared much for it, either. So, we're off to begin a new adventure, and I hope it's with your blessings."

As she turned to walk to town, Stern ran barking from around the barn and startled the wits out of her. "Oh, my goodness, Stern! What if we had left you here? C'mon boy, walk with me toward our new future."

***

"All aboard! Train leaves in ten minutes. All aboard!" the conductor yelled as people hustled to board the smoke belching monster. None of the Newcombs had ever ridden on a train, and Cullen was delighted to accompany them on their maiden journey. It seemed to be a treat for them but he doubted they would feel that way when the journey was all said and done. Train rides could be boring and terribly uncomfortable.

Cullen had warned them of the horrendous food served at watering stations, so Edith had done her best to pack enough food for the trip. Hopefully, it would keep. She brought fresh fruit to snack on, cheese sandwiches, and enough oatmeal cookies to keep everyone's sweet tooth satisfied. She brought two gallon jugs of water to drink and those, together with the food stuffs, had to be kept beneath their seats. Stern would be passed around the group during the trip, each taking turns holding the little fella.

Cullen would do his best to keep them entertained so the trip wouldn't disappoint them too badly. To that end, after everyone was settled and calm, he began telling them in detail about his land, the weather, Southern people and their food, and anything he could expound upon to keep their minds focused on their goals and away from the hard seats on which they were sitting.

"I'm not going to fool you, Virginians may think you're carpetbaggers at first until they find out you're my kin. Just smile and nod in greeting and keep going. It will only take a short while before you're accepted and then you'll become a downright curiosity, especially because of your northern accent. I know, I know, you don't have the strong New England accent, but to a Southerner, it may as well be.

"Know that when a Southerner says, "Well, bless your heart," they're trying to soften the blow of a coming insult. If I was to say, 'I like my tea unsweetened tea, please,' a Smight say, 'Well, bless your heart, ya'll aren't from around heah, are ya?' because sweet tea is the state beverage, I believe.

"Another saying is, 'I'll pray for you.' It means they feel you've either said or done something stupid. You'll catch on, I promise. I bet you even pick up the accent before long."

His family just stared at him as if in deep thought, wondering if he was serious. "What? What's the matter?"

Mason scratched his head and offered, "Oh, nothing. We're just wondering if we might not belong in a zoo, or something. I thought Southern people were hospitable."

"Oh, they are, Mason. They are. They just don't tolerate ignorance and stupidity very well and will call you on it, especially if they feel you're looking down on them. Trust me, you'll get used to their manners and mannerisms. The war was terribly cruel to them and they have long memories, so please be kind.

"Northerners came down in droves to buy land and plantations for back taxes and you can't blame the people for resenting it. They truly are good people, and they don't mind showing their affection by placing a hand on your shoulder or arm, or even giving you a hug."

Continuing on to another subject that might be less troublesome, he began telling the ladies about the food and how much pride women took in the preparation and enjoyment of same. "If I remember correctly, the women are quite competitive when it comes to who is the best cook in the county. There are baking contests, cooking contests, and prizes given for the distinction of being the best at what they love doing. Just compliment a Southern woman on her cooking and she'll love you for life.

"Edith and Beth, I'm sure you'll give them a run for their money. I think you'll enjoy it." Sherry looked quite piqued by that last comment. "Oh, and Sherry, maybe now you'll have time to learn how to cook. I'm looking forward to it."

Sherry was having none of that. "Oh, I'm sure ye ahrr," she replied in her best Irish accent. "Mebee I can learn ta milk cows and win contests doin' that, yeah? I bet dem blue ribbons are a sight ta see." Everyone tried to stifle their laughs as it appeared Sherry was truly offended, but they finally succumbed and laughed until their sides hurt. Cullen had gone a bit overboard in his praise of the girls, giving none to Sherry.

"Aww, I'm sorry, Sherry. I didn't mean anything by it. You should be proud that the reason you don't know how to cook is that you were too busy working your fingers to the bone helping to support the family. It's not likely you'll ever see a Southern gal sailing a trawler. You and Mason worked like the devil to keep money coming in while Edith kept you all nourished and comfortable. I'm so very proud of all of you."

That seemed to smooth Sherry's ruffled feathers a bit and she settled back down to listen to the rest of his descriptions of their new home.

"Like I've said before, the weather is temperate and we generally enjoy milder winters than in New England. Planting is done earlier and we usually have enough rain to keep the crops green and growing. Mason, I thought maybe we'd plant a garden big enough to put food by for the winter months, and then use about seventy-five acres to grow hay. What hay we don't use, we'll sell. We still have time to plant along with rebuilding what needs to be fixed.

"I don't know how many cattle are left on the property, but we'll buy more and let them graze on the rest of the land.

"Ladies, there are enough fruit and nut trees near the farmhouse to also put up for the year. There's pecans and walnuts, pear, plum and apple trees, and I think even a fig tree if it hasn't died.

"Now I'm going to ask you all to have some vision when you first see the farmhouse. It's in bad shape, as I told you before. I don't know if it's even worth fixing. Perhaps we'll just have to tear it down and start over. We'll see. But the land? Oh, the land is something to behold. Just wait until you see it. We can always build a new house, but God gave us the land and by His grace it will stay as it's always been; fertile and lasting.

"So, if you all agree, I would like to live in the barn first so if we need to tear the house down, we'll have shelter during the construction. It'll be rough for a few weeks but we'll survive. It's going to be hard work so I hope you are all up for it."

Everyone was quiet as they each contemplated the meaning of Cullen's words. Mason was looking forward to it. He was excited by the fact he would be building his own home in which to share life with his new bride.

Edith was wondering how she would keep all of them fed while the building, refurbishing, and planting were taking place. Perhaps Beth would help in that regard.

Sherry wasn't worried one bit. As long as Cullen was by her side, she didn't care how long it would all take. It was enough for her to just be with him. He had become her rock, her protector, and she would stand by him in all his endeavors.

The train rolled along, *clickity clack, clickity clack,* as it ate up the miles away from Castine. The temperature was changing and they relished the warmth and evidence of spring as wild grass was already turning green, and Forsythia, already budding.

Edith's cache of food had dwindled, but not the complaints about eating the same thing day in and day out. It seemed unanimous that if they never saw another cheese sandwich, it would be too soon. Fortunately, there were enough towns around water stops where they could buy a quick meal before the train once again chugged toward their destination.

Cullen and Mason took turns checking on the horses in the boxcar to make sure they were fed and watered between stops. They had left a pitchfork lying next to the boxcar door for mucking the corner Honor, Daisy, and Sadie occupied, laid down fresh hay, and rechecked the ropes that tied furniture and belongings away from them.

Cullen gave Honor as much attention as he could during those stops and made sure he brought enough peppermint sticks for both he and Daisy. Lord, would this trip ever end?

Chapter Twenty-Eight

"Last stop Alexandria! Ten minutes! Alexandria!" the conductor said in a booming voice, notifying passengers that it was the end of the line.

As uncomfortable as the ride had been, Cullen dreaded the trip home from Alexandria. He had made arrangements by telegram for wagons and oxen to pull the family and their belongings on the last leg of the trip and it was going to be arduous, to say the least.

There were only two men and four wagons. Sherry and Edith were going to have to learn how to drive the oxen in two of the wagons. He had no doubt that they would be up to the task as they were hard working women who rarely complained.

It was decided that Beth would be the cook during their journey and would also look after Caleb. Stern would be their mascot.

After their possessions had been moved from the boxcar to the wagons, Cullen took them all out for a big breakfast before they began the long trek home.

"Mmm, these buttermilk pancakes are delicious!" Mason said with a full mouth. "Can I order some more?" Cullen laughed and said, "Of course, you can!" I want everyone to enjoy this meal. Order whatever else you like. We'll need our strength for the days ahead."

Sherry eyed the square pieces of what looked like fried meat on Cullen's plate and asked, "What the devil is that?" Cullen answered, "Want a bite? It's called scrapple. It's quite tasty." He poured some maple syrup on a bite and held it out for Sherry's consideration. "It's different, I'll give you that, but I don't think I could abide it without the syrup."

Edith smiled at the face Sherry made and then commented on the biscuits. "So, this is what a biscuit really tastes like. Beth, take note. Cullen loves his biscuits."

It was a wonderful family meal with lots of chatter and laughter. Cullen sat back in his chair for a few moments just watching and listening, and said a silent prayer of thanks. He loved these people with all his heart.

After breakfast, Cullen took Mason to a gunsmith's shop and they spent a good hour deciding what was best suited for Mason's ability to help protect the family. Cullen purchased another two rifles, a set of pistols and holster for Mason, and plenty of ammunition for all of them. He was hoping to take Mason hunting several evenings to help his aim and to provide meat for their meals. Little did Mason know how dashing and masculine Beth would find the pistols strapped to Mason's thighs.

"Why are you staring at me like that, Beth?" Mason, not having been married that long or having much opportunity for privacy with his wife, wasn't able to interpret the "look."

Smiling seductively, she replied, "I don't know what you're talking about, Mason Newcomb." Then she winked at him and sashayed away. Mason blushed ten shades of red and tried to hide his grin. Then he puffed up his chest and grasped his pistols where they were tucked into their holster, as if he were protector of the universe.

"Ladies, you better do some shopping for anything you feel you might need on the trip. Alexandria will have more of a selection than most towns we'll pass along the way. Make sure your bonnets are big enough to block the sun from your faces. Maybe a straw hat would be cooler and block more sunshine. Also, it might be a good idea to buy several pairs of gloves. They don't last long while driving a team and wagon." Cullen knew there would be something they forgot and hoped that Edith had checked her list several times to make sure they had what would be needed. In fact, Edith had been adding items to her list as they rode the train south, and she and Beth shopped for the new items, which included a book of Southern recipes. Beth was determined to make the perfect biscuit for Cullen, and buttermilk pancakes since Mason was so crazy for them.

After much consideration, Cullen thought it best to start the trip that very afternoon, even though some might have thought it prudent to spend an additional night in Alexandria, and get an early start on the morrow. The girls might as well get used to things now as later. At least the wagons were covered and offered some respite from the sun and rain. Cullen would sell two of the wagons when they arrived in McKenney, and perhaps he would keep the oxen.

Honor was tied behind Cullen's wagon and he knew the horse wanted desperately to run in the wide open spaces through which they traveled, so he made a habit of stopping for the day during late afternoon so he could jump on his old friend's back and go ripping through the fields around their campsite. Horse and rider were exultant as they flew like the wind across the land. Cullen felt such peace during those rides and was once again glad that Honor was such a young horse. They had a lot of work to do together and Cullen would make sure his friend was fit as a fiddle while doing it.

Mason needed a horse of his own as Daisy would surely be ready to put out to pasture after their trip. She was old but she was a fine lady, and deserved to spend the rest of her days being pampered. Mason was taller than Cullen and was gaining weight and muscle now that he was eating more than what they had previously been able to afford. Cullen hoped Mason would choose a Percheron or other draft horse if they could find one. Mason's size could handle one and it would serve well as a work horse.

***

The days were long and sometimes trying. Sherry and Edith were stiff and sore after driving all day and couldn't wait to make camp at night.

Beth had taken to riding with Edith, Caleb switching wagons each day so he could spend time with everyone. Beth figured Edith was closer to her in age and they would have more to talk about. Of course, the nights belonged to Mason.

Edith had contemplated asking Beth some questions but never quite got up the nerve to do so, until one day she just blurted out, "Beth, what's it like? What is it like to be married?"

Beth smiled and wondered just what it was her sister-in-law wanted to know. "Well, it's like finding your other half. It makes me feel complete, you know? I never imagined it would be so comforting. What is it exactly that you want to know, Edith?"

Edith pulled the front of her hat lower, trying to hide her blush. "Um, I'm glad you're happy, Beth. I truly am. I didn't mean to get so personal with you. And, I…well…perhaps I wanted, you know, to find out how much, er…is it painful?

Beth put her arm around Edith's shoulder and began a tutorial of sorts.

"Beth, it hurts for only a few seconds, trust me. Then it begins to feel very good indeed. Would you like for me to explain what happens? Has anyone had the 'birds and bees' discussion with you yet?"

"Goodness, no! I mean, I never asked Sherry about it. But it would be nice to be prepared, wouldn't it? I wouldn't want to disappoint my husband on our first night. I want to please him. I was hoping you might teach me a few things."

"I'm no expert, Edith. I've only been married a short while and I know there is more to learn. I'm hoping that Mason and I will learn together. But I can explain what I know so far. Would that be all right?"

So began the conversation that would cement the girls' relationship forever. They giggled and gasped, and wondered aloud about things they knew and had yet to learn. Mason could hear them giggling and carrying on, and thought surely they must be talking about recipes or sewing and such. Wouldn't he have been surprised?

One day Cullen pulled his wagon beside Mason's so they might chat for a while. When he pulled close enough to see Mason's face, he saw that the young man was wearing a scowl. "What's the matter, Mason?"

"Nothing. I'm just practicing looking mean and nasty, hoping to scare away anyone who might think to mess with us. I sure would hate to have to shoot someone."

"Well, it's not pleasant, I can tell you that. I've never taken another man's life unless I was defending myself, and the lives I've taken still weigh heavy on my mind and heart. Given the chance, I'll always try to bluff my way out of a sticky situation rather than use guns.

"When a man sees another man wearing dual pistols, he generally thinks twice before starting trouble. It usually means the other man is a gunslinger, and I have no problem having men think that of me. Go ahead and keep practicing the looks, Mason. I do believe you almost have them down pat." Then he laughed and winked at his brother-in-law. Little did either of them know their skills would be put to the test sooner than either would have liked.

Chapter Twenty-Nine

They had traveled for four days without seeing hardly a soul. The couple of riders they did see just tipped their hats and kept riding. On the fifth day their luck turned.

Cullen noticed lush green grass and a willow tree coming up on their left and felt sure there was water nearby. It would be a perfect place to stop for the night. Everyone got down from their wagons, stretched, and began the process of cooking the evening meal by gathering wood, getting supplies from Edith's wagon, and making their campsite comfortable.

Cullen decided to go hunting for some fresh game and told Mason to stay behind to watch after the family. He hadn't been gone a half hour before a group of four scraggly looking men rode into their camp, two of whom had been union soldiers evidenced by the remnants of their blue uniforms.

"What can we do for you, gentlemen?" Mason asked with a smile on his face, feeling instant dread.

"We were just riding up the trail and heard some ladies laughing. Thought we'd stop and see what was so funny, eh Jasper?" One of the other men responded with a near toothless grin, and one by one they dismounted and walked into camp.

Mason's heart pounded as he replaced his smile with one of the sneers he had practiced earlier in the day. "You know women, always giggling and cackling about something. No need for you to stay. I think it would be best if you mounted up and moved along."

The four men laughed like hell at Mason, and proceeded to give the women a good once over. "Hoo wee! Ain't you a beaut?" Beth backed away from the man but he just kept coming. "Aw, now don't be unfriendly. We just want to have some fun. It's been a long boring ride and we need to have some fun, know what I mean?"

Another of the men ogled Sherry, but she stood stock still, just waiting for him to make a move. "This one is spunky, she is. I like a woman with spunk. I'll take her. Come on, pretty lady, let's have us some fun." That left Edith, and she was shaking like a leaf. "You two will have to share the skinny one. Just take turns. You can flip for who goes first."

Mason didn't know where to begin but he knew he had to protect the women. "Look here, this has gone on long enough. Mount up and ride or I'll shoot every last one of you." Again they laughed at Mason, which infuriated him beyond measure. Just as he would continue demanding they leave, one of them came up from behind and used his pistol butt to crack Mason in the head. He went down in a heap and Beth screamed, running to his side, cradling his head and trying to wake him. This, of course, was not in the strangers' plans and they began dragging the women off into the woods to "have their fun."

Edith and Beth started screaming and continued screaming in hopes Cullen would hear them and come running. They both struggled, clawed and bit, and screamed. Sherry tried to be rational with her tormentor. "We're all northern women. Why would you do such a thing to us? We supported you during the war. We clothed and fed you. Why?"

"Sweetie, I don't care where you come from. You could be from China for all we care. You got what we need right between your legs and that's all that matters." Sherry was incensed and took the opportunity to knee the man in the groin which doubled him over in pain. "You bitch! I'll kill you for that!"

Sherry searched for the rifles and found one set up against the wooden box that held pots and pans. She shot it into the air three times in rapid succession, hoping to scare the men before they could do their damage, and hoping to signal Cullen, wherever he was.

Mason was beginning to wake up and tried to stand in an effort to draw his pistols but fell back to the ground holding his head, blinking rapidly as if he were having trouble with his vision. Sherry was able to grab one of his pistols and turned just as her attacker began growling and made a lunge for her. She never hesitated for a moment and shot him twice; once in the shoulder and when the pistol kicked and came back down, once in the thigh. The man looked shocked and managed to say, "You shot me, you little bitch!" before falling to the ground. One down, three to go.

"SHERRY? SHERRY!!!" Cullen rode hard into camp and immediately saw his wife with a pistol in her hand. He could hear screams coming from the bushes and ran like a man on fire toward the sound. After hearing Sherry's shots and the man's exclamation of shock at having been shot, the men pursuing their pleasure with Beth and Edith began scrambling to see what had happened.

Cullen shot both men in the shoulder so as not to kill them and quickly took their guns and threw them as far into the bushes as possible. "Get up you dirty curs. Mount up and get the hell out of here. Take your buddy over there with you, and if you ever come near me or my family again, it won't be your shoulders I shoot…it'll be right through your black hearts. Now, go on, you filthy bastards. Move it, NOW!" The savage Yankees didn't need to be told twice.

Had they a watch, from beginning to end, they would have seen that the entire incident lasted a mere four minutes. However, to the women, it felt like an eternity.

Mason was still on the ground, apparently unconscious, and Beth worried over him like a mother hen. "Cullen, he's unconscious. What will we do?" she cried. "He won't die, will he?"

Cullen stooped to the ground and put his arm around her, knowing she was close to being scared out of her mind. "Beth, he's all right. Just a knock on the head, that's all. He'll come around in a bit." But Cullen wasn't so sure. He lifted Mason's head and searched for injuries and found a pretty good sized goose egg where he'd been hit. "Let's try to get him in the wagon so he can be more comfortable. Afterward, I'm going to mount Honor and have a look around. I want to make sure those men are long gone."

Each one of them took an arm or leg and tried to lift Mason upright. It was a valiant effort but they would never be able to lift Mason into the wagon. He'd have to climb up under his own volition.

Sherry and Edith started preparing the evening meal, Sherry keeping Caleb very close for protection. Fortunately, Caleb had been napping in her wagon when the men had ridden into camp, and Sherry had not wanted to wake him. When the guns went off, Caleb had screamed for her. "Ma? MA?" he screamed over and over again.

Beth walked to the creek behind their camp and got water with which to bathe Mason's wound. It was nice and cold and would be comforting, and hopefully help stop the bleeding. *"Dearest Father, please heal Mason's wound. We only just got married, Father. Please don't take him from me so soon. We have so many plans. We want children. I have faith that you will come to our aid. I'm counting on you."*

By the time she returned to camp, Mason was moaning and thrashing about, and trying to sit up. "Bethy? Sweetie, where are you?" Beth ran to him wearing a huge smile. "Here I am, Mr. Newcomb. I'm right behind you." Mason reached for her and she fell to her knees in front of him. "You're awake. How do you feel, Lovie?" Not wanting to make a huge fuss, she tried to play it down so not to worry him.

"I've got one heck of a headache. What happened? I think I kind of remember." He was silent for a few minutes while Beth cleaned his wound and then all of a sudden he remembered every single thing that happened before he was knocked out.

"Beth? Did they hurt you? If they hurt you I'll ride through the gates of Hell to make them pay. What did they do to you?" Beth, Sherry and Edith all looked at one another and finally Sherry nodded, telling Beth with her expression that it would be best if he knew the answers to all of his questions. Mason now suffered a pain worse than his injury. He had failed them. As Beth would put the cool cloth to his head once again, Mason shoved her hand aside and told her to get away.

"Leave me alone now. Go help with the meal. I'll be all right." The rage inside him was almost too much for Mason to bear. He knew he must push it aside so he could think clearly and rationally, but he wanted to do those strangers egregious harm. In his mind, he could see himself beating each of them to a bloody pulp, but even those images didn't come close to what he wanted to inflict upon them. These were new feelings to Mason. He was normally an even keeled man with a heart full of kindness. Someone would have to convince him he was still that man because at the moment, Mason was sure that part of him was gone, replaced with a red hot burning for revenge.

Cullen rode back into camp wearing a smile for the ladies. He hated like hell they had suffered such a frightening incident and he wanted to help them get over it. "They're long gone. I followed their tracks and could tell they were high-tailing it as fast as their horses could run. We won't see them again."

He walked over to Sherry and hugged her close. Then he kissed her sweetly as if to say how sorry he was and that she had no more to fear. Then he walked over to Beth and held her, too. Edith was diligently working on their meal and acted as if nothing had happened. Cullen would take her for a little walk that evening and comfort her in private. She was so stoic and stalwart. He wouldn't allow her to martyr her feelings for the sake of the family.

Sherry and Beth began the clean-up after they finished eating, and Cullen pulled Edith to the side and suggested a walk down to the creek. At first she hesitated, looking toward the other women and knowing she should be helping. "It's all right, Edith. I want to talk with you for a few minutes. Is that okay with you?" He could see by the last light of evening there were tears welling up in her sweet eyes.

"Edith, I know you had to be terrified by what happened today. There is no sense in hiding how you feel. You're human just like the rest of us and you need to let us know how you're feeling about it." Then he took her into his arms and held her tight, and it was only then Edith broke down and cried. Her body shook, her breathing was deep and rapid, and she started keening as if her heart would break.

Cullen remained with her until her tears were spent and her breathing returned to normal. "Cullen, I feel so out of place now. I feel like a fifth wheel. I feel like my only value is to cook for the family. I didn't know what to do when those men rode into camp. And they called me 'the skinny one!' Even *they* didn't want me! Will it always be this way for me? Will I ever find a place of my own…a man of my own? Why am I so different? I don't want to feel like a house maid for the rest of my life!"

Cullen had missed the verbal exchange about which she spoke, but he could well imagine what she felt like when it was all over. Her mind must have turned cartwheels in an effort to make sense of it all, and what she should have been afraid of she forgot about because a man had called her "skinny."

"Edith, look at me. You know I love you and I would do anything in the world for you, which includes telling you the God's honest truth when it's needed. Right now I need for you to hear the truth, okay?" Edith nodded. "All right, let's begin.

"You are one of the most beautiful women I've ever met. Yes, you are thin, but you're only almost eighteen. You'll fill out soon, very soon. You have more love in your heart than a hundred women and it shows in everything about you. The way you love and care for all of us. How you're so gentle and kind to everyone. You can't expect to be only seventeen and think you're a full grown woman. It will take a while and before you know it, you'll steal a young man's heart. He'll fall madly in love with you because he sees very clearly everything I'm talking about. He'll want you for his mate…he'll want you to have his children…and he'll absolutely, without any doubt, love your biscuits!" Edith laughed at that and finally stopped crying. "Don't be so eager to grow up, little sister. I know you've taken on the weight of being an adult for several years. Promise me you'll relax and let us repay your kindness and diligence from years past."

They walked back to camp, arm in arm, looking to one and all as if they hadn't a care in the world. But Sherry knew the magic that had just happened between the two and her heart fairly burst with love and pride. Edith was one heck of a young woman, and she was sure Cullen had just convinced her stepdaughter of that very fact.

Chapter Thirty

Finally, they were on the last leg of the trip. "I'd say two or three more days at most," Cullen assured them.

The trip, after what they would forever call "the incident," was uneventful and it gave them time to readjust their thinking back to their goals. The only person physically injured was Mason, and he was slowly overcoming the headaches caused by the goose egg on his head.

Cullen made sure to ride along side of Mason's wagon more often than not in an effort to talk some sense into him. He was almost ready to tell Mason to grow the heck up and quit whining like a boy. If Mason didn't know the kind of man he was by now, he'd probably never know. Mason and Edith…forced to act like adults before they were ready after their father died. Now Mason was married and it was time to get a hold of himself and take life's knocks with aplomb, knowing tomorrow is another day.

"Mason, I know you've felt like a man since your father died. I understand that, but it takes more than a few years to make a man into what he wants to be. You've got plenty of time to grow into the image you have of what that is. I've told you before and I'll tell you again, I'll be here with you every step of the way. So buck the hell up and quit this melancholy. It isn't very attractive. If you won't do it for the rest of us, do it for Beth. If you don't, I wouldn't be a bit surprised if she caught the next train back to Castine."

It wasn't two seconds before that last statement registered in Mason's mind. He then put himself in Beth's shoes and thought about what she was seeing in him lately. It wasn't a pretty sight, for sure. "Cullen, would you have Edith pull up along side my wagon?"

"Sure," Cullen replied, and slowed his wagon enough for Edith's wagon to catch up to him.
"Edith, pull up alongside Mason for a while, okay? I think he'd like to talk to Beth."

Then he slowed down again and let her pull around Mason's wagon. He could see the two wagons pulling close to each other at which time Mason's arm sprang out toward Beth, and she instantly jumped into his embrace. When Edith slowed down to get in line behind Mason, Cullen pulled up beside her and grinned.

"What's that look for, Cullen?" Cullen just grinned again.

"Nothin'. Can't a man smile at his sister?"

"Of course, Cullen. You can smile all you want but you have to tell me what you're smiling about."

"I was just wondering about some of the kids who lived in my county. Just wondering if the ones who might be your age now might like to meet a gorgeous young woman. Maybe start courtin' her, ya know?"

"Go on with you, Cullen Macklin. You're so full of manure, your eyes are turning brown, if you catch my meaning. Go on. I'm fine."

Cullen just blew her a kiss and grinned.

After a couple of minutes, Cullen dropped back to Sherry's wagon and rode beside her for a bit. He hated for her to be last in line for any length of time and would take that position for the rest of the afternoon. But first he wanted to just look at his wife. Damn, she was everything a man could ever want. Beautiful, competent, hard working, and steady in temperament.

"Hey there, sugah, what's your name? You sure are purdy. Want to make some time with me?"

"I'm sorry, suh, but I'm married, and if my husband catches y'all talking to me in this mannah, he will skin y'all alive."

"That right? What's he got that I don't?" This was a fun way to pass time and Cullen was going to make the most of it.

"Well, he's the most handsome man I evah met. Y'all know the type; smooth talkah, hard workah, and treats me reeeal fine at night, if ya catch ma meanin'. He's generous to a fault and buys me pretty things. He makes me feel like no othah man could evah do. So you go on and skedaddle. If he catches you, your tail is gonna be on fiah."

Cullen could hardly contain his laughter until she finished. It was part Irish accent and part Southern, sort of.

"Well, I declayuh, maybe I'll stick around and meet this paragon of virtues. But I do hate competition, don't you?"

"You ah no competition, suh. There is no…dammit, Cullen! Do you realize how long it's been since we made love? When can we get away for some time alone?"

"I'm two steps ahead of you, love. The first night after we arrive, I'm taking you on Honor for a tour of the place. Never worry, I have a plan." With that he grinned and slowed the wagon to pull in behind her, hearing her shriek, "You'd better keep that promise, Cullen Macklin! It won't go well for you if you don't!"

***

It was blistering hot and Cullen explained that sometimes in spring, Virginia could experience a few hot and humid days before the season actually arrived.

Caleb was whining and complaining, Edith looked like a limp dish rag, Beth tried her best to overcome the humidity, and Sherry looked stoic, per usual. The men just sucked it up and kept driving their wagons, mopping the perspiration off their faces, and pretending they weren't affected by it all.

"Don't worry, this won't last long. Weather like this usually precedes a nice thunderstorm that will cool things down. The first place I see that might give us some relief, I'll call out for us to stop for the day. We can add one more day to our travels."

Everyone groaned and kept driving. They all thought to arrive in McKenney the next day.

"Oh, come on now! We're almost there and I told all of you that this would be a difficult trip. Do you want to keep driving or do you want some relief from this heat?"

Everyone was silent while trying to decide what they wanted to do.

Sherry spoke first. "I say we stop about an hour before sundown. Then we eat, sleep, and start early to get to McKenney. What do you say?"

More groans and whining. But they all agreed and kept driving. Cullen started singing, *loudly*, and made them laugh.

"Oh, there once was a girl named Colleen,
On her hair there was such a bright sheen,
She had freckles on her little nose,
And little teeny tiny toes . . ."

"Ach, that is horrible, Cullen! At least sing something where we can all join in!"
"All right, all right! Gosh, you'd think I committed a crime or something!"
Sherry laughed and replied, "You did commit a crime…against our ears, boyo!"

Then she started singing an Irish ballad, "The Girl I Left Behind," and brought the girls to tears.

I'm lonesome since I crossed the hill,
And over the moorland sedgy,
Such heavy thoughts my heart do fill,
Since parting from my Sally.

I seek no more the fine and gay,
For each just does remind me
How sweet the hours I passed away,
With the girl I left behind me . . .

"There now, what are all the tears about? I can hear ya sniffin' all the way back here, I can."

Cullen was silent, still hearing her clear sweet voice. "Sherry, I had no idea you could sing like that. Why have you kept it from us?"

"Ulright, Boyo, I'll sing fer ya whenever ye want, I will. Now leave me be while ye look yonder at that black sky. I do believe one of those lovely thunderstorms is about to roll in."

And so it did. The thunder and lightening were miles away but they at least they got some cool rain. Actually, it was a bit of a deluge, but it was welcome. Even the oxen looked as though they appreciated the respite from the heat.

Honor got frisky and danced behind Cullen's wagon for a bit. Cullen laughed and brought his face up to the rain. "Dern, this sure feels good!"

As Cullen had predicted, the air turned cooler after the rain. Preparing the evening meal was a bit soggy, but was tasty as usual. Beth didn't lie when she said she was a good cook. Mason considered himself extremely fortunate in that regard.

When the plates and utensils were washed and put away for the night, they didn't linger around the fire as usual. They were tired and, more than that, they were excited to be so near their destination.

"Let's not tarry over breakfast tomorrow. I want to get an early start and hopefully reach McKenney by late afternoon," Cullen announced. He would get no argument there. They would be ready to roll by dawn.

***

The mood was bright and lively the next morning as they loaded up and made their way home. McKenney, for all intents and purposes, was right around the bend, and they were joyful to be so close.

"There it is!" Cullen shouted. "We're here! Yahoo!"

McKenney was within sight now and they pushed the oxen a bit faster, not wanting to waste another minute before arriving.

They were quite the spectacle as they drove into town and people came out of establishments to see what the all the ruckus was about. Sherry smiled and waved to the women in front of the mercantile, and they waved back, wearing bright smiles of welcome.

The first thing Cullen wanted to do was check in with the sheriff to see if anything had happened on the old place since they last communicated. Mason moved to follow him into the sheriff's office but Cullen stopped him.

"Please stay with the women, okay? I won't be but a minute." Mason nodded and went back to stand by their wagons, keeping guard.

"Hey sheriff, we finally made it!"

"And you look no worse for the wear, Macklin."

"I'm checking in with you to see if anything has happened since we last spoke."

"Well, I hate to be the bearer of bad news, but you've got some squatters at your place. I done rode out there and told them to leave, and they made like they were going to, but when I checked again within the next few days, they were back. If you have any trouble getting rid of them, let me know and we'll take care of it together. Other than that, everything is fine.

"I've been watching your cattle, and there's a few left. Someone's been feedin' and waterin'em. Don't know who, though. Anyway, welcome home. It's good to see you again."

"Thanks sheriff, and thank you so much for responding to my telegrams and watching over the place. I owe you for that." They shook hands and Cullen left feeling lighter than he had in years.

***

When Cullen walked out of the sheriff's office, everyone turned to him as if to ask, what next? He smiled and said, "I guess the first order of business is to go to the grocer and mercantile and get whatever we need. I don't know when the next trip to town will be so you better stock up." That got Sherry, Edith and Beth moving. It's all they needed to hear.

"Mason, let's go to the lumber yard and get an idea of the cost of materials we'll need. No tellin' how long the girls will be. Actually, how about a beer?" Mason grinned and thought that was a fine idea.

As they walked down the boardwalk, a woman coming the other way saw them and stopped dead in front of Cullen. "My lands, you're back! Charlie Macklin! Thought I'd never see the day."

"Mrs. Garver? Well, I'll be!" Cullen replied, and swung the woman up in a hug and twirled her in circles before putting her back down.

"Yes, I'm back and I'm here to stay. I got married and brought the entire family with me. You'll meet them soon enough. Right now the women are shopping for supplies before we ride out to the old place. I'll see you soon, though. Don't doubt it. You still makin' that wonderful peach pie? Still getting the prize every year for it?"

"What do you think, Charles Maklin? A'course I am! I bet your mouth is just watering for some, too." They embraced once again before parting and Cullen thought it was a good beginning.

"I'm *not* calling you Charlie. I told you that," Mason said under his breath.

"I have a plan for that. I just need Sherry to go along with it."

Soon they were stepping up to the bar of a saloon, ordering two beers, and toasting their arrival. "I'll say it, Cullen. I thought we'd never get here. I'm so glad the trip is over. Now all I have to do is find a place for me and Beth to have some privacy and I'll be good. How about you? It's been a good while for us both."

Cullen smiled and thought it was a manly thing for Mason to say. "Yep, it's been too long, that's for sure." He ordered them another round figuring it was as good a way to wait for the girls as any. "When we come back into town for lumber and such, we'll have Honor re-shoed and then try and find a horse for you. Got any idea of what breed you'd like?" Mason mulled over the question and decided, "I want a horse just like Honor. He fits me just fine and we can use both of them for work horses." Cullen smiled, thinking Mason just made a good practical choice, one that he had already thought of himself.

Chapter Thirty-One

Although he hated to admit it, Cullen was a mite nervous about seeing his old home. It would be embarrassing, yes, but it was more than that. How would they all feel about the place? Would they wonder whether they had made a mistake? Lots of feelings and worries were whirling around in his mind and he was silent for the rest of the trip.

Before they loaded the wagons with supplies in town, Cullen had warned them about the squatters. He said they probably wouldn't be a problem, so they shouldn't worry.

When his wagon climbed the rise that would mark their final descent to the farmhouse, he stopped and just looked at it for a good while. Sherry, Mason, Beth, and Edith, climbed down from their wagons and stood beside Cullen's wagon, waiting for him to say something. When he didn't, they started asking questions.

"Is this it, Cullen? Is this our new home?" Sherry asked with excitement in her voice.

Mason chimed in with, "Those people must be the squatters. Might as well send them on their way right now."

Edith was more concerned with getting there and unpacked. There was so much work to do.

Cullen spoke up then and said, "Get back in your wagons and let's do this."

He let Sherry go first, then Mason, and then Edith. He followed behind them and hoped to high heaven they were satisfied with the choice they had made.

The closer they came to the house, the more Sherry felt the squatters looked familiar. Another fifty yards and she knew why. "Ma? Da?" Climbing down from her wagon, she ran like the wind toward the couple who were waiting with open arms. "Oh, Ma," she cried as she ran into the woman's arms. "Da!"

The three stood together, hugging and kissing. It was a glorious sight for Cullen to see. Her parents had made it with time to spare. He worried they wouldn't be able to make it in time as a surprise for Sherry.

"Colleen, dearest! What a sight fer sore eyes ye ahrr. Does me heart good to hold ye again."

"Oh, Ma, ye look beautiful, ye do. Just like the last time I saw ye. And Da! Still the strong and capable man, as always. I'm overwhelmed with joy ta see ye. How long have yea been here?"

They continued chatting until Cullen walked up to Sherry and put his arm about her waist.

"This is Cullen Macklin, he's my husband," she beamed. "Cullen, this is my Ma, Brannagh, and Da, Liam Darcy."

When she saw the rest of the family holding back, she motioned for them to come forward and introductions were made all around. Da spoke up and asked, "Oy, ye wouldn't be part of the Dublin Macklin clan, would ye?"

Brannagh picked Caleb up and held him close, tears running down her face. "Me grandboy. Never tawt I'd see the day." Liam chucked Caleb under the chin and said, "Ye look just like me son, Brandon, God rest his soul. Come here to yer grandda."

Sherry pulled Cullen away from the crowd and hugged him tight. "Ye did this fer me, ye did. Just fer me. 'Tis the greatest gift I've ever been given. I'll never forget it, ever. You made me dearest dream come true. I love you Cullen Macklin. I'll always love ye."

Then she went back to her parents and they started speaking rapidly in another language. Cullen had heard it plenty during his travels. They called it Gaelic. He could see right then he would either have to learn the language or have them agree to speak English only.

Then something caught Cullen's eye; a young man coming out of the dilapidated barn. Sherry saw it, too, and asked her ma who it might be.

"Ach, in all the excitement, I nearly forgot. You remember the Donnellys, don't ye? Well, 'tis wee Aedan, all growed up, it 'tis. Come, boyo, come meet your new family." Then Brannagh whispered to Sherry that she'd explain it all later.

Cullen rubbed his whiskery chin and thought, *"The more, the merrier, I guess."* He and Mason could sure use the help.

Edith felt sorry for Aedan. He must feel like such a stranger to this clan. She knew how it felt and was going the make a special effort to welcome him and make him feel like he belonged.

"Hello, my name is Edith, and I'm so glad to meet you," she said as she thrust out her hand for him to shake. "I'd love to hear about Ireland soon, and I was hoping you might be the one to tell me all about it."

"Hullo fair Edith, and thank ye for the welcome. I promise not ta be of any trouble and will do me fair share of the work, I will. And when time allows, I'd be happy ta tell ye about me homeland."

"Well, then, let's start unpacking the wagons; that is, if we can get everyone on task," she grinned.

☙ ☙ ☙

Cullen was anxious to see the inside of the house and was pleasantly surprised to find that Brannagh and Liam, had cleaned until things nearly shined. He looked at Liam, and asked, "Have you had any rain? Does the roof leak?" Liam smiled and with more than little pride said, "She leaked a wee bit but I fixed her up in a twinkle. Hasn't leaked since. And when ye have the time, I'd like ta talk to ye about adding on ta the house. I'm a carpenter by trade, ye see, and t'wouldn't take no time a'tall ta knock this house down and begin again. What do ye say to that, Cullen Macklin?"

Cullen was never one to look a gift horse in the mouth and exclaimed,

"Liam, you'll save my hide! Frankly, I didn't know what I was going to do when I arrived, but now here's the answer standing right in front of me! Much obliged, sir," he replied as he furiously pumped Liam's hand. Liam laughed and said, "Boyo, me daughter picked a peach, she did. You'll do just fine as a son-in-law."

Most of the boxes had been taken into the house and supper, as it was called in the south, and to which Sherry rolled her eyes, was cooking. Everyone worked together slick as a whistle, and Cullen was amazed.

When the dishes were done and everyone found bedding and a place to sleep, Cullen grabbed Sherry's hand and pulled her outside. Honor was saddled up and Sherry knew exactly what would happen; his promised tour of the land…at night…where she couldn't see anything, but that was just fine with her. She needed some loving and it didn't matter where they went, as long as it was private.

Mason yelled from the house, "No fair, Cullen!" and Cullen laughed out loud. "What's he talking about?" Sherry thought it quite strange. "Oh, just a little joke, is all."

The sky was a lovely shade of peaches and purples as they rode away from the house, and Sherry breathed deep of the air that now smelled like home. Cullen found a special spot he remembered from his childhood and helped Sherry down from Honor's back. "This is where I would come when I didn't want my father to find me. Sometimes I just couldn't take it anymore; his hatred and cruelty. But now it's going to have a new purpose. Now it's going to be our little hideaway. We have a big family and privacy is probably a thing of the past."

Before he could say another word, Sherry put her arms around him and pulled him close. "Let's try it out, shall we?" Cullen was instantly inflamed with passion. It had been so long since they were together. No matter how much he needed it to be hard and fast, he took his time and loved her like she deserved to be loved.

"I'll make sure to bring a blanket next time. Sorry about that."

"You needn't apologize for anything, love. It was wonderful."

"I want you again, already."

"Then you shall have me."

So was their first real lovemaking since they left Castine. It was soft, it was sweet, and it was definitely memorable.

***

Edith got up early to put on the coffee and start breakfast when Aedan came through the kitchen door. "Couldn't sleep?" she asked. "Nah, I always get up this early. Thought I'd gather the eggs."

Edith was surprised. "Eggs? I didn't see any chickens."

Aedan laughed, "Brannagh wasn't going to leave Ireland without her prize chickens. Wait until ye see'em."

"Sit down and I'll get you a cup of coffee. Sorry there's no cream but Sadie hasn't settled down from the trip. We milked her every day along the way to Virginia, but could only get a little bit. She'll give some after she's settled down in her new pasture."

"That's all right, I don't drink coffee. We drink tea in Ireland. Got any?"

They had about an hour to chat in the kitchen before the rest of the family woke up. Edith and Brannagh cooked breakfast and Beth served it. It was quickly eaten, the men having other things on their mind, like a trip back to town for lumber, nails and anything else they would need to build a new house. Cullen would judge by the cost of the materials about how much it would cost to build a new barn. Things felt like they would all go smoothly. How could they be otherwise? He talked with God every day, giving Him thanks for everything He provided, and he meant *everything*.

When he, Liam and Aedan walked into the lumber yard, they were met by a man who Cullen thought looked familiar. "Macklin! I heard you were back! Good to have you home. I was sorry to hear of your father's passing."

Cullen squinted, trying to place the face, and finally had to admit, "Sorry, I've plumb forgotten your name."

The man chortled, "I guess you would. Our families never did get along too well. The name's Wilson, Jake Wilson."

Cullen grinned and said, "I trust the feud is over now that pa's gone?"
Jake laughed, "Hell yes, it's over. Never made a bit of sense to me anyhow. How can I help you folks today?"

"This is my father-in-law, Liam Darcy, and our cousin Aedan Donnelly."

After Liam's and Aedan's salutations to Jake, it was obvious something was amiss. "You from Ireland?" Liam smiled and said, "You bet. Right off the boat, we are." Jake's demeanor changed instantly.

"Charlie, you married Irish?"

"My family calls me Cullen now. Seems my wife knew a 'Charlie' back in Ireland that was a hateful lout. And yes, I married a beautiful Irish woman named Colleen. Do you want my money or not? If not, I can go elsewhere with my business."

"Don't get testy, '*Cullen*.' Let's not start another feud, all right? I'm just surprised is all, knowin' how your father hated the Irish."

"My father is dead. I'm nothing like my father and please never forget that. Now, can we get on with our business?"

When their business was concluded and a delivery date settled, Cullen took them to the hardware store, and was embarrassed to find the same attitude from that merchant about the Irish.

On the way home, Cullen felt the need to explain. "I'm sorry. I should have told you that there are some people in America who don't like the Irish. I have no idea why but they're downright hated in some places." Then Cullen took a deep breath and blurted, "I'm asking that you please ignore these morons and just kill them with kindness. I know it sounds like a lot to ask but I know these people. If you act like what they say bothers you, they'll keep saying it. Is it too much to ask to turn your cheek the other way and kill them with kindness?"

Liam laughed like hell, "Well, boyo, seems like they didn't know the name Macklin is an Irish name! 'Spose they would've strung ye up if they had, huh? We knew of feelings about the Irish. We were made slaves just as your negroes were. Some called it indentured servitude, but few were ever released as somethin' always come up to keep them from paying off the indenture, ye see. Don't let it bother you none, boy. It doesn't bother us. We know who and what we are. People who hate us are just ignorant. Now let's get on to other business, like building a new house."

Before they left town they found a livestock business that sold chicks, feed, and various other livestock. Cullen bought some chicks, four piglets, and feed for both.

On the way home, Cullen spoke with Liam and Aedan as if they also owned the farm. "Let's plan our garden soon. The potatoes should have been planted by St. Patrick's Day, but we have a little bit of time before the rest is planted. The potatoes will be all right planted this late." Liam got a far away look in his eyes and Cullen was moved to ask if he was feeling all right. "Yes, I'm all right. I was just remembering the famine in Ireland. 'Twas a horrible thing, it was. Do potatoes do well in Virginia?"

On and on they talked about what had to be done in order to provide housing and food for the family. At one point, Liam leaned over and whispered in Cullen's ear, "Don't think I'm not appreciatin' what you're doing for us, but I'd like to build me and Brannagh a wee place of our own if you've got the land for it. We like our privacy, we do. Brannagh can get noisy of a night, if ye know what I mean."

Cullen laughed so hard he almost fell off the wagon seat. "Of course! I have the land, and I wouldn't want anyone to hear Brannagh in the throes, if you know what I mean."

Liam laughed, and Aedan felt left out but figured it was manly stuff they were talking about. Actually, he was more than ready to learn some 'manly stuff' himself. Maybe he would talk to Mason some time.

Chapter Thirty-Two

While the men were gone and Mason was outdoors cleaning the yard of dead tree branches and high grass, Sherry spoke to her Ma about Aedan.

"So Ma, you were going to tell me about Aedan and how he sailed with you to America. What happened?"

"Well, both his parents died from putrid fever and he had no family nearby that he knew of. You and your brother had left Ireland, and me and your Da were lonely, and that's the truth. So we took Aedan in as our own. He's such a good lad and has been a tremendous help to me and Liam. I hope you don't mind that we brought him."

"Heavens, no! He is most welcome and we will all be sure to treat him like a brother. Don't worry, we will love and respect him as if he has Darcy blood."

The girls were washing, drying, and putting away dishes and such in an old hutch that would have to do until the new place was built...or refurbished, or whatever Da had in mind. "How old is he?"

Brannagh closed her eyes, trying to remember. "He's coming on nineteen years, I believe. I know his birth date but I keep forgetting how old he is. But I'm pretty sure he's going on nineteen this August. Be a dear and ask him for me? I'd hate for him to think I forgot, which I did, because I'm old."

"Ach, Ma, don't be silly. You've nary a grey hair on your head, and your skin is still smooth as silk. And I see that Da still gives you the eye now and again."

Brannagh laughed and thanked her daughter for the compliment.

"Well, this smooth skin needs a rest. How about we stop for a while and have a cup of tea. I want to talk with Edith and Beth, to better know them. What say you, girls? Time for a cuppa?"

Both girls laid their dishes on the table and made for the stove to put a kettle on. "We thought you would never ask, Brannagh!"

Apparently the girls wanted the opportunity to sit and chat with her, probably hoping on some level she might fill the need of a mother figure. Certainly, Sherry was too young. She was more like a sister, than mother.

Brannagh smiled knowing how they must feel, and she was overjoyed to fill that space in their hearts. "I've been watching you two, and what I see are two of the loveliest young women I've ever seen. Smart, strong, hard working, and also gentle. Beth, Mason is lucky, he is. And Edith, just wait until the lads from town get a look at you. Why, we'll have to carry a stick with us wherever we go!"

The girls tittered and then settled down for tea and girl talk. Sherry sat silent and watched as the girls' faces lit up with curiosity and enjoyment as Brannagh spun some tales. Ma had always been a good storyteller.

"Now, Colleen, you must tell me why everyone calls you 'Sherry.' Can't say that I like it but if I know why, I might learn to accept it."

"Well, Jacob, my first husband, thought my eyes were the color of Sherry wine, and so he started calling me that. It stuck and now that's what I go by. However, if you and Da start calling me Colleen again, you might get them to start calling me by my birth name. Or maybe not. You never know, eh?"

Beth interrupted to ask Brannagh about Irish cooking. "Brannagh, I love to cook and wondered if you would teach me some Irish dishes. First I have to work on biscuits and the perfect pancake for Mason, and then I'd like to try to make something you might teach me."

They talked and talked until it was almost time for the midday meal when Mason entered the kitchen and said, "No lunch? What have you women been doing?" Turning around and leaving the kitchen for the pump outside, he muttered, "With all a man has to do around here and you're sitting around peckin' like hens." Beth started giggling and then they all started laughing. Brannagh told Beth, "You best be takin' care of your man, Missy. They can get a mite testy when their stomachs are empty."

***

After much deliberation and a family vote, it was decided the old farmhouse would be torn down and a new house constructed that would better suit their needs.

An inside pump in the kitchen excited Edith more than anyone could have imagined, and Sherry was beside herself with joy at the idea that Da would build a bathing room next to the kitchen where cold and hot water could easily be carried. A rubber hose would be connected to the bottom of the big brass tub (a gift from Cullen to Sherry) and would run outside so it could be drained with ease.

"Can you imagine, Sherry? A pump in the kitchen! And a new modern stove with a large reservoir for hot water! I'm in heaven, I tell you, heaven!"

Sherry caught Edith's hands to stop her from dancing around the front yard.

"I'm so glad it brings you such joy, Edith. I'm going to love the bathing room, too, but we have to be patient. Remember, we'll all be sleeping in the barn until the house is finished. I really wish they had built the new barn first, though. It's going to be a misery. We also have to get the garden planted and build a chicken coop, a hog pen, and…and…oh my Lord, we'll never get it all done!"

Sherry was used to the pressure of working to keep the family going, and she had taken to trawling very easily. It was repetitious and boring, but it brought money in. Now she hardly knew where to start and it was as frustrating as it was embarrassing. She was used to being in charge and now she felt useless. In her mind, she was letting her family down.

One day she was standing in the yard, turning three hundred and sixty degrees in an effort to find something she could do to contribute when Cullen walked behind her and wrapped her in his arms. "I can see the wheels turning, Sherry. What's the matter? Come on, spit it out."

"Oh, Cullen, I'm so useless! I don't know where to start and I wouldn't know what I'm doing if I found something to do. I'm just drifting each day, letting the family down."

"Really? I thought you were dancing."

"Don't you make fun of me, Cullen Macklin! I'll come after you with the broom, I will!"

"Well, your arms were out, very elegantly I might add, and you were turning in circles. What was I to think?"

"Seriously, Cullen. What am I to do?"

Still in his arms, he turned them both in a slow circle so Sherry could see what each person was doing.

"Seems like Edith and Aedan are building the chicken coop. Mason and Liam are measuring the foundation of the new house, Beth and Brannagh must be in the barn sectioning it off as living quarters and a kitchen, and I'm setting up the cutting station where wood will be sawed and stacked.

"The garden needs work. We have to get the dirt prepared to plant and I'm waiting on the owner of the feed and garden store to deliver the plow and disc I'm renting.

"Rome wasn't built in a day, Sweetheart. It will all get done, don't you worry." Turning her in a circle again, Cullen noticed the feed store wagon coming over the rise.

"Ah, speak of the devil and he appears. Come on, let's go say hello."

As they walked in the direction of the incoming wagon, Cullen yelled for the men to come and help unload the implements. Work stopped and everyone gathered to see if they could help.

"Sherry, I think you would be most useful helping Beth and Brannagh in the barn. So after the delivery, why don't you just go see what needs doing, all right?"

Sherry nodded and hung her head. "If you say so, Cullen. I promise I'll make myself useful yet."

As the days went by, Sherry joined in the rhythm of the work being done and found plenty of things she could do to help. She put on a pair of Aedan's old dungarees, used a piece of twine to keep them up, and rolled up the legs. Every little thing that needed doing had to be done some time so she looked for anything and everything that needed attention. Soon she had a sense of pride and accomplishment that motivated her to continue. She was also learning.

"Ma, you used to know a lot about planting a garden. Do you think you and me could plow and disc the garden and get it planted? Cullen's horse is a sweetheart and I think I could handle him and the plow. What do you say? Feel like giving it a whirl?"

Brannagh knew how her daughter had been feeling and knew that to accomplish preparing the ground for a garden would make her feel like she was taking care of her family.

"Colleen, you're not alone anymore, love. The whole world isn't sitting on your shoulders now. You can relax and enjoy the building of your new house. You've got four men and three women behind you now. Relax, why don't you?"

Sherry rolled her eyes. "What would you have me do, Ma? Just ask."

"Well, another grandchild would be nice. How about you work on that?"

Brannagh winked at her and walked back to the barn, leaving Sherry to think about what she said. Was it time for another baby? Or should they wait; maybe get in the family way come winter? Caleb had turned five during their trip south. Even as she thought it, she spied the little sprite working beside Cullen, jabbering his ears off. "Caleb! Come on, it's time for your nap, little one!" She would talk with Cullen about it and hear his thoughts on the matter.

Chapter Thirty-Three

"Ach, I've torn my only work dress and think it's beyond repair. I should have stayed in the dungarees, I suppose." Sherry appeared crestfallen over the old dress, and Brannagh knew just the thing to cheer her up.

"I've been wanting to go to town and shop at the mercantile. I've always loved to window shop and if we can find suitable fabric for a work dress, I'd be happy to have a new one sown in just a twinkle. Come, let's take a break, gather the girls, and go to town." Not waiting for Sherry's answer, she yelled for Aedan to come rig the wagon for the trip.

Cullen would have preferred to have Aedan or Mason go with them but feared it would ruffle Sherry's feathers to act so protectively when he knew she could handle driving the wagon. He would just have to trust her but it would be a long wait until she got home.

When the women rode up to the mercantile and tied Honor to the hitching rail, all eyes turned to them and Sherry assumed they were looking at Honor. The horse attracted attention wherever he went. Sherry gave him a few pats on his neck and whispered, "I'll not forget the peppermint sticks, my friend. So be a good boy and wait patiently."

A bell tinkled above the door as they entered and once again all eyes turned their way.

"Mornin' Mrs. Macklin. Nice to see you again. Let me know when you're ready to check out." The owner looked apprehensive for some reason but Sherry dismissed it as being stress since the store looked very busy.

Beth and Edith went off by themselves and looked at the usual geegaws that young ladies were attracted to. Sherry and Brannagh headed straight for the fabrics. Silently perusing the ginghams, they overheard three women who were clutched in a corner indulging in gossip…about them.

"Old Mr. Macklin is probably rolling in his grave. Can you imagine his only son marrying Irish? Why, I never!"

"I heard they had once been slaves. White trash, they are."

"Lands, I hope they stick to themselves."

Brannagh looked at Sherry with a mischievous twinkle in her eye and started giggling. Sherry couldn't help herself and joined her mother.

"What are they laughing about? Certainly there is nothing funny about being Irish!"

The old hens stayed in their corner like sentries guarding town society, watching every move they made.

"Well, lass, 'tis time ta go look at the china, eh? 'Twill please Cullen a great deal ta see his kitchen so well turned out. Oh, and don't forget we need pickling spices for the corned beef. Ah, yer Da sorely misses his corned beef and cabbage, so he does."

As they walked to the front of the store, Brannagh noticed a bulletin tacked to a message board. "My, will ye look at dis? They're havin' a dance in four weeks time! Come, let us go back and choose fabric for new dresses. Yer da just loves to dance, he does."

"Don't forget Cullen! He loves ta dance just as much as Da. How exciting it tis! New dresses and a chance to meet all the town folk. What a boon, eh?"

They could hear the old harpies, still in their corner, gasp when Brannagh said they would be attending the dance, and Sherry knew her Ma was enjoying the entire scenario.

When the girls were finished shopping and it was time for them to purchase their items, Sherry pulled about twenty sticks of peppermint from a jar on the counter and added them to the tally. "Cullen's horse dearly loves the peppermint sticks, he does. I've told him 'tis a dear cost to indulge an animal so, but he insists. He's like that, ye know. Always so generous. 'Tis one of the reasons I love him so dearly."

When the Macklin women left the store, Sherry felt several pairs of eyes on them as they placed their purchases in the back of the wagon, and just for spite, she pulled out two peppermint sticks and fed them to Honor, who smacked his lips in pure delight. She was certain she heard a couple of "Well, I never's" coming from behind the storefront window so she turned around and gave them a curtsey. Old biddies.

Later, Cullen heard loud laughter and turned to the rise to see all of the women in his family laughing heartily as they approached the yard. It was a beautiful sight to see and he hoped it would always be that way for them; plenty to laugh about.

***

"I believe the boards should go that way, Aedan. I think it makes more sense."

"Oh, do ye now? I know what I'm doin' Edith, so let me at it, eh?"

"Seriously, I think it would be better to run the boards further out to give the pigs more room."

"I've already talked with Cullen about it, and they're goin' *this* way. Now that's an end to it."

"You think you're so smart? Well, I've seen smarter coming from an old mule we once had. Don't you talk down to me like that, Aedan Donnelly!"

"I'll talk to you any way I please, Miss Newcomb. Now get out of me way!"

Edith was incensed and never gave her next move a second thought. With every bit of her strength, she shoved

Aedan to the ground and then went to her knees and started beating him about the head and chest.

"Edith! Stop! What the devil has gotten into ye?" Aedan was brought up to never touch a woman in anger and he wasn't about to start now but, Jaysus, the girl was whoopin' him pretty fair!

Cullen and Liam were coming out of the barn and merely stood watching. "'Tiz one of two things, Cullen. They hate each other or 'tis love that has'em so twitchy."

Cullen smiled and continued watching. "Want to make a bet on it, Liam? I'll give you five dollars if it's love." Liam laughed and said, "Yer on, boyo!" He then spit in his palm and shook Cullen's hand on the bet. They then went about their business and let the two continue battling in the dirt.

Brannagh had been watching from the barn door and was whispering to herself, "C'mon, Edith! Give'im what fer, lass!"

Caleb thought it was a game, sat on Aedan's belly, and started jumping up and down.

"Enough!" screamed Aedan, as he swiftly flipped Edith over, straddled her waist, and pinned her arms to the ground. Both were heaving for air and if looks could kill, one of them would be dead. But as their breathing slowed, Aedan's eyes turned from anger to something else entirely. Edith never looked away as her face lost its furious mien. Instead she gazed into Aedan's azure eyes with something akin to wonder.

"Have you had enough, Edith?"

Licking her lips, she took her time in answering. "I don't know."

Aedan knew he better get up before something happened that would change their relationship forever.

Giving her a hand up, he blurted, "Don't trifle with me, Edith. I won't have it."

What the heck did he mean by that? "I'll do as I please, Aedan Donnelly, and don't you forget it." With that, she turned around and stomped away from the would-be hog pen. "Do it yourself if you're so smart."

Edith didn't know how to feel, several emotions assaulting her at once. Why did Aedan make her so angry? Why did she feel justified in harping on him so often? What was she trying to do? Get a rise out of him? If so, for what reason? She was perplexed, for sure. Their relationship had turned sour as soon as she had started her fault finding.

Aedan's hands were shaking, probably from exertion. But he knew he was stronger than to shake after a tussle with a wee lass, and wondered what had gotten into him. He vowed to stay away from Edith from then on. What man needed such grief? He must stay focused on his work. Everyone was depending on him.

***

The weather held and provided the men with warm dry days in which to build and plow.

The fields to be used as a vegetable garden had been plowed and the women held seeds in their aprons, planting them as they walked along the rows. As they walked, Sherry sang in a clear and lilting voice:

Ma'am dear, I remember when
The summer time was past and gone
When coming through the meadow,
Sure she swore I was the only one
That ever she could love,
But oh! The false and cruel one,
For all that, she's left me
Here alone for to die . . .

When she had finished all the verses, Brannagh joined in and started the song over again. When Edith and Beth had heard it a couple of times, they joined in. Sherry sang melody and Brannagh sang harmony, and their voices rang out in the field as if a choir of angels had come to earth.

Cullen and Liam stopped their work, Liam lit his pipe, and they sat on the new front steps of the farmhouse they were building. Liam puffed and nodded in time with the song, and Cullen just closed his eyes and took the song into his soul, so much did he enjoy hearing it. Looking over at Liam, Cullen finally spoke, "I pray to the Good Lord that our days will always be filled with such happiness." Liam replied, "Cullen, they will. They will."

Within the next two days the hay fields were turned and planted which signaled the end of planting and the start of prayers for enough rain to nourish the fields and garden.

Cullen had built the front porch first, which was kind of backwards, but he wanted so badly to have a place for the family to rest and chat in the evenings. Liam said he could do it that way and construction was moving right along thanks to the men's hard work.

During another trip to town for building materials, Cullen went to the feed store to see if they had any plants Sherry could put in the ground now that the front porch was complete. As luck would have it, the owner had just taken delivery on two dozen rose bushes, six of which Cullen bought for his wife. "Now ya gotta feed'em, Mr. Macklin. I recommend horse manure. Best fertilizer for roses that I know of, yes sirree." Sherry would be mighty pleased.

***

"I haven't seen you and Cullen on his horse for a ride lately. Don't you think it's time for a ride, Colleen? Time's a waistin', it tis."

Sherry laughed, "Ma, I think Mason and Beth are using our 'special place' too, and I'm afraid of all four of us arriving at the same time. I'm not that old and there's plenty of time for babies."

"Then how about a swim down at the creek? Take a blanket and I'll make sure you're not interrupted. That's what me and yer Da do." Sherry's eyes got round as silver dollars and she gasped.

"What? You think I'm too old for lovin'? Don't be daft, lass. Lovin' tis lovin' no matter at what age." Brannagh went back to peeling potatoes and let Sherry think on it for a bit.

Sherry was quiet as she sat with her Ma, peeling potatoes. Her birthday was coming up and she would be another year older and perhaps another year closer to having trouble conceiving. Maybe Ma was right. Maybe it was time to begin in earnest to conceive. Cullen certainly would appreciate the trying and the thought brought a huge smile to her face. Well, the creek it shall be, she mused. No time like the present.

***

Cullen was alone on their new porch one evening after supper, the women were inside the barn washing dishes, and Liam, Mason, and Aedan, were setting up a horseshoe pit in the front yard just a bit up from the family cemetery. It was a glorious evening and he appreciated the time and space for some solitude.

No one could hear him if he spoke aloud, so he did just that. "Dear God, it's been a long time since we've had the chance to talk together in this manner. I have to admit I like it better when I speak the words aloud. I don't know, it just makes me feel closer to you. Anyway, I hope you can read my heart when I say that I'm profoundly grateful for all of your gifts. I'm especially grateful for my expanding family and, of course, my beloved wife, Sherry. What treasures they are.

"During all my years of traveling, I rode with a big hole in my chest where love and family should have been. All my life I've wanted love and thought for several years it just wasn't in the cards, so to speak. You've watched over me all my life, I know that now, and you saw fit to answer my prayers, even though they really weren't formal prayers at the time. You looked deep inside of me and found something worthy of your love. I promise you today, sitting right here on my new porch, that I will prove worthy of that love. I will endeavor to keep holy all of your gifts and I will always keep you close in my heart. You will forever be my church, my guiding light, my comfort, and my strength. I love you, God. I always will. Amen."

The gravity and joy of his words had tears welling in his eyes, and he knew without doubt that his life would always be full of grace. Sure, there would be problems, and there would be frightening times, but all of that he would turn over to God and allow Him to handle it. It felt good to surrender himself into God's keeping. It was a tremendous relief.

He wished he had another few hours to just sit and wonder at God's loving ways, another few hours to revel in the feelings he was experiencing, but time marches on and he was late in feeding Honor and the rest of the stock. "Oh, and God? PS: Thank you for my companion, Honor. Amen."

He was smiling when Sherry approached the porch. "Whatcha doin' Cullen? You look mighty happy."

"I am happy, Sweetheart. So happy I could burst into a million stars. Come here and sit on my lap for a bit. We'll watch the sunset together."

"Cullen, we need to go for more 'rides.' I've been thinking, and I hope you agree, that it's time to start making babies. How do you feel about that, hmm?"

"I feel it's a grand idea, Sherry. Just grand. Let's walk down to the creek tonight if your ma and da don't beat us to it."

Sherry gasped, "You knew about that?"

"Of course, I did. I can always tell by the grin on Liam's face the next morning."

Chapter Thirty-Four

"'Tis glad I am that we've got these dresses almost made. I hate working until the last minute, don't you?"

"Yes, Ma, I agree. Just think of how beautiful the Darcy and Newcomb women will be at the dance. I can't wait."

After another trip to the mercantile, and hearing more chirping magpies gasping their displeasure at having Irish attend their dance, additional material was purchased and dresses for all the women in the family had been made. Brannagh was determined they would outshine all of the old biddies.

"Ma, what are we going do about Edith and Aedan? They're at war with each other and it's putting a strain on the rest of the family. I haven't the slightest idea what has gotten into Edith. Aedan has been a hard worker and deserves her respect instead of her constant harping."

"Aye, but 'tis no mystery. Edith has feelings for our Aedan, and I do believe they are reciprocated. They're so young they don't know how to deal with it yet. I say 'tis time for Aedan to grab her, kiss her soundly, and tell her the way it's going to be. That'll shock the words right out of her mouth, it will."

Both mother and daughter laughed but Sherry wondered if it just might work. "I'd dearly love to see them have a good time together at the dance. I hope he'll 'make his move' in time." Then they laughed again.

Lord, how Sherry appreciated her mother being there with her. It was certainly a dream come true. Cullen had seen to it. She smiled when she thought of how lovingly Cullen treated her and wanted the same for dear Edith. Although Edith had a few years before she had to make a decision, it would be good practice to learn to live with

Aedan in friendship and fellowship. Who knew? They just might end up together in the end.

"I'll talk to Cullen about it. Maybe he can talk with Aedan, and offer some suggestions.

***

"What? You want me to talk with Aedan about what? Leave the boy alone, Sherry. If I were him I would stay as far away from Edith as I could. She's being a shrew, for gosh sakes!"

"I know, Cullen, but I think she really likes or perhaps even loves him and doesn't know what to do about it. I think she is trying to get a rise out of him and she's going about it all wrong."

"Then how about you talking to Edith and telling her to stop this foolishness. Personally, I'm getting tired of it."

"Okay. I'll talk to Edith and you talk to Aedan, all right??

"What do you want me to say? 'Please be kind to my sister who is acting like a shrew'?"

"Ach, Cullen. Don't be daft. You'll know what to say when the time comes."

Sherry decided to take the bull by the horns the next afternoon by asking Edith to help her weed the garden.

"Edith, come help me with the weeding, will you?" Edith shrugged and followed Sherry into the field. "I need to know what's going on between you and Aedan, and I don't want any prevaricating, you hear? Now, tell me why you are acting the way you do with him. Has he done something that he shouldn't have? Has he been unkind? What?"

Edith hung her head, took a deep breath, and replied, "I don't know, Sherry. I like Aedan a lot. I mean a lot, and I keep wanting to get closer but mess up when I finally have any time with him. He hates me and that only makes things worse. I want to move closer but am terrified of rejection.

So I guess I've been beating him to the punch? I don't know. It's frustrating the daylights out of me."

"So that's how it is. Ma thought it might be this. How about calling a truce and starting fresh? I'm sure Aedan would be agreeable to that. But this has to stop. It makes the rest of the family tense when we should all be getting along and working well together."

Edith turned toward the barn and watched as a shirtless Aedan worked digging a trench for pipe to the kitchen water pump. Sherry followed her gaze and thought the boy was quite a specimen, if she were to say so herself. "He's lovely, isn't he?"

Edith blushed but looked totally defeated. "Yes, he is. Quite lovely, in fact."

Sherry felt sorry for Edith. She had been so lonely over the years and wanted so badly to have what the rest of the family shared. A loving mate.

"Go on, go over there and ask to call a truce. Tell him you'd like to start over again. I'm sure he'll agree."

Just minutes previously . . . "No, absolutely not, Cullen. The girl hasn't all her marbles, I tell ye. She's mean as a two headed snake, she is, and I'm not goin' ta mess with her."

"Come on now, tell me you have no feelings for Edith. I'm not blind, you know. Me and Liam have noticed how your eyes follow her around the yard and in the barn. You can't tell me you have no feelings for the girl."

"Yeah, I follow her with my eyes! A'course I do! She's likely to attack me at any moment, she is! What the devil is wrong with her?"

Cullen was hard pressed to keep from laughing. "I hear you, I hear you. Truthfully, I've never seen her act the way she does with you. She reminds me of a rooster spreading its wings and pecking at a particular hen, trying to get her attention. Actually, I think she loves you, Aedan. Now,

what are you going to do about it? I have a suggestion if . .
."

Oh Lord, here she comes . . .

"Hello, Aedan, I..." Before she could go any further, Aedon grabbed her by the shoulders, and said, "Woman, can ya shut yer gob for five minutes? Jaysus!" Then he kissed her. Not a simple peck, either. He kissed her hard and it was packed with plenty of meaning. When she didn't try to escape, he softened the kiss and ran his tongue across her lips as he had been dying to taste her since the day they first met.

"There," he said as he put her away from him. "I suppose I'll have to do that from now on when yer mouth is flappin' with some complaint or another. Now go on, go back to weedin' with Sherry, and leave me be. This is man's work and it's got to be done, it does."

"Yes, Aedan," Edith replied with a sweet smile on her face. "I'll let you work, but first I want to tell you..." Aedan stepped up and kissed her again. "Didn't I tell ye, Edith? Don't ye listen to a word I say?"

He then turned her toward the field and smacked her bottom. "Git. Go on with ye."

Edith walked slowly and then gained momentum as it dawned on her how Aedan must feel. She touched her mouth and ran the rest of the way, anxious to tell Sherry what happened and what was said.

Later that evening as Cullen and Sherry were headed to the creek for a bit of privacy, they shared what each of them had said to Edith and Aedan, and laughed at how it all turned out. At least there would now be peace in the family. But Cullen would keep an eye on Aedan to make sure he was treating Edith like a lady.

***

Cullen called a meeting after supper one evening and gathered the men on the front porch of the new house.

"It's time to take stock of what's been done and what there is still to be done. Liam says this house should be ready to move in within the next two weeks. That means it's time for Mason and Liam to pick a piece of the land on which to build their own homes. I'm sure you two have already scouted the acreage and have a good idea about where you'd like to build. So check with your wives and make sure they agree with your choice."

Mason grinned and replied, "Me and Bethy have already decided on a spot and we're ready to start as soon as this house is up and finished. How about you, Liam?"

"Well, me and Brannagh would like to build on that hill across the hay field. That way Brannagh will be close by when all of the babes are born. I'm hopin' we all stay close but not too close, if ye get me meanin'."

Everyone laughed and a schedule of sorts was agreed upon for the rest of the construction.

"I've learned a lot from Liam as we've built this house, and I think I could start on our foundation by myself. At least I'd like to try. Liam will you supervise my efforts?"

"'Tis a good eye you have, Mason. I think you can handle it just fine. I'll make sure of the right of it."

Everyone dispersed and Cullen stayed on the porch as was his habit in the evenings. He told Sherry it was his "personal" time when he might just sit and contemplate things. She had no objection and made sure everyone respected that time.

"Father, things are coming right along. Thanks again." He sat back on the chair legs and lit the pipe Liam had fashioned for him. As he puffed, he began humming an old tune his mother had taught him. It made his heart ache for all that had happened since her death. Still, even though it was bittersweet, he enjoyed allowing his heart to remember her and would look forward to going through the boxes Brannagh had packed away before they had reached home. He was sure there must be something in them to remember her by.

Chapter Thirty-Five

It was the afternoon of the dance and the women were in the barn giggling and whispering among themselves, fixing hair and sewing last minute adjustments to their dresses. Cullen looked at Liam, and said, "I think there is a secret society that's taken over our barn."

Liam laughed, choking on a puff of smoke from his pipe, "'Tis the Secret Society of Women, lad, and we'll never be invited to join, I'll tell ye that. Best leave them be until they're done and, sure, God only knows when that will be."

The women had been cooking and baking all morning, making sure their contributions would be fresh and inviting. They made a caramel cake, three pies, and roasted a huge piece of beef with all the trimmings. The new stove Cullen had bought for the house had been a godsend. Beth had mastered the Southern biscuit and made three dozen to take along. Sadie had been milked two days previous and the cream had been gathered to make plenty of butter to which Edith added a good amount of honey.

Mason and Aedan had ridden into town the day before and rented a nice big buggy to carry the entire family who were dressed in their finery, to the dance. Everything was ready.

The sun was hanging low in the sky by the time they arrived at the feed store where merchandise had been moved to a local barn, and the floor swept clean for dancing. Tables were lined up against a long wall where women could place the food they had prepared, and a large punch bowl was brimming with what looked like lemonade with chunks of ice floating on top.

Children ran to and fro, getting into everything that captured their interest, and mothers clucked over them like hens, making sure they stayed out of trouble. All in all, it was a wasted effort as the children would have their fun and mothers were actually loath to stop them. Caleb ran behind the children, trying to catch up and join in their fun. All mothers watched every child to keep them safe.

A platform had been built for the band, which consisted of a banjo, fiddle, and piano. Everyone was busy getting it all put together so the dance could begin and hadn't noticed who had yet to arrive. There was too much going on to notice. Too much excitement.

Finally it was time to begin the affair as people started gathering near the walls so the dance floor could be used, and it gave neighbors a chance to look around to see who was attending. It didn't take long for the old biddies to notice that the Darcys and Newcombs had arrived. Whispers went from person to person like a chain of bad news, and before long the place became silent, all heads turning their way.

The fiddle player grabbed his instrument and began playing "The Irish Washerwoman." It was the most well known Irish song in America and Sherry knew it was meant to mock her family. Instead of being embarrassed, Sherry yelled, "Listen, Da! He's playing it just for us, he is! Come, let us show'em how it's done." Liam took her hand and they performed an authentic Irish jig.

Cullen started clapping his hands in time with the music, and Brannagh pulled Aedan onto the floor and joined Sherry and Liam. They whooped and hollered while they danced and appeared to be having the time of their lives.

Cullen walked behind Mrs. Garver, put his hands on her shoulders and whispered in her ear, "Would the beautiful Mrs. Helen Garver grant me a dance?" Without hesitation, she took his hand as he led her to the dance floor, laughing as he gathered her up and twirled her around. "Why, Charlie Macklin, you bad boy!" she squealed with delight.

The young people, who had no idea of their parents' bigotry, joined them on the dance floor, trying to imitate their steps. Soon, they too were stomping, twirling, and having a good time. This really chapped Lolly Goodman's behind. She was the mayor's wife and felt entitled to mandate her views as law. Her eyes threw darts of hatred toward the dance floor as more and more people joined in the dance. Even the banjo and piano player had picked up the tune and joined the fiddler, not knowing it had been meant as an insult. Rather, everyone seemed to be enjoying themselves.

***

"It ain't right," Jake Wilson said under his breath.

"What ain't right, Jake?" asked the man beside him.

"It ain't right our folk have to mingle with white niggers, that's what!"

"Whatdaya mean, Jake? They look all right to me."

"What the hell do you know, Howard? Ain't you ever heard of the Irish and how much they like to drink whiskey and fight?"

Howie shrugged and walked off, not wanting Jake and his prejudices to ruin his fun for the evening.

Jake was certainly riled up and becoming more so every minute. He took a flask of whiskey out of his pocket, not even realizing the irony after his statement to Howie regarding the Irish, and took a long pull from it. When that didn't quench his hatred, he took another pull and stood to the side of the dance floor, watching with utter contempt.

The musicians took a break to eat and drink before all the food was gone, which gave the crowd time to chat with one another, or gossip, depending on who was doing the talking.

Cullen watched as the girls joined groups of women who seemed to accept them just fine. Edith looked like she might pull back but he noticed Sherry inconspicuously take her by the arm and pull into the group.

Liam had struck up a conversation with some gentlemen across the room, and Mason and Aedan, gravitated toward a group of young men who were more their age. That left him alone, but not for long.

He noticed Eustace Garver talking with Herbert Scaggs, the owner of the town mercantile, and went over to get a feel for how the town was feeling about his family's arrival.

"Mr. Garver, how nice to see you again," Cullen smiled as he grasped the old man's hand in greeting.

"Charlie Macklin, it's been a long while, hasn't it? We're so happy you've come back to fix up your father's place and make it your home. How's the work goin' out there?"

"It's slow, but going just fine, sir." Cullen was glad to receive such a reception from Mr. Garver, whom the town's people had always thought of so highly.

"Oh really? Too slow, huh? Whatcha buildin' out there, son?"

"Well, we tore down the old place and have a new house almost completed. We should be moving into it within the next two weeks, but we still have two more houses to build, not to mention a new barn, which we need very badly. I'm not worried, though. It'll all get done eventually."

When Cullen mentioned the barn, a sparkle appeared in Mr. Garver's eyes, and he wondered what was on the man's mind.

"Did ya hear that, Herbie? They need a new barn. What can be done about that, do ya think?" Herbert Scaggs' face lit up when he realized what Eustace was suggesting, and replied, "I think this calls for a good old fashioned barn raising, Eustace! Why, we haven't had one for years, have we? Yes sir, I used to so enjoy a good barn raising. Just thinking of all the food makes my mouth water." Both men laughed and clapped each other on the back, then looked to Cullen once again for his reaction.

"I don't know, Mr. Garver. It seems as though we have some people in town who don't cotton to the Irish. They've already shown their displeasure at my return with a new family. Do you think there are enough men in town who don't care about such things? If so, I'd be pleased as punch to have their help."

"Hell, Charlie, we know who you're talkin' about and they don't matter as much as a pinch of salt. McKenney has always welcomed new neighbors and we're not going to stop now because of some senseless bigotry. Why, the name of the town is Irish! They don't own this town and they won't stop us from helping an old friend. By the way, I'm sorry for the loss of your father. He was just passin' time until he could go home to your Ma, and that's a fact. Stubborn, hardheaded, nasty son of a bitch, he was. None of us had to guess why you left, son. Everyone knew."

"Thank you, sir. I've made my peace with our relationship. I'm glad he's home with Ma."

"Tell you what, Charlie. Come to the house after church next Sunday and we'll make all the plans over some coffee and peach pie. Helen would love to have you."

"Heck, Mr. Garver, I don't care whether we talk or not! I just want some of Miss Helen's peach pie!" The three men laughed together and Cullen felt elated at their acceptance of his family while some in town had been so cold and judgmental.

Just then, Sherry walked up to them and Cullen introduced her.

"Gentlemen, this is my wife, Sherry."

"It's a pleasure to meet you. Cullen told us all about you and your wife, Mr. Garver, while we rode for days and days to get here. I understand I have some competition in the pie department, eh?" Her smile was bright and Cullen couldn't have been more proud of her.

"Cullen? Your name is Charlie Macklin, am I right?" asked Mr. Garver, as he gave Cullen a quizzical look.

Sherry said before Cullen had a chance to, "Well, ye see, 'tis because of a 'Charlie' I knew back in Ireland, that I won't call him by the name anymore. Ach, he was a weasel, so he was. So I call my husband Cullen, which is a good Irish name, by the way."

"I'll try to remember that, Mrs. Macklin."

"Oh, do call me Sherry, sir. I'll be called nothin' but Sherry by the people Cullen thinks so much of. You were always so kind to him, so caring. He told me all of it, he did."

Sherry knew she was laying on the Irish accent a bit, but she wanted to be accepted as Irish, and the accent would always be a reminder of her heritage, despite the fact that some in town seemed to think it was a stain on her humanity.

The music started up again and Sherry asked the gentlemen's pardon to take her husband onto the dance floor. "I just love to dance, don't you?" she asked, dazzling Mr. Garver with a beautiful smile.

As the evening wore on, it became clear there were only a few people that openly snubbed the family, Lolly Goodwin being the leader of the hatred camp. Jake Wilson couldn't seem to find anyone who would listen to his complaints so he just drank himself silly and ended up passed out on the front steps of the feed store.

The ride home was animated as they shared what they had learned about the people of McKenney. "'Tis a nice town of people, it tis," Liam stated as the buggy whisked them along the road toward home. "Seems to me tis only a few who have sticks up their arses." They all murmured their agreement and promised not to worry about it anymore.

Cullen could hear a couple of yawns coming from the buggy and wondered if he should wait until the morning to tell them of Mr. Garver's idea of a barn raising. But he was so excited, he could wait no longer.

"Liam, we're to go to the Garver's after church on Sunday. He and Mr. Scaggs have an idea about having a barn raising for us. What do you think?"

"Jumpin' Leprechauns, Cullen! 'Tis just what we need, it tis! By all the saints, we'll have us a grand barn, will we not?"

Chapter Thirty-Six

The family worked like an army of ants carrying everything from the barn into the new house, and soon the old structure was empty.

"Liam, I'm thinking since the barn is so old, dry, and rickety, do you think hooking up a rope to Honor, and having him pull it down would work?"

"'Twas just me thinkin', Cullen. I think it would work quite well. Want to give it a go?"

Making sure there was enough rope between Honor and the barn so the horse wouldn't be injured, they rigged it up and attached it to a makeshift harness Liam made. Cullen checked it all to make sure everything was tight and fastened correctly.

After visiting with Mr. Garver, the week previous, enough wood was ordered to build the barn the way Cullen wanted it, and it had been smart to have it unloaded on the far side of the yard instead of next to the old barn. After staring at the entire setup for a good five minutes, Cullen said, "Okay, let's do it!"

The family was outside and far enough away to be safe as the procedure was started.

"Saints preserve us, this better work or I'll be without a husband, I will."

"Don't worry, Ma. They know what they're doing. Watch and see." Sherry put her arm around her ma's shoulder as they stood together, silently saying goodbye to the old barn that had given them shelter.

Cullen whispered in Honor's ear and then gently pulled him into action. The moaning and groaning of the old wood was pitiful, as if it were protesting its demise. Soon the top of the front wall was coming forward as that side of the roof sagged precariously. Finally it fell to the ground in a great whoosh of air and dust. "One down and three to go,"

Cullen smiled as he scratched Honor behind the ear. He looked just as proud of the horse as he would be of his own child.

Once the structure was completely down, each member of the family started to break apart the wood with hammers and crowbars, throwing it all into a great pile where the barn had stood.

It was hard work, and everyone was ready for some rest by the time the job was completed. The girls were drenched in sweat and looked like wilted sunflowers. The men were thirsty and hungry.

"Let's take a rest and have some supper. Brannagh made fresh bread for some meat and cheese sandwiches." Sherry pulled Caleb to her and slowly walked to the new kitchen. *Ah, her new kitchen.*

"No cheese for me, thanks!" Mason laughed. "I think I'll just have meat on mine." Everyone agreed as the memory of all the cheese sandwiches eaten on the trip from Maine came to mind.

Liam looked beat and Cullen decided right then to put off starting the fire until the next day. It would be an all day affair tending a fire of that size, and everyone should be rested and on their toes when it was lit.

After they had eaten supper, Cullen suggested a cool dip in the creek. The spot he had created as a boy was big enough for everyone to splash around for some relief. "Let's head to the creek and have some fun!" he said with an impish smile on his face, his dimples making it impossible for anyone to deny him.

***

It felt so decadent to swim in the same place she and Cullen came to make love. Just thinking of it made her blush, said blush not escaping Cullen's attention. He smiled and waded over to her, the look in his eyes saying everything she was feeling.

"What's the matter, wife? Experiencing some memories, hmm?"

Sherry swatted him on the shoulder and said, "Shh! Don't say another word! I'll die of embarrassment if someone should figure out why!"

"I don't see Liam or Brannagh blushing, do you?"

"No, but they're not me, Cullen Macklin. Keep your distance." Then she winked at him.

Cullen waded behind her and held her around the waist, her dress floating on the surface of the water. Should he have decided to, he could have sampled her softness without anyone's knowing better but…he dunked her instead.

Sherry came up spitting and wiping water from her eyes, and yelled, "Why you just wait, husband! I'll get you for that!"

Cullen was laughing like crazy, and so was everyone else, as she dipped back under the water and yanked his feet out from under him. Not to be left out, Mason and Aedan grabbed Beth and Edith, dunking them and backing away before the girls could retaliate.

Liam just hugged Brannagh, and whispered, "Let the children have their fun, eh? Tonight we'll make our own fun." Brannagh took a deep breath as Liam nuzzled her neck, imagining what the night might bring. She closed her eyes and silently thanked God for the amazing way her life was turning out. As they swayed from side to side in the water, Brannagh whispered,

"Ain't this life grand, Liam? 'Tis everything we ever wanted."

***

The next day dawned bright with not a breath of wind. Cullen was thankful for that since it would keep the fire from spreading to old trees that stood nearby.

"Everyone got their buckets?" he called. "Let's get this fire started."

Caleb looked crestfallen that he wasn't allowed near the fire and wanted a bucket of his own so he could help. Cullen bent down beside the boy and told him, "Caleb, you have the most important job of all, son. You need to sit far away so you can see the whole picture of what is happening. What if we are too close to see embers flying through the air toward the trees and dry grass?" He then gave the boy a hug, noticing the pleasure on his little face at having such a big job to do.

It took a good half hour to get the entire blaze going since they used no accelerant to speak of; only a small amount of kerosene. It was more a matter of starting a small camp-like fire and using coals and wood that had already caught flame.

Cullen and Liam stood together watching the inferno, judging the safety and progress of the procedure. Liam nudged Cullen, "So far, so good, eh?"

Edith noticed a few boards that hadn't been placed on the pile and moved to get them. Everyone else was watching their section of the fire, making sure it wasn't spreading when she leaned too close to the flames to throw the boards in the middle of the blaze, never realizing that when she turned back around to get another piece, the back of her skirt had caught fire.

Suddenly a scream rent the air as Edith slapped at her skirt, trying to put out the flames that licked at her back and legs. Aedan was at her side in a trice, ripping the skirt at the waist and pulling the burning fabric away from her body. When it was done, he laid her on the ground and began checking for burns, not noticing she was unconscious.

"Edith, *cailin,* wake up! Edith, do ye hear me? Oh, what will I do without you? Wake up," he said as he patted her pale cheek. He could feel tears welling in his eyes but would not let them fall. No one knew how he felt about Edith, and he would be a man, not a child in front of the family.

Brannagh ran to Edith and bent down to see if she was breathing. "She's just passed out, Aedan. Not to worry. Let's get a blanket and use it to get her in the house." Aedan wouldn't leave her side so Brannagh called for Caleb to be a little man and fetch a clean one from the house. Everyone else was gathered around Edith, and didn't want to move. They just kept staring at her, frozen in fear.

Suddenly Edith screamed, "Oh, my God! The pain! Please help me! I'm in so much pain!" Aedan then let his tears fall. "Brannagh, do something! She's suffering so badly!"

Caleb came running from the house and made a beeline for Brannagh.

"Thank you, grandson. You did a fine job, ye did. I'm so proud of ye."

Cullen and Liam gingerly lifted Edith from the ground, onto the blanket, and grabbed the four corners of it quickly, making their way toward the house. "Easy, now, easy. Don't hurt her anymore than she's sufferin'," Aedan instructed.

Cullen called back over his shoulder to the rest of his crew, "Don't take your eyes off that fire! Watch it every second, okay?" Everyone nodded as if in a daze but dutifully swiveled their heads back to the fire. Except for Mason. His little sister had been burned pretty badly by the looks of it, and he wanted to help her. He was her big brother who had always loved and protected her from harm. Sherry noticed the worry on his face and yelled above the roar of the flames, "She's in good hands, Mason! Ma is a gifted healer. She'll take good care of her, never doubt it."

The fire went on for hours, as did Edith's searing pain. Brannagh had cut the remaining clothes off the young woman and was distressed to have to ask her help in turning over so she could inspect the damage done to her backside and legs.

The room smelled of burnt flesh and hair but, fortunately, the smell appeared to be worse than the actual injuries. Yes, Edith would be in pain for a long time until she was healed, but Brannagh didn't think the scaring would be too bad. However, she wanted the doctor to come and see her to give his own opinion. Hopefully, he would have a soothing salve and some laudanum to help with Edith's pain.

"Oh, Brannagh, it hurts so badly. I know I'm acting like a baby but I've never been in so much pain. Please forgive me for acting like a child."

"No need to apologize. I'd be screamin' me head off, I would. So go on and do whatever eases your pain, even if it's cursin' like a sailor. I'll be right back. I need to have one of the men go to town and fetch the doctor back to look at those burns."

Aedan was waiting outside the bedroom door and quickly volunteered to ride to town and bring the doctor back. "Please, Brannagh, let me do it. I'll ride like the wind, I will."

Brannagh hugged him tight and whispered, "Go fetch the doctor for your woman, son. Your love will give you wings to fly faster. Go on, now. I'll take care of our Edith until you get back."

"I love her, Brannagh. I didn't know what it was, really, but now I do. I can't live without her. God, save her, please!"

Brannagh moved to the window to watch Aedan run for Honor. The lad jumped on the giant's back without a saddle and kicked him hard to start down the road to town.

After a few seconds, Edith cried out in pain again. "Oh, I don't think I can take anymore of this. It burns like the devil." Then tears flowed down her cheeks as she expressed more than physical pain.

"Who will want me now with so much scarring? I'll be ugly and worthless if it leaves me with a limp. What if I never walk right again? I'll be a freakish monster that no one will want to look at." Carefully reaching her hand to her head, she asked, "Do I still have my hair?" She patted her head the best she could and found almost half of it gone. "Brannagh! I've lost my hair? It was the only thing that was pretty about me!" Then she cried and moanrd, the sound breaking Brannagh's heart.

Soon, Edith lost consciousness again. Brannagh figured it was for the best until the doctor arrived. *God, give her a little bit of peace until the doctor starts his pokin' and prodin'.*

Chapter Thirty-Seven

The sun was setting low in the western sky and the fire had almost burned itself out. Cullen let it burn as long as it took to reduce everything to ash. It would make clean up easier.

He looked at his beloved brother-in-law and saw the worry etched around his eyes and mouth. "Mason, go on up and see Edith. We can finish up here. The fire is almost out now. Go on."

Mason ran to the kitchen door and opened it so hard it banged against the house. Running up the steps, he made it to Edith's room just as the doctor was finishing his examination. Aedan stood close to the side of the bed opposite the doctor, waiting for his prognosis.

"Doctor, will she soon be fit again?" he asked Doc Harding as he washed his hands.

"She's going to be fine but it will take a good while. She's going to be in terrible pain for at least a couple of weeks, and I'm leaving some salve and laudanum for her to take when needed. Just ride into town if she runs out of either one.

"There will be scarring, there's no way around it. The burns are bad but the fire hadn't had the chance to actually go deep enough that it will affect her strength or gait when she walks. It won't be pretty, I can tell you that. And I suggest you cut her hair in some short style until it grows back again. I know how women are about their hair," he grinned, trying to let them all know that she was going to recover with what he hoped was minimal damage.

Mason took the doctor's place at the bed while he packed up his medical bag and left the room. Both he and Aedan just stared at Edith, hoping she would open her eyes.

"I'm going to marry her, Mason. Nothing in the world will keep me from having her as my wife, so ye just as well get used to the idea."
Mason grinned. "Aedan, I'll be happier than a pig in mud to have you as a brother-in-law. What the heck took you so long to figure this out? Everyone else in the family suspected it a long time ago."

A blush crept up Aedan's neck to his ears. "It didn't really take *that* long. I knew the day I kissed her to shut her up that it was what I wanted to experience for the rest of my life. I must admit, though, she was a hard one to figure out, eh? Damn near beat me senseless that day."

Both men grinned as they looked at each other.

"I promise you, Mason Newcomb, I'll be good to her and I'll provide for her as long as I live. You have my word on it," at which point he held his hand over the bed, his intended lying asleep below, and shook Mason's hand in a tight, meaningful grip.

"I'll be twenty in August, and Edith is soon to be eighteen. I know we're young, but both of us have lived lives that make us older than our actual years. I'm sure you know what I'm talking about. Edith is a woman full grown in many ways. And, me? Jaysus, I almost feel world weary at twenty. But Edith will change all that, she will. We'll be happy, Mason. I know it deep in me soul."

Mason's heart was full beyond measure. His little sister would have the life she had always dreamed about. A loving husband, a farm to grow crops, and children of her own. It was exactly how she dreamed it would be for so many years.

It appeared the trauma was over except for poor Edith's healing process.

***

"I'm exhausted, how about you, Mrs. Maklin?"

"Yes, I certainly am. This has been a busy and trying week."

Cullen and Sherry got undressed and crawled under the sheets on their new bed.

"Mmm, this is so soft and comfortable. I'll be asleep in no time."
Sherry smiled at her husband as she snuggled close, lovingly extending an arm over his chest.

"Me too. I'd love to do something else but I think sleep is all I can manage tonight."

Each of them fell into an immediate deep slumber, knowing that tomorrow was going to be another hectic day. The neighbors were coming for the barn raising and the girls would be busy cooking and baking to feed the volunteers.

Cullen dreamed that night of how the barn would look when it was completed, picturing himself in the dream standing before the building and feeling a sense of great pride. Then he heard a horse screaming and was panicked that it might be Honor. He looked and looked but couldn't find his beloved companion. *Honor! Honor, where are you?* He ran back and forth across the paddock and couldn't see the horse anywhere. *HONOR!* A sense of dread woke him from the dream and he sat straight up in bed. Drenched in sweat, he heard what he thought had been a dream. *Oh no!* Honor *was* screaming! Cullen jumped from the bed, went to the window and lifted it open with a crash. *Oh God, no!*

"Fire! Fire! Everyone wake up!" He threw on his trousers and boots and ran down the stairs. "Buckets! Everyone grab a bucket and a blanket!"
Liam was right behind him. "I'm right behind ye, boyo!"

The pile of lumber they had purchased to build the barn was ablaze, flames licking high into the midnight sky. If they didn't hurry, all of the wood would be useless.

Cullen had never seen Mason move so fast. He, Aedan, and Liam had formed a line to the water pump and ran buckets of water one after the other while he stayed at the pump, drenching blankets that would hopefully help smother the flames.

Sherry had grabbed a bucket and took her place in line, Beth not far behind her.

It took thirty minutes to extinguish the arsonist's efforts. Someone purposely set the fire, but why? Who would do this? For what purpose?

When the fire was nothing but a smoking, hissing pile of ash and bits of wet wood, Cullen could still hear Honor snorting and running along the fence line of the paddock. "What's the matter, boy?"

Just then a bit of red caught his eye along the wood line, and he could hear the snapping of twigs as someone ran away from the scene. "Liam, did you see that?"

"You bet I did. Let's get our rifles and give chase. We'll catch the bugger what done this to us, we will."

Cullen never waited for the rifles but immediately began running through the woods in the direction the culprit had escaped. Bare chested, the limbs from the trees he ran through digging and scratching him, but he wouldn't stop. Whoever did this would pay, and pay dearly.

Just as Cullen would give up the chase, clouds passed over the moon and provided enough light through the trees to see the man he was pursuing, a bright red shirt like a beacon in the night. "STOP! Stop right there!" The man in the red shirt was tiring which made him stumble, having to right himself to continue on. "Go to hell, Macklin!" he shouted. "Go back to Ireland, if you love it so damned much!"

Mason wasn't far behind and began shooting a pistol in the air, yelling, "The next one is for you, you bastard! Stop running and let us see your face, coward!"

Just then Cullen heard the creak of leather as the man mounted his horse and kicked it into action. He heard hoofbeats as the sound grew further and further away, and knew there would be no catching the man that night. Unfortunately for the criminal, Cullen thought he recognized his voice and would hunt him down tomorrow.

***

It was an ordinary Saturday when Cullen arrived in town. People were shopping and gathering on the boardwalks to visit and chat with neighbors.

Cullen tipped his hat as he passed them by, and was headed straight for Jake Wilson's lumber business. He was more than sure it had been Jake last night who started the fire. He just hadn't counted on Jake's hatred and bigotry being so strong.

It didn't surprise Cullen to find the lumber yard deserted, not even an employee in sight. That meant the only other place he could imagine Jake to be, was the saloon.

He nodded to a man outside the batwing doors of the saloon and entered, scanning the room for Jake. Not disappointed, he found him at the bar working on his third shot of whiskey, if the number of shot glasses in front of him was any indication.

"Jake Wilson!" he called.

Jake turned around and gave Cullen a smarmy grin. "What do you want, Macklin? Can't a man have a drink in peace?"

"You set fire to the wood you delivered last week at my place. You knew there was to be a barn raising this morning, and you decided to ruin my plans, isn't that right?"

"I don't know what the hell you're talking about Macklin. I was home last night, all night. You can ask my wife."

"You wouldn't happen to own a bright red shirt, would you, Jake? You know, like lumberjacks wear? I saw you run from my place last night and I chased you through the woods. Too bad I didn't catch you, but I heard your voice as you told me to move back to Ireland, if I loved it so much. That was you, wasn't it, Jake…"

"What? You lookin' for me to provide more wood or somethin', 'cause I'm not gonna do it."

"Yes, you are, Jake. You're going to replace every bit of it."

By this time the saloon was silent, every head turned to watch the conversation between Cullen and Jake. Cullen could hear a drunk whisper to the fella sitting next to him, "Damn, Jake hates the Irish, don't he? Never thought he'd go this far, though, no sir."

"Shut up, Sullivan! Keep your drunken trap shut!" Jake yelled.

The drunk laughed, and replied, "Did you know, Jake, that I dropped the 'O' in front of my last name? Do ya know what that means?" Jake turned and looked at Sullivan.

"That's right, Jake. I'm IRISH!" then howled with laughter as the remaining customers in the saloon joined him.

Jake could have withstood Cullen's interrogation fine, but to be the brunt of such a joke and have men laughing at him? This he couldn't abide.

"You got no proof, Macklin, no proof at all."

"So, if I were to go to your house and see a red shirt hanging on the clothesline, or if I were to ask your wife if you owned such a shirt…"

"So what? Yeah, I own a red shirt but so do other men in town. That ain't no proof."

Cullen knew this was going nowhere and that he would have to push Jake to his limits to get him to come clean.

"You hate the Irish so much that you would do most anything to rid this town of them, wouldn't you. You feel like it's your duty to wash this town clean of the Irish. After all, they're just drunks, picking fights everywhere they go. They don't even deserve to walk the streets of McKenney, isn't that right?"

Jake's face was red as a beet and Cullen thought for sure the man would go for his throat.

"You're goddamn right, Macklin! They're not worthy of spit shinin' my boots! And you married one of'em. Damn, man! What's wrong with you?"

"You did it, I knew you did."

"You're damned right, and I'd do it all over again. Now get your sorry Irish lovin' ass away from me and let me enjoy my drink in peace."

Cullen exhaled a long breath and looked behind him. The sheriff pushed open the batwing doors and stood staring at Jake. He breathed on the cuff of his sleeve and polished the star on his chest before saying, "Jake Wilson, you're under arrest for arson. Put your drink down and come along with me."

"I ain't goin' nowhere with you sheriff. You know what I'm sayin' is true! Them Irish will turn this town into a slum if we let'em!"

The sheriff grimaced, and added, "Jake, we all know you were once in love with Sullivan's sister, Mary, and she spurned you; thought you weren't good enough for her. You knew she was Irish and you've hated the Irish ever since. Come along now, peaceably."

Sullivan sat straighter in his chair, as straight as possible in his inebriated condition. "What? You loved my sister,

Jake?" Then he burst into laughter. "A'course she wouldn't have your sorry ass! You ain't Irish!"

The entire saloon broke into laughter, drunks clinking their shot glasses together as they enjoyed the joke.

As the sheriff tied Jake's hands behind him, he shouted to everyone in the saloon, "You're just a bunch of white nigger lovers, aren't ya! And that makes you just as bad as them, don't you understand that?"
"Come along, Jake. We'll talk about this more when you've sobered up."

***

Word had pretty quickly gotten to Jake's wife, Jenny. She knew what her husband was capable of and if he wasn't stopped, she'd never be able to show her face in McKenney, again.

Just as Jake was being hauled out of the saloon with the sheriff, she walked right through the open doors and found Cullen.

"Good morning, Mr. Macklin. My name is Jenny Wilson. I'm Jake's wife. I want you to know how sorry I am for what he's done and I'd like for you to come to the lumberyard and take whatever you need to build your barn. I heard folks say that there was to be a barn raising at your place this morning and I wouldn't want to have it ruined for you."

"That's mighty nice of you, Mrs. Wilson, and I believe I'll take you up on the offer. However, everyone's already been told the barn raising is off for today. We'll just schedule it again when everyone has the time." Cullen tipped his hat to the woman and said, "Good day, ma'am."

Walking out of the saloon, Cullen felt sorry for her and hoped she had the good sense the Lord gave her to cut loose of Jake, or her life would be a continuous misery.

Chapter Thirty-Eight

True to her word, Jenny Wilson had looked at the lumberyard's books and copied Cullen's previous order to a tee, having all the wood delivered to Cullen within three days. She also visited the town lawyer and suggested a settlement wherein Cullen got the remaining wood necessary to build anything he desired on his property at a very generous discount, hoping it would persuade the judge to treat Jake with kinder consideration. She and Jake would have to do without a few things for a while but she hoped the town would agree that she and Jake were making amends.

***

"Edith, Aedan wants to visit with you. Won't you let him, dearie?"

Brannagh hoped Edith would finally say yes, because Aedan was truly beside himself with worry.

"No, Brannagh. Not today. I don't want to see anyone, thank you."

"But Edith, Aedan misses you so. Won't you at least say hello to him? Let him come into the room and sit with you for just a few minutes?"

"No, I don't want to see him. Him, especially. I don't want to see the pity in his eyes." Edith closed her eyes as a tear escaped down the side of her face.

Then she heard the steps of a long stride as someone approached her bed. Aedan motioned for Brannagh to leave the room and she did, feeling Edith needed to face her fears.

"Open your eyes, Edith, and look at me." Edith remained still and apparently unmoved by his plea.

"I know you hear me, so open your eyes." Still nothing.

Aedan moved closer to the bed and bent down to kiss each of his love's eyelids, and then decided to just begin talking whether or not Edith replied or even acknowledged him.

"I've picked out a piece of land, Edith; a piece of land where we can build our house. It's bonny, lass. I really think you'll love it.

"I'm thinkin' you should be healed well enough to be married soon. Brannagh says she'll be happy to make your wedding dress. I don't even care if you wear your faded gingham as long as you stand beside me and say 'I do'.

"You see, I love you, Edith. I've loved you since that first kiss and it's only grown deeper as the days have passed. I didn't know what to call it at first and I doubted it was actually love because I've not experienced it before, but I know it for sure now.

"When I saw your dress in flames, the thought of losing you ripped through my heart and almost killed me. When we realized you would be all right, I knew immediately that I wanted you for my own. I swear, my love, as my wife, nothing bad will ever happen to you again. I'll protect you with my life, if need be. Please say you'll be mine? Please lift this sorrow from my soul and speak to me…tell me you love me?"

Still Edith didn't move or respond.

Aedan inhaled a deep breath and then exhaled in sorrow. The burden of her rejection would be hard to overcome but he doubted he would give up hope. Putting his hat back on his head, he turned to leave the room when he heard…

"I don't want your pity, Aedan. I don't want anyone's pity."

"'Tis not pity, Edith. 'Tis love, deep and abiding, I promise you that."

"I'll have scars, bad scars that will be hard to look at. Lord knows how short my hair will end up being after Brannagh takes the shears to it. I'll not be fit for any man to look at. Save yourself the pity you feel and don't ask me again. I won't marry you. I'll never marry."

Aedan braced himself and then let her have it. "All right, Edith. It's time you stopped feeling sorry for yourself. Buck up, lass! You think a few scars will be the end of the world? You think you'll be ugly and not worthy of love because of some accident? Well, let me tell you this, dear lass, you need to wake up and act your age. You're a woman, not a child. You're a strong woman who should be doing everything in her power to heal and join the living once again.

"I'll tell ye what, when you decide to grow up and quit acting like a little girl, I'll be waiting for the woman I want to marry. Until then, I hope ye enjoy wallowin' in yer misery."

With that, Aedan stomped from the room only to find Brannagh had been listening in the hallway. When he looked at her, she grinned and pumped her fist in the air as if to tell him, "good job!" He winked at her and went down the stairs, a new purpose in his step. He'd reach the stubborn girl one way or another.

***

"All right, Edith, we're getting up today and walkin' around a bit. We're going down the stairs and then back up again after we go for a wee stroll outside in the fresh air. Come now, don't be stubborn."

"I'm not getting up. It hurts too badly."

"Edith, you know the doctor said it's time for you to get some exercise and fresh air. Look here, I've made a pretty dress for you to wear. See? It hangs straight from the under the bosom so it will be more comfortable while you finish healin'."

"Good Lord, Brannagh! Why not hook it up to a basket and add gas and hot air! Augh, it's ugly! Get it away from me!"

"Don't you be sassin' me, girl! I've had enough of your sulkin' and feelin' sorry for yerself. Everyone has had enough of it! I'm tellin' ye that we're getting you dressed and we're walking outside for a bit."

Then Brannagh ripped the covers off Edith, and grasped her under the arms and around the chest. "Those burns are healin' quite nice, they are, and you're going to start healin' in yer head, Missy!"

Sherry stood outside Edith's room and listened as the war was on to get Edith up and out of her bed. Her Ma was right. Enough was enough, and she was grateful for her Ma's stubbornness that matched Edith's own. Sherry feared she wouldn't have the heart to be so determined and risk hurting the girl.

***

"It stings, Brannaugh!"

Brannagh had brought two kitchen chairs outside and provided Edith with two fluffy pillows to sit on to ease her pain.

"It stings, does it? How on earth do ye think you'll do with laborin' a child into this world, eh? Stings my arse…"

Everyone stopped what they were doing and stared at the two women sitting there, catching the fresh breeze and sniping at each other.

Cullen thought to himself, "*Oh hell! I'm gettin' out of here!*" then promptly turned in the opposite direction and disappeared.

Liam was grinning. *'Tis true. No one denies me Brannagh when she's in charge,* he thought to himself.

Mason took a few steps in their direction and immediately stopped when he saw the look of warning in Brannagh's eyes. It said, *"Do NOT approach here!"*

Aedan ignored Brannagh's looks of warning and walked right up to them.

"What say ye, Brannagh? Think we might have us a weddin' soon?"

Brannagh looked as though she was giving it considerable thought and cautioned, "I'd say at least two more weeks, lad. Maybe even a month *if* we can't get those wounds aired out, that is!" she said, staring straight into Edith's eyes.

Edith was wearing down. It was hard to keep up her pledge to not let anyone see or speak to her. Her burns *were* feeling better and, if she was honest with herself, Aedan's persistence felt more like love now than pity.

Suddenly, she broke into loud and heartfelt laughter, slapping her knee several times in the process. "All right! All right! I give up! I'll marry you as long as the dress Brannagh makes me doesn't look like *this one!*

So was the beginning of a short courtship that ended in the marriage of Aedan and Edith Donnelly.

Chapter Thirty-Nine

Summer was at its zenith and life was rolling along in a pleasant rhythm. There was much work left to do but the family felt it would all get done before winter, so they paced themselves to accomplish so much in a day, storing their energy in the evenings to begin again the next morning. There was plenty of love, laughter, and motivation. In other words, the family was one heck of a team.

It was a Sunday morning when the men stood in front of the new barn and silently appreciated the efforts of their neighbors in getting it erected.

"Sure is pretty," Cullen sighed.

"She's a beast, she is," Liam replied.

"When can we have a dance?" Mason asked.

"Imagine the horses we can raise with all the room," Aedan finished.

Then silence once more. It was enough just to gaze upon the barn's beauty and size. Liam was right; she was a beast.

"Should we paint her?" Cullen asked.

All three responses were quick and simultaneous.

"Not yet," they answered. Then they all took deep breaths of the aroma of new wood and continued their admiration. Silence . . .

"There's still the smoke house and hot house to build," Liam reminded the men.

"Yep, I guess that's the next job, huh?" Cullen sighed again.

"Me and Aedan can build those. Don't worry about it," Mason answered.

"'Tis true, it's a small enough job. Me and my brother-in-law can do it justice." Aedan beamed and put his arm around Mason's shoulder.

∗∗∗

"Look at those eejits, will ye? You'd think they'd never seen a barn before. Men. Just when ye think ye got'em figured out, they start actin' queer again." Brannagh stood drying a teacup, watching the men worship the new barn; because, to her, that's exactly what it looked like, worship.

"Reminds me of how Jacob used to look at the Mermaid. It left me feeling wanting. Who can compete with the likes of that? It's brand new, it's sturdy, and it's gorgeous." Sherry laughed at her own foolishness and then admitted,

"Ach, let them have their time with it. I'll be having Cullen tonight, and that's all that counts."

The women laughed with Sherry but stood gathered by the kitchen door, watching the somewhat sacred scene.

"I wonder if I kept a clean blanket out there…" Edith mused. "Do you think loving would be better out there?" That was it. The girls started laughing until their sides hurt.

Beth chimed in, "Well, if Mason doesn't get that look off his face, I might have to accuse him of cheating on me!" That started another round of laughter that was loud enough for the men to hear.

∗∗∗

"They're laughin' at us, Boyo. Is it that obvious?" Liam asked Cullen.

"Let them laugh. This is a one time thing and I won't be denied it."

Mason turned around and saw the look on Beth's face and wondered aloud, "Uh, are we going to get in trouble for this? I mean, I love this barn, but Beth looks like she could chew nails."

Aedan looked over his shoulder and then at Mason, "Are ye a man or are ye a mouse? 'Tis a barn for the Saints' sake! A brand spankn' new barn that smells like Heaven itself! Let them be mad, I don't care."
"What if they don't give us supper tonight?" Cullen wondered aloud as he sniffed the air and caught a whiff of chicken frying.

***

Brannagh took pity on them for being subject to such manly fascinations and said, "Why not serve them outside tonight. T'would be easy enough to do, yeah? That way they can keep on lookin'…at whatever it tis they're lookin' at."
All the girls nodded in agreement and plates were piled high with fried chicken, and all the trimmings. The men appreciated it so much that the women thought for sure the coming night in the privacy of their rooms would be well worth the effort.

***

"Ladies, would y'all grab a rake and help us rake up the sawdust around the barn?"
"What for? It'll wash away soon enough," Sherry told Cullen.
"Nope, it's for the walls and floor of the hot house and smoke house. It makes good insulation. I'm hoping you gals can go into town and bring a wagon load of sawdust back from Wilson's lumber yard.
Sherry just stood staring at Cullen.
"You know, the hot house? Where you keep all the canned vegetables during summer and winter?"

Sherry nodded in understanding, "Oh, you mean like the pantry we had indoors? Why keep it all outdoors?"

Cullen smiled at his adorable wife, and replied, "Because there will be too much to store in the kitchen or root cellar. Trust me, okay?" He kissed her on the cheek and added, "Try to get as much as you can. There's a canvas tarp to cover it with in the barn."

Hot houses, smoke houses, good Lord! Supplies for an irrigation system for the vegetable garden, damming off the creek; when did Cullen learn how to do all of these things? She had to admit that the irrigation system Cullen had developed worked like a miracle. The amount of water flowing from the creek could be adjusted at any time, and the plants were growing lush and fruitful.

She still felt out of her depth but was learning more every day, and Cullen was always more than glad to teach her all he could.

Things other people took for granted, Sherry had to learn and memorize. She would comfort herself most times by betting no one could sail a trawler as well as she. Unfortunately, in this part of Virginia, there was no water and no trawling. Then she would remember how much she hated trawling and would thank Heaven that she was now here with Cullen and her beloved family.

"Girls? Who wants to go into town with me?" Sherry called from the kitchen door.

Edith and Beth were always the first ones to squeal with delight and beg, "Me! Me! I'll go!"
Brannagh laughed and said, "Go on with ye. I'll watch Caleb and start on supper while you're gone."

***

"Look at this list of things Brannagh wants! Where will we fit it all if the wagon is full of sawdust?" Sherry silently went over the list again, shaking her head. "What *is* all this stuff?"

Beth looked at the list and recognized supplies for canning. "It's canning supplies. After buying all of this, only lids will be needed next year. Boy, it looks like we'll have our work cut out for us come the first harvest. Then we'll have a second harvest according to the time between the two plantings that was marked on the calendar. We'll have food for the entire winter without any worries. Doesn't that feel good?

"I saw some berry bushes down by the creek and I can't wait to make jam. Mason just loves jam on his biscuits. Oh, and I can't wait to make apple jelly! I saw the recipe in that Southern cook book we bought in Alexandria. I've never made a jelly before so it will be exciting to try . . ."

Sherry's mind was elsewhere. Bless Beth's heart, but she wasn't interested in jams and jellies. Her mind was meandering through the stolen minutes she and Cullen had enjoyed down at the creek last evening. Never in her wildest imagination would she have ever thought that making love would be so wonderful…no, amazing! She wished they had an entire week to themselves with no work to do, no family around. Just one week, that's all she would ask for. And she would spend it in bed with Cullen. They would have to eat, of course, but . . ."

"Sherry? SHERRY!? Where is your mind? Me and Beth have been trying to get your attention for the last two minutes. Where were you?"

Sherry blushed beet red. "I was…well, I guess I was…I can't remember now. Why'd you interrupt me? Dern!"

Edith and Beth almost fell off the wagon seat laughing. "We know where you were! You're lucky Honor knows his way to town or we might have ended up in North Carolina!"

Edith put her hands to her cheeks and laughed again. Beth giggled because she often disappeared to the same place when she saw Mason working in the field or using a hammer to build something. Or when he stopped at the pump to pour cold water over his head on a hot day. Or when he…oh gosh! There she went again, off to that "*place*." She grabbed the list from Edith and began fanning herself. Sherry and Edith exploded into peals of laughter that embarrassed her no end.

"What about you, Mrs. O'Donnell?" Beth asked. "Tell us you don't disappear sometimes to that same place! You're a liar if you say you don't."

Now it was Edith's turn to blush. "Why, I don't think I've ever gotten lost in such daydreams. Why daydream when the real thing is only hours away? Or maybe minutes away if you can sneak off somewhere?"

Beth gasped. "No fair! Mason works so hard we don't have time to sneak off! That's totally unfair, Edith O'Donnell. We should at least take turns!"

Sherry hadn't been so amused in ages. "This brings up a good point, Beth. Taking turns, that is. What happens when we have babies? Can we take turns watching each others' babies so we can sneak off?"

Edith stared at Sherry with a deadpan look. Beth looked around Edith to stare at Sherry with a curious eye.

"What? I'm just asking. Would that work?"

"Sherry, are you expecting?" Edith murmured while Beth shook her head up and down as if asking the same question.

"No, not yet. At least I don't think so. How about you two? Are you trying?"

Edith's mouth was hanging open at the question and Sherry put her gloved hand under Edith's chin to close it before she drooled. "I guess I was waiting for you to be the first, Sherry. That sounds silly, doesn't it? I guess I wanted to watch you experience it first so I'll know more what to do when it's my own time. I guess I should have paid more attention to what you went through having Caleb. How about you, Beth?"

"Well, I'm the oldest child in my family, and I watched my mother go through the process four times. I was there to take care of the little ones when Mother would go into labor. There's not much to it besides some sickness in the first few months and then the pain of delivery. But Mother says that a woman forgets the pain as soon as she's holding her newborn. So I pretty much know how it goes. And, no, I haven't been trying, exactly. Just enjoying."

That sent the girls into another laughing fit, and before they knew it they were riding into town.

Chapter Forty

It always amazed Sherry how the town was bustling with people each time she visited. There were people everywhere, chatting on the boardwalk, shopping, and walking to and fro among the shops.

Suddenly, her blood ran cold when she thought she saw a familiar face in the crowd. But then the man turned and walked into the barber shop. She was just being silly. He wouldn't be alone. He would have his friends with him. She nervously scanned the crowd to see if she could spot any of the others but didn't see them. *I'm just being silly. A nervous Nellie, is all.*

Taking a deep breath and telling herself to relax, she jumped from the wagon seat and tied Honor's reins in front of the mercantile. Still scanning the boardwalks, she gave the girls a hand down and they all walked into the store.

Beth seemed to know exactly what to shop for so Sherry let Edith and Beth go on by themselves to have a good time. Meanwhile, she looked out the front window, keeping an eye out for that familiar face. *It couldn't possibly be. No, her mind was just playing tricks on her. Just forget about it.* Perhaps she would go to Wilson's and have the sawdust loaded while the girls browsed the mercantile. It would keep her busy and would also give her a chance to continue searching through the people milling around town.

Sherry was silent on the way home but Edith and Beth never noticed because they were chattering like magpies about this piece of fabric or that bonnet. Sherry listened with half an ear because she was trying to talk herself out of the remaining chill of fear from what she *thought* she saw in town. Should she mention it to Cullen? Would he immediately ride into town to look for the man? Maybe he should tell the sheriff about it so he could keep an eye out.

Surely those men were wanted by the law for crimes committed against others. She doubted that her family had been their only victims.

But what if she was mistaken? What if it wasn't the same man? Silently chiding herself, she spent the remaining ride home in denial that what she had seen in town was real. Perhaps she would sleep on it and see how she felt in the morning.

***

It was the end of August, when on the rise looking down at the farmhouse, four riders sat scanning the property for its inhabitants.

"Well look at this, fellas. A brand new barn and farmhouse. What luck!"

"It sure is, Tom…I mean, General. It would be a nice place to spend the winter, wouldn't it?"

"Jasper, I guess it depends on how hard it will be to convince the owners that generous hospitality would be in their best interests."

"Look there, sir," said the simpering sycophant. "Don't she look familiar? I think it's that red headed woman who shot you. Don't you think she looks familiar?"

"Private, I do believe you are correct. My leg aches just looking at her. Let's ride on down and say hello."

***

Sherry walked out the kitchen door with a bucket in her hand. It was laundry day and she dreaded the long and arduous task of filling the wash tub and heating the water, let alone the actual scrubbing, rinsing, and hanging the clothes on the line. It was the least she could do since the other women in the family always did the cooking.

Tomorrow she would wash all the bed sheets. Perhaps she wouldn't mind it so much after she, Cullen and Caleb lived alone in the house. It would more than cut the chore in half.

She was conflicted about the time when Ma and Da, and Mason and Beth, would move into their own homes. She would miss them terribly but she wanted to start hers and Cullen's married life with space of their own. She consoled herself with the thought that she would be able to see Da's house across the field when the hay was cut. Mason's property wasn't too far away and it would be a lovely stroll in the springtime. Aedan's and Edith's house was last on the list to be built so she would at least have Edith for a while longer after the others moved out.

While the water heated, Sherry grated laundry soap from a large bar and collected it to mix in the washtub. Before she picked up the paddle to mix in the soap flakes, she glanced across the field to where Cullen, Aedan, and her Da were working on her parents' new house. Mason and Beth were also working on their new home, and Mason was proud as a peacock of his new skills and the progress he was making.

Inside the kitchen, Sherry could hear her Ma and Edith giggling over something witty Caleb had said, and all seemed right in her world. In hindsight, she should have been paying more attention to what was happening behind her.

"Well, look who it is," said the General as Sherry turned to witness her worst nightmare.

"I thought my husband chased you north the last time we met." Sherry was *not* going to show this man fear. She didn't the last time she saw him and she wouldn't do so now.

"North isn't the only direction one can travel, my dear. Just so happens we are wanted up north for war crimes. Guess whether or not we committed them?"

Sherry was terrified, and kept glancing across the hay field hoping Cullen would see the arrival of their new *guests*.

"There's no doubt in my mind whether or not you committed such crimes, mister. No doubt at all. There's nothing for you here so why don't you turn around and ride away. You'll get no cooperation from this family."

"Oh, but I disagree. You see, I live with pain each and every day because of you. I'll see it as a sign of Southern hospitality that you put us up for the winter seeing as how the cold weather will probably make my leg ache like hell. On second thought, I think we'll just take over this house and property as settlement for all the pain and suffering. Isn't that right, Jasper?"

"Yes sir, that's right."

"Jasper, why don't you and Ted dismount and go in the kitchen. Bring us the other ladies so we can become better acquainted."

Sherry hoped Edith and her Ma had seen the group of riders and were running upstairs for a rifle or two. She looked once more across the field and saw Cullen and the men running toward the house. My god, they had no guns. They were totally unprepared for this.

"Well, how do, gents? Everything looks just wonderful. The house, the barn, the fields…just grand. I'm so glad we waited until you were finished. Now we won't have to stand around and watch you work so hard. Fortuitous, wouldn't you say? And since I now have a bum leg thanks to your wife, well, I guess you're just going to have to run things around here until I get back on my feet, so to speak.

Every gun the riders had, pistol or rifle, was trained on the family.

"Jasper here will follow you into the barn with our horses where you will rub them down real good and feed them well. Jasper, see to it, will you?"

Cullen knew the smartest move right then would be to keep quiet and do as he was told. If they ever got out of this mess, he would never again go anywhere, *anywhere,* without his guns.

"Ladies, we sure could use a hot home cooked meal," the General said, as he tipped his hat toward the women. "Much obliged.

"Looks like laundry day. I swear, I don't think I could be luckier, do you?" the General said as he nonchalantly sniffed the cuff of his uniform. Sherry noted his sarcastic grin and knew she was his main target. He would make her rue the day she ever pulled the trigger on that pistol some months ago. He would make her feel pain just like the pain she had caused him.

"Ted, you search the house for weapons and bring any you find out here. We'll store them all in one place where we can always see them."

"Holt, you go in the barn with Jasper and take a good look around. Then help him bring the men back. And watch out; they're going to be planning and scheming as to how to stop us from having this place as our own."

Sherry stood stock still, just staring at the man who, in her mind, comically called himself the General, since the faded stripes on his jacket proved otherwise. Just then, she could hear Mason and Beth laughing together as they walked around the bend, and wanted to scream at them to turn around and run into the woods.

"Don't say a word, you bitch. I'm warning you."

Sherry looked at him and then at his bum leg and let just the tiniest bit of a smile cross her lips.

"What are you going to do? Jump off your horse and beat me? If I run, can you catch me? You certainly don't want to shoot me. That would ruin your plans, wouldn't it. If you shoot me dead, where's the fun in that? You want to make me pay, isn't that right?"

The General smiled and said, "That's right, ma'am. That sure as hell is the plan. And I'll relish each and every time you wince in pain. Never doubt it; you *will* pay for my pain."

"We'll see about that. By the way, I won't call you 'General' because I can't see the Union ever promoting such a pig to that rank. So, what's your name?"

"Thomas Quintin Oliver, at your service," he grinned. "But I won't be serving *you,* now will I. And you would be correct that I wasn't a general in the war. But I sure do like playing like one. Gives me an immeasurable sense of power and accomplishment.

"You'll call me General one day soon. You'll call me anything I want you to call me. You'll do anything I want you to do, and you'll do it with a smile and a curtsy. You'll moan when I take you, and you'll pleasure me in any manner I'm in the mood for. Is that clear?"

"I wouldn't count my chickens, Mr. Oliver. Not just yet, anyhow." And then Sherry turned her back on him and walked into the kitchen.

"Hey, I didn't dismiss you yet!"

The General was then met with howling laughter as she continued walking away. He just smiled and thought, yes sir, he sure did love a spunky woman.

Chapter Forty-One

Later that evening when supper was over and the General had taken a leisurely hot bath, he thought how good it was to eat a home cooked meal, to be clean, and sleep in a soft bed. He missed feeling this way. It had been so many years since he had felt such comforts, he was surprised he could even remember them. He guessed it had been since he was a kid, before the war.

"Jasper, keep an eye on these people. Make sure they don't get together and start plotting my demise. And tell Ted to guard my bedroom tonight. Take shifts if you have to. I need a good night's rest."

The women were to sleep in the house, and the men were to sleep in the barn. Sherry felt this was nerve wracking since she didn't know if Cullen was planning a solution to their current situation. She would be damned before she allowed these foul smelling animals to take from her what she had worked so hard to build.

Walking into the kitchen later that night Sherry was met by one of the more odiferous members of Oliver's motley gang. "Good evening, sir. I'm hungry and wanted to get an apple, if you don't mind? I promise I won't take long."

Holt grinned and gave her a lascivious once over with bloodshot eyes. "I don't see why not, pretty lady. But don't pull any fast moves or I'll have to shoot you, understand? The General would be mighty disappointed if you was to die before he…uh, he'd be madder than a wet hen, so behave yourself."

"Sir, I totally understand my predicament and am not so stupid as to jeopardize my life over an apple. Please let me pass."

Holt stepped aside to let Sherry pass as she made for the kitchen counter where a bowl of apples awaited…near the knives. She made a good show of choosing an apple and even engaged Holt in conversation while she was looking through the bowl. "Did you enjoy your supper tonight, sir? Beth is certainly a good cook. Wait until you taste her pies and cakes."

"You're sure right on that account, Missy. It was a meal fit for a king. Or a general!" He bent over laughing so hard at what he thought was a witty remark and was thus distracted as Sherry slid a paring knife into the pocket of her dress. Turning to leave the kitchen, she polished the apple with her apron and left the room, taking a noisy bite to let Holt know she really had been hungry. If they could just keep Mr. Oliver occupied and distracted, perhaps the rest of the gang might be easy pickings. It was obvious they weren't the brightest of men.

***

The man named Jasper had told Cullen and the rest of the men in his family to sleep in one of the horse stalls so he could keep a close eye on them. That was his first mistake. Had Jasper been more astute, he would have separated them to keep them from talking with one another.

Cullen waited until he could hear Jasper snoring, which by the sound of it, Jasper had chosen to sleep near the barn door, meaning it was safe to make a bit of noise without him hearing it.

"Liam," he whispered. "Are you awake?"

"Of course I am. Who could sleep with that eejit snoring like a freight train?" Liam whispered back.

"I have a plan."

"Oh good. I was wonderin' whether or not we'd make it through this, I was."

***

"Good morning, ladies. A cup of coffee, if you please. And perhaps some pancakes, eggs, and bacon. Sure sounds good." Oliver was feeling very pleased with himself. A good night's rest had been just the thing to begin a day full of revenge.

As Sherry walked by his chair, Oliver's arm snaked out to grab her around the waist. "You and I will have a long talk after breakfast. Actually, I think we should invite the other ladies, too. After all, it involves all of you."

Sherry recoiled from his touch and gave him a deadly look.

"Now don't go getting all huffy. It would be best if you were to relax and resign yourself to your fate…just as I had to do when you shot me. Just as I've tried to do each and every goddamned day since."

Oliver grabbed Sherry's wrist, painfully. "Tonight you will sleep with me…in my room…in my bed. You will sleep with me each and every night until I'm through with you. I imagine even a beautiful woman like you might lose her charms after a while. Do you understand me?"

Sherry was on fire with rage and hatred. "You're a fool if you think I would let you touch me. I'm repulsed by your mere presence. I find you exceedingly revolting," she spit out through gritted teeth. Escaping his grasp, she continued helping to prepare breakfast.

Oliver, the *General*, stared at Sherry and rubbed the hardness in his pants. "Oh, Miss Sherry, if you only knew how your attitude inflames my lust for you. No simpering miss, are you. Keep it up, my dear. A little punishing tussle between the sheets is just what I've been dreaming about.

"Now, as to the rest of you ladies, you will make yourselves available to my men any time and anywhere they like. If they say bend over, you lift your skirts and bend over. If they want to squeeze a ripe breast, they'll grab one whenever they desire. If they tell you to get on your knees, well, you can guess the rest of that one. And to show you I'm not totally heartless, I'll have them bathe daily. Won't that be nice?"

Beth started to cry and as Edith made to hold her, Oliver snapped, "NO! There will be no coddling here. My men want experienced women and you will be by the time they are finished with you. So you better grow up quick. Now serve me my damned breakfast and give me another cup of coffee. Step lively!"

***

All of the General's men, except for Holt, joined him at the breakfast table. Just as they were finishing up and draining their cups of the last drop of coffee, they heard laughter coming from the direction of the barn.

"You two get out there and see what's going on," Oliver demanded.

Apparently, Oliver had been sitting too long and his leg had stiffened. Sherry enjoyed the sight of him trying to rise from his chair.

He hobbled across the kitchen floor to the screened door to see what was going on while the women looked through the kitchen window toward the barn. When Sherry realized what might be happening, she took the paring knife from her skirt pocket and quietly walked toward Oliver, ready to…what, stab him? With a paring knife?

"You men are pathetic. Can't you control a group of laughing men, for God's sake?" Oliver shouted at his men.

Brannagh knew what Sherry was thinking and grabbed the knife from her hand, continuing the silent steps toward Oliver's back. Without a second thought, she raised the knife, caught his forehead from behind, jerked his head back, and sliced the knife cleanly across his throat. His hands flew to his neck and he began gurgling as he turned to see if it had been Sherry that dealt the fatal blow. "Sh…Sher…" he rasped, as he fell to his knees. He then looked at the spurting blood that flew from his neck and fell face first to the floor.

***

While Oliver and his men were having breakfast and Holt was supposedly watching them, Cullen and the men retrieved the guns he had hidden deep behind a mound of hay. There weren't enough for Aedan to have one so he brazenly walked out of the barn with a sickle. Holt was so simple minded it probably wouldn't register, anyway.

As Oliver's men walked toward the barn, Liam said in a loud voice, "Oy, do ye remember the time I stepped on the hem of Lolly Goodwin's dress and ripped the whole shebang from her waist? Jaysus, Joseph and Mary, but the woman has an enormous arse, does she not?" Cullen started laughing, encouraging Aedan and Mason to join in.

"Hell yeah, I remember! Her face turned ten shades of red! Damn, that was funny." Cullen noticed Oliver's men coming closer toward them now.

"Hey! What the hell is goin' on out here?" Ted asked.

Liam lit his pipe and made a great show of savoring a puff. Mason put his hands on his hips in a stance that said, *it's none of your damned business.*

Aedan slid his thumb across the scythe to test its sharpness, and Cullen just stood there looking nonplussed.

Then as one they turned toward each other again and continued the story of Lolly Goodwin's behind.

"Hey, I asked you a question, dammit? What the hell are you doing out here. This ain't no tea party!"

"Ach, go on with ye, we're just enjoying a moment of peace. Step away, why don't ye. I've taken about as much shite from you eejits as I'm gonna take, and that's the truth." Liam sneered.

Mason spoke up and added, "Why don't you come over here and do something about it, huh? Big bad Union soldiers. Bah!"

Cullen waited until all three of Oliver's men went for their pistols before he grabbed his own from where he had stuffed it in the back waistband of his pants. Aedan, who was standing the closest to Holt, turned and swung the sickle down hard against the man's right arm, effectively stunning him senseless. He enjoyed the look of shock on his face as blood dripped from the wound.

For a split second, Cullen wondered whether or not to kill or just maim them. The trouble was that Oliver was still in the house and had to be taken care of. In the end, Cullen shot them all in the chest and left it up to God whether or not they survived. Before the unfortunates even hit the ground, he was running toward the kitchen door.

"Sherry!" he yelled as he pulled the door open. And then he stopped suddenly as he almost tripped over Oliver's body.

Cullen looked from Sherry to the rest of the girls and knew they were all in shock. Brannagh still held the paring knife in her hand and was covered in blood. Beth and Edith just stared right through him, and Sherry finally said, "We took care of it. Well, Ma did. She took care of it for us, Cullen. I've never seen her so brave. She wasn't going to let anything happen to her girls. She wasn't going to let me commit such a crime. She saved us." Cullen stepped over the General's body and captured Sherry in a tight embrace.

Chapter Forty-Two

Cullen sent Aedan to town, telling the young man to get the most speed out of Honor that he could. It was important for the sheriff to come to the farm as soon as possible.

There was no medical treatment for Oliver's men. Holt was dead, and the other two were damn close to it.

Cullen seriously dreaded the sheriff's reaction to what he'd done. He was thrown back in time to when another four men lay dead by his hand, and hoped to heaven the result would be the same. After all of God's gifts thus far, he could hardly believe the Father would let him spend the rest of his days in prison; or worse, hang from a rope.

He had dragged Oliver's body from the kitchen to the side yard. The girls would get busy scrubbing away the last evidence of the man's wasted life. What turned a man from being God fearing to being a rapist and killer? What happened in a man's past to turn him so sour on life?

Within the next hour, Cullen heard horses approaching from the direction of town, and knew it was Aedan and the sheriff.

"Howdy, Maklin. Heard you had some trouble out here. By the looks of it, a war was waged. Nice to see you were the surviving army. Now tell me everything…all of it. Don't spare one detail."

Cullen was having trouble deciphering the sheriff's mood which sent him into a downward spiral of anxiety. "Sheriff, would you like to go in the house? Maybe have a cup of coffee? Then I'll tell you all of it that I know. The girls were kept separate from us so you'll have to ask them their part. But please don't upset them more than they already are. They're in shock, actually." The sheriff nodded and said he would be gentle with them.

When all was said and every detail given, Cullen hooked Honor up to a wagon and the men picked up Oliver's gang, who were all now deceased, and hoisted them into the wagon bed as if they were so much grain.

"Macklin, I'll make some inquiries but I'm pretty sure I know who these men were. Heard tell of their raping and tormenting women all through Virginia. Seein' as how your wife was told by the leader that they were wanted for war crimes in the north, well, I can't see as how anyone would blame you and your men-folk for what ya done. Like I said, I'll make inquiries up North to verify they were wanted men." Then he smiled, "Don't look so down in the mouth. If everything pans out, you'll likely be a hero."

Once again Cullen was faced with the consequences of taking human lives. No matter how much he told himself that it was a necessary action to take, to save the lives of his family, he just couldn't reconcile it. But now wasn't the time for self recriminations. He had to see to his family. He had to be strong and loving so they would one day, hopefully soon, forget the trauma and tragedy of what had happened that day. He prayed it didn't taint all of their accomplishments.

***

Liam kept a close eye on Brannagh, for the rest of the day. He knew she was suffering and also knew she would put on a good face for the rest of the family. He had to get her away for some privacy. He had to hold her while her tears could finally flow.

"Come, *Anamchara*. Let us take a walk down by the creek, eh?" Brannagh said nothing as she turned in the direction of the creek. She just walked slowly like a ghost through a mist.

"Brannagh, my love, with all me heart and soul, I have to tell ye that what you did today saved our family. T'was brave, and that's a fact. I've never been so proud of ye. Never."

Brannagh looked up into his eyes and saw all the love she ever wanted shining there. Then she bent over and gasped for air. She couldn't catch her breath for love nor money.

Liam held her at arms length and shouted, "Brannagh! Look at me! Look at me and breathe with me!" Brannagh stopped thrashing in his arms and listened as he started taking long deep breaths. Soon her breathing matched his and her complexion returned to normal.

"That's it, me love. In…and out…in…and out. That's it. I'm going to hold you now. Will that be all right, Lovie?"

Brannagh nodded her head, giving him permission to move closer.

"I know you're sufferin', lass. I know how difficult it must have been. And I know why ye did it. Colleen told me, she did. Oh, the love we feel for our children is enormous, eh? You didn't want her beautiful soul stained with the taking of another's life." He began rubbing her back in soft circles and was relieved when she began to sob. It seemed as though all of the pain and anguish she had tolerated over the years was being spent in one huge rush.

Liam continued to hold her, murmuring to her in Gaelic, and then softly crooning an Irish lullaby. He could feel her muscles relax and her sobs turned to a mere trail of tears down her face and onto his shirt. "That's it, love. I've got you."

"Ach, Liam…'twas an evil in me that just came out of nowhere. I don't really remember my thinkin' at the time. I just remember the feel of slicing the man's throat and it's something I'll never forget. But God will forgive me, eh? He knows what's in my heart. He knows how much I love me family. Surely I won't burn in Hell, do ye think?"

Liam smiled and moved a finger over her forehead to push some wayward locks of hair out of her face. "My love, those men made their choices long ago. Surely they knew 'twould end badly for them. What right did they have to steal our homes and land? What right did they have to rape the women in our family? None, that's what. You did what you had to and that's an end to it. I'll hear no more from you about burning in Hell, do ye hear? Now come, we have a family to look after."

They held hands on the walk back to the house, each with their own thoughts and fears. But Liam knew his wife would heal. In a couple of weeks she'd be right as rain, she would.

***

After supper that evening, Cullen bade the family to remain seated at the dining room table. Everyone was listless and distracted and he thought it would be healing for each person to perhaps share any concerns about what had happened that day.

"I'm so sorry we had to endure the hell we experienced today. It was so callous but necessary. We were forced to do things we would never have imagined, and it's left us feeling terrified and guilty.

"It will do no good to hold in what we are feeling and act like nothing happened. We may think it's what is good for the rest of the family, but it's not. I want to hear what you're all thinking about this morning. I want you to let it all out here and now so we can begin to heal."

"This is so much cow manure, Cullen. You're not a preacher and we aren't your damned sheep." Mason was angry and Cullen figured it was as good a place to begin as any.

"Shut up, Mason!" Edith shouted. "Don't you care how we feel? Don't you care that the women in this family were going to be reduced to whores for those filthy men? Yes, that's right. We were given instructions on how to make ourselves available to them any time and anywhere. Sherry was to sleep with the General, and was to please him in any manner he desired. His goal in the end was to kill her when he became bored with her."

"I'm glad he's dead," Sherry hissed. "But I wonder…is there anyone else out there who wants us dead? Or who wants to take away everything we've worked so hard for? Maybe Jamison will come back to life and hound us to the ends of the earth! I can't stand it anymore! I just want peace in my life! I just want…oh my God, I was going to kill Oliver!"

"Colleen, don't you dare take that on yourself. I was the one who killed him, and it will be on me to stand before God and give him an accounting of it, it will. And if you want to know how I feel about taking the man's life, well, I look at it as self defense. He had no right to . . . "

"All right, all right!" Liam said as he stood from the table. "What's done is done! 'Tis no sense in crying over spilled milk. So this is what we're gonna do, it tis. We're gonna go on with our lives. We're gonna pick up where we left off like this never happened.

"I want ye all to say a prayer tonight that God wash away any sin, real or imagined, and promise to live the rest of your lives in a Christ-like manner. 'Tis all anyone can ask of ye. Personally, I think the eejit bastards deserved what they got. Now let there be an end to it. Come on Brannagh. It's time to wash the dishes and then be off to bed."

Brannagh stood and took Liam's hand. "I have to agree with Da. 'Tis a waste of time to hold on to feelings of guilt, shame or anything else. Da's right. Surrender it to The

Father, and he'll give us comfort. Now let's clear the table and wash the dishes. Tomorrow's another day, it tis."

Chapter Forty-Three

It was the end of September, which was apple harvest time. Brannagh made sure that it was a festive time although it would be one of hard work.

They were to make and can apple butter, and apple sauce, and would dry apples with which to make apple pies and dumplings during the next year.

The men were in the vegetable garden digging up the last of the potatoes to put in the root cellar, when Liam said to Cullen, "'Tis a miracle these potatoes are. Never saw the likes of them in Ireland, I'll tell ye that, boyo. Look at'em! Big and hard and not one sign of blight." He then wiped a tear from his eye from remembering Ireland's tragic potato blight. "If I haven't thanked ye lately, son, let me thank ye again for bringing us over to be with our Colleen. You've made us so happy. You truly made our dreams come true, ye did."

Cullen blushed a bit and replied, "Liam, it was my gift to your family. The smile on your daughter's face and the joy in her heart made it all worth while, and I've finally found a family that is full of love and acceptance. It was my pleasure to bring you to your new home."

"All right, 'tis enough blubberin', it tis. Let's get these potatoes down to the house and into the cellar. Maybe Beth will mash up a few with cream and butter. Ach, it's makin' me mouth water just thinkin' of it!"

***

"Your Da says our house should be finished by the end of October, or so. I'm sure you'll be glad to whittle down the number of people in your house, eh?"

"No, Ma. I won't be glad. I mean, I do want to be in our home as a family, you know, Cullen, Caleb and myself, but I'll miss you all terribly."

"Look out the kitchen window and tell me what you see," Brannagh said with a smile.

Sherry looked up and saw Cullen, Aedan and her Da, working like bees in a hive, getting Ma's house finished. "I know, I know. I can look out my window and see your house any time I want to. I can walk across the field and be there in ten minutes."

"So what's botherin' ye so, lovey? I won't be gone so you won't be able to miss me, am I right? Somethin' else is troublin' ye, eh?"

"I haven't taken the time to learn to cook yet! What am I going to do when you, Beth, and Edith leave? My family will starve!"

Brannagh laughed, although she shouldn't have. Her daughter was truly distraught. "Hmm, I see what ye mean, lass. Poor Cullen will have to steal away across the field for nourishment and Caleb will wither away to a nubbin, he will."

"It's not funny, Ma! Everyone will be gone and here I'll be, rattling around in the kitchen, big belly bumping into everything, not knowing the first thing about feeding my family."

"Don't worr…*what?* Your big belly? Colleen! Are you with child, dearest?"

Sherry grinned, "I think so. I'm late for my monthly. But don't tell anyone until I know for sure, all right? I would hate to disappoint Cullen if it's not true."

Brannagh stared at her daughter's breasts, trying to judge whether or not they were a bit larger than usual. "All right, mum's the word, then." She then looked out the window and saw Liam walking across the field toward the barn. "Oh, look! Tis your Da comin' to the barn. I swear, he's still a strikin' fella, eh? I'm feelin' like I need a kiss. I'll be right back."

"Ma, don't you do it! Don't you tell Da! Ma? Come back here, Ma!"

So much for keeping secrets in the family. If her mother told Da, Da would tell Aedan, and Aedan would…ach! Sherry watched as her ma ran up to Da, giving him a kiss and telling him something that pleased him mightily. Oh well, the deed was done. She just hoped she was truly with child and that it wasn't a false alarm. Da better keep his mouth shut. It was all she could hope for.

Brannagh didn't mean to betray her daughter's confidence, really, but she knew the family needed something joyful to hold on to. This would be the final step toward forgetting the recent past. It would give everyone hope and something to prepare for. Why, she could just see all the girls sitting in front of a fire, knitting and sewing tiny pieces of clothing for the coming new addition to the family. Oh, what fun it would be! She smiled to herself over such musings, and then made her way to the outhouse. She was going to have to cut down on drinking so much tea and coffee. It had her running to the john much too often.

***

It was now the middle of October, and Sherry knew without a doubt she was with child. The smell of food made her even more nauseous than usual and she had to keep a slop jar under the bed to empty the contents of her stomach each morning. So far she had been able to hide the fact from everyone except Ma and Da, although Cullen kept a close eye on her, so her parents had probably told him about it.

When she was pregnant with Caleb, she was fortunate to have had no symptoms at all. Now she felt sick as a dog and was so tired she almost fell asleep at the supper table.

That evening while the dishes of food were being passed around the table, Sherry was looking quite green around the gills.

"Sherry, you're not looking too well. Are you sure you're okay?" Cullen asked with concern.

"He's right, Sherry. You look awful, no offense." Edith grinned at Sherry, and gave her a knowing wink.

Sherry rolled her eyes, and said, "All right! I'm with child! Are you happy now?"

Everyone spoke at the same time, expounding on what a wonderful thing it was to soon have another member of the family and what they needed to do in preparation.

Brannagh was buttering a biscuit but put it down on second thought.

Edith looked about to burst with something she wanted to say.

Beth looked from one person to another around the table and appeared to be deciding on something to say in response to the news.

"Are you sure, Sherry? Is that why you look and feel so bad?" Cullen grinned.

"Well, now, it does me heart good to know that ye ahl think I'm such a beauty. Ahhr the rest a'ye gonna tell me how bad I look? Suints preserve us!"

Edith smiled and touched Sherry's arm. "Now, now. We're just happy you aren't sick with some disease, is all. I'm sorry you're the one who feels so bad when I'm feeling just fine. I thought I would be sick like you."

Beth's eyes got as big as saucers. "Edith? You, too?"

"Yes, me too." Aedan looked like he had just swallowed a goldfish and jumped from his chair. "Edith! 'Tis true?" Edith nodded and Aedan got to his knees and put his ear against her stomach. "It's me dearest wish, it tis! What a gift yer givin' me, wife!"

Beth waited until everyone quieted down before she cleared her throat. "Um, it certainly is a happy occasion. I mean, three babies being born so close together will be fun, right?"

Every head swung in Beth's direction. "You, too?"

"Yes, me too." Mason just stared at his wife and asked, "How did this happen? How did all three of you get pregnant at the same time?" Everyone at the table burst out laughing at such a comical question. "Okay, okay, I know *how it happened,* but it is kind of strange, isn't it?"

Brannagh coughed slightly into her napkin. "Tis not so strange. I've heard that women who spend a lot of time together get into a rhythm, so to speak. So it doesn't really surprise me. Now, if you'll excuse me, I'm not feeling very well right now."

Liam looked concerned but it was Sherry who jumped from the table and ran after her mother. "Ma? Are you sick? Please tell me what's going on!"

"Girl, I think I've hit the time of life when a woman changes and stops having her monthlies. I haven't bled in two months now. I never knew that a woman could feel so sick with it."

"Ma, that doesn't sound right to me. We're going to take you to the doctor first thing tomorrow morning. And don't argue with me, either! I won't take no for an answer. Now let's take you to lie down for a bit."

Liam looked at Cullen, and the men exchanged a look of concern. "I'll just go up and sit with Brannagh for a bit. Save me some dessert."

Everyone got quiet as they contemplated what might be wrong with Brannagh. She was the head of the family in so many ways, and it was worrisome to know she wasn't well.

***

Sherry and Brannagh both walked into the doctor's office, looking and feeling like hell.

"Next?" asked the doctor as he looked into the waiting room. Sherry raised her hand and helped Brannagh stand up. "We are, doctor."

"Well, come in. Come in. Now what can I do for you ladies today?"

"My mother hasn't been feeling well for a good while now, and I thought I should bring her in to see you. Would you please examine her and see what you find?"

"Of course. If you'll just wait here for your mother, she'll be back in a few minutes."

Sherry sat in the waiting room wondering what was wrong with her ma. She just couldn't lose her, not with the pending arrival of her baby. She needed her ma. She would be lost without her.

After a half hour or so, the door to the examining room opened and a grinning Brannagh made her way into the waiting room.

"Now remember, Mrs. Darcy, take plenty of sips of liquids and eat small portions until you're feeling better. And come see me in another month or so. You'll be fine, I'm sure. Good day, ladies."

"Ma, what's wrong? What did the doctor say?"

"You're not going to believe it, Colleen."

"Of course I'll believe it but you have to tell me first!"

"I'm with child."

"Ma, is that possible? I mean, can you get pregnant at your age?"

"It seems you can, dear girl. The doctor says I'm fit as a fiddle, he does, and that he's sure I'll be just fine. I'm not so old, you know. I was just sixteen when I had you."

Sherry did the mental calculations and grinned from ear to ear. "A brother or sister! Oh, my gosh! I'm going to have a little brother or sister!" Sherry was beside herself with joy. "Let's hurry home. I can't wait to see the look on Da's face when you tell him!"

Liam was indeed surprised to hear of his wife's pregnancy, and felt blessed that God would bestow yet another blessing upon them.

Chapter Forty-Four

It was almost Christmas, and all the houses had been built and everyone had moved in to their new homes.

Christmas would be celebrated at the Macklin's this year, and Sherry was busy reading recipes and making practice dishes in preparation. The other girls had volunteered to help cook and bring side dishes but Sherry declined their offers. She would do this on her own, no matter what the outcome.

Cullen sneaked up behind her in the kitchen and put his arms around her growing belly. "What's cookin', darlin'?

"Fried squash and onions," she replied. "It looks simple enough to make but I'm thinking I'll ruin it just the same." Sherry sighed heavily, brushed her hair out of her face and kept reading.

"I'm sure it will be fine. Christmas isn't about food, after all," Cullen replied kindly. "Caleb has been pestering me to go cut a Christmas tree for the house. I think I'll take him in the woods and find the perfect one. Happy cooking."

On the way to the wood line, Caleb was chipper and talkative. Cullen asked him if he was excited for Christmas to arrive and the boy stopped walking, had a perplexed look on his face and said, "Yes, I'm excited. Aren't you? I love Christmas. Doesn't everyone?"

Cullen pulled the boy's woolen hat farther onto his head and replied, "Why do you love Christmas?"

"Well, cause there's a tree all decorated, and there's lots of good food, and the family comes together to celebrate. It's just fun, is all."

Cullen wondered if Caleb was too young to understand the significance of Christmas, and decided it should be up to Sherry to make the choice of whether to explain it at this point or not. Would the words *Christ*, and *Baby Jesus* make any sense to him? He would talk with Sherry about it later.

Caleb walked on in silence, obviously contemplating all the fun he would have on Christmas Day, which gave Cullen a chance to think about what the holiday meant to him. He remembered all the lonely Christmas holidays he had spent before meeting the Newcombs, and felt mournful. Christmas Days spent in saloons, trying to make enough money to be able to eat. He thought about all the times he had walked upstairs with a dance hall girl to slake his physical hunger, and wanted to throw up. But before his memories could drag him further into despair, he remembered meeting Ken and Charlie. He remembered the love and companionship they offered, and his heart expanded a little.

Then he remembered meeting the Cummings family and everything they did for him. And his heart expanded a bit more.

Then he remembered his faithful companion, Honor, and grinned from ear to ear.

Then he remembered arriving in Castine, and meeting Sherry and her children, and he felt a joy that bloomed in his heart. He remembered all the times he was guided in the direction in which he needed to go in order to realize his hopes and dreams. *I am truly blessed.*

As always, Cullen felt profound gratitude when he remembered all his blessings. He marveled at how much he had accomplished, and felt energized by what lay ahead. He had a child on the way. Imagine that! A child of his own and one, no matter girl or boy, he would lavish with love and acceptance. He would undo all that his father had done to make him feel so lonely, unworthy, and unloved. He would make it his life work to provide his children with everything they needed. He would love and protect them with his last breath.

***

Cullen looked out the living room window and noticed a buggy approaching the farm. His first instinct after the trauma with the General and his crew made him tense with anxiety. Then he noticed one of the passengers was a woman who sat holding the arm of the driver. Perhaps they were lost.

The woman's bonnet was pulled low and the man's ten gallon hat almost obliterated his face from view. *What the devil?*

Cullen walked out onto the front porch and waited to see who they might be. Within another minute or so, he knew exactly who there were and jumped off the porch and ran to meet them.

"Charlie? Ken? Is it really you?"

Ken pushed his hat higher on his head and grinned like a Cheshire cat. Charlie held her arms out to Cullen and he caught her as she almost flew from the buggy into his arms. He held her close and spun her in circles, so glad to see his friends again.

"Cullen, we're a Christmas surprise, you might say. We just couldn't stay away any longer. I hope it's all right," Charlie said through her tears.

Ken sat on the wooden seat and just shook his head. Charlie would probubly huve left him if he hud refused to make the trip. "I'll just ride on toward the house. You two can stand there blubberin' if you want." He clicked the horses and rode the rest of the way, grinning with joy. Damn, it was good to see the boy again!

Sherry looked through the window and was ready for a cat fight. *Who the devil is Cullen hugging so close and so long?* When the man drove the buggy close and jumped down to hitch the horses, she saw he was smiling so he couldn't have been angry. Sherry opened the front door and introduced herself, hoping the man would do the same.

"Well, if you aren't the prettiest thing I've ever seen! Well, except for my Charlie, that is. Cullen's done found himself a gem, I see. The name's Ken Hutchinson, and that woman who appears to have attacked Cullen, is my wife, Charlie, short for Charlotte.

"Please forgive our showing up unannounced, but Charlie wanted it to be a Christmas surprise. Evidently, it worked." The man's dimpled cheeks put Sherry at ease and she welcomed him into their home. "Please, take off your coat and sit by the fire. I'll put a pot of coffee on."

Instead of moving, both of them watched Cullen and Charlie make their way toward the house, both talking a blue streak. "There's a lot of catchin' up to do, Mrs. Westover, an awful lot."

Sherry smiled, knowing that there certainly was a lot of catching up to do.

Later, during dinner, Sherry invited them to stay for a good while, announcing that their arrival was the best present Cullen could have received for Christmas. Well, that and the fact that she was going to give him a son or daughter.

Cullen was proud as punch of his wife for inviting them, and Charlie's acceptance of the invitation put the icing on the cake.

When dessert was finished and second cups of coffee poured, Ken looked at Cullen, and said, "Cullen, how much does an acre of land cost out here? Me and Charlie, well, we're plumb wore out with all dust the hot weather back home and were thinking of making a change. Is there any land near your property for sale?"

Epilogue

Cullen was sitting on the porch, enjoying a bowl of fragrant pipe tobacco, and watching the children playing in the yard. Little redheaded Beatrice Fiona Maklin, was the light of his life and he never tired of watching her play.

All the children were born within the same month and today all of their birthdays were being celebrated together, as they would always be.

The children had adopted Charlie and Ken as their second grandparents, which pleased them no end. She and Ken doted on the children and visited often, always bringing a bag of sweet treats with them.

Their ranch was only a half hour away, on the other side of McKenney, and Cullen was always glad to see them; Charlie loving to hook Nocount up to their buggy to show how well he had come along. She changed his name to something or other, he couldn't remember. Something like *Miracle,* or some such, and the thought made him grin.

The real miracle had been the direction in which his life had taken since meeting all of the beautiful people he called his family. As always, the only thing missing was his beloved mother. At times of such thoughtful meanderings, he would talk to her like she were sitting right beside him.

"Mama, can you believe the luck? Did you ever imagine that your loving son would make this much out of his life? For a long time I never thought it would come about. Never thought I'd have all the love and abundance I now enjoy. Sometimes I like thinking that it was you who was guiding me from the other side. I can feel you so close, sometimes. It's a true comfort until I see you again.

Sherry is with child again. I hope it's a boy this time. I spend a lot of time thinking of names for him. If thinking and hoping can make dreams come true, his name is already Edward Cole Maklin. Has a nice ring, I think. Sherry had wanted to name our little girl after you, Mama, and I hope it made you happy. This time I will name the child…*the boy*."

He closed his eyes wearing a smile. Somehow, he knew she heard him. At least that's what he delighted in believing.

Just then he heard Ken yell from the horseshoe pit, "Liam, I declare you have a sixth sense with these damn horseshoes!"

"'Tis nothin' but skill, boyo. Now quite yer yappin' and let's play."

Bea ran up to her papa and screamed, "Papa! The bear is going to catch me!" as she ran into his lap. Sure enough, Aedan was running after her, growling like a bear and showing his teeth.

"Aedan, you'll give my baby girl nightmares, now quit!"

"Ach, yer gettin' old, Cullen. "Twas just havin' a bit o'fun."

"Oh, it's a bit of fun you want? How about this…"

Cullen put Bea aside and went after Aedan until they were rolling around on the ground and laughing like loons.

"Supper is ready!" Edith called from the house.

Aedan sniffed the air, "By the Saints, 'tis corned beef tonight! First one there gets the end piece!" and took off running.

Cullen laughed, laid back on the grass, and said heavenward, "Thank you, God, for everything, just the way it is."

www.ingramcontent.com/pod-product-compliance
Lightning Source LLC
Chambersburg PA
CBHW050757080726
47590CB00020B/180